# The Night Girl

# Praise for The Night Girl

*"A charming urban fairy tale about tolerance, acceptance, and discovering the wonders that may just be hidden in plain sight."*

— J.M. Frey, author of *The Skylark's Saga*

*"It's an excellent fantasy adventure packed with humor, unforgettable characters, and more twists and turns than an underground amusement ride. You'll never look at a gargoyle in the same way. Or the city of Toronto. So much fun!"*

— Arthur Slade, author of *Amber Fang*

# The Night Girl

SHADOWPAW PRESS *Reprise*

JAMES BOW

THE NIGHT GIRL
By James Bow

Shadowpaw Press Reprise
Regina, Saskatchewan, Canada
shadowpawpress.com

Second edition

First edition: REUTS Publications, LLC, 2019



Cover by Bibliofic Designs
bibliofcdesigns.com



Trade Paperback ISBN: 978-1998273-39-3
Ebook ISBN: 978-1-998273-40-9

Shadowpaw Press is grateful for
the financial support of Creative Saskatchewan.

# Contents

**Part Four**

## The Goblin Market



**Part Five**

## Drop the Veil

*To my mother, who didn't get to see this.*

*And to Sir Terry, who made me ask: "What Would Pratchett Do?"*

# Part One
# In the Office of the Mountain King

*We must not look at goblin men,*
*We must not buy their fruits:*
*Who knows upon what soil they fed*
*Their hungry thirsty roots?*

— "Goblin Market," Christina Rossetti, 1862

# Chapter 1
# Leaving North Bay, Ontario

Departures, Perpetua decided, deserved a train.

Dr. Zhivago had a train. He also had Russia in winter, with billowing steam, a longing whistle, and longing looks. In *Casablanca*, Bogart had Ingrid Bergman and a plane.

*I*, Perpetua thought, *have a rolling suitcase with a stuck wheel and a bus station at the edge of town.*

The sun beat down on her as she waited for the light to change. When it did, she crossed the highway, her long skirt swishing, her suitcase going *scraggle-scraggle-scrape* behind her.

But the Ontario Northland train had left North Bay years ago. And a plane would blow her wad of cash before she even stepped on the tarmac in Toronto. All that was left was the Northland bus.

She walked down the hill to the old train station that now served as a bus depot. She waited, alone, at the bay marked for the Toronto express. The breeze brought the sharp smell of old rail creosote mixed with the fresh scent of pine trees she knew she was going to miss.

She perked up when she heard an approaching car, but it peaked and faded away, out of sight over the hill.

"Not that I should care," she muttered. "I'm twenty-one. This was going to happen eventually."

"*We'll see how brave you are*," her mother had said—after, Perpetua had to admit, much goading. Still, it stung.

*Yes*, she thought. *We'll see*.

A rising roar and the gleam of reflected sun made her look up. A bus was coming down toward the depot. The sign on its windshield read: TORONTO.

It stopped at the bay with a chuff. Perpetua looked up the hill for that one red car that would tell her that, in the race with the Northland, her mother had at least shown up at the starting line.

The driver pumped the brakes. "You getting on, or what?"

Perpetua shrugged. "Guess I'm going to Toronto."

The driver rolled his eyes. "That magical town."

She found a seat halfway back, stuffed her suitcase in the overhead rack, and sat down with her backpack on her lap. She looked out the window as the bus groaned onward.

"Magic? Why not?" She tilted her seat back. "I could use a little magic right now."

## Chapter 2
# The City of Light and Magic

Perpetua had come to Toronto looking for a job. Instead, she found gargoyles.

They leered from the corner of the terminal as Perpetua stared up at them. *Seriously? Gargoyles in a bus terminal?*

But the terminal grumbled with idling engines. People filed onto a bus to Montreal. A driver flipped through his clipboard. Nobody gave the faces even a passing glance.

She shrugged. *Must be some forgotten art installation.*

She took a deep, steadying breath and coughed out a lungful of diesel exhaust. She headed for the sidewalk, cutting a wide arc past a grizzled homeless man sitting against the wall.

She kept her spirits up by thinking, despite her mother's comment, about how brave she was. After all, how many people came to a strange city with $500 in their pocket (well, technically, their bra), and set out to make a new life?

*Lots, actually. That's what immigrants do. Except, maybe, for the money in their underwear part. And they work themselves to the bone, if they're lucky.*

She turned onto the main thoroughfare and stopped in her tracks.

She'd known Toronto was a big city, but she hadn't appreciated just how big until faced with this river of humanity. Men and women in power suits, stockbrokers leaning into cell phones, students striding to the beat of music on their earbuds, their shoes battered the sidewalk in a steady rhythm as they all strode north, eyes down or glazed, letting nobody and nothing stand in their way.

Perpetua stared, appalled, until she spotted a fish swimming against the stream: a young woman in a stylish green skirt and blazer, striding confidently, ruby lips set firm, parting the crowd like an icebreaker. She caught Perpetua's gaze. Her eyes narrowed, and her smile tightened. She quickened her pace and vanished down the street.

Perpetua squared her shoulders. *So, that's how you do it: step out like you own the place*, and *people will make way for you*.

She stepped out like she owned the place.

The rhythm of feet broke into a staccato of stumbles and body checks.

"Ow!"

"Watch where you're going!"

"Oof!"

"Get out of the way!"

"My foot!"

"Hey!"

She darted through a gap in the stream and found herself teetering on the curb, trapped between cars moving at the speed of battleships in harbour, and people charging like cavalry.

At least here, she could walk without the risk of being run over, so walk, she did.

"Hey! Need a ride?"

She stopped and looked around to see who'd said that. Nobody was looking at her. The car windows were all closed against the heat. She shrugged and walked on.

"Take you wherever you need to go!"

She slowed. The traffic around her squealed, drawing together like a coiled spring.

"Taxi for hire!"

She looked to her left and saw an orange-and-teal taxicab keeping pace with her in the curb lane, its windows open.

"No thanks," she said.

The driver's head swivelled toward her. "What?"

She kept walking. "You asked if I wanted a cab. I don't, thanks."

He frowned. "I didn't ask if you wanted a cab."

Perpetua peered into the open window.

A young man sat behind the wheel. He was about her age, light-skinned, with a beaky nose and a face so narrow it looked like he'd shut it in a book. His top half, which was all she could see, wore a sweatshirt with McGill University emblazoned across the chest. His mop of dark curls would have looked good on, say, Tina Turner, circa 1985.

"You did," she replied. "You asked me three times. And you're following me."

"I'm not following you!"

She stopped. So did the cab. "Oh yeah?"

"But—"

She walked on, faster. The cab kept pace with her. She stopped again, glaring, hands on her hips. "Look, I'm warning you—"

"Honest, I'm not following you! I don't have any choice where to go." He gestured out the front window. "Look!"

She looked. The cab was a foot from the back bumper of a limousine. The limousine was stopped even closer to the back of a cube van. The cube van was behind a bus.

*And the arm bone's connected to the . . . leg bone*, she thought, and then subtly shook her head to rid it of the earworm. She flashed the taxi driver a withering glare, turned, and walked on.

As she did, the bus closed its doors and moved ahead. The cube van's brake lights came off. It pulled forward, as did the limousine. She looked to her left and, sure enough, the taxicab was once again keeping pace with her.

She stopped. The cab stopped. So did every other car in the lane. Engines idled. Ahead of her, someone honked a horn. She looked up and down the line of traffic. “Well, that’s weird.”

She gave the driver an accusing glare, and he shrugged apologetically.

She looked ahead again. “Okay, it’s a red light at the next intersection. I’ll go this way, and you wait until I get to the next intersection and turn right, okay?”

He looked nervous. “Uh . . .”

“It won’t take long. Nice meeting you!” She strode away.

Ahead, the cars stopped at the intersection suddenly flashed their signals and turned right. The other cars pulled into the space after them. The limousine pulled ahead, and the gap between it and the taxicab widened.

Behind the cab, drivers leaned on their horns. Someone shouted, “Move on, you jerk!”

Perpetua glanced back and saw the cab driver’s cheeks redden, his knuckles whitened on the wheel. He peeled forward, tires screeching, and then filled the gap behind the limousine with a squeak. This again brought him level with Perpetua, and the traffic kept pace as she walked forward.

“I’m sorry,” he said. “They come after you with pitchforks if you hold up the line.”

Perpetua stopped. Traffic stopped with a squeak.

Hands on her hips, she looked up and down the jammed laneway. She cocked her head. “What would happen if I walked backward, I wonder?”

The cab driver blanched. “No! Don’t!”

She lifted her foot. “I really think I ought to try . . .”

But before her heel touched the sidewalk, she heard a squeal and a thump behind her. Horns blared. People shouted.

“Geez!” The cab driver waved at her, frantic. “Get in! Quick!”

She yanked open the back door, tossed in her suitcase, and leaped onto the seat, backpack and all. She pulled the door shut. Immediately, traffic moved, and the cab drove on.

"So, where to, miss?"

"Um . . ." Perpetua looked out at the street. Traffic was now moving at a good clip. "What just happened?"

The driver shrugged. "Toronto traffic. It's got a mind of its own."

Perpetua looked at the cabbie. He seemed harmless enough, but looks could be deceiving. His name was Fergus, according to the information beside the photo on his licence. Actually, that was his last name; his first was so scuffed, it was illegible.

She shifted her backpack onto her lap. Inside, she had her emergency cell phone and an emergency can of mace. "If you weren't talking to me out there, then who were you talking to when you said, 'need a ride,' and 'taxi for hire'?"

The light dawned. "Oh!" He chuckled. "Sorry. I was just practising the patter."

"Patter?"

"Half this job is patter. Connecting with customers. Getting them to relax. It brings in tips. Or so I'm told."

She raised an eyebrow. "So, you were pattering . . . at yourself?" She told herself it wasn't nearly as dirty as it sounded.

Fergus sent her a grin by way of the rear-view mirror. "If you hadn't interrupted me, you would have heard me say, 'So, you new in town?' and 'Going to see anything interesting?'"

"Catchy."

"So, you new in town?"

"Kind of." Perpetua glanced out the window.

"Going to see anything interesting?"

"Sort of." She held her breath, then let it go, slowly.

Fergus's brow creased. "You okay?"

She looked at him again. She shouldn't talk to strangers; that was one of her mother's rules, and one of the few she still respected. Still . . . her instincts threw up no warnings about this guy. Perhaps it would be okay. "I'm making a new start."

"A new start?"

"I'm starting a new life."

His eyes widened in the mirror. "Just like that? It's a big city for that sort of thing."

"Come on! I can't be the first person to do this!"

"Point. Still, it's brave. I came here for an education. Instead, here I am, driving a cab."

"Aha. Is the cab company hiring?"

"Not really. I got this through a friend of a friend."

"Oh." She sat back, disappointed.

"So, you never told me." He angled through an intersection. "Where to?"

"Um . . ." She straightened up. The thought of contending with the crowds again didn't thrill her, but she was on a budget. "Sorry." Honesty was the best policy, right? After all, it was why she'd stormed away from home: a question of honesty. "You should let me out. I can't afford this trip."

"How much *can* you afford?"

She mulled it over. "Ten dollars? I have to go to—" Her street smarts vetoed the idea of telling the cabbie exactly where she was heading. "King and Church?"

He flipped a hand on the steering wheel. "Fair enough. It's more than I'm making just sitting here in traffic."

She settled back in her seat. "Huh." She smiled. "Thanks."

She liked the way Fergus's eyes said "*You're welcome*" in the rear-view mirror.

They turned another corner, and Toronto's skyline shifted into view. She leaned forward with a gasp. "Well, hey!"

She knew Toronto's streets weren't paved with gold, but now that she was here, she had to wonder about the buildings. The towers ahead glowed orange in the setting sun, so bright she had to squint.

"Maybe there's a little magic in this city, after all," she said.

That hope dried up soon after.

"What do you mean, 'there's no room'?" she yelled.

The desk manager shrugged. "The room you asked for is no longer available."

"But . . ." Her fists clenched. "I booked it on the internet!" It was a struggle not to stamp her foot; she'd outgrown that, or at least thought she had. "I have the receipt and everything!" She slapped the folded paper on the counter. "See?"

The manager barely looked at it. "That's not a receipt. That's just a reservation."

Perpetua arched an eyebrow. "Doesn't the term 'reservation' imply that you've set aside a room in reserve?"

"Yeah, but not the price for it. If you don't pay a deposit, conditions may change without notice."

"On a whim, you mean!"

"There is a room available," the manager deadpanned. "For the reasonable price of $100 per night, you can—"

This time, Perpetua *did* stamp her foot. "That's *four times* what you advertised! At that price—" She stuttered to a stop.

*I'd be out of here in less than a week!*

"Nothing I can do. It's the height of tourist season. Everything is booked. Take it, or leave it."

Perpetua glared at him. A hundred dollars a night, for at least one night, when she had just $500 to her name? Take it, or leave it, indeed.

She leaned on the counter. "Would you like some feedback on that? 'Cause, you know, there *is* a third option . . ."

On reflection, Perpetua had to rate the hotel's security staff as "better than average."

She even resolved to say so on Yelp, right after the part about the manager trying to swindle her. The way the two big men gently, but firmly, bundled her out the door and onto the street . . . that, at least, was professional. They were even kind enough to hand her backpack to her. Then they stood, watching her, maybe to make sure she didn't try to barrel back inside.

"What?" she told their stony faces. "He said, 'Take it or leave it.' Is it my fault he couldn't take it?"

The two guards straightened their identical red blazers and stepped back inside.

Perpetua looked around. The sun was down, and the city's skyline sparkled like a Christmas tree. A streetcar glided past. A homeless man struggled to manoeuvre his shopping cart across the tracks.

Across the street, a cathedral's spires rose into the sky. They looked magnificent, a mass of complicated shapes rich with carvings under the eaves, and the grotesque stone faces of gargoyles leering from niches above the porch. But despite its soaring steeple, it was dwarfed by the skyscrapers behind it. And Perpetua had to admit, in that moment, that she felt as though she were dwarfed by everything.

She took a breath and let it out slowly. "Okay. This is okay. So, plan A didn't work out. There are other letters in the alphabet. *Y*, for instance."

Cars breezed past, and the wind plucked at her skirt. This was the height of summer, yet Perpetua felt a sudden chill.

*Sure, you could find a place tonight. But what about the next night? What will you pay, then? What if a job doesn't materialize in the next five days?*

She stared at the small park beside the cathedral. Its natural beauty was spoiled only slightly by a raggedly dressed figure sprawled over the nearby bench, snoring.

*You could go home*, said a little voice at the back of her mind.

But she couldn't. The bus back to North Bay had left long ago. Like it or not, she was stuck in Toronto.

"Oh my god!" She pressed her hands over her mouth, but the words spilled out anyway. "Oh my god! What am I going to do?"

Something caught her eye. It was the homeless man, still

struggling to manhandle his cart up onto the sidewalk. Her gaze tracked up the street. "Oh my god!"

She darted forward, grabbed the near end of the cart, and pulled. The cart leaped with a clatter onto the sidewalk. The man came with it.

Behind him on the road, a dump truck smashed past.

"Watch where you're going!" Perpetua yelled after it. *The creep didn't even slow down*.

She turned back to the man. "You all right?"

He looked at her with eyes that glittered through the mass of his hair and the deep shadow under his broad-brimmed hat. They stared at each other.

"You all right?" she asked again.

He nodded at her, then up at the gargoyles on the cathedral. "Gotta go," he mumbled. "Places to meet, things to go, people to do." His words slurred as he shuffled away—remarkably fast, Perpetua thought.

She turned to watch him amble away, and a wave of stink washed over her. She backed up, choking, and only then remembered the greasy feeling of the cart against her fingers. She rubbed them on her skirt. "Ew! Well, you're welcome."

She took a breath of fresher air and then let it go. "What am I going to do?"

There was a scruff of stone against stone.

She straightened up, glanced at her backpack, where the kind-of-illegal mace was stashed, and then looked around. She was alone on the sidewalk.

She looked up at the cathedral, and then frowned at a gargoyle perched above the door, its shoulders white with bird poop. A pigeon strutted across its neck and pecked at its ear.

The gargoyle's stony gaze was focused on something past Perpetua, and its outstretched arm pointed over Perpetua's shoulder.

*That's weird*, she thought. *I don't think it was pointing before . . .*

*It must have been. What other explanation is there?*

Still, she followed the direction of its pointing finger to an alleyway across the street. The building closest was boarded up and plastered with signs advertising it as "The Future Site of St. Lawrence Station—Don River Subway." The building next to it, however, did not look abandoned. A sign on its wall seemed to say, "HOSTE—" The rest was obscured by a lamppost.

Perpetua crossed the street, dragging her suitcase after her.

The sign was painted, and not backlit, but she could read it clearly. "Hostelry. Rooms for rent. Safe. Clean. $20/night." An arrow pointed to a well-lit door, which opened smoothly. The carpet in the hall beyond was dark and old and a bit worn, but clean.

*Worth a look, I suppose. I can always back out.*

She waved at the gargoyle across the street. "Thanks!" She turned back to the door. "Here's to a little bit of magic, after all."

The door slammed behind her.

Across the street, a pigeon cooed. A stony, grinding sound echoed, followed by a squawk. Feathers fluttered to the ground, and all was still.

The desk manager gaped at her as though he'd never seen a customer before.

"What are you doing here?" He had a young boy's squeaky voice and an old man's wrinkled face. "You—you shouldn't be here!"

She frowned. "I can't imagine how you keep the crowds away."

"Seriously, hu—" He shook himself. "How did you find this place?"

Perpetua backed away. "Well, I . . . it's . . ." She felt her cheeks flush as she tried to figure out what to say. She was too tired to come up with a convincing lie. "The fact is, I saw a gargoyle across the street. It was pointing at this place."

The manager drew back. "Seriously?"

"Yeah, I know. Sounds stupid, but—"

"Excuse me." The manager hopped over the desk, agile as a teenager, and scurried out the front door. The door had barely closed when it burst open again, and the manager was back. "So it is. That settles it. You can stay."

Perpetua remembered to close her mouth. "Really?"

"Yeah." He flipped open the desk register. "For two weeks, or until you get a job. You can't stay here forever. Plenty of other people need the room."

"I—uh . . ." She could barely follow this conversation. "Thanks . . . I really appreciate this. I—"

He spun the register to face her and held out the pen. "Sign here, please."

"Sure. How did you know I need a job?"

"Doesn't everybody?" The wrinkles on his face shaped themselves into a smile that reminded her briefly of the gargoyle.

"Well, thank goodness I found this hotel. What's the name?" She looked at the register and did a double-take. "Amnesia House? Why the heck did you call this place Amnesia House?"

"I forget."

She wasn't sure it was a joke.

## Chapter 3
# Fergus's Journal Entries

At home, Fergus picked up a black, hardcover book with the word "JOURNAL" embossed on the front in gold. He grinned at the Post-it Note in his own handwriting that said, "My Journal! Keep Out! Fergus."

Turning it over in his hands, he flipped through it. Page after page of handwriting strobed past. He closed the book and frowned at it a moment before taking a seat in his armchair and opening it to read.

*Saturday, February 2*
*Dear Future Self,*

*Here are some things to know. I'm a taxi driver. I have $300 in my bank account, but no balance on my credit card. Don't overuse the credit card. I live at 108 Albany Avenue in Toronto, and my cell phone number is (416) 555-9681. Rent is due at the end of the month, so it's time to get back to work.*

Fergus flipped ahead.

*Friday, March 1*
*Dear Future Self,*

*The rent is paid. Can it really be that much for a basement apartment? Looking at the classifieds, I see . . . yes, it can. I'll see if I can get some extra time scheduled from Jay down at dispatch. Still no balance on my credit card, though, so that's good.*

Fergus flipped ahead some more.

*Wednesday, April 10*
*Dear Future Self,*

*It feels really strange to write that, like I'm talking to myself on paper. But they say this is a good way to make sure these journal entries get done, and to turn writing a diary into a habit. I admit that I've not been keeping up, and they say that I have to. And, well, who am I to disagree with the experts?*

*They tell me to write about discoveries. Well, today, I discovered I could navigate Cabbagetown. When I turned off Parliament onto Winchester, I knew which streets were one-way only, and even the best place to let off my passenger. I was impressed. My passenger's tip was less than impressive, however.*

*Honestly, I wouldn't have chosen this job if I'd known what it would be like. So, hear this, Future Self: driving a taxi? Not the glamorous life you'd think it'd be.*

Frowning, Fergus flipped further. Finally, something caught his eye, and he smoothed down the page.

*Tuesday, July 2*

*Taxi-driving isn't all bad, actually. It's neat to see the city at night. There's a pulse to it. And everybody looks forward. People walk or drive with a part of their mind already at their destination. You can see in their faces the places they're going. Hopeful. Sad. Stressed. Exuberant. In love.*

*Speaking of, I met this cute girl today. She just jumped into my cab. Literally.*

*She wasn't tall, but she wasn't short. She was thin, but not skinny. She had on a long black skirt and had slender legs that made her look tall, but really, she was just right. She had brown hair pulled back in a ponytail, green eyes, and a smile you didn't want to get on the wrong side of. Her face was . . . mixed. Stressed, nervous, but . . . excited at the possibilities.*

*She didn't have much money, so I gave her a discount, which might be why Jay was mad at me later. She talked about coming to Toronto with not much, of making a new life, so how could I not help her out? I didn't warn her off it, either.*

*We all have to start over sometimes.*

*And maybe it's wishful thinking, but I hope I get to see her again.*

*Anyway, not a bad day for my six-month anniversary of losing my memory.*

# Chapter 4
# Looking for a Job in Toronto

The next day, Perpetua printed off copies of her resume, dialled up her "heroic montage" playlist on her battered iPod, plugged in her earphones, and headed off for her first job interview.

"Thank you. We'll be in touch," the interviewer said after only a few short minutes and even fewer questions.

Perpetua frowned, but she stood when the interviewer did, and shook the man's hand.

*That's okay,* she told herself as she turned onto King, tired of trying to analyze what had gone wrong. *There are plenty of fish in the sea.*

Back at the hostel, Perpetua tapped on the front desk. The manager looked up. "Any messages?" she asked. The manager shook his head, and she slouched to her room.

"What do you mean, do I have any experience in the food service industry?" Perpetua goggled at the interviewer. "Aren't you a bank?"

"We're trying a new business model," the interviewer replied. "After the success of establishments like Hooters, we thought we'd have our tellers circulate around the floor, engaging customers, just like waitresses. How does that sound to you?"

Perpetua searched for just the right word. She settled for: "Interesting."

The interviewer held up a T-shirt and very short, cut-off jeans. "This would be your uniform."

Perpetua's eyes widened.

"So," the interviewer went on. "Can you see yourself in one of these?"

Her eyes narrowed. "Depends. Can you see yourself in one?"

He laughed. "No, I couldn't possib—" He stopped, blanching at Perpetua's expression. Then he stood up and extended his hand. "Thank you. We'll be in touch."

In her room that night, Perpetua sniffed the air, startled from her thoughts by an alarming, acrid smell. Her gaze shot toward the hotplate, and the pot that was starting to smoke. She yanked her lentils free and doused them with water from a bottle. She grimaced at the contents and moved to throw them in the waste bin. She hesitated. Looking in the pot again, she picked up a plastic fork and began sorting through the contents for something edible.

"You're a temp agency in Toronto!" Perpetua stared across the desk in disbelief. "How can you *not* have any openings?"

The manager shrugged. "We're temporarily overstaffed."

She let out a sigh that was almost a growl and stormed from the office.

Back at the hostel, Perpetua crossed out three listings on a folded classifieds section. She looked at the bed, at the roll of bills and the handful of coins that lay there, and sighed. She took the bills and shoved them back beneath her bra. Then she shrugged on her black T-shirt and headed out to her next round of appointments.

The interviewer gingerly held her resume in his white latex gloves, and Perpetua marvelled at the things she could put up with while in search of a job. Really, were there any limits?

He looked up at her. "So, Miss Collins: do you have any objection to working with radioactive materials?"

What was truly frightening was the length of the pause before she said, flatly: "Yes."

Perpetua sat alone inside a cafe dubbed "Coffee Thyme." She watched a young man step inside, frown at the decor (or lack thereof), and head to the register. "Yeah," he said. "I'd like a venti, half-caf double cappuccino. Easy on the froth?"

The man behind the counter glared. "Get. Out!" he intoned, and threw a day-old muffin at the customer's retreating back.

*Yup*, she thought. *Definitely the anti-Starbucks*. But the tea was cheap, assuming you were brave enough to order one. She leaned forward and rested her head in her hands.

The man behind the counter cleared his throat. Perpetua looked up and saw him look at her and then, pointedly, at the clock. Beneath it was a sign: "Loitering prohibited. No more than 20 minutes per drink!"

She returned an even more pointed look, then rose with dignity, shouldered her backpack, and swept out.

The afternoon sun had settled behind a high-rise apartment, putting the street in shadow. Perpetua tossed her crossed-out newspaper into a recycling bin and meandered along the sidewalk, scuffing her feet.

Time was running out. If she didn't get a job soon, she

wouldn't be able to afford the bus ticket back to North Bay. She'd have to call her mother for a lift.

"Which would complete the humiliation," she muttered.

A horn honked behind her. She jerked up, then stepped back as a cab pulled up.

"I didn't order a—" She spotted the driver. "Cab Guy?"

Fergus gave her a grin. "Traffic Girl!"

"What are you doing here?"

"This is Adelaide Street. If I'm looking for a fare, I cruise Adelaide."

She glanced both ways along the sidewalk. Most of the streets of downtown Toronto were full of people, catered to by prosperous-looking shops. This part of Adelaide wasn't one of them. What few stores there were, buried amongst the loading docks and the oddly shaped parking lots, were all closed. Some were even shuttered. She looked at Fergus. "Does it work?"

He grimaced. "Not really, no. King Street is where the action is. But I'm the new kid, so . . . seniority, you know?"

Her brow furrowed. "Why not just cruise King? Who'd know?"

His grin was edged now. "Oh, they'd know. Cabbies . . . they're the eyes of the city. So, what are you doing out here?"

"Job hunting."

"Lots of good opportunities on Adelaide?"

"Shut up."

"You look like you could use a break." He nodded at the back seat. "Get in."

She drew back. "I can't afford to pay you."

"Where you heading?"

"King and Church."

"Get in," he said. "On the house. Or rather, cab. It gets me onto King. They can't accuse me of cruising if I drop off a passenger, can they?"

She opened the door and slid in. "Thanks."

They drove off, and Fergus glanced at her through the rear-view mirror. "So, what am I supposed to call you, if not 'traffic girl'?"

Perpetua thought about saying, "your client," but since she was technically riding for free, maybe that didn't apply. "Call me Perpetua."

"Per . . . petua?"

"My mother named me. It's not my fault. What do I call you?"

"Fergus."

She wrinkled her nose. According to his licence, Fergus was his last name. His first name was Smudge. "Not 'Mr. Fergus.' You're no older than I am, and I just told you my first name."

"Just Fergus."

"What Fergus?"

He focused on the traffic ahead. "It's . . . Aloysius."

"Whoa!" Her eyebrows flew up. "Let me guess: your mom named you?"

He matched her grin. "Kind of, yeah."

"Mothers," she said. "They can haunt your life forever with just a name. Still, it could be worse. My middle name's Tallulah."

"Ouch!"

"Yeah."

He twisted the wheel. "So. Job hunting."

She looked out the window. "I don't want to talk about it."

"That bad, huh?"

"What did I *just* say?"

"Sorry."

She sighed. "No, I'm sorry. I shouldn't take it out on you. I knew coming here was a gamble. Doesn't make it hurt any less, though."

"I suppose knowing that others are in the same boat isn't much of a consolation."

"Not really." She looked back out the window. A dishevelled

man pushed a shopping cart along the street. Another man, lying in a dark alleyway, turned over and wrapped himself in a dirty blanket.

"Still," she said, after a moment, "it could be worse." She smiled at him. "Thank you for the lift."

She liked the smile she saw in his reflected eyes. "You're welcome," he replied.

The brakes squealed softly as they eased to a stop. "Here we are," he said. "King and Church."

She pointed at the alleyway by the hostel. "Can you pull up to the hostel, there? That's where I'm staying."

He turned around and looked at her. "Really? *That's* where you're staying?"

Her brow furrowed at his sudden interest. "Yeah. It's not bad. The manager's a bit prickly, but the place is clean. It's about the only good thing that's come my way in this city, so maybe save the judgment."

"You can see it all right?"

Her frown deepened. "Yes."

He stared at her. He looked . . . impressed, but Perpetua felt uncomfortable. "Is there a problem?" she asked.

"I think I may have a job lead for you," he said.

She jerked up. "Really?"

"Yeah. Wait, hold on a minute . . ." He shuffled through some papers on the seat beside him. "Here." He passed over a folded newspaper. "What do you think of that?"

She took at the newspaper. It wasn't one of the mainstream titles, but an alternative rag full of listings of adult stores and escort services. She was about to tell Fergus what she thought of his "lead" when she saw it, at the bottom of the page:

WANTED: NIGHT GIRL

*Personal assistant job. Keyboarding and computer skills*

*required. Duties include: managing finances, contacting clients, answering phones.*

*Must be able to tolerate deep underground environment.*

*Steady nerves an asset. Non-screamer preferred.*

*Full time: 9 p.m. - 5 a.m., $24/hr plus benefits. Bring resume today, 7:30 p.m. Successful applicant hired on the spot.*

*T.P. Earthenhouse: Bouncers, Rare Coins, and Art Installations*

*Toronto Dominion Bank Tower, Subbasement Three*
*King and Bay, Toronto Financial District.*

She nodded when she saw the salary. But then she looked closer. "'Night *Girl*'? What the heck's a 'night girl'?"

"He probably means it like the term 'Girl Friday,'" Fergus said. "You know, a personal assistant, Jill-of-all-trades—"

"I know what it means," she replied. "I've seen *His Girl Friday*. He'd better not be getting any ideas." She took another look at the ad. "'Steady nerves an asset'?"

"You got those, right?"

"'Non-screamer preferred'?"

"Somebody's got a sense of humour!"

She put the paper down. "Are you having me on?"

"No, really! I think they're looking for somebody like you."

She looked at the ad again. "But where is this place? Subbasement Three?" She looked at him, raising an eyebrow.

"Probably in the Underground City."

Her other eyebrow joined the first. "There's an *underground* city?"

"You haven't heard about Toronto's big, underground shopping complex?" His eyebrows shot up in turn. "It's in the Guinness Book of World Records, just like Yonge Street and the CN Tower used to be."

"But what *is* it?"

He took a deep breath, then looked up thoughtfully. “So . . . you know how a tree has as much going on belowground as it does above?”

“I guess.”

“Well,” he said, “there’s something you need to know about this city . . .”

## Chapter 5
# The Underground City

At the corner of King and Bay, in the thick of Toronto's financial district, Perpetua heard the opera singer.

She stood beneath the stone and steel towers, pressed up against a marble wall to let the crowds pass. At first, she thought she was imagining things, but then she heard the lyrics.

*Vesti la giubba e la faccia infarina.*
*La gente paga, e rider vuole qua.*
*E se Arlecchin t'invola Colombina,*
*ridi, Pagliaccio, e ognun applaudirà!*
*Tramuta in lazzi lo spasmo ed il pianto*
*in una smorfia il singhiozzo e 'l dolor, ah!*

She looked about, puzzled, before she spotted the tuxedoed man on the roof of a low building jutting out from between two black skyscrapers. He belted out the words. And he was actually quite good.

The crowds passed below him on the sidewalk, lost in their own worlds.

The light changed, and Perpetua joined the stream of homebound people rushing into building stairwells like snowmelt down a drain.

Once on the escalator, she was startled by how far down she could see.

All of Perpetua's interviews had been above ground. As she'd struggled through the downtown crowds, she'd noticed stairs and escalators leading down, but had thought they were just the way to the subway. Turned out, she was right, but that wasn't the half of it.

Fergus had quoted her numbers, like a walking Wikipedia. Over twenty-nine kilometres of tunnels connecting over fifty buildings to seven subway stations. Over four million square feet of stores, handling 100,000 commuters on an average weekday. But these numbers told only a fraction of the picture. She'd seen rivers of humanity on the streets; down here, it was a torrent. Down here, the footfalls echoed and re-echoed in a frenzied drumbeat.

At the bottom of the escalator, she made the mistake of stopping to stare. People shouted. People shoved. She ducked behind a marble pillar and watched people flow from the escalator into the larger river heading beneath signs that pointed the way to Union Station.

"Wow," she breathed.

She'd been in Toronto for a few days now. She was beginning to understand its rhythms. She focused on gaps between the walkers, and then took the leap—several leaps. Skipping and dodging between the commuters, she emerged into a food court. Grabbing a cheap tea from a coffee vendor, she found an empty seat and watched the people stream past, like a girl on a riverbank, tempted to skip stones.

On the PA system, the Beatles told everyone about the lonely people everywhere. Display monitors showed a local news channel, with a live feed of the mayor of Toronto.

"You get a subway! And *you* get a subway!" he shouted,

pointing in turn to people in the mob of cheering supporters. "Everybody gets a subway! Because I have the cash! Oh, yeah!"

Beneath him, the caption read, "Scarborough Rejoices: Bloor and Sheppard Subways Meet at Town Centre."

Perpetua glanced back at the passing crowd. The clumble of footfalls, the burble of voices, proved strangely lulling. She picked up a discarded newspaper and looked through the classifieds. Many of the listings were ones she had already seen. She turned to the front section and settled down to wait.

When she looked up a little later, she set the paper down. "What . . . the hell?"

The food court was deserted. The shops were closed. Where once there had been a river of people, there was now nothing but empty floor space. Someone had turned the Muzak off.

She walked to the corridor, held her arms out, and turned a full circle. Nobody ran into her; nobody cursed her. She was completely, utterly alone.

"Did somebody call an apocalypse and not tell me?" she muttered. "This is straight out of *Dawn of the Dead*!"

A door squealed open, and footsteps approached at a swift clop. Shadows flickered on the wall of a side corridor. Perpetua tensed. She glanced at her backpack on the food court table. Did mace work against zombies?

The shadow burst from the corridor: a businessman with blazer tails flapping, briefcase bouncing, tie swept over his shoulder. He looked at his watch, muttering, "I'm late! I'm late!" He clattered past Perpetua and was gone.

From other side corridors, sounds and shadows emerged. Straggling workers and shoppers, all, some rushing to the trains, others taking their time. The world hadn't ended, after all.

And somewhere far away, someone sang.

It was a woman this time, her soprano voice rising and falling through the corridors.

*So bist du meine Tochter nimmermehr*

*Verstossen sei aug swig*
*Verlassen sei aug eqig*

Perpetua shook her head. "Somebody should get those two opera singers together."

She checked the time on her cell phone: 6:30 p.m. She retrieved her bag and set out along the corridors, looking for the Toronto Dominion Bank Tower and Subbasement Three.

She walked, and she walked, and she walked.

None of the elevators she spied went to Subbasement Three. She wasn't even sure if she was in the right Toronto Dominion Tower (turns out, there were four).

A half-hour into her journey, she was cursing the map designers of the PATH network. What possible use was it to designate north, south, east, and west in an environment where the stores looked the same and you couldn't see the sun? There were plenty of exits to the surface, but that didn't help, since she had to go back underground to start the search again.

An hour into her journey, she stopped by a bench, ripped a page from her notebook, wrote "I WAS HERE" on it, and left it on the bench. She was not surprised to come upon that paper from a different direction a half hour later.

*I'm walking in frickin' circles! I'm going to be late for my appointment, but who the heck am I supposed to ask?*

Ahead of her, at a door offering an exit onto King Street, a group of teens gambolled down the stairs, skateboards tucked under their arms. They glanced up and down the corridor.

"All clear," one shouted.

They plunked their skateboards on the marble floor and kicked off with a whoop. They hit a wheelchair ramp and gathered speed. Perpetua smiled as their cries echoed into the distance. *At least someone here is having fun*, she thought.

Ahead, a door marked "SECURITY" swung open, and two guards ran out. They glared at the disappearing skateboarders.

"Not again," huffed one. He rushed after the teenagers,

holding a radio to his mouth. "Trespassing skateboarders. We're in pursuit."

"It's like a daily workout," said his partner, running after.

"Hey, wait!" Perpetua shouted. Then she lowered her hand. The officers hadn't paid her the slightest bit of notice. *Well, perfect*, she thought.

She came to the wheelchair access ramp and looked at its gentle incline, its short marble wall. She paused a moment, thinking about the skateboarders and a much simpler time.

She backed up a couple of steps and then made a running start. Cresting the top of the wheelchair ramp, she jumped up, perched sideways on the top of the marble wall, and let momentum carry her down, like sliding down a banister. She hopped off at the bottom and looked back up, grinning.

A shadow fell over her. She turned. A security guard stood there, arms folded. "Shouldn't you be somewhere else?"

*Okay, the guard's ability to materialize out of nowhere was a little creepy. But it's been years since I've been put off by crossed arms and grim stares, and I'm not going to start now.*

"Yes," she said. "You can help me find the way. I've got a job interview."

The man's frown deepened. "A job interview. At this hour?"

"Yeah." Perpetua pulled out the newspaper and held it up, the Night Girl ad prominent.

The two guards returned, panting. "This woman giving you trouble, Patrick?" said one.

Patrick held up a palm. "Wait." He took the paper and stared at the advertisement. "Subbasement Three? Well, how about that!"

Perpetua rolled her eyes. "Yeah. And as you can see, I have to get going. So, if you'll just point me in the direction of the right elevator—"

"Not elevators, miss," said Patrick. He handed the paper back to her. "Stairs."

"Stairs?"

"The elevators don't go down to Subbasement Three. You want the door beside the elevators. That way." He pointed.

"Okay," she said, still wary.

The other guards looked sullenly at each other. "Did you see which way the skateboarders went?" asked one.

A skateboarder rolled behind them and tapped the taller guard on the shoulder. "You're it!" Then he was gone.

"Wh—I'll get those little—" The two officers gave chase.

Patrick turned to go. Then he turned back and flicked his hat brim in salute. "Good luck!" He ran off after his partners.

Perpetua found the elevator bay and opened the door on the side marked "STAIRS." Beyond was a typical stairwell: glossy white walls and harsh fluorescent lights that hummed like enormous insects.

She checked the time on her cell phone and then galloped down the stairs.

"Subbasement One," she muttered, one flight down, noting the words that had been painted on the wall. She peered through the window in the door and saw rows upon rows of cars. "Parking garage." She clattered down the next flight.

"Subbasement Two." Here, she noted dustier walls and a bare light bulb in the ceiling. The garage outside this window had fewer cars.

She looked dubiously down the final flight of stairs. "I think somebody's played a trick on me." She squared her jaw and trotted on.

"Subbasement Three." Here, the sign had almost faded to the same colour as the wall. "Parking—" She glanced through the window and did a double-take. "Oh, wait! Shopping corridor!"

She pushed the crash bar and entered.

It was as if she was back in the underground mall, except . . . this corridor was short, ending abruptly fifty feet away at a utility door marked, "EXIT." But it had the same marble floors, the same gleaming walls, and the same recessed pot lights.

There were three stores here: two on the left, one on the right, all with signs saying they were open. The remaining space held a shuttered food court full of tables and chairs. A sign pointed the way to the washrooms.

Perpetua stared at the door to a store called House of Limericks. Curious, she poked her head inside.

A man looked up from his desk. "There once was a man from Nantucket—"

Perpetua let the door slam.

The next storefront was the office for The Tooth Hurts, Dentistry. Running along the bottom of the sign was a slogan: "We can handle the tooth!"

She crossed the corridor to the third office. The words "T.P. Earthenhouse: Bouncers, Rare Coins, and Art Installations" stood out in black-bordered gold against the frosted glass. The letters were in some formal font, with fancy little serifs. It looked expensive.

She reached for the door, only to snatch back her hand as it swung open.

A young man stood there, eyes wide. He wore regulation interview attire: a shirt and tie, a briefcase. The briefcase had been hastily closed, trapping a piece of paper that poked out from a corner. He stared at her before he found his voice. "Are you here about the job?"

"Uh . . . Yeah. You?"

He nodded.

"You interviewed for a job labelled 'Night *Girl*'?"

"I was desperate," he said, edging past her.

She watched him go. "And now?"

"You don't want to go in there. Trust me. It's *crazy*!" He rushed for the stairs.

Perpetua looked at the door to the office, then back at the stairwell.

She shrugged. "I've seen worse."

She stepped inside.

## Chapter 6
# Fergus Journal Entries II

Fergus flipped past a couple of pages and then leaned back. Idly, he twirled a pen in his hands.

*Monday, July 15*
*Hey, Future Self! How's it going?*

*Nope. That's not me. Still, I've tried it out, and now I know.*

*Let's try again.*

*Dear Future Self,*

*It's been another day of driving and checking out the big city. And I have to wonder, how easy would it be to disappear in a city like Toronto?*

*I've been thinking about it. I meet a lot of people in my job. Consider, on a twelve-hour shift, with cab rides that last an average of twenty minutes, and an average of 1.5 passengers per ride, that's fifty-four passengers to meet every day. And that's assuming that I'm giving rides for every minute of those twelve hours. The reality, of course, is much less.*

*So, fifty passengers, in a city of three million people. In a region of nearly seven million. That's a drop in the bucket. What are the chances of seeing someone more than once?*

*How easy would it be to just slip into those crowds and disappear forever?*

*Whether you wanted to or not?*

*That's a disturbing tangent.*

*So, really, if you think about it, it's a miracle to meet somebody more than once in this job. Depending on the person, of course. And I was lucky enough to see that cute girl again. Remember, she jumped into my cab a few days back? I just happened to pick her up again. In my cab. Not actually pick her up, you understand.*

*But I did learn her name. Perpetua. A weird name, but a nice one. It fits. Per. Pet. Tua. It rolls off the tongue.*

*Anyway, I could tell that the past few days have been hard on her. Like the city wants to make her disappear. She told me she hadn't found a job yet, which sucks.*

*Why does the world have to be so hard for people like her?*

*I know life is hard, but some people have it so easy, and they get so many perks, stuff to make things go even smoother. Beauty is squandered on the rich. People with the power to move the world don't need the looks that go with it. Beautiful poor people, like Perpetua, should have more lucky breaks in their lives.*

*So, I gave her one.*

*I showed her a job posting I'd had my eye on for a while. She seemed interested.*

*And she saw the want ad for what it was. She didn't look at me oddly or chastise me for handing her an ad for some garage sale. She saw through the veil immediately.*

*Which shows how special she is, even though she doesn't seem to know it.*

# Chapter 7
# The Job Interview

The office looked sane, at least.

Slate-grey carpet covered the whole floor, with neither blemish nor stain. After walking through marble corridors in moderately stylish shoes, its softness was welcome. The frosted outer glass softened the lights of the corridor, allowing recessed pot lights to show off the waiting area.

The room was mostly empty, save for a reception desk at the back and a stack of boxes in a corner, each bearing an incomprehensible Swedish word and a picture of a chair. In the opposite corner was a photocopier-fax machine.

Perpetua went to the reception desk and ran her hand along its mahogany surface. The company's name was embossed across the front in gold letters. Behind it, a green swivel chair faced a phone switchboard and a stylish computer.

*The place looks sane. More than that, it looks well-financed.*

*But where is everybody?*

She glanced at her cell. Almost 8:30. But the office remained stubbornly deserted.

Three doors faced onto the reception area. The door on the right had an embossed sign reading, "TRAINING ROOM." The door opposite said, "WASHROOM." The third door, located behind the reception desk, was sturdier than the other two. It bore a plaque that read, “T.P. EARTHENHOUSE.”

“Must be where the boss lives.” She stepped around the desk and raised her hand to knock.

“Is someone there?” a voice asked.

Perpetua stood poised, knuckles still inches from the door. She lowered her hand. “Yeah. Me. I’m here about the Night Girl job?”

“Ah, excellent!” The voice was deep and smooth as a hundred-dollar bill. “Is anybody else with you?”

She looked back at the empty reception area. No shadows on the frosted glass windows; nothing to suggest waiting bodies.

“Nope,” she called. “Just me.”

“Oh, well,” the voice replied. “Still, you’re here. Please find a chair and come in. I’ll be with you presently.”

Perpetua brushed back stray strands of her hair and smoothed out her dress. *This is it*, she thought. *Possibly my last chance, my last interview before I slink back to North Bay and Mother’s smug satisfaction. I’d better make it good.*

*Wait. What did he mean, please find a chair, and* then *come in?*

She opened the door. Earthenhouse’s office was dimmer than the reception area, but it held a rich-looking, executive-style mahogany desk with an even richer-looking leather swivel chair behind it. A fruit basket with fresh apples, oranges, and bananas perched on the corner of the desk.

There was no other chair.

There was no Earthenhouse, either. Perpetua looked around before she saw a second doorway. A light was on behind it, and the sound of running water could be faintly heard; possibly an in-office washroom.

*Swanky!*

But all the other chairs were in boxes. *He doesn’t expect me to stand through my interview, does he?* Instead, she grabbed the green swivel chair from its place behind the reception desk. It made a sound like a dozen mice caught in a rusty hamster wheel.

She stared at the chair, gave it another tug. It let out another mousy squeak. She shrugged and dragged it, squeaking, into the office.

She sat in front of Earthenhouse's desk and sorted through her backpack for her resume. *Right. Get ready. You want this job, but you're not cloying. Just keep your cool and show him you're a professional.*

Behind her, the sound of running water stopped and was followed by that of a towel flapping. The door swung open.

"Ah," came Earthenhouse's deep voice. "I see you brought in the chair from reception. Excellent. Shows initiative."

Perpetua stood up gracefully and turned to offer a handshake. Her eyes widened.

T.P. Earthenhouse was three-quarters leg. He stood at Perpetua's height (five feet, four inches), and was about her width, but his waist was where his chest should be. He stood like a box on stilts, wearing a white shirt, red tie, and pinstripe pants with suspenders that made his legs look even longer. He was bald, and his skin was the colour of mossy stone. His eyes were black as a shark's, and his nose jutted halfway to his chin.

"T.P. Earthenhouse, at your service, madam." His smile revealed jagged teeth. Before Perpetua could react, he clasped her outstretched hand and bowed, kissing the back of it. His lips chilled her skin. "A pleasure to meet you, Miss . . ." He waited.

Perpetua recaptured her hand and found her voice. "Collins. Perpetua Collins, sir."

He tilted his head, and his neck made a sound like stones clicking. "Are you all right? You're looking a little green."

*He's one to talk!*

But she banished the woozy feeling and looked Earthenhouse in the eye. "I'm fine, sir. I just . . . haven't had dinner today." Which was true.

"Oh, well, after this, you should eat." He pointed behind her. "Have a seat. I'll make this as quick as I can."

Perpetua felt behind her for her chair and sat with a squeak. The chair squeaked, too.

Earthenhouse loped around his desk and sat on his haunches in his leather chair, his long-boned hands draped over his protruding knees. He leaned forward to pick up her resume, and somehow didn't topple his chair over.

"Miss Perpetua Collins . . ." He paused and peered past the resume at her. "Perpetua . . . family name?"

"My mother named me. It's not my fault."

"Ah." He gave her another glance before returning to her resume. "You're awfully young."

Her eyes narrowed. A plethora of comebacks danced on her lips, but she gave no voice to any of them. For one thing, she needed this job. For another . . . it just seemed cruel.

"I'm twenty-one," she said at last.

"That's young, isn't it?"

"It's older than twenty. That a problem?"

"I guess it isn't." He looked back at her resume. "There's no phone number here."

"Yeah." *On the other hand, that* could *be a problem*. "I've only just arrived, and I'm staying at a hostel. I don't know their number."

He tilted the paper, looked at her above it. "What about the number where you used to live?"

Her knuckles tightened on the armrest of her chair. "Trust me, it's not worth calling there. I don't have anything to do with that place now."

"Ah." He set the resume down and peered at her, propping his chin in his hands. "Let's talk about your experience, then. Have you worked in an office environment before?"

"I've done temp work," she replied. "I know how to use Microsoft Office. I can put together letters and spreadsheets. I know my way around a phone switchboard." *In that, the phone part is kind of obvious. And what I don't know, I can fake until I learn.*

"I see." Earthenhouse took a deep breath. "So, tell me, Miss Collins: have you had to deal with someone experiencing amnesia or other forms of memory loss?"

She gaped. "What kind of question is *that*?"

"Shall I take that as a 'no'?"

*It wasn't in the job description. Then again, what sort of job* has *that description?* "Lots of amnesia cases among your employees, are there?"

"No," he said quietly. "It's just good to be prepared."

Her heart sank. "Does this mean I don't get the job?"

"Not necessarily. This will just be something I'll handle."

"Uh—"

"Shall we move on?"

Perpetua wasn't sure. The amnesia question was so out of left field. Why did it even have to be asked in the first place?

*But I need this job. There's nothing else lined up. This is my last chance.*

She looked at her knees to regroup.

"I see you have some experience serving the public," said Earthenhouse. "Can you tell me more about that?"

Perpetua looked up. Her brow furrowed. Earthenhouse was suddenly wearing a top hat.

"Well . . ." She eyed the top hat. "I worked at McDonald's." She folded her arms across her chest. "I know that doesn't sound like much, but it's an active job. You never know who might come in. You've got to be prepared for everything." *You end up dealing with some pretty challenging people, and not just the customers.*

"Good." He peered at her resume again. "I see you left within two months."

*Two weeks, actually. Fortunately, those spanned two separate months, so I could report them as two months.* "Summer job. I had to go back to school."

"I see you have three years of university education . . ." His brow furrowed. "Why haven't you graduated?"

*He doesn't miss much, does he?* "It's on hold." She looked down at her lap, grinding her teeth. *Three years studying International Relations, as if jobs at the UN grew on trees. What was I thinking?*

"Why did you put it on hold?" Earthenhouse asked.

Perpetua looked up and blinked. Earthenhouse's top hat was striped. It had been black before. Same size, same shape, but now black and white, like a referee's shirt.

Silence stretched. Earthenhouse looked at her. "Miss Collins? Did you miss the question?"

"Um . . ." As job interviews went, Earthenhouse was playing dirty. She struggled to put something together. "I needed some paying work. Which is why I'm here."

"I see." Earthenhouse picked up her resume again. "It's a shame. I see your grade point average was in the mid-nineties."

"Thank you." She glanced at her knees again, then looked up. This time, Earthenhouse's top hat was red. More importantly, she saw Earthenhouse's hand hit his lap.

"Excuse me," she said.

He tilted his head. The hat tilted rakishly. "Yes, Miss Collins?"

"You're quick-changing your hat while conducting this interview."

"You noticed that."

"I did."

He leaned back. "And you called me on it."

"Yeah."

He took off his top hat and vanished it beneath his desk. "Most impressive. Most candidates don't say a word. They just become uncomfortable."

"So, this was a test?"

He steepled his fingers. "Of a sort."

"You know, when most interviewers want to challenge their

subjects, they say things like, 'Please tell us about your weaknesses, and where you think you'll be in five years' time.'"

"That doesn't tell me much," he said. "Most candidates just go on and on about how they push themselves too hard and want to actualize their potential."

In spite of herself, Perpetua grinned. "Point. But still: top hats?"

"How else am I going to ascertain your suitability for this job on such thin credentials?"

She straightened up. "You know, I may be thin on credentials, but I'm not thin on *experience*. Yes, I'm twenty-one. Yes, I don't have a long job list. But I know my way around computers." She pointed at the paper in Earthenhouse's hand. "I drafted that resume myself, using out-of-date software and a wonky printer at a local library. There are no spelling mistakes and, if I do say so myself, I think it's well formatted."

He glanced over her resume again and nodded.

She went on. "Your listing asked for somebody who can type, who knows computers, and can handle the phone. Oh, and it asked for somebody who can manage finances." She tapped her chest. "I've been here for two weeks. I came here with just five hundred dollars in my pocket. I know how to manage finances. Strong nerves? Got those, too, trying to live in Toronto with just five hundred dollars in my pocket. And 'non-screamer'?"

She took a breath. "Well, I haven't screamed yet, though I have to admit, you're giving me plenty of reason to. So, there you go: with all those skills and all that experience, I think I'm your girl."

She folded her arms across her chest.

Earthenhouse leaned back in his chair. He tilted his head again, taking her in. He nodded. "Most impressive. Well, Miss Collins, I confess, the top hats are more than just a test. They're a security measure."

"Security measure?"

"Yes. My business relies on keeping things in confidence. If people aren't willing to commit to this office, I don't want them giving away too much about what they've seen here. Rather than go through the process of nondisclosure agreements, I make sure to insert as many bizarre elements into the interview as possible."

She'd heard of this technique before—on a comedy program. "So, you're saying that if I tell anybody about this interview, people will think I'm crazy?"

Earthenhouse nodded.

She jerked her head at the stores across the corridor. "Does that explain the House of Limericks?"

He took a deep breath before saying, "No."

She stared at him. "Mr. Earthenhouse, may I ask you a question?"

"Always."

"What the heck is this job you're interviewing me for, with all of these tests and bizarre security measures?"

He looked her over, appraisingly.

*I should just go. I don't care if this is my last chance to not slink home to Mother. What kind of a boss plays mind games like this?*

Finally, he leaned back. "I apologize, Miss Collins. I can see you are not easily put off by strangeness, but you don't tolerate foolishness, either, and you face problems directly. Believe it or not, that makes you eminently qualified for this position. At the least, you deserve a proper explanation, and here it is: I have to be careful who I hire because of the nature of my business."

Her chair squeaked. The desire to walk out increased, but so too had her curiosity. "You aren't about to tell me this is a front for the Mafia, are you?"

He looked shocked. "No! Nothing of the sort. This business is about providing employment to a special class of underprivileged."

"Underprivileged?" She thought back to the words on the glass outside. "Well, I've heard of starving artists, and I suppose rare coin dealers might have a hard time, but I thought bouncers were a booming business."

Earthenhouse's smile was brief. "It's not the career that is the problem, Miss Collins. Those are the fields in which my group has, in general, been able to find a living."

"And this group is . . .?"

"One of which I am very familiar," he said. "A group of which I am part, in fact. You see, Miss Collins . . ." He leaned back. "I am a goblin."

Silence descended. With a clunk.

*So, there it is. I'm being interviewed by a crazy person. My choice is either to slink back to North Bay or accept that special hell of working for a boss that is certifiable. Like those two weeks at McDonalds, with the night manager who was convinced he'd been abducted by aliens, freaking out every time lights pulled up to the drive-thru window. Ten meltdowns I stood—ten!— before I stormed out and never came back, not even to collect my paycheck.*

But that was then. Today . . . today, she'd collect that paycheck, if she could.

Interviewer and interviewee stared at one another. Perpetua began to count the number of times she breathed while she waited for somebody to say something—not her, clearly, because what was there to say? She was up to nine when Earthenhouse said, "I must say, Miss Collins, you seem to be taking this revelation rather well."

She kept her expression neutral. "I do my best."

"That's better than most people," he replied. "Your reaction pleases me, Miss Collins. Doubtless, you have heard stories about my race, but you shouldn't judge me on what you've heard. We live amongst you. As such, we need to play by human rules to make a decent living. This is what my company provides." He smiled. "My business connects my people with various opportunities in this city, while maintaining humanity's ignorance of our presence. This raises challenges, and this is where you come in."

"How?"

"Well, Miss Collins, we would like you to become our human face," he said. "Not literally, of course; that would be messy and hardly an effective disguise. But I can take this business no further without outside help. You would be dealing with our human contacts: talking to them on the phone, sending out invoices, making appointments, arranging temporary employment for our goblin and troll clients."

"Troll clients," she deadpanned.

"Yes." He went on. "That's the position, Miss Collins, and I have to say that you are by far the most promising candidate I've interviewed. I would like to offer you this job if you are interested. I hope you can start tomorrow."

Never in Perpetua's wildest dreams could she imagine a stranger job interview, or a stranger job in general. Walking out meant walking straight back to the bus station, but staying meant —who knew what staying meant?

But then she thought that, after all of Earthenhouse's tests, there was one she could yet try on her own.

"I'm interested." She leaned forward. "But there are conditions. I'm new to this city. Came here with one suitcase, and just a little bit of money."

He nodded, so she continued, "As frugal as I've been—and I've been frugal, believe me—it's been two weeks. I barely have enough to pay for the bus back to North Bay, much less pay the rent to stay in Toronto. If I'm to work for you, I'm going to need something that can help me stay here until my regular paycheck arrives."

Earthenhouse drew a finger thoughtfully down his cheek. "You're looking for your first pay in advance? That's a bold request, Miss Collins."

Despite the butterflies in her stomach, she met the raised eyebrow with a raised chin. "People lining up out the door, are there?"

He chuckled. "Fair point. All right. I'll grant your request." He sorted through the papers on his desk. "Let me draw up the contract." He nodded at the fruit basket in the corner. "Have some fruit while you wait."

As she peeled her banana and ate it, Earthenhouse pulled out a long, closely written paper from a drawer, followed by a quill pen and a bottle of ink.

*He really is a refugee from the last century. Early in the last century.*

He muttered as he pored over the paper, making corrections. "Twenty-four dollars per hour, check . . . paid breaks, check . . . paid vacations, check . . . spawning leave, check. All is in order."

He turned the contract around, but pulled back the quill pen as she reached for it. "I'm sure you'll have no objection to sealing the goblin contract the traditional way: with spit?"

She raised an eyebrow. "Isn't it usually blood?"

"That's a myth."

"Fine." She looked over the contract. Twenty-four dollars per hour, including breaks, check. No references to blood sacrifice, check. Job to start tomorrow. "Looks good!" She gathered herself and spat on the line over her name.

Wiping her mouth on her sleeve, she stood up and extended her other hand for a shake, only to have Earthenhouse grip it for another old-world style kiss. "Just—" She took his wrist and rearranged their hands so they clasped. Then she let go of his wrist and pumped his arm. "I'll see you tomorrow, sir."

He looked at her, perplexed, but then inclined his head in a formal bow. "I look forward to working with you, Miss Collins."

# Chapter 8
# The City of Magic in the Dark

Perpetua burst from the Underground City into the streetlight-lit evening. After the antiseptic cool of the shopping corridors, the muggy warmth wrapped around her like a shawl.

*That was the weirdest interview I have ever had*, she thought.

But she smiled at the feel of the thicker wad of bills tucked beneath her bra strap.

*Still, if he can afford that office and paying me on time, he can afford to be a little crazy.*

She thought about heading to Adelaide Street to flag down Fergus, but decided she shouldn't spend all her cash in one night. She'd splurge on streetcar fare instead. She shouldered her backpack and set out for the stop.

The gargoyles on the cornices winked at her as the traffic lights changed. She passed the public square at King and Bay. In the middle stood a fountain, where a lumpy stone statue sat, looking like a double-sized, couch-potato version of *The Thinker*.

The Lumpy Thinker had a heavy forehead and glowering eyebrows. He sat on a stool in the middle, two fish shooting jets of water from their mouths, bathing his shoulder blades.

Perpetua stared at the art installation, cocking her head, and then turned away. She almost crashed into a shopping cart.

"Oh, sorry," said the hunched, dishevelled man who shambled past. It took her a second, but she recognized him as the homeless man she'd pulled out of the way of the dump truck on her first night. She opened her mouth to say so.

Instantly, the stench hit her, pushing her away as effectively as a force field. *Well, let's not stay here!* She ducked her head and dodged back to the streetcar stop. Cart wheels squeaked as the man ambled away, muttering in a mad, guttural voice.

Perpetua shuddered. "Lord! If they ever catch me talking to myself, get me some medical help, please."

As the traffic ebbed and flowed, she caught snatches of his words.

"Jesus saves, you know." Throaty chuckle. "The world is his oyster." Another chuckle. "Moses spoke to the Samaritans in the great white desert. His first commandment: thou shalt eat salad." He cleared his throat. "Right, Gunther: dinner time."

The change in the homeless man's voice pulled Perpetua around. She saw him standing before the Lumpy Thinker, back straight, looking focused and intelligent, holding out a head of wilted lettuce. Not that this was an intelligent thing to do, but he looked far more lucid than he had before.

"C'mon, Gunther," he coaxed. "Don't keep me waiting. I've got my rounds."

Before Perpetua's eyes, the Lumpy Thinker shook himself awake. He looked at the lettuce and opened his mouth. The homeless man tossed it into the Thinker's maw. "There you go! Here's another!"

The Thinker slavered and bobbed with pleasure. He opened his mouth and scooped the air with both hands, clearly demanding more food.

Perpetua's mouth dropped open. Before she could shout, a small but firm voice spoke up at the back of her mind.

It said: *Hold on. One of two things is happening right now.*

*Either you've snapped and are hallucinating, in which case, shouting about it will win you a one-way trip to the loony bin, or you are actually watching a homeless guy feeding heads of lettuce to a statue and—more importantly—the statue eating them. In which case, this very big, very muscular, and apparently very mobile statue might object very strongly to you sounding the alarm.*

"Good selection today," said the homeless man. "Loblaws just threw out its stock. To think, the food banks don't want this stuff."

Perpetua closed her jaw with an effort. She rubbed her eyes and looked again, desperately hoping to see something different, but it was still feeding time at King and Bay.

The homeless man tossed in the third head of lettuce. Gunther gnashed it, then held out his gigantic hand, palm out.

"No more?" The homeless man set the last head of lettuce back in the cart under a garbage bag tarp. "Oh yeah, right: your diet. How's that going?"

Gunther tensed and turned toward Perpetua. His warning rumble resonated in her chest. She stepped back, then flinched as a passing car sounded its horn. A streetcar pulled up and opened its doors, but she didn't move.

The homeless man looked at her across the square. Pinned in his gaze, Perpetua saw his baggy cheeks, protruding chin, and long, hooked nose. How had she not noticed those before?

In a low voice, he said, "Nobody is going to believe you."

Behind her, the streetcar driver called out, "Hey! You getting on, or what?"

The homeless . . . whatever he was . . . reached up a gnarled, long-boned hand and tipped his broad-brimmed hat at her. His mass of hair came off with it, like a wig. She saw pointed ears, a bald scalp, and tufts of wiry hair poking out from beneath the hat.

The spell broke, and she dashed for the safety of the streetcar. She took her seat, her heart racing. But when she looked back at the square through the window, the Lumpy Thinker had resumed his thoughtful pose in the middle of the fountain, and the homeless man was shambling away toward Front Street, pushing his cart ahead of him.

Perpetua was still thinking about the Lumpy Thinker when she jumped off the streetcar and headed up the alleyway to the hostel. Was she going mad? Perhaps she should have said something. A ticket to the loony bin included medical attention, after all.

She'd gone halfway to the next street when she realized she'd somehow missed the hostel's front door.

She came back to King Street, then turned again, frowning. No matter where she looked, she couldn't find the hostel door with its dim light. The hostel wasn't there.

"What the heck?" She looked at the buildings in the alleyway. She stepped back, tripped, and fell over with a yell.

She picked herself up and stared to see her suitcase set out on the sidewalk. She hefted it. It felt as heavy as it should, if packed with all her belongings.

"What the hell!"

She looked at her suitcase, at the alleyway where Amnesia House had been and was no longer, then up at the glittering skyline of Toronto.

She remembered the desk manager's words: "*You can stay. For two weeks, or until you get a job. You can't stay here forever. Plenty of other people need the room.*"

*Two weeks. It's two weeks to the day since I came to Toronto.*

"But *I* needed that room!" she whispered. "What am I going to do now?"

The breeze nipped at the back of her neck. She pulled up the handle on her suitcase and walked off along King Street, the case going *scraggle-scraggle-scrape* behind her.

# Part Two
# The Haunted Office

# Chapter 9
# Twenty-One Hours Awake

After much hunting, Perpetua found a room with doors that locked. A room that allowed her to sleep. The sleep had been enough to almost convince her that what she'd seen at King and Bay had been part of a dream. Almost.

That sleep had cost her $95.

*It could have been worse*, she thought, as she set her fork down at a cheap breakfast restaurant the next morning. *At least there's a place where I can eat eggs and bacon for $2.99.*

She picked up a newspaper and turned to the classifieds.

Again.

She pulled a pen from her ponytail and looked for apartment listings. *So what if I've been kicked out? I've got a job now, and Toronto has space to house three million people. There has to be a place for me.*

She went through the list and crossed off candidates: too expensive, too expensive, too expensive, too . . .

She stopped when she saw that the first two rows of candidates had been crossed out, as had most of the third. She could detect a pattern here, and it wasn't a good one.

But there were circles of possibility. Perhaps something was hidden amongst all those crosses.

“Time for some more heroic montage music!” She put on a smile and hooked up her iPod. After paying the bill, she put on her earphones and swept from the restaurant.

“Heroic montage” was a long playlist. The last chords of it found Perpetua in a food court in the Underground City with her face in her hands. “Shit.”

She knew she couldn’t afford to be picky, and she hadn’t been. However, there were still lines she wouldn’t cross. Some of which had been helpfully marked off with police tape.

But at the places she did think she could tolerate, she ran into other problems: requests for references (she had nobody local, and she wasn’t going to use Mother), credit checks (what credit?) and, worst of all, first and last month’s rent.

She’d forgotten about the first and last month’s rent.

Even with a week’s wages in advance, she had less than a thousand dollars on her. She had no bank account. She needed at least another week of work before she had enough money to make a deposit, and this was assuming she didn’t eat, drink, ride a streetcar, or do anything else that required her to spend money.

In the shopping corridor behind her, the footfalls faded. Around turns and through doorways, the woman began to sing.

“Well, at least I have a roof over my head for the night,” she said. “Maybe I can sleep there after work.”

She slugged the last of her coffee, pulled up the handle on her suitcase, and headed off.

The House of Limericks was advertising a special on haikus as Perpetua arrived in Subbasement Three. At the door to Earthenhouse’s office, she found a yellow, handwritten note stuck to the frosted glass. She pulled it off.

"Miss Collins: I am meeting with clients. Welcome to your first day of work. I've left you some instructions to help you along. —TPE."

"Huh." She had the place to herself, then. She felt awkward about that, like being asked to walk the high wire without a net, but she unlocked the door with the key he'd given her the night before and stepped inside.

As she reached for the lights, something crinkled underfoot. Another yellow note clung to her heel. "Miss Collins, please be careful not to step on the Post-it Notes. —TPE."

"What the—?" The lights flickered on, and she found herself surrounded by a swarm of yellow slips. They were stuck to the walls. They were stuck to the chairs. They were stuck to the floor. There was even one lonely slip on the ceiling, which she couldn't reach, even by jumping.

"Weirdo." She crumpled the note and swept to her desk. The chair squeaked sharply as she sat down. "Now, don't you start!" she snapped at it.

There was another Post-it Note on her monitor with the words, "User ID: pcollins; Password: underground." She plucked this from the screen and pasted it over the Post-it Note identifying the computer's on-off switch.

"I guess this counts as my job training," she said.

Her top drawer contained a box wrapped with a bow, though the effect of the present was diminished by the note that said, "Business cards! Take some home with you! —TPE."

She nodded appreciatively at the stylish cards. They bore her name (correctly spelled), her job title ("Secretary"; it appeared Earthenhouse was still stuck in the last century), and the phone number to the office. The ink was shiny and raised; it felt smooth on her thumb.

She turned the card over. On the back were the words, "In case of amnesia, call 416-5WHOAMI."

She stared at the card. Then she looked around for weights suspended from the ceiling, or clubs or poles that might fall and hit her on the head. Seeing none, she shrugged. The box had a brass business card case; she filled this up and stuffed it into her backpack.

Her other desk drawers contained office supplies and a place to hang files. Beside her computer was an in tray (helpfully marked "In Tray" by a Post-it Note), a phone (no messages save for a Post-it Note reading, "No messages"), and a plastic file folder. The in tray contained a file of "Documents to be Faxed," while a second file contained "Items to be Mailed (After Work)," and a third contained "Items to be Proofread before Mailing." There was also a sheet of paper listing office supplies that needed to be ordered. At the top of the list was "Post-it Notes."

She looked around at the office and the responsibility that was all hers. And despite the weirdness, she smiled. "Tuesday, July 16," she muttered. "The first day of my professional life."

She got to work.

There was a lot of it. There were several letters to officials at Toronto City Hall. "Dear Madam, we have identified several potential art installation sites in Grange Park. Would you please consider this proposal to fund a number of displays from the cultural budget?" Others were to big financial companies in the office towers above her. "Dear Sir, we have noticed that your building is looking bare. Perhaps you would consider the installation of a few art displays on your building . . ."

Earthenhouse's pitch seemed to be working. She typed up invoices to the City of Toronto for art installations in the downtown. There were also envelopes containing checks from many of the nightclubs. These were attached to invoices labelled: "Bouncer Division" (colour-coded black and blue). They were decent-sized checks, as well.

*All-in-all*, she thought, *it's been a productive . . . well, I suppose I have to call it "evening," even though it feels more like a morning.*

At noon (midnight), she pulled her bagged lunch from her backpack (an apple and a bottle of water) and ate at her desk.

Still, as she faced an afternoon (morning) in the office with yet more paperwork, her eyes fell on the classified section of the newspaper she'd brought with her, the one with candidate apartments circled and crossed out.

*It's hard enough working in front of a computer for eight hours straight*, she thought, *and Earthenhouse isn't here. I could spend some time finding a place to stay. Who would know? It's not like anybody's watching me.*

She picked up the newspaper.

*But I'd know*. I'm *watching me.*

She set the newspaper down.

*And it kind of feels like somebody else is, too.*

The hairs on the back of her neck prickled.

A woman alone, she knew enough not to ignore that feeling. Slipping out of her seat, she ignored its protesting squeak and opened the door to Earthenhouse's office. Fumbling for the light switch, she shoved up the dimmer and blinked as the bright lights pushed back the darkness.

The office was empty. Earthenhouse's desk and his leather-backed desk chair were exactly as she remembered them. The bathroom door was open, and the bathroom itself was empty. She dimmed the lights and shut the door, but the nervous feeling didn't go away.

She crossed the reception area and poked her head into the corridor. Nobody was standing outside.

She shut the door and turned back to her desk. She bumped into her desk chair and fell face-first into it.

She shoved herself up. Her chair had somehow rolled out from behind her desk and into her path. She gave it a push, and its wheels squeaked. Her brow furrowed.

*I'm imagining things. Right?*

Before she wheeled her chair back behind her desk, she locked the front door. If anybody wanted to come in, they could knock.

She got back to work.

At 5 a.m., Perpetua locked the office door, stretched, and let out a yawn.

The proprietor of the House of Limericks was also locking up. He smiled at her and then bounded up the stairs in iambic pentameter. Perpetua followed more slowly, dragging her suitcase.

She was looking for the nearest exit in the corridors above when she heard a machinery-like noise rise around her. It had a bass-thrum rumble that caught at her chest. She put her hand to the wall and felt it tremble, like the growl of a gigantic animal turning over in its sleep. A moment passed, and the rumble faded away.

"What the hell was that?"

A skateboarder rolled past. "Subway," he replied. "You hear it all over the city. Heavy trains rumbling underground."

"Oh." She looked at him sidelong. "Thanks."

"You're welcome," he replied. "See ya!" And he skidded off.

She came out onto one of the back streets. It was deserted here, but she heard engines in the distance and the *ding* of a streetcar's bell. A glow in the eastern sky suggested dawn was near.

As she looked about, another yawn hit her.

*Twenty-one hours awake*, she thought, after a quick calculation. "I need a place to rest."

*And to find an apartment.*

"I can't find an apartment if I'm fighting to stay awake," she muttered.

*And you can't sleep unless you find a place to sleep.*

"Well, what are my choices?" she muttered, irritated with the voice inside her head. "A park bench?"

She looked across the square. All the benches were taken. Even if they had been free, she wasn't comfortable with the idea of sleeping on one. She hated camping, and roughing it in the city seemed worse than roughing it in the woods.

"Hotel?" she muttered.

*Another $95 you can't afford to spend.*

"Someplace indoors?"

*Now there's a thought. Stores are unlikely, but restaurants . . .*

She headed away from the downtown. The glass towers were shut up tight, but within a few blocks, she spotted a flashing "OPEN" sign in the window of a shabby brick building.

The building might have been a home a century ago, but now, it held two restaurants, one on top of the other. The bottom one looked too chic to belong to even the twenty-first century, and it was closed, anyway, but the second had people inside. Coffee was being served. The smell pulled Perpetua in like a fishing lure.

The restaurant was called "Corned Beef House," and every window had painted messages celebrating this fact. "Toronto's Best Kept Secret!" shouted one. "Try our World-Famous Corned Beef!" said another. At the door, a waitress stood before a blackboard that advertised corned beef sandwiches, corned beef hash, and plates of corned beef.

Perpetua grinned at the waitress. "So . . . you have lobster rolls?"

The waitress's eyes narrowed. "You'll eat our corned beef, and you'll like it!"

Perpetua held up her hands. "Okay! Okay! I see you serve breakfast. Could I have two eggs and some corned beef hash? And coffee?"

With a "Hmph!" the waitress led Perpetua to an empty table and stalked off.

Breakfast bought Perpetua two hours of shelter, but no sleep. She looked through the classifieds, lingering as long as she dared, before she headed back out to the street.

The morning rush hour had begun. She dodged pedestrians who glared at her and the bulky suitcase she dragged behind her. A few blocks later, she was glaring at her suitcase herself. Her arms were tired, her legs ached, and the other candidate for a sleeping spot—public libraries—hadn't opened yet.

She boarded a streetcar, looking to check out the nearest candidate on her apartment list, found a seat at the back, and woke up on the other side of the city, with the streetcar driver poking her in the arm.

"Miss?" *Poke!* "Miss?" *Poke! Poke!* "Miss? We're at our last stop."

"I—wha—?" Realization hit her, and she winced. She'd missed her stop by several miles, and for the silliest of reasons. "Sorry. I actually wanted to get off at Lansdowne."

"We passed that," the driver replied.

"So I gathered." She gave him a hopeful smile. "Any chance you could take me back there?"

"Sure!" He held out his hand. "Fare, please?"

She gave him a beseeching stare, but he went on standing there with outstretched hand until, finally, she fished around in her bag and handed over a token with a glare.

After another discouraging search for apartments, Perpetua showered at the YWCA, using her membership card from the branch in North Bay for access. She'd learned the shelters were full that night and were not open during the day.

Still, she was relatively alert when she showed up for her second day of work. As she opened the door, she heard grunts and words of a language she didn't recognize, but whose tone sounded distinctly like swearing.

Earthenhouse sat, surrounded by torn bits of cardboard, scattered papers, bits of metal, and one assembled chair. As she watched, he gave this chair a final thwack. "There!" Seeing Perpetua, he stood up proudly. "Miss Collins! I was just putting together the waiting room chairs."

The stylish wooden chair with metal legs chose that moment to fall apart. Earthenhouse stared at the wreck. "How am I going to have this done in time for the grand opening? It's less than a week!"

Perpetua tamped down her cheeky grin and offered a sympathetic smile instead. "Your chair giving you problems, sir?"

"Yes." He glared at the pile of parts. "The company promised that everything I needed to set up these chairs would be included in the box, but they seem to have misplaced the hammer and nails. I tried to make do."

She sifted through the parts and picked up a bent metal stick, hexagonal in cross-section. "Didn't you use this?"

His brow furrowed. "You call that a hammer?"

Her eyebrows arched up. "I call this an Allen wrench. It works like this . . ." She pulled two parts from the pile, fitted a screw between them, and twisted them into place with the wrench. She held this out to Earthenhouse.

"Remarkable." He took the parts and stared at them before shrugging. "Well, with my cultural background, we do better with things we can hit."

"If you say so, sir."

He looked at her hopefully. "Can you tackle this, Miss Collins?"

"Sure!" It wouldn't be hard, and it would make her look useful.

The chairs occupied her "morning." After lunch, she was back behind her desk, typing up letters and preparing the outgoing mail.

That's when the fatigue really hit.

She'd just hit "save" when she looked up and found that the lights were suddenly too bright. Her skin felt like it had taken on a sheen of plastic. "Aie!" She pressed her hands to her eyes. "Ooo. Okay. So this is what it's like to hit the wall."

She took a deep breath, then let it go.

"Fortunately, I'm prepared for this contingency." She pulled over her backpack and brought out a thermos. "Thank goodness for tea."

*Even if it's only a temporary solution.*

Doggedly, she powered through. At the end of her second day, she knocked on Earthenhouse's door. "Sir? I'm heading out."

"Thank you, Miss Collins!" came Earthenhouse's voice from within. "Another fine effort on your part. Good work."

She smiled at that. As she passed her desk on her way to the front door, she waved vaguely and said, "Bye, office!"

Her chair squeaked goodbye.

She stopped and stared at it a moment, then turned and walked out the door.

## Chapter 10
# Fergus Journal Entries III

*Thursday, July 18*

*So, Future Self, you remember what I said about this city being a good place to hide? I guess it goes without saying that this city is also a hard one for finding people again.*

*I've been looking for Perpetua. Not because I'm some creepy stalker, mind you. I'm just curious how she's getting on in her job. How does she like working for the people she's working for?*

*Anyway, I've been keeping an eye out for her while cruising Adelaide, around the time she gets out of work. Which makes for a quiet and costly night for me.*

*I've thought about visiting her in her office, but that would be a little weird. There'd be too many questions.*

*I did get close, though. Today, as I was about to give up and head back to dispatch, I spotted her, slouching up the street in front of me. She looked sad. I was about to honk my horn and offer her a ride when . . .*

*Would you believe it? Somebody got in and told me to drive. I had a fare! Fresh from the clubs and smelling of alcohol, but not behaving badly enough for me to be able to order him out.*

*I did honk my horn and smile at her as I headed along Adelaide, but she didn't look up. She didn't smile.*

*And the bastard in the back seat only wanted me to take him five blocks.*

## Chapter 11

# Six Hours of Sleep in Three Days

Thursday was like Wednesday. After breakfast at Corned Beef House, Perpetua stole sleep on a streetcar and dreamed about Earthenhouse showing up to work wearing a suit made entirely of Post-it Notes. That made her wake with a shout. There were more discouraging visits to apartments she could not afford. There was a shower at the Y, and still no shelter space available.

By late afternoon, tired and disheartened, she let the crowd guide her back to the financial district and the Underground City. As she walked, she didn't notice the person ahead, striding the other way, letting the crowds slip by around him.

The businessman's suit and green tie were immaculate. His shoes shone. Perpetua didn't look up until she was almost nose to nose with him, and by then, it was too late. He gave her a haughty glare. Perpetua braced herself for the crash.

And then suddenly, the businessman was behind her, striding away. Perpetua looked up and around. "How—?"

The crowd plowed into her from behind. There were shouts, trips, and suddenly, Perpetua was spat out of the mass of people and into a streetlamp. She clutched her reef between the human stream and the traffic jam while she gathered her senses.

"Coffee," she breathed. "Coffee! That will make the hallucinations go away!"

She focused on the stream of people, gauging her first step. Finally, she strode forward, slipped back in amongst the walkers, and headed for her third night of work.

Coffee helped. A little. At the door, Perpetua leaned against the frame and worked on her "professional face." Fixing a smile in place, she swept inside. "Good morning!" she called. "I mean, evening!"

The new chairs now ringed the room. At the foot of her desk, she spotted a huge box sitting on the floor. She tried shoving it aside with her foot, but when it didn't move, she had to drop to her knees and shoulder it out of her path.

Earthenhouse poked his head out from behind his door. "Ah, Miss Collins! On time as usual. Excellent!"

Perpetua gave the box another shove and stood up. "Package for you, sir?"

He nodded. "Probably the new coffee maker."

She stared at it. "What's it made out of? Depleted uranium?"

"I'm told it's a top-of-the-line model," he replied.

"You sure they didn't mean 'top heavy'?"

"Pretty sure, yes," he said.

She scowled. *Perhaps I should get my boss a sarcasm detector for Christmas.* She shook off that thought. *No need to be snappish. Just my fatigue talking.*

"Can you put this together, Miss Collins? You did such a good job with the chairs."

*Probably wise, given how he tried to use an Allen wrench like a hammer.* "Yes, Mr. Earthenhouse!" She grabbed a letter opener and slit open the top of the box. The coffee maker inside was short, stout, and gleaming. There were four separate carafes and several packages of beans. She flipped open the instruction manual and realized she'd picked up volume two.

"I have an additional assignment for you, Miss Collins," said Earthenhouse. "I need to confirm with a client about a series of job assignments. All the paperwork is ready; it just needs signatures. Send it off by courier to City Hall, and have them send it back. I've left instructions on who to call and what, exactly, to say."

"Sure thing, sir." She looked back at the instructions for the coffee maker. Her brow furrowed. "This thing actually needs a level and a plumb line?"

"Miss Collins," said Earthenhouse.

She looked up. "Yes, Mr. Earthenhouse?"

"There may be a client visit involved with this contract, an appointment for which still needs to be made." He paused, appearing to weigh his next words carefully. "I just want to make it clear," he said at last, "that on no account are our business contacts to come to this office after midnight. Do you understand?"

*Why? Is that when the vampires come out?* Out loud, she said, "Whatever you say, Mr. Earthenhouse."

"Thank you, Miss Collins." He loped back into his office and shut the door.

She turned back to the coffee maker. "He's paranoid, but he pays well. Just keep telling yourself that."

Her desk chair squeaked.

An hour later, grunting, she hauled the completed coffee machine onto the table in the corner, then yelped and tugged her fingers out from under it. After waving them in the air, she sucked at them a moment, giving the coffee maker a baleful look. Then, after flexing her fingers to make sure nothing was broken, she filled the hopper with coffee beans.

Turning over a metal sprocket that she hadn't been able to make fit, she eyed her handiwork, shrugged, and plugged the machine in. The display lit up, and water began to chug and gurgle.

She nodded. "Not bad for an hour's work without pliers."

"You look like you could do with a nice cup of coffee!"

She squeaked at the sudden voice, all chirpy with an electronic edge. She peered closer at the side of the coffee maker and found herself staring at a little red dot within a clear dome, like HAL-9000 from the movie *2001*.

The coffee maker went on. "I am ready and willing to offer you a wide selection of coffee products! Would you like an espresso? Would you like a cappuccino? Would you like a mocha?"

Perpetua's eyebrows arched upward.

"Would you like more foam in your milk? Would you like less foam in your milk? Would you like soy *instead* of milk?"

Perpetua tilted her head and eyed the buttons around the display. "Huh," she said. "I've got to remember this model." *So I can make sure that I don't buy it.*

"It is my pleasure to serve you!" the coffee maker chirped. "I am the voice-activated BEAN-There 5000! The world's most advanced maker of coffee and coffee-related products! BEAN-There 5000 is a trademark of—"

"All right!" she shouted. "Coffee. Black. Hot. Got it?"

"Yes, ma'am!" sang the coffee maker. "And may I say—"

"Just shut up and make it!"

The coffee maker shut off its voice and began to gurgle.

Later that night, Earthenhouse returned from an errand and plunked a heavy box on her desk. "Good news, Miss Collins! The advertisements are here!"

She jerked up. *Not asleep!* Out loud, she said, "That was quick!" She'd only proofread them yesterday.

He shrugged. "I know a good printer."

She opened the package and picked up a handful of sheets. *Grand opening! New centre for goblins and trolls! Come sit and chat in peace!* "Sounds like fun," she said.

There was a picture of the office, including her desk, with her desk chair posed prominently in front of it. Beneath that was the address, a date, and a time (midnight, to be extra creepy and mysterious). The printer had done a good job, with crisp colours on good paper. "This will definitely catch the eye," she said.

"That's what I was hoping you'd say," he replied. "I need you to send these out to a distributor." He gestured to a Post-it Note. "I've written down the contact inf—"

He stopped suddenly, his head jerking back. He let out a croak. He jerked back with another croak.

She frowned. "Sir? Are you all right?"

He wrinkled his nose and shook his head. "I'm fine. I think we're on schedule for our grand opening next week, and the arrival of our goblin clients. I'll write up announcements, and you can send . . ." He sniffed. "Send . . ." He croaked again.

"Sir?"

The croaks came louder. That's when Perpetua realized that Earthenhouse was about to sneeze. She ducked back.

Earthenhouse relaxed and let out a sigh of relief. The moment stretched.

She straightened up. "Anyway—"

"ACHOO!"

The sneeze blew back Perpetua's hair. She stood there, advertising flyers in hand. A stray sheet of paper slipped from the pile and fluttered to the floor.

Earthenhouse rubbed his nose and looked up. His eyes widened in horror. "Miss Collins! I'm so sorry!"

"It's okay." Perpetua's voice was tight.

"No, it's not," he babbled. "That was beyond rude, and I—"

As he came forward, he jerked back and let out the croaking noise again. This time, Perpetua ducked for cover.

Fortunately, Earthenhouse sneezed into his sleeve. He

straightened up, pinching his nose. "Are you wearing . . . lavender, Miss Collins?"

"Uh . . ." She frowned. "Yeah. It's a soap that I . . . bought." Or, more accurately, found in one of the YWCA's shower stalls. "You're not scent-sensitive, are you?"

"Just to lavender," he replied. "Many goblins are. June is not a good month to be around us. Could you . . .?" He gave her a pleading look.

"I'll find a different soap," she said, stepping further back.

"Thank you," said Earthenhouse, sounding even more congested. "Keep up the good work. Now, if you'll excuse me."

He turned back into his office. His third sneeze made the door slam.

She shuddered, then put the papers back in their box. Spotting the one on the floor by the bathroom door, she picked it up, then decided that a visit to the bathroom might not be a bad idea. She plunked the lonely sheet down by the bathroom sink and washed her hands and face. Once she'd tossed the paper towel in the trash, she used the mirror to adjust her ponytail.

*What is that in the mirror?*

It took her a moment to realize she was looking at a reflection of the flyer. But this wasn't what she'd prepared.

She looked at the real paper, then at its reflection. The paper at hand was the flyer advertising Monday's grand opening in crisp colours and bright designs. The reflection looked like it had been written with a black magic marker.

She frowned as she tried to read the reflected paper, but of course, it was mirror-wise.

She pulled a banged-up makeup compact from under the elastic of her skirt and opened it up to reveal the mirror. Turning, she peered into this mirror and aimed it at the reflection of the paper.

"Garage . . . sale," she said, slowly, as each word came into view. "Monday . . . July 23 . . . 1072 Brimorton Drive." The hand-drawn flyer advertised: *Games! Comics! Knick-knacks!* And told people to come between 10 a.m. and 3 p.m.

She picked up the paper from the counter and peered at it close, trying to see the writing beneath the print. Only holding it up to the mirror revealed the reflections of the marks of a black pen.

"What the heck?"

She left the bathroom, staring at the advertisement, and went up to Earthenhouse's door. She raised her hand to knock.

"What is it, Miss Collins?" said Earthenhouse, inside.

Opening her mouth to speak, she hesitated. What, exactly, was she going to ask? After a moment, she stepped back. "Never mind, sir. I'll figure it out myself."

She went back to her desk and sat down.

The sky was lightening toward dawn when Perpetua heaved open the door and stumbled out onto the street. She paused as the sticky air wrapped around her. The day promised to be hot, humid, and stifling.

*Which is just what I need. Thanks, Mother Nature!*

What she wanted was a bed. A couch. Anything she could call her own, at least for a few hours. Someplace indoors, with air-conditioning, that wouldn't be targeted by police officers or mall cops telling her to move along.

What she was likely to get were a few short spurts of fitful sleep at the back of a bus, or in a library somewhere, and next to no productivity in finding that bed or couch. She needed an apartment to find an apartment, and that was a textbook definition of irony.

Dejected, she slouched along the street toward the night bus stop.

Her footfalls on the pavement echoed off the glass and steel buildings around her. Perpetua kept an eye on her surroundings

—one of the few pieces of motherly advice she still followed religiously. It was strange how a city as big and full as Toronto could be so lonely, and it was strange how that loneliness could be so frightening.

But nobody stepped from the shadows. No footfalls followed her. She saw no one. Until, that is, she found herself surrounded.

She started, looking around, her heart thumping, before she realized that she'd just walked into a square full of statues. They stood on plinths in a circle, gargoyles all of them, with long, pointed ears, sharp, grinning teeth, and hooked noses. Some sat on their haunches, elbows resting on their knees, all points. Others stood, looking up, pointing at the cornices.

She'd been through this square before, a week or so ago, when she was still looking for work. The plinths had been empty and roped off with yellow tape. Signs had been set up saying that statues had been "removed for cleaning." Now, someone had put the statues back.

And she had the shivering sensation that they were looking at her.

*Don't be silly. You're being paranoid, and isn't that a symptom of sleep deprivation?*

But she did a slow turn. The statues didn't move, didn't speak. The square was wide open. There were no alleyways where someone could hide, but she couldn't shake the sensation that someone was watching her. Someone close.

She turned sharply, focusing on the gargoyle nearest to her. It was standing, one hand crooked over its chin, looking past Perpetua as if into the future.

She came closer.

This gargoyle had been carefully carved to look like it was wearing clothes—shapeless overalls, in fact. The points of its ears reached as high as the top of its head. Its hooked nose jutted down over its mouth. It looked so real, she thought the fabric might move if she blew on it.

She peered closer . . .

Wheels squealed, and horns honked. She jerked around, startled, but the two cars that had almost hit each other sped off with a roar of engines and the echoes of epithets. Perpetua had no idea why her heart should be beating so rapidly.

"Just tense from lack of sleep, maybe. Just—"

"ACHOO!"

The sneeze sent her staggering, clutching at her chest. She whirled around, searching for whatever it was that had blown back her hair.

But she was alone. Only the statue stood, crouched, its eyes locked forward. Its hand crooked under its nose.

She frowned at the statue, then backed away. Turning, she left the square, using the walk you used when you didn't want anyone to see you run.

# Chapter 12
# Four Days. Five

The coffee didn't seem to be working. Perpetua stood at the transit stop, watching streetcar after streetcar pass, before realizing she'd fallen into a daze.

She pushed herself away from the lamppost, feeling almost drunk. "This is silly. I need a bed. I need a hotel, now. I don't care if it costs me another $95."

She staggered off in search of one and soon got a nasty surprise.

"What do you mean, every hotel room in this city is booked?" she yelled at the manager.

"Every hotel room in this city is booked," he repeated. "No rooms at all, because of the ABBA reunion concert."

"Concert?" She stamped her foot. She was beyond caring how infantile that looked. "How dare they book the reunion concert in Toronto the one day I need to sleep!" She turned away and then turned back. "Can I sleep in your lobby?"

His gaze soured. "No loitering."

Perpetua revised her impression of him from apologetic to just plain dick. She stamped out into the street, trailing dark clouds of fury and desperation. "Goddamn ABBA!"

Sleeping in streetcars was the best she could do. But by the time afternoon rolled around, Perpetua found herself leaning against a telephone pole at the King-Bay intersection, staring across the street at the Lumpy Thinker. The singer on the low rooftop serenaded the oblivious.

The crowds slipped past around Perpetua, strobing her vision. In one flash, she thought she saw the Lumpy Thinker glance at her, but another blink showed the statue in its habitual pose.

She shuddered.

"Nine hours of sleep in four days," she mumbled. "I think I need help."

It was also her last weekday.

*If I don't find an apartment soon, I won't even have the luxury of Earthenhouse's office as a roof over my head in the middle of the night.*

She frowned. *Maybe I could ask to sleep in his office.*

Just as she'd asked for a week's wages in advance. *He's going to think I can't take care of myself. He's going to think I'm a freeloader.*

*Well, maybe I need some freeloading*, snarled a rebellious voice at the back of her mind.

She stared ahead, the rest of her mind fuzzing in fatigue and doubt. *Maybe*, she thought.

The light turned green.

Perpetua stumbled into the food court, exhaustion messing with her rhythm. Not only had she been awake for over eighty-four hours over the past four days, she'd also been on her feet a lot. Her legs ached. Her head ached.

On the display monitors, the mayor joked with reporters.

"What's with the whole shovel motif?" a reporter asked. "It's not like you dug the subways yourself."

"Of course not," said the mayor. "But you should have seen the hands that did."

The reporters laughed. The caption below the video feed read, "MORE SUBWAY EXTENSIONS ANNOUNCED."

"I'm going to fall asleep," she muttered. "I am going to fall asleep *on the job*, and then Earthenhouse will find me and fire me, and I'll be forced to go home, an utter failure. I've got to make it through this night."

She spied the coffee stand and marched over with such purpose that the barista looked nervously at her and started casting about for escape routes.

She slapped a ten-dollar bill on his counter. "Give me the strongest thing you've got!"

Outside Earthenhouse's office, Perpetua struggled to unlock the door. Shoving it open, she tripped on the threshold and barely caught herself before she went sprawling. She leaned on the doorframe a moment and wondered where the ticking sound was coming from.

She found it at her fingertips. The hand that held her keys trembled, jackhammering against the metal of the doorjamb. It was only when she reached up and pressed her hand down that the noise stopped. "Oh, this is going to be a long night."

She shoved herself away from the door and staggered inside.

The coffee maker perked up. "Can I interest you in a lovely cup of coffee?"

"Oh, God, no!" She slumped into her chair.

"What can I make for you that would make your day brighter?" said the machine.

"Tea?" she croaked.

The coffee maker burbled, and a cup popped out. "Mint tea on order!"

She closed her eyes. "I love you."

"I regret that I cannot return your feelings of affection! Sugar?"

"Yes, please." She heaved herself out of her chair to get the cup.

Back at her desk, she found a handwritten Post-it Note at the top of her folder of letters to proofread. "Miss Collins, I have more meetings with clients. Will be back later. —TPE."

"Oh, no," she breathed. *This will be just like the first day, only worse. How am I going to stay awake without somebody looking over my shoulder?*

*Well, maybe this is an opportunity,* another thought surfaced. *I can sleep, and who'd know?*

*I'd know.*

She leaned forward, sighing, and rubbed her eyes. "Well, then. I'd better get to work."

Two hours later, the caffeine cut out. Perpetua felt as if weights had been hung on her eyebrows. She leaned on her elbows and used her fingers to prop her eyes open.

She groaned. She looked at the time and groaned louder. "Six hours to go?"

A thought struck her. It was close to break time. And given that break times were times when she didn't have to work, that time could be put to better use sleeping.

"That's assuming I wake up again," she muttered.

She focused on her computer for a moment, and then on the settings of her cell phone, which she still used for emergencies only, and to tell the time.

*I need to buy a cell phone plan,* she thought, then scotched that thought back into the hole it had crawled out from. *I need to stop being tripped up by distractions. God, I'm so tired!*

"Good night, world," she said, pushing her keyboard back. She flipped over a sign she'd written and taped so it could hang over the front of her desk. It read, "On break. Will wake up at 11:15 p.m." *At least, I hope so.*

She put her head in her arms on her desk, closed her eyes, and breathed deep.

Within minutes, she was snoring.

Fifteen minutes passed, and the alarm she'd set on the computer rang.

Without looking up, Perpetua slapped her keyboard. The alarm stopped.

She snored a moment longer.

Her cell phone beeped loud and long.

Perpetua swung an arm out and knocked her cell phone into her wastebasket. The wastebasket amplified the sound until Perpetua's leg shot out and kicked the basket over. It continued to beep on, muffled.

Perpetua snored some more.

In the corridor outside, the stairwell door crashed open. Someone came clumping down the corridor, humming to himself.

The desk chair beneath Perpetua squeaked.

The humming got louder. A silhouette appeared on the frosted glass and approached the door.

The desk chair squeaked again, more loudly. Perpetua mumbled and batted away imaginary flies. The chair squeaked a third time.

At the door, a key snicked into the lock.

The chair rocked back sharply. Perpetua's head swung back. The chair pitched forward, sending Perpetua face-first into her keyboard.

She shot up. "What the hell!"

The door swung open, and Earthenhouse loped in. Perpetua leaped to her feet.

"Hi! Sir!" She just barely stopped herself from saluting. "I wasn't expecting you!"

"I finished my tasks early!" He grinned at her and handed her a pile of envelopes. "Today's incoming mail. Work coming along well?"

"Yes, sir," she said. "I've been printing off your letters." She picked up a paper, saw that she'd misspelled "invoice," and hid that sheet behind her back.

"Excellent." He stepped past her. "Well, carry on!"

She stood to attention until the door to his office clicked shut.

Then she slumped against her desk, clutching at her chest. *That was a close one. At least Earthenhouse didn't catch me sleeping on the job. Somebody was looking out for me.*

"Thank you, whoever you are," she said, beneath her breath.

Her desk chair squeaked.

At the end of the day, Earthenhouse stepped from his office. Perpetua tapped away robotically. She didn't look up until Earthenhouse nudged her. "Miss Collins?"

She stopped typing and turned in her chair. "Sir?"

"It's five o'clock, Miss Collins," he said. "Time to end the day."

She blinked. "Yes, sir?"

"I must say, Miss Collins, I've been impressed by your performance. You know your way around computers, and you've turned around every assignment quickly and accurately. I made a good choice hiring you."

Perpetua blinked at him. "Yes, sir?"

"Yes," he replied. "It bodes well for next week, when we have our grand opening. I trust you have everything ready?"

"Yes, sir?"

"Good. Well, rest up, Miss Collins. You've earned it." He patted her shoulder. "Have a nice"—he paused over the next word, as though trying it for the first time—"weekend." He loped back to his office and shut the door behind him.

Perpetua kept staring at the place he'd been. "Yes, sir?" she said a moment later; then, "Yes, sir?" a moment after that.

Then she shook herself. "Wait, what?"

She looked around the office. "Was somebody just talking to me?" She staggered. "Oh, God! The day is over. I need a bed. Now."

She gathered her things, clumsily, and turned to the office door. There, she hesitated, looking back at Earthenhouse's office.

Her own words echoed in her head. *He'll think I'm a free-loader. He'll think I can't take care of myself.*

But she tamped those words down. *This is getting desperate.*

She marched back across the office and knocked on Earthenhouse's door. "Sir? Can I ask you something?"

There was no answer.

"Sir?" She knocked again. Then, boldly, she opened the door and entered. "Sir, I've got to ask you something. Can I stay here—?"

She stopped when she realized she was talking to the air.

The office was empty. Earthenhouse's chair rocked gently, as though someone had just left it.

"But he was just here," she said to herself, out loud. "I *saw* him come back here!" *Did I hallucinate him?*

A doorknob clicked, and movement drew her eye. Her heart jumped as she saw the bathroom door swing open of its own accord. The bathroom beyond was empty.

Perpetua backed away.

She left the office, walking slower than she ever had before. The bright lights of the stairwell made her cry out and squint. Her legs felt like they wore anklets of lead as she pulled herself up the stairs. Her shoulder brushed the walls of the shopping corridors as she lurched toward an exit—any exit.

On the street, the air felt as thick as cotton batting, and just as warm. Dark clouds blocked the sunrise, and the streetlights speared rays through a pale yellow fog. She was alone on the sidewalk. A few engines growled in the distance, but the street around her was quiet. She put her head down and stepped and stepped. Her suitcase scraggled, then scraped. After what seemed like an eternity, she looked up and found herself across the street from Corned Beef House.

Her stomach churned, and she put her hand to her mouth. No. She couldn't eat just yet. Sleep first. Somewhere. Somehow.

She took a deep breath, then wiped the sweat from her brow.

She leaned against a lamppost and looked up. *Think*, she told herself. *You just need to think!*

*Hotels. Full. Shelters. Full. Streetcars. Not good enough. Which left . . .*

She sighed and trudged onward, looking for the nearest park with an empty bench.

Walking north on John Street, she saw a large park tucked in beside some high rises immediately north of Queen Street. There was a long, cobbled promenade . . . and benches! Yes! She picked up the pace . . .

And halted at the gate of the park. The benches all had occupants.

"Damn!"

She pushed on, shuffling along the path, eyeing each bench in turn. The piles of clothes and the smell warned her away. But farther in, she looked ahead and saw . . . green-painted wood.

"Am I dreaming?" She broke into a run and pounced on the bench at the end of the row. It was solid, dry, and long enough for her to stretch out on.

She shoved her suitcase under the bench and set her backpack at one end. Mushing it up so it was as soft as it could be, she lay down and settled her head into her "pillow."

One moment, she lay there too tense to even breathe. Then she exhaled. And with that breath, all tension left her body. At last: she was going to sleep.

Lightning flashed.

Perpetua's eyes shot open. "Oh, no."

Thunder rumbled.

She shook her head slowly. "No! Don't you dare!"

Rain poured down.

"Son of a—" She spluttered as rainwater hit the back of her throat.

The downpour drenched her. Lightning flashed again, and thunder boomed almost instantly, but she was beyond caring. She bounded to her feet. This was it. This was enough. She was going to tell Mother Nature what for.

She threw her backpack at the clouds, only to have it land a few feet away from her. She shouted at the air. “What did I ever do to deserve this? Just a few hours is all I ask! Just a few hours of goddamn sleep! But do you give it to me? No, you goddamn, son of a—Mother Nature on a stick! You know what? You want to rain on me? You want to flash lightning? You want to blow? Go ahead!” She threw up a rude gesture. “Blow this! I’m standing right here, so pour on down! Go ahead! See if I care!”

“Not like that,” shouted a voice from one of the park benches. “Like this!”

A heavyset man with a white beard bounded up. He could have passed for Santa Claus if it weren’t for the ratty trench coat. Or the smell. But he faced the skies and bellowed in full theatrical mode. “Blow, winds, and crack your cheeks! Rage! Blow! You cataracts and hurricanoes! Spout ’til you have drenched our steeples, drowned the cocks! You sulf’rous and thought-executing fires! Vaunt-couriers to oak-cleaving thunderbolts!”

Perpetua stared. The rain plastered her hair to her cheeks, her clothing to her skin. The other homeless people on the benches sat up, staring.

“Perpetua?”

She turned and found Fergus standing beside her. His taxi was at the curb, the door hanging open.

She looked at the homeless man declaiming at the rain. “Is he . . . quoting King Lear?”

“Singe my white head! And thou, all-shaking thunder, strike flat the thick rotundity o’ the world! Crack Nature’s molds, all germens spill at once, that makes ingrateful man!”

Fergus didn’t take his eyes off her. “You don’t look so good.”

“I—” She struggled to speak. Even as lightning flashed, she stood stunned, that her thunder had been so completely stolen from her. “Why is he quoting King Lear?”

Fergus took her arm and gently led her away. “Out-of-work

actor. We get a lot of those around here. Let's get you out of the rain."

She pulled away, grabbed her suitcase, and retrieved her backpack. The other homeless people watched, rapt, as the homeless actor continued his speech.

Fergus led the way as Perpetua squelched up to his taxicab and climbed into the back seat. Fergus closed the door. He got behind the wheel, and the cab pulled away from the curb.

"So, where to?" He gave her a tentative smile through the rearview mirror.

She had her mouth open before she realized that she had no clue.

"I . . . I don't know," she said, drooping. "I'm so tired. Please, just . . . just drive. Okay?"

"Okay." He turned the wheel. "How about—?"

What he asked, Perpetua never knew. She was asleep before her head touched the headrest.

# Chapter 13
# The Awkward Lifeline

Perpetua woke with a snort and winced as sunlight hit her eyes. She shaded them and sat up. Her hand bumped her backpack, which she realized had been placed there as a pillow. There was also a blanket on the floor of the back seat, lying in a rumpled pile, as if she'd kicked it off in her sleep.

She was in the back seat of a cab parked in a gravel parking lot, under the shade of a tree. She spotted a pair of street signs at the nearby intersection: Front and Cherry. How did she get here?

Except for her, the cab was empty. The windows were rolled down, and the keys were in the ignition. She looked around the front seat and saw a clipboard with receipts and . . . a camera.

She picked it up. It was a black camera, thick, with a large lens that could screw on or off. It had heft, and clearly was not some cheap knock-off.

*Why would he have a camera in his cab?*

She turned it on and flipped through the most recent pictures, but they only showed the rooflines of buildings, the gargoyles looking down. No shots of her asleep. That was a relief.

She heard gravel crunch outside and looked up. Fergus was walking back across the parking lot, holding a tray bearing two cups and two paper bags.

Hastily, she turned the camera off and set it back where she'd found it. She leaned back in her seat. He came up to the car, juggled the load to get a hand free, and knocked on the door. He grinned to see her staring. "Well, hey there, sleepyhead!"

She felt her cheeks heating up. "Hey! What time is it?"

He handed her a cup and a paper bag through the window, then opened the door and slid in beside her. "About seven."

She jerked up. That wasn't right. When she'd lain down on that park bench, she'd been under the impression it was seven o'clock—in the morning.

"Wait . . ." She worked it out. "Is this *evening*?"

He nodded.

"You let me sleep in your cab for twelve hours?"

"You looked like you needed it."

She ducked her head. "Did I snore?"

He laughed. "Did you?" He caught her gaze and got serious. "Not too bad." He pointed at her bag. "There. Eat."

She pulled a muffin from the bag. Her stomach reminded her that she hadn't eaten since around midnight. But as she ate, she thought through the implications. She started to say something, with her mouth full, then took the time to swallow before saying, "I ruined your business. I'm sorry!"

His brow furrowed. "What do you mean?"

"I was asleep in your cab for all of Saturday! I cost you a whole day's worth of fares!"

"Oh, that." He shrugged. "You didn't ruin my business . . . much. Like I said, you looked like you needed the sleep." He held up a hand as she reached for her money. "And I won't have you paying me for it. You couldn't afford a day's fare."

She stopped. He was right; she couldn't. She felt grateful, but also a little shy. "Thanks."

Silence fell. They shifted in their seats. Perpetua brought her coffee to her lips. It was a liquid chocolate bar—a mocha caramel, a favourite of hers, but too expensive for her to splurge on. How had he known? "Why are you so nice to me?"

Fergus smiled, but shrugged. "Can't I just be nice? I thought you could use the help."

*Help.* Despite feeling better with both sleep and coffee, the rest of the weekend stretched out ahead of her, containing nothing but bleak desperation. More fruitless struggling, and another night where she had to choose between a hotel she couldn't afford and a bed exposed to the elements. She glowered at the seat back in front of her. "Well, thanks," she said bitterly.

He frowned at her. "Bad day?"

"I don't want to talk about it."

"Sorry."

"It's just that . . . I'm having a really sucky time, okay?"

"Okay. You don't have to talk about it if you don't want to."

"I mean, it's just not fair!" She thumped the armrest.

"Umm . . . still respecting your request to not talk about it. Or not, if you prefer."

But now she'd started, the words flowed out like water through a broken dam. "I can't find a place to stay. Every cheap place is either a deathtrap or has a landlord that sends my intuition running for the hills. I can't afford the first and last month's rent, and I can't find any place to sleep. I'm a walking zombie during office hours, and I think my office is haunted, and the statues are all staring at me. I knew coming to Toronto wouldn't be easy, but I thought I could cut it, and if this keeps up, I won't be able to. And that's just not fair! It's not fair at all!"

She touched her cheeks, and her fingers came away wet. Her breathing was ragged. "F—" she snapped. "I'm crying. Just like—I'm not a crier. That's not the person I'm supposed to be!"

"Hey." He reached out to touch her arm, hesitated, and then let his hand fall. "It's a big city. It's okay to cry."

"Really?" She cleared her nose with a sniff. "When was the last time *you* teared up?"

"A month ago, Thursday."

She stared at him. "Why?"

"A good person told me to go to hell." He tilted his head. "Now that I say it, I'm less sure she was a good person."

She faced forward. "Well, at least *you* have a roof over your head."

"You know," Fergus began. Then he halted. "No. Never mind."

She frowned at him. "What?"

He shook his head. "It's silly. You're not going to go for this."

She faced him. "Try me."

"It's just that . . ." He ducked his head. "It sounds like what you need is a roof over your head for a few days. Until you get settled. Well, I've got a roof. It's over my head. And I can share it with you."

Silence descended. Perpetua unhooked her seatbelt, turned in her seat, and gave him a hard stare. Fergus wilted in the heat of it. His cheeks went red, and his head lowered to meet his rising shoulders. "Um . . . look, I'm not trying anything funny or anything, okay?"

She kept staring at him.

"Honest!" His voice rose. "I've just . . . I've got a place. It's a one-bedroom."

Perpetua's glare intensified.

"I didn't mean what you think I mean!" he said quickly. "It has a living room, and a couch, and I was only offering the living room and the couch because I think you could use the living room and the couch. It's a good place, really! Okay, the rent's a little high, but what isn't in Toronto? And I was only thinking that maybe you could help me make ends meet. And it can help you, too. You're trying to find a place, and you can't do that without someplace to stay, and I thought that my place is safe and warm and—did I mention, safe?—and it could give you a base, or something, from which to work. Honest! That's all I was offering!"

Silence stretched a moment longer.

He gave her a nervous smile. "Can I go now?"

After another moment to reinforce the stare, Perpetua turned away and settled back in her seat. Fergus slumped back and breathed a sigh of relief.

"So," she said, "what's your place like?"

He looked at her and smiled.

Fergus's apartment was in the basement of a converted Victorian house. The windows recessed near the ceiling let in little light. There were, however, two entrances—the one they were using and a back door beside the stove in the kitchen. She nodded at this: *they paid attention to the fire codes. Good. Mark one point for safety.*

The living room had a sectional sofa, battered and out of style, but also clean. The coffee table was a rescued milk basket draped with a tablecloth, but it held a stout, scented candle on a plate. A scuffed television set with a faux-wood finish sat in the corner.

The bathroom was also clean. The bath was small, but still—a bath. She could stretch out in it, even if it meant dangling her legs over the side. There was no mildew on the shower curtain and, more importantly, the bathroom door locked on the inside. *Mark one point for privacy.*

She didn't go into Fergus's bedroom, but she could see the bed through the doorway. The sheets had been kicked back, and there were clothes strewn across the floor. It was cluttered and a little messy, but still . . . yes, clean. It reminded her of her own bedroom back home, except missing the Pogues posters.

Fergus shifted on his feet behind her. "So . . . what do you think?"

She turned slowly, taking in everything. "Well, it's clean."

"Um. Well, I try."

"I'd have the couch, right?"

"Yeah. And if you want to take things from the fridge, that's okay. Just contribute a few groceries now and then."

"And my rent would be . . .?"

"Rent? Uh . . ."

"Don't go soft on me, now. I'm not a charity case."

He shrugged. "I don't know. One hundred a month? If that's okay?"

That, she thought, was highway robbery, and she was no thief. "How about two hundred?"

"Done!" They shook hands.

She looked around again and smiled. The place was cool, despite the pavement outside being pounded by the summer sun. She could sleep, and not have to worry about being prodded by police officers and who knew who else. She could feel the weight lifting from her shoulders. She looked Fergus in the eyes. "Thank you. If it wasn't for you, I wouldn't have my job. And now, you've given me a place to rest my head. I owe you a lot."

His cheeks flushed. "You don't owe me anything. Just a little help with the rent is enough."

"Sure." She clasped his shoulder. "You know, some people might say that I'm taking a risk here, sleeping on your couch. I hardly know you. But I know in my gut that you're a nice guy. I can trust you."

"Well, yeah." He shifted awkwardly. "Thanks."

Her grip tightened on his shoulder. "But, just so we're clear, I value my privacy. We knock on all doors, especially bathroom doors, before entering. And while I don't think you'll try anything funny, just know that if you *do* get closer than arm's length without my permission—" she gave him a shake, emphasizing her straight arm—"I know jujitsu, and I *will* hurt you. Are we clear?"

He swallowed. "Crystal."

"Good." She gave his shoulder a final, friendly squeeze and then stepped back. "Now, to help pay you for your generosity, I'm going to cook you a late breakfast. I hope you like your eggs scrambled. But first, I'm going to unpack, and I'd really like to use your shower."

## Chapter 14
# Fergus Journal Entries IV

Clicking his pen, Fergus turned the page.

*Sunday, July 21*
*Dear Future Self,*

*I know, I know: what the heck have I got myself into?*

*Jay down at dispatch had a fit. Honestly, I don't see why he cares so much. I'm the one who didn't make any money over the past twelve hours. He only gets a small piece of it. Or, rather, he doesn't get a small piece of it. And I'd like to see how productive he could be with somebody snoring in his back seat.*

*It had to be done. And, yes, maybe I am out of my mind for bringing that cute girl into my home, but it had to be done.*

*Sure, we've only met, like, three times since she jumped into my cab three weeks back. But she needed help. It was blindingly obvious. And if I didn't help her, who would? You understand, right?*

*I think you would, if you had seen her crying in my cab. You'd understand if you had seen the smile she gave me, just before she threatened me with bodily harm if I stepped out of line.*

*Sure, this makes things more complicated for my project, but you know what? I don't care.*

*It's a screwy world. Half the population is too fat, while the other half goes hungry. Everybody is unhappy with what they've got.*

*It's not wrong of me to want to make the world a better place. Sometimes, making that world requires big gestures that change the lives of millions of people. Sometimes, making that world comes in smaller steps, like offering one person a place to rest her head.*

*So, let's hear it for the small steps, 'kay?*

## Chapter 15
# The Truth about Goblins and Trolls

The smell of breakfast roused Perpetua from sleep. She flipped up her sleep mask.

Fergus stood in front of the kitchenette's stove, poking the frying pan with a spatula.

She sat up. "You're up early."

"It's actually two in the afternoon." He pointed at the stovetop clock with the spatula. "But with our sleep cycles, I guess it's time for breakfast."

"Whoa, two o'clock." She rolled up and headed to the bathroom to change into her day clothes. When she came back, she added, "Hard to think of the afternoon as morning."

"You get used to it." The toast popped up, and Fergus buttered two slices, setting one on a plate before he ladled scrambled eggs on top of it, followed by two slices of bacon. "Coffee's ready, too."

"Thanks." She took the plate Fergus offered her and added another slice of toast on top of the eggs and bacon. She stopped mid-munch to savour her impromptu sandwich. "Oh, a girl could get used to this."

She strolled around the living room carrying her breakfast and spotted something on a table in the corner. She picked up a frame holding a picture of a woman a few years older than she was, with a mass of blonde hair and a collegiate tank top. She had blue eyes that sparkled. She looked cute and familiar. An arm draped around her shoulder from off-frame. "Who's this?"

Fergus focused on his eggs. "That's my mom."

"Oh! How's she doing?"

"Um . . . she's dead." He avoided her shocked stare. "'S okay. It was years ago. Cancer, I'm told."

She put the photograph down. "I'm sorry."

"I said it's okay." He fished a fork from a drawer. "How are the eggs? It's the first time I've cooked for anybody."

The eggs were good, and she said so. As they ate, the tension eased out of the air. Perpetua cleaned the dishes, then spent the afternoon on Fergus's couch, circling candidate apartments on her newspaper, but with far less urgency than before. Fergus puttered about, cleaning or sometimes checking email on a battered computer in the corner. Occasionally, their eyes would meet, and they would smile, before turning back to whatever it was they were doing. Eventually, Fergus grabbed a book and excused himself to go read in his bedroom.

Over the top of her newspaper, Perpetua watched him go. She smiled to herself.

When Perpetua entered Subbasement Three the following Monday, she saw that someone had put up banners over the windows of the office. "GRAND OPENING!" shouted one, and "WELCOME ALL!" shouted the other.

"I hope he won't be too disappointed when nobody shows up." She paused as she unlocked the door. "I hope he doesn't decide to lay me off."

The moment she pushed open the door to the office, the coffee maker perked up. "You look like you could use a nice cup of coffee!"

She frowned at it. "So, you weren't a sleep-deprived hallucination?"

"If you're tired from lack of sleep," the coffee maker chirped, "a nice cup of coffee can help kickstart your day!"

"You'd better hope Health Canada doesn't hear you say that!" But she filled a cup and took it to her desk. The fax machine started up, and she picked up the papers. One was an approved invoice to send Earthenhouse's way, which was good. Money was coming into the business.

She turned back to the chair and found it backed out and ready for her to sit.

She stared at it a moment, then sat.

"Thank you," she muttered.

"*Squeak! Squeak-squeak!*"

Perpetua got to work.

A half hour before midnight, Earthenhouse's door creaked open, and he peered out at her, polishing his teeth with a small electric toothbrush. "Good evening, Miss Collins. Did you have any trouble sending the faxes?"

"No, Mr. Earthenhouse."

"Excellent." He turned off the toothbrush. "The first of our clients should be arriving in a few minutes. Are you ready to meet them?"

*Assuming any show up*. Aloud, she said, "Yes, Mr. Earthenhouse."

"Did you make the coffee?"

"Yes, Mr. Earthenhouse."

"Good!" He turned away. Before he closed the door, however, he turned back. "Miss Collins?" he called. She looked up. He held up two fingers. "Make two pots."

She shrugged and got the water for a second pot of coffee. It seemed a waste to her, but orders were orders.

At one minute to midnight, Perpetua pushed back from her computer and stretched, ignoring her chair's protesting squeak.

She looked around the empty office and batted at a balloon that had drifted into her vision.

"Sorry, sir," she said beneath her breath. "Looks like it's going to be a quiet day like all the rest."

The clock clicked midnight.

The door flew open. A horde of grey-skinned creatures swarmed into the office, chattering like magpies.

Perpetua stared. It was a sea of bald heads and grey skin, pointy ears and fangs. The creatures were grinning and cackling, chatting about the ride to work. They shared Earthenhouse's pallor, but not his fashion sense. Instead of pinstripes and dress shirts, they wore grey pants and grey sweaters. Perpetua had to look twice to make sure they were even wearing clothes, and was more than a bit relieved to see that they were.

The creatures came in all shapes and sizes, but most were under four feet tall. That is, until the door swung open again and a seven-foot-tall mountain ducked his head beneath the lintel. He grinned at the others and sat down across three chairs.

Perpetua stared at the throng of strange, bizarre creatures, and then slowly began to slip down in her chair. This hallucination couldn't be blamed on sleep deprivation. No, it was like the Lumpy Thinker in the square, only a thousand times worse. This time, there could be no doubt that she was going crazy.

But before she could hide, one of the creatures flicked its bright gaze to her.

"Ooo!" he chirped, in a gravelly, sing-song voice. "A secretary!"

More eyes flashed. "A human!"

Perpetua was suddenly surrounded by pair after pair of gleaming eyes and wide, cheeky grins. She swallowed hard. "Um . . . hello!"

"Hi!" chorused the short throng.

"W-what are you all doing here?"

"Waiting for coffee," said an impish creature.

The others nodded. "Coffee! Coffee! Waiting for coffee!"

"Uh . . ." She pointed at the carafes in the corner. "I've made coffee. Help yourselves?"

"No, we must wait," said another. "Chim and Chum are coming."

Her brow furrowed. "Who are Chim and—?"

The door burst open. A ball of stone tumbled across the floor, landing on Perpetua's desk, where it unravelled. It was all points, from knees to elbows, ears and teeth. It—no, she guessed it might be he—grinned at her. His body quivered as he inhaled. "Coffee?" His breath blew back her hair.

She stared at him. Then raised a finger and pointed to the corner table where the coffee maker chugged happily away.

The creature launched itself off the desk, landing just short of the corner table. He grabbed the percolating pot and poured half its steaming contents down his throat.

The door burst open again, and a second ball of stone tumbled across the office, landing on her desk with a thump. He was the first creature's twin, down to the ragged, toothy grin, except that he had a tail. A long, pointy tale that swished level with his shoulders. "Did he drink all the coffee?"

Perpetua swung her pointing finger to the second carafe. The creature beamed at her. "Thank you!" He hopped off the desk and snatched up the second carafe, downing half of it in one gulp. Then, holding their carafes like coffee mugs, the two creatures chattered at each other like a couple at a cocktail party in a sped-up film.

Perpetua turned and saw a lineup of ghoul-like creatures at her desk, all smiling at her, all waiting patiently, and each with a mug in his (her? its?) hands.

That would explain the extra carafes Earthenhouse had bought with the set.

She made the extra coffee. The crowd gathered around the coffee maker to watch it percolate and make conversation. Meanwhile, she backed up to the door. The creatures made no move to stop her. She waved quickly to the seven-foot-tall beast that hadn't moved from the three chairs, muttered something about break time, and then grabbed her backpack and ran into the corridor.

She was up three flights of stairs and had reached the public shopping corridor before her legs and lungs forced her to stop. She leaned against a marble wall, wheezing. "What . . . the . . . hell?"

"Are you all right?"

She jumped and clutched at her chest before she saw it was only Patrick, the security guard.

"I'm fine!" She waved him off, then found that she hated this lie. "I'm not fine. But I'll be okay." That, she hoped, was closer to the truth.

He pulled his hands out of his pockets. "What happened?"

*The truth will make him think I'm crazy. Heck, I'm pretty sure I* am *crazy. What other explanation could there be for seeing what I just saw—or think I saw?*

She took a deep breath, then let it out slowly. "I saw something I wasn't expecting." Beneath her breath, she added, "Lots of somethings."

"Goblins?"

She froze. There are many ways one could say, "goblins." There was the incredulous voice. The ridiculing voice. The sarcastic voice.

Patrick's voice was matter-of-fact, with an edge of surprise that "goblins" should come as a surprise to her.

The way he looked at her confirmed it. He wasn't looking at her as though she were crazy. He only looked puzzled.

"Yeah," she said. "Lots and lots of goblins. Am I going crazy?"

"I don't see why. You answered the ad, after all. The real ad?"

"But I—" She stopped. *Real* ad? *What* real ad? Then she remembered: she still had the newspaper with the Night Girl ad that had sent her here in the first place. She rummaged through her backpack and pulled it out. She looked at the clipping, but it was just as she'd remembered. *Personal assistant job . . . duties include managing finances, contacting clients . . . steady nerves an asset . . .*

Then she remembered the flyer she'd seen through the bathroom mirror, and she held the newspaper clipping up to the shiny marble wall. The reflection was backwards, and nowhere near as clear as it would be in a mirror, but she could still make out the words YARD SALE! and EVERYTHING MUST GO!

Patrick went on. "Didn't you know what you were getting into? I mean, you can clearly see through the veil."

Her breath quickened. "Veil? What veil?"

"You know . . ." He gave her a smile. "The thing that keeps most people from seeing them? Only a few people can see past it, like you. And"—here, he looked around, as if to see if anybody was listening—"people like me."

He put his hand on his chest, and it took Perpetua a moment to realize he was pointing at an enamelled pin on his collar: a green shamrock.

She had so many questions. As she formed her mouth around the words, Patrick glanced past her and straightened up. "Well, it looks as though your break is over. I think your chair wants you back at the office."

"Wait, what?" She heard a squeak and whirled around to see her desk chair emerging from the stairwell.

"What—?" She dodged, but it altered course to intercept her. "What are you—hey!"

She glanced back at Patrick, but he was walking away.

The chair squeaked closer, and Perpetua rounded on it. They both froze. She stood in a sumo crouch, ready to wrestle if it attacked her.

Despite having no facial features whatsoever, the chair stared back.

It darted to her left and, as Perpetua reacted, zipped to the right, swinging around behind her to ram at the back of her legs. She fell into the seat, arms flailing, and the chair zoomed toward the stairwell. The door swung open as they approached.

Perpetua's eyes widened as the flight of stairs loomed. "Look out!" she shouted, then, "Ow! Ow! Ow!" as the chair skipped and hopped down the stairs. More doors opened for them as they rolled through the lower shopping corridor and made a beeline for Earthenhouse's office.

He stood up as she entered. "Miss Collins! What happened? Did you take an unscheduled break?"

"My chair is possessed, and you're babbling about break times?" She darted for the door, but the chair blocked her path.

"Well, it is in the contract," he replied. "Although, maybe I should have told your chair not to be so stringent about enforcing the terms of your contract tonight."

Perpetua stared at Earthenhouse. "'Tell it'? Are you serious?"

"The contract specified sick leave and vacation times, and requires two weeks' notice if you intend to resign," he replied. "There's a half-hour lunch break, with two fifteen-minute breaks on either side of it. The contract has been logged, and the office made aware of the terms. Did you go on break before the prescribed time?"

"Let me get this straight: this"—she waved a hand at the desk chair—"*thing* will come and get me if I don't come back from break on time?"

"I am a stickler for punctuality."

She rubbed her backside. "You're down three flights of stairs."

"I know."

Perpetua pinched the bridge of her nose. "Permission to speak freely, sir?"

"Always."

"*What the hell is going on here*?"

"I thought we'd covered that in the interview," he said.

"You mean, *those* are our clients?" She jerked a finger at the closed door. "Hordes upon hordes of . . . *things* with sharp teeth—"

"Goblins," said Earthenhouse.

"And huge, seven-foot-tall creatures—"

"Trolls," said Earthenhouse.

"And—" She waved her arms. "And other *things*, with weird faces, and tongues sticking out?"

"Also goblins," said Earthenhouse. "They tend to be particularly good at sitting as gargoyles."

*Gargoyles? That sneezed when they smelled lavender soap?*

Her hands dropped to her sides. "*Those* are our art installations? We pay goblins to sit in place for hours?"

"It's a living."

She ran her hand through her hair. "What about those two hyperactive . . . rolling things that drank two-thirds of my coffee?"

"Oh, those are Chim and Chum Stonelaughter." He laughed. "Twins from a fine goblin family with a long tradition in the gargoyle business. Unfortunately, I've had difficulty placing them. They can't seem to sit still for long periods."

"No kidding!"

"Miss Collins, I *did* tell you I was a goblin, didn't I?"

"I thought you were crazy!" she yelled.

Earthenhouse's shark eyes gleamed. His smile was razor-thin. "Do you think that now?"

She lowered her gaze. "No. Maybe *I'm* crazy."

His voice softened. "Do you really think that?"

"No." She closed her eyes and then opened them again. "And I'm not dreaming, either. I should quit, but if I don't give you two weeks' notice, that chair will come and get me."

"Well, you can still leave," said Earthenhouse. "Activate your screaming clause."

"'Screaming clause'?"

"If you leave the office at a run, screaming, then the two-week notice period is waived."

"Oh." She drew a breath, held it a moment, and then said, "Seriously? That's in my contract?"

"It's what most people do when they leave here, so I thought I'd write it in."

*A screaming clause*, she thought. *I can do that. A yell of fear and a howl of bewildered rage sound the same. All I have to do is run from this office, screaming, turn my back on twenty-four dollars an hour, and, if I can't find another job, slink back to North Bay and listen to Mother tell me that she told me so.*

Perpetua's eyebrows and mouth narrowed to two thin, level lines.

"Miss Collins," Earthenhouse continued. "Perhaps I did not explain things as clearly as I could have. By that alone, you have every right to activate your screaming clause, but I would be sorry to see that happen. This is a legitimate business. To do it, I need someone humans can deal with. You have been the most promising candidate, by far. Now that you know the true conditions of this workplace, will you stay?"

Perpetua folded her arms. "I want a raise!"

He tilted his head thoughtfully. "I could pay you twenty-five—"

"Thirty! And I get to have a word with your desk chair about enforcing break times!"

"Done," said Earthenhouse.

Behind her, the desk chair made a squeak that sounded oddly like a gulp.

"Fine," she said. "And thank you. Now that that's settled, I'll get back to work."

She spun around and glared at her chair until it sidled out of her way. She nodded, satisfied, and walked out of Earthenhouse's office.

"Miss Collins," he called. "You forgot your desk chair."

Perpetua poked her head back through the doorway. "Come on, Scooter!"

Earthenhouse raised an eyebrow. "Scooter?"

She pointed at the chair. "Now, look here, you: if you can move around on your own, you don't need me pulling you everywhere. So, are you coming?"

The chair hesitated. Then it squeaked past her and into the

reception area of the office. Smiling grimly, Perpetua headed for her desk. Scooter scooted itself into place as she sat down.

In the waiting area, the goblins milled about, sipping coffee and chattering, while the troll sat and stared ahead. Chim and Chum stood in the corner, bobbing like two pistons of an engine, chanting: "Socialize, socialize! Socialize, socialize!"

Perpetua flipped through a fat folder containing work assignments. They were for gargoyle installations across the city, as well as one or two requests by nightclubs for bouncers. Her eyes tracked up to the troll, with his shovel-like hands.

*Well, it's a living.*

She stood and cleared her throat. The goblins stopped chattering. "Right," she called out. "Gather round, everybody. The first temp jobs are here."

## Chapter 16
# The Rules of the World

Climbing out from the Underground City, Perpetua looked up. The silhouettes of gargoyles poked up from the shadowy buildings into the brightening sky. She picked out the addresses she knew and pointed at each one in turn. "That one's ours. That one's ours." She walked toward Adelaide. "That one's ours. And that one . . . isn't."

She stopped across the street from a building that was shorter and older, but still all glass and steel. Gargoyles peered down from the roof level. One picked its nose.

"Freelancers?"

Cars breezed past. After a few minutes, she spotted the cab she was looking for and raised her hand. When it stopped, Fergus leaned over to look out. "Oh, hey! Just in time!"

She got in. The cab pulled away from the curb.

"So, how was work?" Fergus twisted the wheel.

She looked at his eyes, reflected through the rear-view mirror. "You know," she said, "I work for a real troll, eh?"

His brow furrowed. "Do you mean 'troll' like you don't like him? Or 'troll' like he's actually a goblin?"

Her eyes narrowed. "You *knew* who I was working for, and you didn't tell me?"

He looked at her, uncertainly, through the rear-view mirror. "Well . . . no . . .?"

Perpetua took a deep breath for a big, long rant.

He ducked. "Wait! How 'bout I explain?"

She leaned back. "Go ahead."

"Over breakfast?"

Her glare intensified.

"Okay, how about I *buy* you breakfast?" He turned and looked back at her. "It's the least I can do, right? Explanations come easier over bacon and eggs." He gave her a hopeful smile.

She thought about this a moment, then settled back in her seat. "All right. Drive. I know a good place."

Perpetua directed Fergus to Corned Beef House. He read the "Best Kept Secret in Toronto" slogan on the windows, right next to "World-Famous . . ." and pointed. "Um?"

"I know." She waved him inside. "But you've really got to try their corned beef."

Inside the door, the waitress gave Perpetua a grunt of recognition.

Fergus grinned. "Corned Beef House, huh? You guys have veggie-burgers?"

The waitress's knuckles whitened on the menus in her hand.

Perpetua took Fergus by the arm. "He's kidding, and he's sorry. Two corned beef hash and eggs, please! And two coffees." She led the way to their table. "I can't take you anywhere."

They sat, and the waitress delivered their coffee. Wrapping her hands around her cup, Perpetua leaned forward. "So . . .? Spill! Where did all the goblins and trolls come from? When did they get here? And how the hell can they be in this city without people noticing?"

He raised a hand. "You might want to keep your voice down."

Perpetua paused. The volume of the restaurant had dipped.

Everywhere she looked, she saw people talking or drinking coffee and staring into space. But there was a listening edge to the silence. Shouting felt . . . risky.

The waitress appeared, then, setting plates of corned beef hash between them. That snapped the spell. Perpetua watched Fergus as he tucked into his meal, and then picked up her own fork. "So?" she said quietly, between bites. "How is it that nobody notices?"

"Well, you noticed," said Fergus.

"That's different."

"I've noticed," he added.

"That's . . . well . . ."

He looked at her. "You've met others who knew about the goblins, right?"

She thought of Patrick, the security guard. Also, the House of Limericks was right next door, and the proprietor looked human. "Well . . ."

"It's true, you don't see goblins in the news," said Fergus, "but it's not true that nobody knows about them. What's closer to the truth is that the people who know mind their own business. It's a sort of unspoken pact."

She stared in disbelief. "That can't be enough to keep their presence secret."

"And yet, you only just figured out there were goblins around you today."

She glared. "Okay. So, how did they get here?"

"They've always been here. Or, more accurately, they've always been among us. A question you might ask yourself is, 'Why are they hiding?' In answer to that, I would say, 'What do you know about the Battle of Magh Tuireadh?'"

She folded her arms across her chest and stared at him.

He nodded. "Nothing, right? And some people want to keep it that way, because, you know, why draw attention to yourselves? But it was a real historical battle that's faded into myth and legend. It happened in Ireland about three thousand years ago. But we've got to backtrack a bit, first."

Perpetua almost choked on her coffee. "You've got to backtrack from three thousand years ago?"

He grinned. "Kind of, yeah. The thing you've got to realize is that the goblins, trolls, and faeries of legend? They're real people. They lived alongside the humans we know, but they were outsiders. When the Celts marched out of central Europe, they pushed everyone else back until they reached Ireland and ran out of land. The faeries, the goblins, and the trolls had to stand together and fight, or be pushed into the sea."

"Did they?"

"Yup. And they lost. Badly. Even with goblin and faerie magic, and some hefty superweapons, the Celts' numbers and Iron Age swords were too much. The Celts conquered Ireland. And the faeries, the goblins, and the trolls had to live with that."

He leaned forward. "The faeries had an advantage, though: they were beautiful. They married into the Celtic race and raised their children as humans. They were the lucky ones. They got to assimilate."

She frowned. "Assimilation is not so lucky."

"It is when you think of the alternatives. Assimilation wasn't an option for most goblins. And as for the trolls . . . well, you've seen them: how well do you think they'd fit in?"

She winced.

"Exactly," said Fergus. "Those that could pass themselves off as humans did. Those that couldn't . . . well, they went underground. They lived in caves, under bridges. They stole chickens and raided dairies. Over time, they became the stories we use to scare kids at bedtime."

She stared at him in disbelief. "They hid? Behind the furniture? For three thousand years? How could they *do* that? They're sitting at the tops of buildings, Fergus!"

He jerked his head at the window. "Look outside."

She looked. The sky was brightening. Rush hour was beginning. Business people were on the street, talking on cell phones; they barely avoided being run down by the traffic.

"There is magic in this world," said Fergus. "How do you think a free market economy works? It also helps to keep up the veil. Goblins are good at making sure people don't notice them, or the trolls. Only a few people can see through it, like you did when you didn't see an ad for a garage sale in that job ad I gave you. Humans help out, too, though they don't even know it."

"How?"

He leaned forward. "There are three types of people on this planet. There's the group that thinks they control their own lives. They think they know everything there is to know about the world. Point out the goblins to them, and they'd run around in circles, waving their arms. So, nobody tells them about the goblins."

He nodded out the window at a dishevelled man standing at the corner, nursing a paper cup of coffee. "Then there are those who have surrendered control over their lives. They keep their heads down and let things happen. Sure, they know about the goblins and the trolls, but they don't bother the goblins, and the goblins don't bother them. And then finally, there are people like you."

"Me?"

"I saw it the moment I saw you," he said. "Everybody else had their heads down, but you were looking up and around. You didn't have that glazed look in your eyes. You see what's around you, and you don't automatically judge. That's why you can see through the veil. Maybe you have a bit of faerie or goblin magic in you or, more likely, you're just attuned. You see the goblins as the people they are, and that makes you one of the best kinds of people around."

She rolled her eyes. "Flattery won't get you anywhere." But she still smiled.

"So, what's your story?" Fergus set down his fork. "Where did you come from? How did you get here? Only seems fair that we exchange."

"Exchange? All of that was about the goblins. I still don't know much about you."

"Oh, there's not much to say about me." He looked evasive for a moment, but then schooled his features into an affected look of goofily fascinated listening—chin on hands, gazing at her with wide eyes—that was hard to resist.

She set down her fork, in turn. "I grew up in North Bay. You've heard of it?"

Fergus grinned. "It's north of here, right?"

She rolled her eyes. "Yeah. It's a medium-sized town, a bit too far north to be part of Toronto's cottage country, so it makes most of its money from industry. Still, it's beautiful enough in summer. Winter's another story."

He frowned. "What's wrong with winter?"

"It's north," she replied. "We get a lot of snow, and it tends to shut down the highways into the city." She looked past Fergus, remembering. "The wind comes screaming off Lake Nipissing and makes you wish you were dead. So, I moved to Toronto."

He winced.

She laughed. "Sorry. That didn't sound so bad when it was in my head."

"S'all right."

She stared into the depths of her coffee cup. "I think maybe the town drove my father away," she said. "And, really, that's why I'm here."

"To look for your father?"

"No," she said quickly. "To get away from Mom. I sort of walked out on her. We fought."

"What about?"

"Lots of different things. Honestly, it had been building for years, but, really, it had to do with how Dad left us."

"That's a lot of walking out on your mother."

She scowled at him. "Dad left just months after I was born,

apparently. I don't know why. And the thing is, Mom lied to me about why he left."

He tilted his head and gave her an encouraging smile. A listening smile. Perpetua liked that.

She sat forward again and rested her cheek on her hand. "In grade school, I finally pieced together that the other kids had daddies, and not me. So, I asked Mom about it."

"What did she say?"

Her eyes flashed as she looked at him. "She said, and these are her exact words, 'Daddy couldn't stay with us, dear. He had to go underground.'"

"Go . . .? Like a spy?"

"Exactly what I thought. And I'd just managed to sneak-watch James Bond without Mom knowing, so you can imagine how I felt: Daddy was a spy! That was so cool! And I believed it—right up until I became a teenager and pieced it all together."

"So, what really happened?"

"He just left!" she snapped. "One day, he was there; the next day, he wasn't. And for years, Mom never let me know. Even when I was old enough, she never told me the truth. She still hasn't." She leaned back again. "That's why I walked out on her."

"What did she say when you left?" he asked.

Perpetua opened her mouth to answer, but the waitress arrived and plunked their bill on the table.

Both hesitated a moment. Fergus reached for the check, but Perpetua snatched it up. "I'll get this."

They walked together back to the cab. Fergus held the door open for her. Perpetua frowned at this, but got in. He got in on the other side, and they drove off.

Perpetua looked out the window as they passed the King-Bay intersection. She saw the singer on the rooftops, and the crowds of people flowing past the Lumpy Thinker.

"So, they're everywhere," she said. "Even if I were to point them out, most people wouldn't notice that the statues were alive?"

"Nobody's noticed yet, have they?" He gave her a smile, and she found herself smiling back.

She looked out the window again. "Welcome to the big city, I guess."

The gargoyles on the cornice winked at her.

She winked back.

# Part Three
# The Faerie Mafia

*We are actors. We are the opposite of people. We need an audience.*

— Tom Stoppard, *Rosencrantz and Guildenstern are Dead*

## Chapter 17
# Settling into the World

Earthenhouse paid Perpetua at the end of the week. Again, it was in cash.

Now that Perpetua's money roll had grown to a size that could not comfortably (or attractively) fit inside her bra, she decided to open a bank account.

As she headed off, she wondered why Earthenhouse relied on cash. The goblins and trolls' pay had also come in envelopes full of bills. Earthenhouse wasn't hiding things from the taxman, either; she knew this from the forms she'd spent hours on the day before.

She passed another plywood construction fence around a boarded-up building with signs that shouted: "NEW SUBWAYS! GROWING TO SERVE YOU!"

Minutes later, Perpetua sat across the desk from a middle-aged woman dressed in black slacks and a cardigan over a bright green blouse. She bashed at her keyboard. "Print, damn you! I said, print!" Her scowl cleared when she looked up at Perpetua. "How may I help you?"

"I need to open an account," Perpetua replied.

"Oh, lovely!" said the manager. "Have you read about our banking plans?"

"Which ones have the lowest service fees?" said Perpetua.

"That depends on the plan," the manager chirped. "I'll print out a list, and you can compare and see what you like. If I could see some ID, please, that will help smooth the process along. A driver's licence, a passport, a citizenship or permanent resident card, a social insurance number, that sort of thing. Any two pieces of ID will do."

Perpetua pulled out her driver's licence and her social security card. *Thank heavens, I always have those handy*, she thought. *Things would be even tougher if I didn't. I couldn't open a bank account, and would have to be paid in . . .*

Cash.

She sat up straight.

Of course, Earthenhouse paid the goblins and trolls in cash. How on earth were they going to deposit paychecks?

It struck her, then, that this applied to just about every troll and goblin in Earthenhouse's care, and that it wasn't just bank accounts they had to worry about. Imagine Rek trying to get a passport. And what about driver's licences and health cards?

No wonder that homeless guy was feeding the Lumpy Thinker cabbage from his shopping cart. If Earthenhouse was the only lifeline for the goblins in this bureaucratic world . . .

She was still thinking this, ashamed that she hadn't thought about it before, when the manager hit the "any" key on her keyboard hard and repeatedly. "I said, print! Print, damn you!" The manager pointed at her screen. "You *will* print!"

A spark lanced from her finger. For a second, her computer glowed blue, and then the printer spewed out paper as though its life depended on it.

The manager gave a satisfied huff, which turned to a look of wide-eyed horror when she saw Perpetua staring. "Um . . . you weren't supposed to see that."

Perpetua eyed the woman. Her skin was porcelain, her hair red. She didn't look unusual. Maybe a little too thin; almost willowy. But that didn't explain what she'd seen, did it?

It didn't explain the uneasy feeling she had that saying something would get them both into deep, deep trouble.

"Uh . . . see what?"

The manager nodded frantically. "Exactly! Nothing at all! Just some static discharge. We get that here sometimes, in dry weather."

She turned to her computer and typed rapidly. "So, new bank account, then? Let's see what I can do for you today!" The computer beeped. "Here's one! High interest rates and no service charges whatsoever. Would that interest you?"

Perpetua wasn't sure how to react to this, so she picked the safest course of response. "Sure?"

"Lovely! I'll get the paperwork!" The manager hurried off.

Perpetua watched her go. "What just happened?"

Perpetua worked through the evening, until midnight, when the door swung open and the horde (*I ought to think of a better group name for them—a gaggle? Maybe a congress?*) swept into the office and started chatting up the coffee maker.

She picked up the jobs folder from the inbox and flipped through the pages. "Rek Strongrass?" she called.

An impish figure, bald with pointy ears, poked his head up from the crowd and scrambled over. She handed him the paper. "Art installation. Old City Hall. Replacing one of the gargoyles while the stonework is taken away for cleaning."

He snatched the paper and pumped his fist. "Yes!" He scrambled out the door.

Perpetua peered at the next page. "Odin Chickenbane?" She counted it as one of her stronger attributes that she was able to say these names without laughing.

Odin came over, short and bony, with endlessly grinning teeth. She handed over the paper. "Cornice sitter, Strathcona Hotel."

Odin bowed low. "Thank you, Boss Lady!"

The next assignment was for a troll. "Fred?" She did a double-take. "*Fred*?"

The lone troll stood up. He took one step toward her and held out a shovel-like hand.

She looked at him. "Seriously, your name is just . . . Fred?"

He bobbed his head.

She raised an eyebrow. "Do you have a last name, Fred?"

He bobbed again. "Troll."

She stared at him. "Do you have a middle name?"

He bobbed a third time. "The."

Perpetua handed over the paper. "Bouncer. A restaurant called *Le Petit Ennui*. I hear it's a hip place. I'm sure you'll fit right in."

He bobbed at her and ambled out.

She handed out a dozen more assignments, each for various statues, gargoyles, and road workers; that last job included a work uniform. A reflective vest, a hard hat, and a shovel did much to hide the goblin-ness of their clients, something Perpetua wouldn't have believed if she hadn't seen it done.

As the last newly employed clients left the office, Perpetua looked at her empty folder, then up at the horde that remained. Chim and Chum bobbed and ducked, and somehow managed not to spill their drinks. Others stood in small groups, chatting and drinking coffee. Some of them had been there every day this past week. They didn't seem too upset about not getting assignments, but she wondered how long they'd be willing to wait before they got discouraged.

"Miss Collins?" Earthenhouse's voice snapped her from her reverie. She turned, looked Earthenhouse in the face, and then felt her gaze track upward. Behind him loomed a mountain of stone, with knuckles that grazed the floor. "This is Howard," said Earthenhouse. "He's a troll."

"Troooooooll," drawled Howard, extending his shovel-like hand to Perpetua.

"Hello, Howard." She gingerly clasped a finger. Her forehead creased. "Didn't we place you—?"

Earthenhouse cut in. "It did not work out as well as we hoped." He lowered his voice. "He was assigned to the security division. I'm afraid he took the title of 'bouncer' a little too literally."

Perpetua looked up at Howard. He grinned, revealing teeth like granite chips. "Bounce, bounce!"

"Miss Collins," said Earthenhouse. "I need you to run today's training session."

"Um . . . sir?" Earthenhouse had held a training session every day this past week. It emptied out the reception area for half an hour every time. She'd been too busy with her invoices to look into the training room and see what went on there.

"Normally, I'd do it," he said, "but I have a phone meeting I can't postpone. I believe the phrase is, 'I need you to cover for me'?"

"But, sir," she said, "I've never trained anybody before!"

He spread his hands. "Just do what I do: pop in the video and stand back."

*Stand back. That's all?*

Earthenhouse handed her a videocassette, and she stared at it. She hadn't seen one of these since she was ten. She caught the hopeful look on Earthenhouse's face and hated the thought of letting him down. "I'll do my best, sir."

He smiled, then beckoned her closer. "Get Howard to help you. It will help him feel useful after losing the bouncer contract."

She looked up at Howard. He grinned. "Bounce?"

She took the video. As she stepped into the training room, Howard following, crouching to get through the door, a dozen pairs of eyes watched eagerly. She could hear whispers of: "Movie! Movie!"

The video equipment was already set up, which was a relief, because she was darned if she knew how to get a VCR working. Of all the courses she'd taken at university, not one of them was on the archaeology of technology. The videocassette slipped in easily—once she got it the right way around—but it took a moment for her to figure out how to get it to play.

The goblins filed in as she worked. Only Chim and Chum stayed in the reception area, chanting "Movie! Movie!" back and forth at each other. One of the goblins closed the door discreetly.

Finally, with a sound like mice being strangled, the cassette began to play. Perpetua straightened up. "Get the lights, Howard."

Howard pulled a halogen lamp from the ceiling, socket and all, and held it out to her. Trailing wires sparked near the ceiling.

Perpetua stared at the offering. "Put the light down, Howard."

The troll set down the shattered assembly, and Perpetua used the eraser tip of a pencil to flip the light switch. The room darkened. The sparks stopped.

The tape played, albeit with a streak of white static stamped across the bottom of the screen. The training video began with white lettering on a black background.

*T.P. Earthenhouse presents . . .*

The room buzzed with anticipation

*The New Employees Welcome Video!*

The audience clapped.

The picture faded in. Earthenhouse, filmed by an unsteady camera, looked up from behind his desk.

"Oh, hello." His eyes focused off-screen, looking at what may have been cue cards. "Welcome to T.P. Earthenhouse: Rare Coins, Bouncers, and Art Installations. Have you ever wanted to earn a living doing honest human work? Here, you can look forward to a productive career within the human economy. Have you ever wanted a decent wage, reduced hours, and a benefits package? Well, here at T.P. Earthenhouse: Rare Coins, Bouncers, and Art Installations, you can realize"—he paused, and there was a sound of posterboard being flipped over—"your dreams."

On-screen, Earthenhouse stood up and stalked around his desk, reaching behind him to clasp the edge, trying to look casual.

"We've all been there," he continued. "Our attempts to interact with humans are usually met with the same reaction . . ."

The picture cut to a goblin wearing a mask shaped like the face of a little girl. He stood, arms at his sides, screaming in a high-pitched voice.

The picture cut back to Earthenhouse. "If you want to avoid this assault on your ears, along with the commotion that generally follows such incidents, we can help. We provide you with paying jobs that control your interaction with nervous humans."

The picture cut to a gargoyle sitting on a cornice at night. The goblin stopped digging in his ear, turned to the camera, and waved.

The goblins in the training room, and Howard, waved back.

"Our security division offers a number of opportunities for trolls," Earthenhouse went on. "In these positions, humans expect someone big who doesn't say much. The companies that employ our workers have been impressed by the level of protection they've received, though care must be taken to deal with lawbreakers gently."

The picture flipped to a cartoon image of a troll holding a man over his shoulder. The man wore a striped shirt, black pants, and a burglar mask. Underneath this picture was the caption "CORRECT." Beside it was a cartoon of the same burglar lying on the floor after having left burglar-shaped holes in a series of walls. Underneath the picture was the caption, "NOT CORRECT."

"Please be aware that the term 'bouncer' is a human euphemism," Earthenhouse's voice-over commented. "It is not an actual part of the job description."

Perpetua glanced at Howard and saw the troll lower his gaze to his knees.

After more inspiring Muzak and more pictures of goblins and

trolls at work, the movie ended. In the glow from the television screen, Perpetua stepped forward and faced the room.

"Okay," she said. "Hands up: who saw this yesterday?"

Almost every hand in the room went up. The only one that didn't belonged to a goblin who had signed up as a client that day.

"Hands up: who saw this same video the day before yesterday?"

Two hands dropped to laps—also new clients. Earthenhouse had been showing the same video over and over again.

"How many of you have seen this video every day this week?"

Again, most hands stayed up.

"And how many of you found it at all useful?"

She waited. The hands stayed up a moment. Then, as the silence lengthened, they started to lower, slowly and sheepishly.

"So, why are you watching this again and again?"

The horde looked at each other. Glinting eyes blinked. "Pictures," said one goblin at last. The others took up the chant. "Pictures! Pretty, pretty pictures!"

Perpetua sucked her teeth. Then she stepped to the door and opened it. "Okay, everybody: wait outside and . . . do whatever it is you do, okay?"

The horde moved out, rumbling like a landslide. When the way was clear, Perpetua strode across the office and knocked on Earthenhouse's door. "Sir? Can I talk to you?"

"Certainly!" he called. "Come in!"

She entered and stood opposite the desk from him, hands on her hips. "You're running a community centre."

He looked up at her, and then around, as though looking for a label he'd missed. "No . . . I think it says clearly on the door—"

"You have over a dozen goblins and one troll in that waiting room," she cut in, pointing back behind her to the reception area, "some of whom have been waiting for jobs since opening day. Chim and Chum can't sit still, and Howard's too literal-minded to be trusted with heavy machinery. When will their next assignments be?"

Earthenhouse took a deep breath. "Not everyone is suited for the jobs available to us."

"And so they come here. And you let them stay, because to do anything else would be . . ." She struggled to pick the next word.

"Inhumane," Earthenhouse finished, with a trace of irony.

"So, this is a community centre," she said. "And I've looked at the schedule for today."

"We talked about it," said Earthenhouse. "I have a meeting—"

"Not your schedule." She jerked her head back at the reception area. "Theirs."

He blinked at her. She pulled out a notepad and flipped up the first page. "At midnight, our clients arrive. The lucky ones get their job assignments. At 12:30, we run the training video. At 1, the training video ends." She flipped her notepad closed. "And that's all."

For a moment, night girl and boss stared at each other across the boss's desk.

"Should there be more?" he asked.

"Yeah! I mean, what would you be doing right now, if this place wasn't here?"

He thought a moment. "Probably sitting around somewhere. There's not much else to do." He looked up at her. "Maybe hunt for chickens."

She tilted her head. "So, what you've done is set up a place to do what they'd normally do, except with a roof over their heads. That's an improvement, but it's not enough."

"Isn't it?"

"Well, look at you!" She gestured at his pinstripes. "You have things to do, meetings to go to. How much better do you feel, now that you have all this stuff to work on?"

He considered this, nodding slowly.

"It's not enough that they have shelter." She paused. It seemed odd to say it, since it wasn't so long ago that she would have given almost anything for the bare minimum of shelter. But it was still true. "If you want your clients to feel good about themselves, they need things to do."

Earthenhouse rested his chin on his steepled fingers. "I hadn't thought of that. So, what does one do at a community centre?"

She struggled for an answer. "I don't know. Skill-training sessions. Game rooms. Movie nights. Um . . . dance classes." She waved her hands. "Maybe not that, but anything else. Right now, they're eagerly looking forward to repeat showings of our training video."

He sighed. "You'll have to forgive me, Miss Collins. You are right. I have never done anything like this before."

"Okay. Well, I have a few ideas already. I'll get to work."

She walked out of Earthenhouse's office and found the goblin horde sitting on the chairs in the waiting area, drinking more coffee. Some were spinning aimlessly. She kicked herself for having waited even this long before saying anything, but now, she supposed, was still better than never. She cleared her throat. "You folks looking for something to do?"

Several pairs of glittering eyes looked at her. After a moment, heads nodded.

"Any of you know how to use a computer?" she asked.

Heads shook from side to side.

"Any of you know how to use a fax machine?"

Heads shook again.

"All of this techie stuff is a mystery to you, isn't it?"

Glittering eyes blinked at her. Foreheads furrowed.

She took a deep breath. "Okay, well, who here wants to know how to use a fax machine?"

A dozen hands went up.

She smiled. "Good. Then let's get started."

On her way to work the next day, Perpetua stopped at a trendy coffee shop to splurge on a Frappuccino. It meant waiting in line for ten minutes before she could place her order, but she had time, and the air-conditioning was welcome. She sat on a stool by a tall counter near the window while she braced herself to face the sweltering heat outside.

As she relaxed, she let the burble of the customers wash over her, picking out strands of conversation as they went by.

A preening lawyer grinned at his colleague. "Yeah, so, those guys at Howe and Ross—"

A middle-aged receptionist shook her head in disgust. "I'm telling you, it's freezer and furnace in this town! I—"

An IT guy wearing a Dungeons & Dragons T-shirt. "Yeah, that server. It's going to come down when they least expect it—"

"*There are too many of them in this town*."

Perpetua stiffened. The female voice caught at her hearing the way the hissing of a snake pumped adrenalin into a hiker's heart. She could do nothing but listen.

Out of the corner of her eye, she saw a young woman with black hair, a white blouse, and a green jacket and slacks lean across the table toward her partner, a man in a pinstripe suit with slicked-back, ginger-coloured hair.

"How many are too many?" asked the man with a sly smile.

The woman's returning smile was brief. "Point. But there are far more than should be here. It's dangerous; if we get any more, the wrong people will notice."

"It can't be that serious, can it?" asked the man. "The veil's held so far."

"So far," the woman echoed. "Do you want to see how far it can stretch?"

"Well, what can we do about it?" asked the man. "There's nothing to prevent them from locating where they please."

"Something is drawing them here," said the woman. "Something's upsetting the balance. If what I'm hearing is correct, somebody might be getting a visit, and soon."

"You think someone is breaking the Mores?" asked the man.

"Maybe," said the woman. "Hopefully, we'll find out before it's too late. Then we'll—shh. Someone is listening to us."

A chill ran down Perpetua's spine.

"Are you sure?" The man leaned forward. He shielded his mouth. "We're speaking beneath the veil. There are no—"

"Hush!"

The man cut himself short. He went on. "There are only humans here."

"I know my powers," the woman whispered. "There may only be humans here, but one of them is listening right now. Talk sports, while I see who."

"You mean, like how the Blue Jays have an outside chance at the wild card spot? They just need to sweep their swing with the Yankees to overtake the . . ."

The man droned on. The woman shifted in her seat, turning slowly, scanning the shop.

Perpetua felt the tension rise like a boiling kettle. Some instinct inside her made her slip from her stool and merge with a crowd of students bustling toward the door. She was outside before she realized she'd left her Frappuccino behind.

# Chapter 18
# Fergus Journal Entries V

*Monday, August 12*
*Dear Future Self,*

*Had trouble finding this journal today. I was going to ask Perpetua if she'd moved it, but then figured that was unwise. Eventually, I found it on a different shelf from where I usually keep it.*

*See? I'm learning. Also, I don't think she's the sort who'd read my journal entries.*

*Tuesday, August 13*
*Dear Future Self,*

*So, there are a few perils when you share your home with a female.*

*Peril one: hair products. These are to be kept strictly segregated between the sexes. Apparently, theirs contain some secret ingredient that must be applied to women's hair only, on pain of death, or at the very least, glares and huffs. They are not an* acceptable substitute for your own shampoo, even if they do give my hair a more full-bodied curl.

Peril two: television rights. I suppose that since the living room is essentially her bedroom, she should have more of a say in what I put on the television. Watching two different shows on a TV and a computer doesn't work when you have to share the space, earphones or no. And she's right: Law and Order reruns are a dime a dozen. But Cakebusters? Who on earth thought that watching people baking cakes would make for compelling television?

And Josie's flan really should have won.

Peril three: one of you will fail to put food away after taking it out of the fridge, and the other will find that offensive. At the same time, the other will fail to put the cutlery away in the correct drawer. You will be tempted to say: "See? Let she who is without sin cast the first stone."

Do not ever say that. It does not go well.

Wednesday, August 14
Dear Future Self,

There is one more peril you should remember about living with a female, and this may be the biggest one: please, for the love of God, listen carefully when your roommate answers your question of "Are you decent?" after she has had a shower. Make sure you haven't misheard her, or that she hasn't misheard your question.

I'm not sure exactly what happened, but we ended

*up stepping into the living room at the same time, each expecting the other to stay behind a closed door.*

*Fortunately, she had a towel handy.*

*Extra fortunately, she found it within herself to laugh when I retreated to my bedroom so fast I slammed face-first into the doorframe.*

*In the postmortem, as she checked me over for a concussion, we agreed that we would never speak of it again.*

*She's great!*

## Chapter 19
# There's Kissing in This One

Perpetua's first idea for the community centre was "movie night." It wasn't a stretch: she loved movies, and she loved to share movies. After getting permission to dip into the petty cash to buy a DVD player and DVDs, she set up the equipment in the training room and popped *Fantasia* into the player as a surprise substitution for the old training video.

Her secret smile widened into a grin as she watched the goblins and Howard stare, entranced, at the new video. She went back to her desk with a spring in her step. It was about time they had something new to watch.

The clients, she discovered, liked to watch things more than once. When she offered them *Run, Lola, Run*, they asked, begged, and pleaded to see *Fantasia* again. They seemed even more enthusiastic during the third showing.

On the fourth day, however, Howard entered the office wearing a tutu. Perpetua, remembering the dance number with the alligators and hippopotamuses, put two and tutu together and realized she was about to risk property damage.

"No reenactments!" She stood with hands on hips. "And above all else, no tutus!"

"Awwww!" chorused the horde.

"Hey! Who made the popcorn?"

*Run, Lola, Run* went over well that night, and Perpetua felt even better. Maybe the next film could be one of her favourites. The Lord of the Rings, she thought. *The best movie trilogy of all time. Epic fantasy, sword fights, battles against evil orcs and . . . cave trolls . . . and . . . orcs . . . which were actually called goblins in* The Hobbit . . .

*Hmm . . .*

She placed an order for *The Sound of Music*, instead.

The following Saturday, with another week's pay in the bank, Perpetua restarted her apartment search.

It wasn't quite as soul-crushing as the first search had been.

"Not that that's saying a lot." She sneered at the marked-up classifieds section before tossing it into a recycling bin.

It was now Sunday. Two days of fruitless searching. She slouched along Bloor Street as evening set in. She'd have to report her failure to Fergus. Another night of sleeping on his couch lay ahead, and though that didn't seem at all bad, it was still frustrating.

"I mean, c'mon! I'm earning more than I have in my entire life. I have a bank account! That should be enough to get me a decent place!"

Wrapped in her thoughts, she shouldered through the wandering crowds, pushing past street cafes and hipster bars, until she came up against a body that didn't get out of her way. It was like walking into a brick wall.

"Hey, watch it!" the brick wall growled at her. She looked up . . . and up . . . and stepped back. "Sorry!"

The security guard stood beside a door barricaded with red velvet ropes. Blasts of raucous music bombarded the street each time the door opened.

She ducked her head and made to slip past, when something clicked. She looked up at the bouncer again. His eyes were sunk in shadow under heavy eyebrows and the brim of his cap. His arms hung, gorilla-like, to his knees. Each hairy knuckle was as large and as rough as a walnut.

Behind him, she saw the name of the club: *Le Petit Ennui*. "Fred?"

A low rumble slipped from his throat—a warning. He glanced at the lineup beside him. People were chattering to each other or bobbing their heads to the music of headphones. But one young man was blinking at Perpetua and looking up at Fred.

"Oh! Sorry, uh . . ." Perpetua pulled her cell phone from her pocket. Without flipping it on, she put it to her ear. "Better?"

Out of the corner of her eye, she saw the man go back to chatting with his girlfriend.

She looked up at Fred. "So, enjoying the work?"

He straightened up proudly and grunted.

"Well, at least you're having a better evening than I am," she muttered.

Grunt?

"Apartment hunting. But the prey is either out of my league, or hardly worth it."

A long, pondering grunt. Then he raised his arm and pointed across the street.

She followed his point and realized she was staring at a gargoyle-goblin stationed below the third-story window of a brick walk-up.

Looking both ways, she crossed the street, keeping the gargoyle in her view. When she reached the other sidewalk, she was close enough to see that the goblin's eyes were shifting. He looked pointedly at her and then slowly turned his head. Perpetua followed his gaze to a window on the second floor, and saw the "Apartment for Rent" sign that had been partly obscured by a window garden.

She brought up her cell phone and dialled. "Fergus? Get down here. I think I've finally found an apartment."

Perpetua stood in the middle of a mostly beige cube, next to another mostly beige cube and an attached, mostly beige bathroom.

Fergus looked up and around. "Tall ceilings."

"Or short tenants," she replied. "Not that I'm complaining."

The building manager slouched behind them, hands in his pockets. "So, yeah. This is the living room, with attached kitchen." He nodded at the adjoining room. "That can be your bedroom. And there's a bathroom."

Perpetua nudged Fergus. "What do you think? Looks solid."

He tilted his head, considering. "Kind of boring."

"Compact," she said.

"Boring," he repeated.

She frowned at him. "Functional."

"Boring." Then he saw her frown and smiled. "Which probably means it's exactly what you need." His eyes widened, and he stuttered. "Not that you're boring; you're anything but! I-I mean . . . you should take it."

She grinned at him and slugged his shoulder. She turned to the manager. "So, rent: seven-fifty a month, including utilities?"

The manager shrugged. "Sure."

This was looking even better. "Can I hang stuff on the walls?"

He shrugged. "Whatever."

"When can I move in?"

He shrugged again. "Whenever."

"I'll take it. Is tomorrow okay?"

He held out a clipboard. "Sign here, please."

"Sure!" Perpetua pulled a ballpoint pen from her ponytail and scribbled her name. She waited until the door had closed behind the manager before commenting. "I'm starting to understand how the goblins can hide so easily." She turned and saw Fergus staring at her ponytail. "What?"

He pointed. "You keep pens in your hair?"

She raised an eyebrow. "You learn to cope when you don't have pockets. I even have an X-Acto knife."

"*What?*"

"Kidding! Kidding!" She stuck the pen back into her ponytail. "Probably kidding." She turned in a circle, taking in the big beige space. "Wow. All of this is now mine!"

He grinned at her. "Congratulations!" He looked down and rubbed the back of his calf with his other foot. "I'm going to miss you."

She hardly heard him. "My own apartment," she said, awestruck. Then she jumped up and punched the air. "I did it!"

He laughed. "Yes, you did!"

But she wasn't done cheering. She grabbed his hands and swung him squawking around in a mad dance across the empty living room. "I did it! And I didn't have to sleep on the streets! Thank you, Fergus! Thank you!" She gave him a hug that shoved the air from his lungs and, without a second thought, kissed him on the lips.

The sudden silence was deafening. Perpetua held Fergus, held the kiss, and after a panicked moment, realized that he was kissing back, his arms going around her waist to pull her close. She liked that moment and let it linger.

Then, opening her eyes to see his face up close, she saw his eyes open, widen, and she realized what she—what they—had done.

They pushed apart like the wrong ends of magnets, cries of alarm and shouts of, "Sorry! Sorry! I'm sorry!" filling the awkward air.

"I'm sorry!" said Fergus.

"Sorry!" said Perpetua.

Then they stopped and looked at each other.

"Why are we both saying sorry?" asked Fergus.

For a moment, she didn't have an answer. Then she shrugged and said, "Because we're Canadians?"

They snorted with laughter.

She thought about it a moment longer and then said, "Just because you caught me doesn't mean I should have jumped."

He nodded slowly. “Still,” he said. “I caught you. Isn’t that better than the alternative?”

“I guess . . . it’s just that . . .” She looked away, at the big, spacious apartment around her. “This is a big moment for me. Huge! I almost want to call my mother and tell her that I made it.” She looked at him. “And then I went and complicated it by kissing you.”

Fergus winced. “Sorry!”

“Seriously, why?”

He grinned at her glare and chuckled softly. “For making you want complicated things, perhaps?”

“Perhaps.” She sighed and came closer, touched his cheek. “It’s just . . . I wasn’t expecting this. I’ve been sleeping on your couch for weeks now. And you’ve been a perfect gentleman about it. Why did I have to go and shake things up?”

He shrugged again. “Maybe, because you have your own place now, you feel it’s safe to shake?”

They stared at each other as the mangled metaphor clattered into the sunset.

“Seriously, though,” he went on. “You’re an adult now. That’s what this place and the job that lets you afford it mean to you, right? It means more than voting or driving your own car. And, as symbols go, it’s a lot nicer than debt.”

Perpetua chuckled ruefully. She nodded.

“In this place, you get to do what you want,” he said. “You didn’t have that on my couch. So, what do you want?”

The moment lengthened.

“You know,” he added, “you say things are ‘complicated,’ and use scary metaphors like ‘jump,’ but you haven’t once said the word ‘bad.’”

She tilted her head at him. “You’re right,” she said after a while, and she pushed closer.

Their second kiss was softer, longer and slower. The moment stretched, and the only sounds in the apartment were those of breath. The front door opened, and the manager stepped inside before backing out again quickly. "Oh! Sorry!" The door shut behind him.

A long moment later, they pulled apart, but they kept their arms wrapped tight around each other.

"You up for making things complicated?" asked Perpetua.

Fergus nodded—nervous, but eager.

"Then we should totally date. C'mon. Let's go out tonight and celebrate. I know a place. It's crowded, but I know the bouncer."

*Le Petit Ennui* was full of people. Couples huddled together at tiny tables, while hipsters hung out near the wall. Waiters serving drinks sidled through the narrowing gaps.

It was loud, but Perpetua was surprised by the lack of music. Then she spotted musicians in a corner. The tables there had been pushed aside for a stage, and people were setting up microphones and speakers. Someone was noodling on an electric mandolin.

"Huh," she said. "A live band tonight. I guess that's cool."

Fergus leaned closer, raising his voice above the din. "So, what do people do here?"

"Shout over the music, once it starts playing. Drink overpriced drinks and eat food on plates that are too big for the tables." It struck her as odd that anybody living in downtown Toronto should be unclear as to what goes on in bars, but perhaps Fergus hadn't gone out much. She nudged him and nodded at the currently empty dance floor. "You and I are going out there, assuming the music can be danced to. It's such a big space; seems a waste not to use it."

He looked at the dance floor and went a little pale. "If I'm going to go out there, I'm going to need an overpriced drink first. How 'bout I get one for each of us, and you find us a table?"

"Gotcha!"

He headed to the bar. Perpetua found a minuscule empty

table covered with abandoned glasses by the low wall that surrounded the dance floor. It had a good view of the band.

A waiter appeared and began clearing away the glasses. Perpetua smiled encouragingly and mentally noted that she'd have to give the man a tip. Tipping had become affordable when she wasn't looking. And that realization made her smile widen. She leaned on the railing and happily watched the other couples chatting.

Someone sidled up beside her. It wasn't Fergus. Out of the corner of her eye, she saw tight pants and a green satin vest over a purple button-up shirt with no collar. The man tipped the brim of his fedora. "Hey," he said in a rich baritone.

She sighed. *Not again. Can't I just enjoy my date in peace?* She stiffened her shoulders and kept her gaze on the dance floor, tightening her body to say, "Go away."

But the man didn't go away. "I've seen you around. You work in the Underground City, right? At night?"

*Okay, how can I make myself clearer without saying the words "go away"? Not that that option is off the table.* She turned her face away. "Whatever."

"What sort of job keeps such strange hours? You working for some sweatshop owner?"

*He's not getting it. I don't want to have Fergus deal with this when I can do it myself.* She straightened up and turned to glare. The man was handsome, she gave him that. Almost too handsome, like he was showing off. He had the hipster uniform down to a tee, from the goatee to the little gold earrings, and . . . her eyes narrowed. "You're wearing sunglasses."

"Yeah? So?"

"Indoors," she added. "At night."

"Your point?"

"You wear your sunglasses. At night," she deadpanned. She waved her hands. "So you can . . .? So you can . . .? What?"

He offered a minimal half-smile. "So I can wear them ironically."

She nodded, as if this made sense. "Well, I'm not so good at irony. Slapstick, on the other hand . . ." She snatched the glasses off his face and froze.

Bright green eyes stared back at her, wide in shock as she clutched his sunglasses. She'd never seen eyes like that before—or, she realized, maybe she had. Her mind flashed to the bank manager. Same colour, but the manager's eyes hadn't been this intense. These eyes could grab you and drag you to the bottom of the sea.

"What are you?" She caught herself. Hadn't she meant to say "who"?

The man flinched from her stare, then swung away. Shielding his eyes with a hand, he dashed for the exit. The crowd slipped by around him, without anyone dropping their drinks or stopping their chatter. Perpetua realized that she was staring slack-jawed after him, and closed her mouth.

Fergus came up, holding two drinks. He handed her one. "Did I miss anything?"

Perpetua thought about this, then tossed the sunglasses aside. "Not much." She sipped the drink, then held it off and frowned at it. Diet cola. And Fergus seemed to have gotten himself a Sprite. She looked from one glass to the other, then shrugged and sipped again.

Fergus set down his glass. "So, we've got the overpriced drinks. We're going to go out on the dance floor. I guess we'll order food when the waiter finds us? That leaves shouting over the music whenever the music starts. What do you want to shout about?"

She put her elbows on the table and leaned forward, bringing the two of them nearly nose to nose. "The future?"

He grinned nervously, but didn't pull back. "The future's looking good from this angle."

Perpetua tried to hold on to the sultry, but Fergus's shy, sweet smile made her break into laughter. She smiled back at him. "It does, doesn't it? I've worked hard, but I've also been very lucky.

Don't think that I don't know that. I owe you so much. Thank you again."

He blushed. "You're welcome." Sobering, he asked, "So, it's not too strange, working for . . . you know?"

"Well, strange, yeah." She leaned back. "But fulfilling. I feel like I'm helping, especially since Earthenhouse has given me a budget to make changes with. Movie night's a hit, and I've ordered some games."

"Games?"

"You know, like Ping-Pong?"

His eyes widened. "Keep the trolls away from the Ping-Pong!"

"Why?" Then she thought about the possibility of ricochet. "Oh. Okay. Note to self: get Nerf Ping-Pong."

"Good idea."

The waiter arrived, took their order for burgers and fries, and looked awful snooty about it. After he slithered off, Perpetua said, "I've been doing other things, as well. I started getting some of them to help around the office, teaching them to use the fax machine and the computer. They're actually pretty good at it, once you show them how."

"Really?"

"Yeah. And it got me thinking: we've been getting a lot of clients—goblins—showing up. One or two trolls, too, but they don't stay long. Whatever Earthenhouse is doing gets the trolls into jobs pretty quickly. The goblins take longer, but they're smart. They can master a computer after only a few sessions. Maybe I could get more for the training budget and put together a computer lab. Then they could be in line for clerical jobs."

Fergus looked at her as if he hadn't heard her right. "Wait, clerical jobs? You mean, like secretaries and stuff? What you do?"

She wrinkled her nose at him. "The official term is 'administrative assistant,' if you please. My boss gets a free pass 'cause he pays me. You don't."

"But . . . administrative assistants," he said. "Answering phones, sitting behind desks, that sort of thing?"

"You bet! I'm writing up a proposal. I think, if I put in some effort, Earthenhouse could add a clerical division to his business."

Fergus stared at her as though in awe, and Perpetua found herself feeling like she was fifteen years old again. She ducked her head, then looked up at him through her lashes. "What?"

Without a word, he kissed her across the narrow table.

It was so sudden, she leaned back in shock before she realized what was happening. Then she leaned forward and put her arms around him. She grunted when the edge of the table pressed into her stomach, but the kiss lengthened.

Beside them, the waiter waited, two plates of burgers in hand. He peered at the space between them and measured a plate against it. He cleared his throat. No use. Finally, he sighed, hauled over another table, and set the plates on that. Then he slipped off to the kitchen, smiling indulgently.

Perpetua broke from the kiss at last and leaned back, eyes sparkling. "What brings this on?"

"Just . . ." He opened his mouth and then froze. Perpetua stared at him, waiting. He didn't look so desperate as when she'd surprised him earlier, when he'd claimed he'd almost forgotten his name. This, she thought, looked like a confession. The moment stretched out portentously.

But before he could speak, the woman on stage tapped the microphone.

"Hello, ladies and gentlemen." The woman raised her voice over the chatter. "We're Celtic Green. We've just got the band together, and we're excited to be here. We've got some great tunes for you tonight."

Perpetua rolled her eyes. "Great, yeah. I hope they're not too loud—"

The mandolin player strummed a chord, and Perpetua felt her attention pulled around as if it were attached by a string. She stared at the band. So did everybody else in the club. Meals were forgotten. The sound level dropped as conversations went on hiatus. Drinks stopped halfway to lips.

The drummer tapped out a staccato rhythm, and the mandolin player toyed with the beat. The lead singer smiled in a strangely secretive way. Then she leaned into the microphone and sang:

*Up the airy mountain, through the rushy glen*
*We daren't go a-hunting for fear of little men*
*Wee folk, good folk, trooping all together*
*Green jacket, red cap, and white owl's feather!*

The music made Perpetua's heart stutter. It hurt. But she didn't want it to stop.

"Who are they?" she whispered.

Fergus looked uncomfortable. He leaned in close and spoke directly into her ear, like he was sharing a dangerous secret. "You remember what I told you about the faeries who assimilated into the human race in ways the goblins and trolls couldn't?" He tilted his head at the band. "You're looking at some right now."

Perpetua goggled at him, then at the band, and really took them in this time. They looked human. Very human. Better than human. They were tall and fair of skin; so fair, they seemed to glow. The black-clad drummer wore his flaming red hair in a curly mop. The mandolin player was clean-shaven and slim as a snake; he wore dark glasses half as big as his face, yet somehow managed not to look absurd. The lead singer was lithe as a young tree in a bright green dress, her dark hair flowing halfway to her waist and floating like silk as she moved. Perpetua would have stared at these people if she'd seen them on the street, but only to admire them.

But the longer she looked, the less certain she became. The band members weren't inhumanly tall . . . but maybe they were just a little too tall. Maybe the lead singer's legs were just a little too slender to be perfect. Maybe the drummer's arms were just a little too long. Their beautiful faces had beautiful features, and beautiful mouths, and yet Perpetua got the sense that their teeth were sharp.

The lead singer tilted her head and looked straight at Perpetua. Their eyes met across the crowded room, and Perpetua felt pinned. The singer smiled, though her eyes narrowed.

Then she turned up her hands and blew on her palms. White vapour rose from them, thickening to a cloud that billowed out over the stage. The air rumbled. The music softened, and the room grew quiet, as though everyone held their breath.

Then the drummer brought down his drumstick, and lightning lanced the stage. Thunder clapped, a first beat that the drummer followed up with more. The mandolin picked up the pace, and the singer launched into the song's spectacular wind-up. The audience cheered.

Perpetua blinked spots from her eyes. "Whoa!" She looked at Fergus, who looked back at her. "Those were some special effects," she began. "Unless . . ."

"Not special effects."

"You mean, they used . . ."

He raised a hand to shield his mouth and shaped the word "*magic*."

She jerked upright. "They used real magic?"

"Shh!"

"But how can they do that?"

"What can I say?" He kept his voice low. "Faeries. They're magical, and they like being that way. It's not cheating if you don't get caught."

## Chapter 20
# The Human Face

The following afternoon, Perpetua popped a pile of cards into a mailbox—the sort that told people your address had changed. There was one for her best friend, Betsy, now shacked up with Roz half a world away. There was even one for her mother. Then, task done, she set off for work.

Her nerves tugged at her as she slipped between suits and dresses, cell phones and iPods. Things had gone well for her, so far, but she'd gone out on a limb with her proposal for a clerical division.

*It's such a good idea, though. There's no way Earthenhouse can say "no," but . . . he didn't ask me to do this. What if that's a problem?*

To distract herself and because everybody else was looking down, Perpetua decided to look up and count the goblins.

Three atop a brownstone walk-up.

Two in the balcony well of a modern concrete office tower.

Thirty by the time she reached College Street.

Sixty by Dundas.

She stopped, frowning at the Royal Bank Building across the street. Four goblins sat in silhouette against the bright sky.

*That's not one of ours.*

The stream of pedestrians engulfed her and carried her along.

To get away from the crowd, she pulled off at University Avenue and followed a brick path that cut beneath a concrete building. She emerged onto a wide walkway that cut between the buildings and would take her to Toronto City Hall. Shielded from the roar of traffic, her footfalls echoed off the stone walls. For a brief moment, she was alone.

And as soon as she was alone, she felt watched.

She frowned at the rooftops and then slowed. The feeling of being watched didn't come from up there.

It came from the sound of footsteps behind her.

She stopped. The sound of her footfalls stopped. She looked around, but she was still alone. *Just an echo, then?*

She tapped her foot. A second later, the tap echoed back at her from the building across the courtyard. "Huh." *Maybe it's just me.*

She walked forward. Three steps later, her footfalls echoed back from the buildings. She counted her steps. One, two, three, four, five, six, seven, eight, nine, and . . . stop.

The echoes came back: ten, eleven, twelve, *stutter-stop*!

Perpetua whirled and swung off her backpack, hand diving inside to grab her can of mace. But the walkway was empty.

She stared around. The walkway was walled with concrete, the doorways flush against the buildings. There were no alcoves, no grottos, nowhere to hide.

Perpetua took two steps forward and realized that her feet weren't echoing anymore.

She walked briskly into the public square. There were other people here, but she cast wary glances behind her, watching for whatever—or whomever—had followed her through the alley. Finally, she spotted a streetcar opening its doors up ahead, and she quickly hopped aboard. *This should give whatever it was the slip.* She breathed a sigh of relief when the doors closed behind her and the streetcar pulled away.

It was standing room only, but Perpetua found a spot near a

window. In the safety of the crowded streetcar, she felt ashamed for being spooked so easily, possibly even by her own echo. But she cast a last look back at the public square and the walkway entrance, and blinked.

A man stood there, tall and more than elegantly slim. He wore a narrow black suit, a gleaming white shirt, and a dark green tie. She couldn't see much of his face, with his sunglasses and the dark fedora, but it was clear he stared at her streetcar, tracking it as it pulled her out of view.

Her mind was still on surplus gargoyles and invisible followers when she got to the office, so she was surprised when the first goblins of the day arrived early. The office was crowded a half hour before midnight.

Perpetua frowned as she watched the chattering crowd sip coffee while she sorted the mail. This was a sign of success, wasn't it? And the more goblins who came looking for help, the more likely it was that Earthenhouse would agree to her idea.

She picked up the pile of junk mail. "Bax!" she called. "I need a shredder."

A roly-poly goblin ambled up, eager to please. Perpetua handed over the envelopes, which Bax promptly tore into pieces with the sound of a buzz saw. Perpetua brushed pieces of the resulting confetti off her skirt. "Thanks, Bax!"

It looked to be a normal, albeit busy day, until the front door opened and a voice exclaimed: "Whoa! A real person!"

Perpetua looked up and saw a young man wearing a shirt, tie, and pressed pants carrying an envelope on a clipboard. A human.

"Um . . ." She straightened up. "Can I help you?"

He pumped her hand. "I'm sorry. It's just that I've never dealt with real people here before. I usually just drop this on the desk." He handed over an envelope. She opened it. It contained a check and one of their invoices. The return address was City Hall.

The light dawned. "You're a client!" Then her stomach dropped. What was it Earthenhouse had said? "*On no account are our business contacts to come to this office after midnight. Do you understand?*"

But it wasn't midnight yet. It was 11:30. *What am I going to do? Run him out the door?*

*And how is he not reacting to the goblins all around him?*

That's when she noticed that the office had gone quiet. Around her, the goblins sat in their seats, hands on their laps, staring glassily forward. Only Chim and Chum moved, bobbing up and down with the regularity of pistons.

"Uh . . ." She came around her desk and started leading the man toward the front door. "You didn't have to come here, you know? You can send these in by mail."

"My boss prefers the personal touch," said the man. "But he didn't have time, so he sent me." He lowered his voice. "Personally, I think he does it as a prank. No offence, but . . . these statues are creepy. And what's the deal with the House of Limericks?"

"No one knows," said Perpetua. "So, your boss didn't tell you what we do here?"

"Oh, it says it plainly on the door," said the man. "Though what rare coins have to do with bouncers is beyond me. As for statues, I prefer nymphs to gargoyles."

"That's nice. Well, thanks for your payment. Have a nice day!"

The man continued to eye the goblins. "I'll give you this: they look lifelike. I'd swear they move when you're not looking."

Perpetua saw, behind the man, some of the goblins shifting uncomfortably in their seats. She remembered, then, that these were clients who couldn't hold down an art installation job. Rek discreetly moved his hand and was now picking his nose. She glared at him, and he sheepishly moved his hand back.

"Is business good?" asked the man. "I wouldn't have thought there'd be much demand for a whole bunch of ugly statues."

A pair of goblins looked at each other and made faces behind the man's back. Perpetua shot them a fierce look, and they put their tongues away and sat up straight—just as the man turned around to see what Perpetua was staring at.

"Actually,"—she turned the man back to face her—"there's a healthy demand for, um, unconventional artworks, like ours. We're proud of them. Now, I'm sure you're plenty busy—"

"Well, maybe so." He moved toward the door. "Sorry for sticking around. It's just good to have somebody to talk to down here. It's wrong to have the PATH network so empty."

"No kidding." Perpetua glared again at the goblins. More tongues were out, and Rek was picking his nose again. "Thank you again for your business, sir—"

There was an exclamation of stone. A small goblin jerked, then resumed his statuesque pose, hands folded primly in his lap. Too late, Perpetua recognized the scent of the man's aftershave: lavender.

The man stared. "Did that statue just . . . sneeze?"

"Extra-realistic animatronic model." She pushed him to the door. "For winter months."

"What will they think of next?"

"Amazing, isn't it? Goodbye!"

The door swung shut. Perpetua watched the man's silhouette through the glass as he looked about for a moment, then walked away down the corridor. She glared at the goblins, who stared back. Her mouth quirked, and she burst out laughing. The goblins soon joined her.

She went back to her desk, shaking her head, still chuckling. "Now I know why they hired me."

She didn't see Earthenhouse enter, but later, as she was processing the paperwork for a new troll named Trixie, a message popped up on Perpetua's computer screen.

"I've read your report, Miss Collins. Please come to my office so we can discuss it."

She smiled. Leading Scooter, she strode confidently into the inner office.

Earthenhouse sat behind his desk, legs folded up and feet on his chair, leafing through his copy of the report. He laid it down when he saw her. “Miss Collins! An excellent report, well prepared. I was indeed fortunate to hire you.”

She smiled as she sat down on Scooter. “Thank you, sir.”

“You’ve given me a lot to think about,” he went on. “And I appreciate your commitment to this company.”

She frowned. He was taking a long time to say “yes.” Butterflies rose in her stomach, but she resolved, whatever the answer, to respond professionally and with composure.

“However,” he went on, “I cannot support your proposal for a clerical division.”

Perpetua’s hands tightened on Scooter’s armrests until the chair squeaked. “What? Why the hell not?”

He frowned at her. “Miss Collins, such language is uncalled for.” He leaned back in his chair, her report lying on the desk between them. The fruit bowl sat on the corner, its contents looking and smelling a little overripe.

Silence lengthened, and Perpetua shifted uncomfortably. She knew she was out of line, and she composed herself with an effort. “Okay, I’m sorry. Just tell me why. Please.”

He took a deep breath. “A clerical division does not match the mandate of this company—”

“The mandate of this company is to help your people,” she cut in. “The best way to do that is to find them work. They can do clerical work! I’ve spent the past week training them how to use office equipment! As long as you remind them not to try faxing their hands, they’re fine!”

“I know their abilities, being as I’m one of them,” he said stiffly.

*Point*, Perpetua thought. “Of course.”

“But I have my doubts that there would be many businesses willing to hire goblins for clerical work,” he went on.

"It doesn't have to be many," she said. "*One* would help. We can't place enough people with our art installations. We have to expand!"

"Miss Collins!" Earthenhouse cut in sharply. More quietly, he added, "Perhaps you should sit down."

Perpetua hadn't realized she'd stood up. She settled back onto Scooter, seething quietly.

Earthenhouse sighed. He leaned forward. "There is a difference between employing my people as gargoyles or security guards and employing them as secretaries. You walk past a gargoyle and don't notice it. The same goes for a troll in uniform. Secretaries and receptionists are not faceless construction workers. They are the face of a company."

"So? You think a company isn't going to hire goblins because they're not beautiful?"

"That's not what I meant. What I meant is that the jobs we offer allow my people to hide their faces. You can't do that if you're the face of a company. People look at that face. They see that face." He leaned back. "They would see us. And in that case, I suppose you are right: my people are not beautiful by human standards. Quite the opposite, in fact. We are ugly."

Night girl and boss stared at each other across the desk. The light gleamed off a gold band on Earthenhouse's ring finger.

"I'm human, and I don't think you're ugly," Perpetua said.

Earthenhouse chuckled. "I wish I could believe you."

She shook her head. "Sir, we have more and more goblins and trolls coming to the office who aren't finding the work we offer. The number of listings isn't keeping up. Maybe it's time people see them, so they know there are good workers out there who want jobs."

Earthenhouse set his long hands flat on the desk, a gesture of finality. "If we let humans see us, they won't like what they see."

She clenched her fists. This was going nowhere. "Don't say no right now, please." She bit her lip. "Just . . . think about it for a while, okay?"

Scooter squeaked as she shoved herself out of the seat. She turned and stalked out the door.

"Miss Collins," Earthenhouse called. She paused on the threshold. "I'm sorry I can't give you a more supportive answer, but I appreciate you taking an interest in my . . . our clients. I know it wasn't part of your job description, but it was kind of you. Enterprising, as well. Please don't stop thinking of new ways to help the company."

She hesitated, then nodded, and left the office. Scooter trundled after her and was already in position when she flopped down at her desk and took several deep breaths. Around her, the horde chattered and sipped their coffee.

Her gaze fell on her copy of the report. She yanked open her desk drawer and shoved it inside.

"Hey, Boss Lady!"

She jumped at the voice by her elbow. "Rek!" she said sharply. But then she stopped herself. No need to scold him. She gave him a smile instead. "You don't need to call me 'Boss Lady.' Miss Collins will do. Or Perpetua."

"Sure thing, Boss Lady!"

Perpetua rolled her eyes once before refocusing on Rek. "How can I help you?"

"It's movie time, Boss Lady!"

She perked up. "Shoot, you're right! I'll set up. Let everyone know it's going to be a couple of minutes late."

"It's okay," said Rek. "*I* set it up. You just press play!"

Her eyebrows rose. "You . . . set it up?" Rek had panicked the first time he saw a keypad. Too many choices! She'd had to talk him down from the ceiling. Literally.

She sprang up and went to the training room, visions of mangled wires and broken displays gambolling through her head. But the TV had been set up, and the DVD of the planned movie was on the menu screen, all shiny and ready to go. She felt guilty for not trusting him. "That's amazing!"

"Hey, you taught me!" said Rek.

Behind them, the goblins filed in to take their seats.

"You ready to press play, Boss?"

Perpetua picked up the remote control, thought twice, and passed it over. "Here. You deserve the honour."

Rek took the remote control reverently, as if handling a holy relic. He aimed it at the DVD player and pressed play. Perpetua stepped back and proudly watched Rek beam as the movie started, and the horde clapped and whistled.

She walked back to her desk and sat down on Scooter. She cast one more glance at the drawer holding her failed proposal, but after another glance at the horde in the training room, she allowed herself a small smile of satisfaction.

As the end of the workday approached, the goblins filed out, followed by Trixie (she with a bouncer assignment in hand). When the office was empty, Perpetua stood up and stretched.

Behind her, the door to Earthenhouse's office opened. She'd checked earlier; it had been empty, but she wasn't surprised when Earthenhouse stepped out.

"Meeting go well, sir?" she asked.

He looked up at her, distracted. "Hmm? Oh, yes. As well as could be expected. But I must be off. I'm afraid I've left some extra filing for you."

Inwardly, she sighed. "No problem, Mr. Earthenhouse."

He loped out the door. "Good night, Miss Collins."

"Good night, sir."

The door clicked shut after him.

She stepped inside Earthenhouse's office and crossed the carpet to the desk, her long skirt swishing in the silence. With any luck, this wouldn't take long.

Sure enough, a small pile of file folders lay on his desk blotter. She picked them up, along with a few that were tucked away beneath the inbox. She went to the filing cabinet and glanced at the titles before slipping them into place.

The files were for individual clients—goblins and trolls—and sorted by division. Each division had a special code, as had been helpfully explained by Post-it Note several weeks back. B for bouncers, AI for art installations, and RC for rare coins (which didn't come up often). Each division had a special combination of colours striped along the top: gold-green for rare coins, red for art installations, black and blue for bouncers, brown for EM . . .

She frowned at the file in her hand. It was just like the rest, except that Earthenhouse had never told her about an EM division before. She didn't know what the initials stood for. Opening the folder produced another surprise.

"Howard?" she exclaimed, and then looked around to make sure nobody was listening.

She was looking at something Earthenhouse hadn't shown her —maybe something she wasn't supposed to see. *But he told me to file these . . . no, wait.* The file in her hand was, she remembered, one of the handful she had picked up from underneath the inbox.

Still, there it was. EM wasn't a typo, either, given the specially coloured label. The next folder was just like it, for a troll she'd never met before named Jack, assigned to a worksite of "TTC: Eglinton-Bayview." The one after that was for a troll named Phyllis.

"That's weird." She flipped to the next file and saw something even weirder. "What the heck is IAC?"

The labels on these folders were grey. The contents provided yet another surprise. Where the EM files were standard employment files, primarily for troll clients, the IAC files weren't work assignments at all. Instead, each file listed a goblin's vital statistics (and it was mostly goblins), their most recent work assignments, and a date. Pasted on the files were Post-it Notes with messages written in bold print.

"Temporary removal from client base. Reason: amnesia reset —TTC: Yonge and Eglinton. Return to active status: six weeks.

Action: restore name, reassign." Another read, "Suspension from client base. Reason: voluntary amnesia reset—depression. Return to active status: indeterminate."

She remembered the number on her business cards, the one to call in case of amnesia. But what the heck was an "amnesia reset"?

Then something else clicked inside her mind, and she looked at the EM files again. Howard's assignment was to a work site labelled "TTC: Yonge and Eglinton."

She flipped back to the IAC files and frowned at the names. Then she recognized one. "Klaus?" Klaus was a goblin. He'd been in the office for the first couple of weeks after it had opened. Now that she thought about it, he had looked a little depressed, and he hadn't landed an assignment. When he hadn't shown up on the third week, she'd assumed he'd found something, but . . .

Wait! Client base. Active status. Removal and suspension. IAC stood for "Inactive Client."

And "suspension"? "Depression"? Perpetua's blood ran cold.

*No. There has to be a better explanation for this. I'm making a mountain out of a molehill. There's no way Earthenhouse would hide clients from me. Why would he?*

She tapped the folders against her fingertips. What should she do about this? What *could* she do? She worked for Earthenhouse. There was probably a perfectly good explanation, and if Earthenhouse didn't want to share the details, it was, quite literally, his business.

*But, where do I file these? There's no partition for IACs or EMs in this filing cabinet.*

Her eyes fell on Earthenhouse's desk. She'd never looked inside those drawers. He'd never mentioned anything in there that she might need to know about.

The office was quiet. The waiting room was empty. So she crossed to Earthenhouse's desk and knelt by the drawers.

The deep drawer was locked, but Perpetua worked her YWCA card into the gap and scratched at the lock shaft. Seconds later, the drawer slid open.

Dozens of folders rocked back and forth, rippling like a paper slinky. The labels at the front were all brown, all marked EM, while those at the back were all grey, all marked IAC. She flipped through the IAC labels, telling herself that she was filing. She found more names she knew. The notices were all similar: temporary removal from client base, suspension from client base, reason: amnesia reset; reason: voluntary—depression. Most were linked to a handful of worksites, many of them connected to the TTC at Yonge and Eglinton.

She remembered Earthenhouse's question back at their job interview, weeks ago. "*Tell me, Miss Collins, have you had to deal with someone experiencing amnesia or other forms of memory loss?*"

Beneath her feet, the deep rumble of machinery picked up again. She felt it in her chest cavity more than she heard it. On the walls, the pictures of bridges and railway tunnels vibrated, causing the reflected light of the spot lamps to shudder.

Perpetua filed the rogue folders where they belonged, closed the drawer and reset the lock. Taking one last look at Earthenhouse's office, she closed his door, picked up her backpack, and left for the night.

## Chapter 21

# Fergus Journal Entries VI

Fergus turned the page in his journal, only to have another page slide out on his lap. It had been torn from the book and neatly folded before being put back. He picked it up.

*The subjects have gathered at the Yonge Street Mission, just south of Gerrard.*

*They have a clear view of passersby and amuse themselves by watching the crowds as they shop and mingle. I counted fifteen on the building today. There were ten a week ago. Seven a week before that.*

*There seem to be more subjects on the other buildings, as well, but I didn't count them. Maybe I should, though that might attract too much attention.*

*What attracts them to crowded places? Do they enjoy watching people? Maybe they just don't have anything else to do. And besides, what other chance do they have to look down on people, even if only literally.*

*Anyway, I snapped my pictures and moved on. I don't think they noticed me.*

*This entry is not for the journal.*

## Chapter 22
# The Belle of St. Brigid

The next day, Perpetua walked through the Underground City. Over the echo of her footfalls, she heard the woman singing around corners.

*Un bel dì, vedremo*
*levarsi un fil di fumo sull'estremo*
*confin del mare.*
*E poi la nave appare.*

Perpetua hesitated at a side corridor. She looked back toward the source.

*If I can solve even just* one *mystery, it would be a load off my mind.*

She followed the smaller corridor. She walked, and she walked. The singing grew louder. The storefronts grew smaller. High-priced tailor outlets gave way to a print centre, a newsstand outlet, and yet another Starbucks.

*Poi la nave bianca*
*entra nel porto, romba il suo saluto.*
*Vedi? È venuto!*

*Io non gli scendo incontro. Io no. Mi metto*

Then, at a set of glass doors, she stopped. The corridor beyond was dark, the outlines of stores vanishing into the gloom. There was no sign warning people away; the darkness was enough. But the singing came from the darkness.

*là sul ciglio del colle e aspetto, e aspetto*
*gran tempo e non mi pesa*
*la lunga attesa.*
*E . . . uscito dalla folla cittadina*
*un uomo, un picciol punto*

Perpetua reached for the handle. The glass door opened easily. "Hello?" she called.

Her voice echoed back. *Hello? Hello . . .? Hello . . .*

The song broke off with a gasp. Feet scrabbled. Somewhere in the distance, a door slammed.

Perpetua stood in silence, staring guiltily into the dark. Eventually, she let the door swing shut and headed back to Earthenhouse's office.

At her desk, Perpetua sat on Scooter and savoured the silence. She knew it would be broken in two hours' time—ten o'clock, now, instead of the original twelve. She didn't mind the clients' chatter, but the lack of it let her get more work done. Five more invoices for art displays. A dozen for road construction workers. Two more bouncer contracts. She tapped away at her keyboard.

"Miss Collins!"

The woman's voice made Perpetua jump and Scooter squeak.

A woman stood before Perpetua's desk, arms folded across her chest. She tilted her head, giving Perpetua a look that was equal parts appraising and disdainful.

Perpetua hadn't heard the door open. She hadn't heard footsteps.

"Miss Perpetua *Tallulah* Collins?" The woman worked her mouth over the name as if tasting it; she didn't seem to like the flavour.

Perpetua remembered to breathe. "How do you know my name?"

"We like to be informed."

This woman reminded Perpetua of the one she'd seen effortlessly navigating the flow of the city's downtown traffic. But this one's hair was blonde, not dark, and it was twisted up in a severe, but elegant knot on the back of her head. Thin eyebrows arched over sparkling green eyes. Her expensively tailored green jacket and knee-length green skirt suggested command as well as style: something a CEO might have worn, if she had been blessed with a body like a steel blade.

She wasn't alone, either.

Flanking the door were two men so tall and thin, they made Perpetua think of whippets. Their pinstripe suits accented their length, as did the ribbon-thin ties. They wore matching sunglasses, black fedoras, and emerald cufflinks that glittered at their wrists. Their skin was transparently pale, and the hair bristling from under the brims of their hats was so curly and so vibrantly red that Perpetua wondered if they were wearing wigs. They stood, arms folded and motionless, faceless behind the black insect-eyes of their sunglasses, like the man who had seemed to appear out of nowhere after she'd heard footsteps in the empty courtyard.

The silence stretched. Perpetua struggled to fill it. "I-I'm sorry. Can I help you?"

"I'd like you to accept this coupon." The woman handed Perpetua a slip of paper. "For your earlier inconvenience."

It was for one free Frappuccino.

Scooter squeaked as Perpetua shot to her feet. "Who are you?" she demanded.

"Christina Bell." The woman stepped closer to the edge of the desk, using her extra inches to tower over Perpetua. "Director of the St. Brigid Social Club and Cultural Institute." Her smile was razor thin. "Toronto branch."

Perpetua kept her eyes on the woman as she would on a wild animal. *A cougar in the woods.* The thought gave her a jolt. She made herself look at the brilliant green eyes that were so hard to meet, but even harder to look away from. At the long, thin arms, and the long, thin fingers, beautifully manicured, that were just a little too long and thin, the red nails a little too pointed. At the mouth, at the thin red lips that were parted slightly now in amusement to show perfectly normal, even, white teeth that yet still suggested . . . fangs.

"You're a faerie," she said flatly.

Christina's smile tightened. "You're very perceptive, for a human."

Perpetua willed her racing heart to slow, but every alarm had gone off inside her, and the woman hadn't even done anything yet —well, besides loom and look contemptuous. She gathered her breath and looked Christina in the eyes. "What can I do for you, Ms. Bell?"

"You can answer a simple question." The woman leaned closer, and Perpetua caught the scent of new-mown hay. "Do you know who you work for?"

Perpetua's mouth clamped shut. It seemed an innocent question, but something in her balked at it.

Christina Bell's smile thinned and sharpened. "Well?"

Behind Perpetua, Earthenhouse cleared his throat. "She works for me."

Christina's gaze jerked past Perpetua, who staggered aside. Christina and Earthenhouse faced each other across the reception desk. Scooter, sitting in the visual line between them, squeaked nervously and inched away. Perpetua grabbed its back and hauled it to safety.

Christina's smile was tight and fierce. "Mr. Earthenhouse."

"Ms. Bell."

Her smile widened. "An interesting operation you have here, Thorsen."

He clasped his hands behind his back, standing straight, but rocking slightly on his feet in an effort to appear nonchalant. "I do my best, Christina. Not to try to make my operation look interesting, you understand, except maybe to my clients. But I work hard. I do my job."

"It's rare for a goblin job to involve an office." Christina tilted her head at Perpetua. "Particularly one that hires pretty little humans."

Perpetua wrinkled her nose at being called "pretty" in the third person. And "little," in any person.

"It's all legitimate," said Earthenhouse. "I paid the rent with my own money, and she answered the advertisement in spite of the normal magical security precautions. So, therefore, she has clearance."

Keeping her hand on Scooter's back, Perpetua eased further away, toward the coffee machine.

"Are you willing to face the auditors to have that tested?"

"Are you?" Earthenhouse snapped back.

Christina's lips tightened. It could no longer be called a smile. Her head tilted. "I'm curious. It takes a lot of money to pay for a place like this. I've checked the gold market. No one has dumped their hoard."

"I had no need to sell my hoard," Earthenhouse replied with dignity. "I am running a legitimate business. I provide a service. People pay me. *Humans* pay me."

"All without violating the Mores?" Christina's non-smile could have cut throats. "All without lifting the veil?"

"All without violating the Mores. All without lifting the veil."

The silence sucked the air out of the room. Christina and Earthenhouse locked eyes across the reception desk, as though the first person to move would break the dam.

Perpetua banged two mugs down on the desk. "Coffee!" She stood between them. "Thought you could use some!"

Christina jerked back. So did Earthenhouse. They stared at her, bewildered, as though they'd forgotten she was there. She pressed her advantage.

"Listen, folks. I know I'm just an admin assistant, but I have a job to do, and I can't do it if I'm kept in the dark. So, I have to ask: who are you, what is this St. Gidget Society—"

Christina's eyes flared. "Saint *Brigid*!"

Perpetua didn't skip a beat. "And what the heck are these Mores that we're not supposed to break?"

Earthenhouse started rocking on his feet again. He turned a lighter shade of mossy stone.

Christina narrowed her eyes at Perpetua and then turned the look on Earthenhouse. "You didn't tell her about the Mores?"

"I didn't get to that part of the training manual," Perpetua cut in. Maybe it was on a Post-it Note she'd missed, but she doubted it. "If you want to enlighten me, I'm standing right here."

Earthenhouse coughed warningly.

Christina swung back to Perpetua, who almost regretted calling the woman's attention. Christina's eyes were intense, but Perpetua stiffened her spine, thought herself tall, and stared the faerie down.

"The Mores were established in the Treaty of Magh Tuireadh," Christina said at last. "They govern the behaviour of faeries and goblins, and those who work beneath them."

Perpetua wrinkled her nose at the phrase "beneath them."

"The Mores exist to ensure that humanity remains oblivious to our presence. It prohibits the unlicensed use of magic in public."

"Oh, really!" Perpetua sniffed. "How's that working out for you?"

"Have you seen any examples of unlicensed use of magic in public, Miss Collins?" Christina asked silkily.

Perpetua's mind flashed to the people who walked with ease

upstream through the crowds. She remembered the faerie band and the bank manager. She remembered how fearful the woman had seemed when she realized that she'd been twigged. As much as she valued honesty, Perpetua knew in her heart that now was not the time. Now was a good time to lie. "Uh . . . no."

"Then it's working for us." Christina smirked.

Earthenhouse coughed again. "Ms. Bell, my office exists solely to provide employment to the goblins and trolls under my care. The watchword has been to find jobs that keep goblins and trolls out of sight of humans who would react badly to their presence."

"And I'm here to make sure you stick to that," said Christina.

"What happens if we don't?" asked Perpetua.

"This place gets shut down due to code violations," Christina replied.

Earthenhouse's eyes were as dark as onyx. "Have there been code violations?"

Christina met his stare for a long moment before turning away. "Not as such," she said carelessly.

*Which means "no,"* Perpetua told herself with a smile. But other things nagged at her. *I've seen goblins gargoyling on a building that wasn't ours. I've seen more and more goblins hanging around. Is it only because I'm finally looking? I can hardly be the only human who can see them. How can it be that everybody who sees something says nothing?*

"Then you have your answer," Earthenhouse said. "My business is clean."

Christina stabbed him with another stare. "I'll be watching to see that it stays that way, Thorsen. You are taking serious risks. You know what will happen if you violate the Mores."

"I'm doing the best I can, Christina. Have a nice day."

Christina turned to go, and then, after a pause, turned back. "Just so you know," she said, mostly to Perpetua, "unlicensed magic is not tolerated. When we see it, we remove it. Like so."

She pointed at Scooter. The desk chair squeaked and trembled. The squeak became a howl as a beam of crackling light lanced from Ms. Bell's fingers and struck the chair. The light pulsed and flared, flowing from Scooter to the faerie's fingertips. Like something being sucked away. Scooter's movements became slow and sluggish.

"What are you doing?" she shrieked. "Do something!" she yelled at Earthenhouse.

Earthenhouse sucked his teeth. "I can't."

Perpetua whirled at Christina. "Stop it!" Without thinking, she lunged into the charged space between the chair and Ms. Bell.

It was like sticking her finger into a light socket. She grunted. The next moment, she was sprawled in Scooter's arms. Earthenhouse and Ms. Bell stared, open-mouthed. Perpetua's head swam, and her ears buzzed. *I must have flown . . . what? Five or six feet? Funny. I don't remember landing.*

But the beam of light was no longer shooting from the faerie's fingers. Whatever she'd done had stopped whatever it was Ms. Bell was doing.

And the shock on Ms. Bell's face told Perpetua something else. She shook her head hard to dislodge the cobwebs and stood up. She had to move carefully, countering a tendency to tip over, but she faced Ms. Bell.

"Let me guess." She put on her fiercest grin. "You said 'auditors.' You called yourself the head of the Toronto branch. You're not the only one in charge, are you? Am I right in guessing that one of the rules on the use of magic is that it's not to be used as a weapon against humans? How much trouble would you get into if I go looking for these auditors and tell them what just happened?"

Ms. Bell's mouth thinned to a red line. She snapped her fingers. Her two agents, who had been standing silent and motionless throughout, snapped to attention so fast, they nearly twanged.

"This isn't over." Ms. Bell stalked from the office, a brilliant flash of green followed by her black-clad agents. One of them glanced back and sneered with a gleam of sharp white teeth. Then they were gone.

Perpetua stared, straight-backed and aggressive, until the door swung shut. Then she took a step and stumbled. "Whoa!"

Earthenhouse caught and held her as Scooter squeaked up behind and pushed its seat against the back of her legs. She sat heavily. She tried to shake the dizziness from her head, and failed. "Okay, that packed a punch!"

"You should not have done that," Earthenhouse said quietly. "You could have been badly hurt."

She blinked up at him. The air between them was full of drifting purple spots. "Guess I should've known that." *Because who sticks their finger in a light socket?* "But I wasn't going to just stand there while Scooter got . . . whatever it was she was doing to him."

"I'm sorry it happened."

She sucked in a breath. "What *did* happen? Who was that? The godmother of the faerie mafia?"

A hint of a smile bent his stony lips. "I don't think she'd take kindly to being called that."

"Like I care. Seriously, what's going on? You never told me about anything like this!"

He avoided her gaze. "I've told you how we've worked to keep most humans oblivious to our presence, Miss Collins. Some of that relies on the willingness of humans to ignore things they don't understand. Some of it is . . . very hard work."

She glanced at the door where the faerie contingent had just left. "So, they're the heavies."

Earthenhouse looked grim.

"Well, I've seen faeries," she said. "Now that I know what to look for, I know I've seen them in lots of places. They're doing just fine. Why do they get to walk around in public like they own the place? Why do you have to hide?"

He stepped back. "It's the way of our world, Miss Collins. I just do what I can."

She frowned at him. “Sir? Is she right? Are you doing something risky here?”

“That doesn’t concern you,” he said, too quickly.

“The hell it doesn’t!” She held up her hands. “Language, sorry. But my fingers are still tingling from whatever she did. Not to mention my head. I deserve an explanation!”

“I’ve given you all you need.”

“Like hell you have—”

“I apologize for what happened, Miss Collins,” Earthenhouse said crisply. “But these are the conditions we have to work with. Unless you’d care to activate your screaming clause . . .”

The threat hovered in the air. *Unless I want to quit. Lose my job.* Perpetua stared at her boss as though he’d hit her. She tried to ignore the dollar signs that flew through her mind and the phrase, “But I just bought a futon!” But it was hard.

“No,” she said at last. “Sir.”

Earthenhouse pinched the bridge of his nose and took a few deep, slow breaths. “I’m sorry, Miss Collins. Now, I have to leave for an important meeting. Our clients will be here momentarily. Will you look after them, please?”

She stared at him a moment longer. Then nodded curtly.

“Thank you, Miss Collins.” He took a step back, hesitated as if about to say something, and then turned away. His office door clicked shut behind him.

Perpetua heaved herself to her feet and took hold of Scooter’s armrest. She guided the chair around the reception desk, made sure it was back in place, and carefully sat down again.

She patted Scooter’s armrest. “You okay?”

Scooter squeaked faintly. It sounded like an “I’m fine, I think” sort of chirp.

And then the door opened, and the clients swarmed inside.

# Chapter 23
# The Dinner Date

The next day was Saturday. Perpetua woke up close to noon and looked around at her still mostly empty space.

*My space*. She smiled at the thought.

Then she remembered yesterday's confrontation, and Earthenhouse's evasiveness, and her smile disappeared.

She lay still a moment, fretting, before deciding that fretting went better with coffee.

After coffee, she decided that company would help, and texted Fergus to invite him to dinner. She got steaks from the market and set to work cooking, all the while trying not to stew.

The steaks sizzled as the sun sank toward the rooftops. Perpetua cooked until Fergus knocked on the door. She crossed the room quickly and opened it.

He stood on the other side with a bottle and a bouquet of daisies, and he lit up when he saw her. "Hi!"

"Hi!" she replied, beaming. The way he looked at her made her cheeks feel warm. "Come in!"

"Sure, uh . . ." He juggled the objects in his hands. "I brought wine." He thrust it out to her. "And . . . do you like flowers?" He held out the bouquet.

She took the white and yellow blooms and looked them over.

"I haven't thought much about flowers, but I can learn to like them." She grinned at him. "Thanks!"

"And . . . something else." He held out a small box wrapped in gold paper and tied with a silver ribbon.

Now it was her turn to juggle the bundles in her arms. She set the wine on the floor and took the box. "What is it?"

"Something for your office desk." He smiled hopefully. "To be displayed prominently, with pride."

She laughed. "You shouldn't have!" She set the bouquet beside the bottle and unwrapped the gift. Fergus watched anxiously as she opened the box to reveal . . .

"Um . . . it's a toy taxicab."

He held up a finger. "Not just any taxicab!"

She peered at it. The colours looked familiar. "It's *your* cab!" The number on the tiny door confirmed it. "How'd you do that?"

"I'm good at model work, apparently. Surprising, right?"

She slugged his shoulder as a reward for his sarcasm, and then flung her arms around him. "It's sweet! I love it! Thank you so much!" She pressed closer, and their lips met.

For a long moment, there were no words. Only holding, breathing, and lips moving.

Perpetua released the kiss after what felt like a long time. Touching her nose to the tip of his, she looked him in the eye. "This evening's getting better fast."

Fergus blushed, but smiled. Then he raised his head and sniffed the air. "Something smells good!"

Perpetua remembered her cooking. "Oh, yeah! You're just in time!" She hurried to the kitchen and whipped the contents of the pans onto two plates. "Congratulate me as I serve my first meal in a month that doesn't involve lentils!"

"Congratulations? I thought you liked lentils."

"Not after the umpteenth time. Now that I have a bank card, I can buy steak! Yay!" She waved Fergus toward a blanket spread out on the floor. "Dinner is served."

Fergus raised his eyebrows. "I've never had an indoor picnic before."

She slugged his arm. "Shut up. It's romantic!"

They ate, and they talked: about traffic, about good places to eat in Toronto, and about bank service charges. But when Fergus asked about her work, Perpetua grew silent. After a moment, she said, "If I told you a few things, would you promise not to tell anyone else?"

"What kind of things?"

"I can't tell you until you promise. Really." She looked hard at him. "I'm giving away secrets talking about this. I could get into trouble."

"All right, I promise!"

She thought through her next words, careful to choose the right ones. "Something happened at the office last night. Something strange." She took a deep breath and let it out. "We were visited by a faerie."

Fergus's eyebrows flicked up.

"And not just any faerie, either. A big shot. Her name's Ms. Bell, and she quoted the name of some society at me. And when Earthenhouse saw her, he . . ." She searched for the right word. "He wasn't happy. Not a bit."

Fergus's eyes widened. "What happened?"

She tensed up thinking about it. "She tried to de-magic Scooter!" She took another deep breath. "It was like a shakedown. Straight out of *Goodfellas*."

"Is Scooter okay?"

"Yeah." She shrugged. "I . . . stopped it."

"What? *How*?"

She shuddered, carelessness evaporating. "I sorta got in the way."

The colour drained from Fergus's cheeks. For a moment, he

just looked down at the floor, silent, his fists clenched. Then he reached forward and clasped her hands. "Are *you* okay?"

"Physically?" She gave him a quick, tense smile. "I'm fine. So's Scooter. But I've been stewing about this all day. I mean, what's with this St. Brigid society? Why are they so interested in Earthenhouse? Is this a turf war? I didn't sign up to be part of a turf war. Or any war."

"It's, um, probably nothing like that." He dropped one of her hands and gently touched her shoulder. "Did they say anything? Did they do anything?"

She glanced at Fergus's hand, still gently cupping her left shoulder, but didn't push it away. Instead, she scooched closer to him on the blanket and moved his hand to her other shoulder so that his arm wrapped around her. "Nothing really happened," she said. "They just growled at each other. This Ms. Bell character seems to think humans aren't supposed to know about goblins." She looked up at Fergus's face. "And that goblins aren't supposed to tell them."

He looked away. "Well, they're not."

Her brow furrowed. She leaned forward to look him in the eye. "But *you* know. Patrick the security guard knows. Plenty of humans know."

"Remember what I said? How many humans know, but they're not the type of people to talk about it, or react badly?"

She wrinkled her nose. "But it's all a great big lie. I don't see how it holds together."

He flipped the hand that was empty. "I suppose, with the psychological equivalent of bailing wire and duct tape."

"Maybe more than that. Ms. Bell talked about the Mores. A set of rules, apparently, that she seemed to think Earthenhouse might be breaking. You heard of them?"

He looked blank. "They get mentioned. Basically, it amounts to 'keep your head down and don't get caught.' But, you know, when you're down on your luck, it doesn't matter who or what you are: you just keep your head down."

She pulled at the edge of the blanket. "Is Earthenhouse breaking the Mores, do you think?"

He looked at her, still blank. "What do you think?"

"I don't know." She looked down at her plate, where the steak lay cooling, and then shook her head. "No. Because I saw Fred. He's looking good. He's got a job, and he's happy. It can't be wrong to get people honest work. But . . . I wonder if there's something Earthenhouse isn't telling me."

"Like what?"

Perpetua squeezed the rolled edge of the blanket. "I've done some math. There are over two thousand clients earning a small wage at our company, around $20,000 per year per client. That's over $40 million. That's a lot of money. Ms. Bell said that she'd checked the gold market, and nobody had 'dumped their hoard.' That's a direct quote, by the way." She looked at Fergus. "And while I was looking at this, I figured out something else, something that Ms. Bell might have been trying to get at."

"What?"

"There aren't that many art installation contracts," she replied. "I mean, yes, the city's running some sort of arts program that's provided revenue, but the number of goblins actually hired by the City of Toronto? Not that many. Earthenhouse is paying corporate clients to take the art installations on. He's paying the goblins directly, from his own pocket. That could be why Ms. Bell was asking after a hoard of gold."

Fergus looked confused. "But you just said—"

"I think I found some of that money," she cut in. "While I was cleaning up the office the other day, I found a bunch of files for a separate department I hadn't heard of."

Fergus shifted and looked at her closely, sympathetically. Perpetua liked that. He was a good listener. "I don't know much about it," she said, "except that it has the initials EM, and it hires mostly trolls. A lot of trolls. More than the bouncer and art installation departments combined."

"And there's no chance they were just old files for old jobs?"

"The dates were recent, and the jobs are current. More than that, it's huge. There's enough work there to keep two of me employed. Earthenhouse said he hired me to be the human face of the company, but half the company is hidden. Who's paying him to do this stuff, and why is he keeping it quiet?"

Fergus opened his mouth, but she cut him off. "There's more. I also found a set of files labelled 'IAC.'"

His brow wrinkled. "There's an IAC division?"

"I don't think so," she said. "These files didn't have invoices or work histories. I eventually figured out that the letters stand for 'inactive clients.'"

He looked unperturbed. When she paused significantly, he tilted his head. "And?"

"And? Isn't it weird?"

"Maybe he has a high turnover."

She sat back. "There's at least as many files for inactive clients as there are for active ones. Most of these files were dated within the last six months. No business has that kind of turnover unless something's wrong. And a bunch of those files—almost half, I think—talk about something called 'amnesia reset.'"

Fergus took a deep, gusty breath, as if he was suddenly short on air. "Okay, this might sound a bit insensitive, but . . . why do you care so much?"

She opened her mouth to snap back at him, and then closed it. *Fair question. It deserves a fair answer.* She thought for a long moment. "I didn't sign up to be part of any war. And I didn't sign up to do anything illegal. If something iffy is going on, it'll be people like me who appear on camera, being taken away in handcuffs."

"Ah."

She hugged her knees to her chest. "But what can I do?"

He was silent for a moment. "You could have a look for yourself."

She looked at him sharply.

"Did these files say where these work sites were?"

"Roughly."

"How many goblins and trolls are we talking about, here?"

"Dozens. At least."

"Well, an operation that large would be hard to hide, wouldn't it? Especially to somebody who knows what she's looking for." He gave her an encouraging smile. "So, look for it."

She tilted her head in disbelief. "Just walk in? To one of those work sites?"

"I doubt you could just walk in. You might have to get more creative in your entry."

She straightened up sharply. "You want me to *break* in?"

"I'm not suggesting you break anything." He grinned faintly. "I'm just saying that, if you're curious, you should have a look around and satisfy your curiosity."

She widened her eyes at him. "Aren't you curious, too? Why don't *you* break in?"

"I can't. If I do it, I'd be trespassing."

"And I wouldn't?"

"Not technically."

She raised her voice. "What do you mean, 'not technically'?"

He looked her in the eye. "You work for Earthenhouse. That gives you a cover story. If you're found out, it limits the damage. Maybe you weren't supposed to see those files, but you work there, and maybe you just accidentally stumbled on something you weren't supposed to see, and got curious. No big. But if *I* go, then they'll think that *I've* seen those files, and I don't work for Earthenhouse. That's worse for you. That's not taking initiative, that's releasing confidential information."

She looked away, frowning. It made sense. She'd hoped it wouldn't.

He gave her shoulder a squeeze. "You could always quit, you know."

"I can't." She was surprised at how quickly she said that.

"Do you need the money that much?"

"It's not about the money," she said, and again was surprised at how quickly that came out. So she thought about it. She could quit. She'd saved enough from her earnings that she could cope without a job long enough to look for another one. So, why not quit?

Her mind flashed back to Scooter's shriek of pain and terror, Earthenhouse's almost-cowed glower, and, most of all, the mean look in Christina's eyes.

"I think I would be leaving the wrong people behind," she said at last.

Fergus said nothing. He just sat there, his arm around her shoulders. When she looked up at him, she found him looking back at her. And the look in his eyes was part understanding, part sympathy, and part . . . pride.

"Well, there is that," he said quietly.

The ground rumbled beneath them. It felt as if a heavy truck was bumping past on the street, or the subway was roaring somewhere far below. She flinched, momentarily startled. Then looked again at Fergus.

"Okay," she said. "I'll do it."

After dinner, Fergus brought out his laptop and set it up to use as a DVD player on the tablecloth-draped banker's box. Perpetua put a packet of popcorn in the microwave. When she came out of the kitchen, Fergus had finished setting up his laptop and was looking into the corners of her apartment.

She arched an eyebrow at him. "Didn't I already give you the grand tour?"

He jerked upright, then flashed a bright smile. "Oh, it's nothing. I was just wondering where the taxi toy went."

It took her a moment to remember, and she felt bad about forgetting his gift. Then she spotted it sitting on one arm of the futon. "Here it is!" She caught at it awkwardly, and it rolled back, falling between the futon and the wall with a clatter.

Fergus sucked his teeth.

"Oops!" She reached for it, but the popcorn began to pop. "Wait! I'll be right back!" She dashed into the kitchen.

When she came back, a bowl of popcorn in one hand and a pair of mugs holding iced drinks in the other, she found Fergus on his stomach, peering under her futon and reaching with one arm. "What are you doing?"

He jerked up, hitting his head on the frame. Clutching his head, he staggered to his feet. "Nothing!" Before she could call him on lying, he grinned sheepishly. "I was just trying to fish out the toy. I'd hate for it to be lost."

He was so cute, looking sheepish and abashed like that. She tilted her head back and smiled at him. "It's okay. I'll get it later, I promise. It'll be on my desk, first thing Monday morning."

He looked at the futon. "It's no trouble. I was thinking it might have gotten scratched when it fell. I could get it fixed. Maybe get you another one."

*Okay, maybe he doesn't get the cues.* "Honestly, don't worry about it. It can wait. I'll fish it out later."

"If I can just—" He started toward the futon.

Perpetua set the popcorn and drinks beside the laptop and took two steps. Fergus looked down, startled, as she wrapped her arms around him and touched her nose to his. She kissed him lightly and locked eyes with him. "Honest. It can wait." Then she kissed him again, more deeply.

He didn't ask about the taxi toy after that.

Much later, Perpetua and Fergus sat on the futon, kissing. The movie flickered on the screen, forgotten. Perpetua wrapped her arms around Fergus and pulled him closer.

"Mmm!" she said. "Enjoying our dinner and a movie?"

"Yeah," he said, between ragged breaths. "What . . . what are we watching again?"

She laughed. "I don't remember. But what about this . . .?" She pushed forward.

He squeaked as she straddled him and pressed him back into

the futon, kissing him hard. His hands traced her shoulder blades through her shirt.

"Per—" he began, before she cut him off with a kiss. "Perpet—" She kissed him again. He pulled her tighter. Then, with obvious and great effort, he pulled back. "We . . . maybe we . . . we should slow down a bit?"

She looked at him through narrowed eyes, her nose touching his. "You didn't seem to want to slow things down before."

"It's just that . . ." His voice was hoarse. "It's just that—"

She arched an eyebrow. "Haven't you done this before?"

He shook his head.

Both eyebrows soared up. "What? Ever?"

He chuckled nervously. "Not as far as I know?"

She leaned back. "So, you're a—"

He nodded.

"Huh!"

He blushed. "I don't want you to stop, honest! I just . . . I guess I just want to slow down a bit. To savour things."

That made her smile a little. "Savour things." It was a good thing to say.

"Yeah . . . you understand?"

She looked down at him, her eyes moving lovingly over his face. "Okay." Then she slipped off his lap and sat on the futon beside him.

He looked heartbroken. "Um . . .?"

"No, no!" She grabbed his hand. "You said we should savour things. We're watching a movie. Let's take some time to savour that, okay?"

"Uh . . ." He looked from her to the screen, uncertain. "Okay." After a moment, he relaxed and settled back.

He yelped when she leaned over and kissed his earlobe. "Ah! Wait, what?"

"Shh . . ." She nibbled his earlobe. "Savour it."

# Chapter 24
# A Letter of Resignation

*Saturday, August 24*

*Please forgive the fact that this is written on a page torn from my journal. Sometimes, you have to write something, and you only have one piece of paper handy.*

*I would like to thank you for the journal. I never thought I'd like writing in a diary, but if I go too long without writing now, I find I miss it. It has been a great way to organize my thoughts.*

*And I'm sure it's been helpful to you, as well. It's a great way to get me to open up, and not just to myself.*

*That's why you suggested I start my diary, isn't it? So you could read it?*

*I know I have a lot to be thankful for. You gave me a lifeline to this city, and for not much in exchange. I was asked to do things, and I did them. It wasn't hard. At first.*

*But looking back on my letters, I can see that*

*when you found me and asked me to help, I was in no condition to say "no." I had nobody to turn to. I didn't know what to do.*

*Yes, you've helped me get my old job back and settled me in my apartment, but thanks to you, I've betrayed a good person. I don't know what Earthen-house wants, but I do know that Perpetua is a good person, and you scared her. I helped you scare her. And I hate that.*

*Thanks to you, I have lied to good people. I can't come clean to Perpetua because . . . well, you know.*

*But I'm not going to do this anymore. So, when you get to this paragraph, if you haven't already guessed, consider this my letter of resignation.*

*So long, Christina.*

# Part Four
# The Goblin Market

## Chapter 25
# The Earth Movers

Perpetua rode the subway to Eglinton Station. The crowds, heavy even during a midday Sunday, pushed her from behind, until she shouldered her way to a small, still patch by a pillar, where she could collect herself.

A voice broke into her thoughts.

"Fifty thousand? That's outrageous!"

On a plasma screen hanging from the ceiling, a news reporter was trying to interview a hefty, red-faced man in a brown suit.

"Fifty thousand?" the man repeated. "The homeless head count two years ago was only five thousand. I questioned that count then, and I question this count now!"

The reporter tried to cut in. "But, councillor—"

"How can thirty-five thousand people show up without anybody noticing?" the councillor stormed. "In this day and age, when we're building new subways, expanding the downtown core, and building towers everywhere? It's not possible! You know what the real problem is? It's these bleeding hearts on the mayor's executive committee inflating the numbers so they can get more funding for their agenda; that's the real crime, here! They've allowed sloppy work, basing their numbers on the hearsay of other homeless!"

Perpetua frowned. She recognized the building the councillor and the reporter were standing in front of.

"That's a serious accusation," the reporter began.

"Well, I *am* serious! Look at where we are: this is one of the areas the report says is loaded with homeless people! I ask you, can you see people sleeping on the streets right now? Can you? Because I can't!"

Her eyes narrowed. She began to count the goblins she could see on the cornice of the building behind them. The camera cut away as she got to seven.

She turned away, slipping into the crowd that pushed up the steps from the platform to the mezzanine level. Behind her, the TV reporter said, "Councillor Fjorde, thank you for talking to us." A pause, then: "It must be noted that the mayor's office downplayed the report, saying that the numbers were preliminary, and that the report had been leaked . . ."

The councillor's words echoed in Perpetua's head. How could thirty-five thousand people suddenly show up on the streets without anybody noticing?

They were goblins. They had to be. Where else could that many new homeless have come from? No wonder she was seeing so many more gargoyles on the rooftops. They were good at hiding from those who'd freak out if they saw them. But other homeless people could see them, Fergus had said, because they were the type of people who could keep the secret.

Still, thirty-five thousand? And why now?

At the top of the stairs, the air pulsed with footsteps. The warm smell of a cinnamon bun concession stand overpowered the station's scents of creosote, body odour, and cleaning fluids. The stand had attracted a long lineup of people interrupting their commute, and no wonder.

Across the mezzanine was a temporary wall of plywood, complete with signs and a map announcing a new subway project, "GROWING TO SERVE YOU!"

And that was it. No construction workers. No hammering.

No roar of power tools. No other hint that this was a construction site, much less a site hiring dozens of goblins and trolls.

She crossed the stream of commuters to the plywood hoarding and ran her hand along the wood. It was solidly built, but sounded hollow to her taps. She put her ear to the wall, but could hear nothing. She came to a door set in the middle, a smooth rectangle of grey veneer, punctuated by a stainless steel doorknob. Probably locked.

She reached out to try the door, but then stopped.

*This is stupid. I'm spying on my boss. I'm risking my job, my financial independence, and for what?*

The door swung open. She ducked back fast.

A construction worker came out, wearing grimy denim overalls and an orange utility vest. A hard hat shadowed his deep-set eyes. He kicked a wooden wedge under the door to hold it open.

Perpetua stared.

The construction worker was a troll. Howard, to be exact. So *this* had been his assignment! He lumbered through the crowd in his overalls and utility vest, making a beeline for the cinnamon bun stand.

The cashier stopped chewing her gum long enough to ask, "So, whatcha like? A dozen?"

Howard grunted and inclined his head.

"And coffee, too, right?"

Howard grunted twice, reached out his huge hand, and dropped a handful of bills on the counter. The cashier pulled out a box and loaded it up with pastries. "Hey, Jill!" she called.

Another young woman came out of a back room, spotted Howard, and started filling coffee cups. She stuck these in a cardboard tray, which she set on Howard's ample palm, followed by the box of cinnamon rolls.

Howard grunted, gave a little bow, and let the women keep the change. Perpetua pressed herself against the wall as he waded back into the crowd, heading for the open door.

*Okay, this is it. No time to practice those breaking and entering skills I learned from the internet last night; it's do or die. Go inside, take a quick look around, then get out. Be smooth. Be brazen. Go.*

She sidled along the wall, keeping on the edge of the stream of people, while Howard leaned against the open door and worked at the wooden wedge with his foot. Finally, he kicked the wedge free, sending it skittering across the floor. It vanished down the corridor. He peered after it, then shrugged and stepped through. The door swung shut behind him.

Perpetua went down on one knee, as if to tie her shoelaces, though she was wearing Velcro-fastened short boots. The toe of her boot caught the door just before it closed and held it ajar. She stood up, trying to be nonchalant about having her foot in the door, but nobody took any notice.

*Be smooth. Be brazen.* She counted to ten to give Howard time to walk away, thought about the speed of trolls, and counted to ten again. Then she ducked inside.

She breathed a sigh of relief as she watched the door click shut. Then she turned and ran face-first into a man—a human—wearing a hard hat and carrying a clipboard. He wore denim jeans, a white shirt, and a green tie, and looked like some sort of manager. "What the hell are you doing here?" He looked her up and down.

Perpetua said the first thing that came to her: "I work for Earthenhouse!"

She stopped just short of slapping herself on the forehead. *Great move, dumb-dumb! You get caught trespassing, and the first thing you do is blurt out the name of your employer?*

But the man's face cleared. "Oh!" He held out a hand. "I'm sorry! I wasn't expecting you. I'm Gary Thompson, the foreman here, Miss . . ."

*Right. Plan B.* She clasped the man's hand. "Collins. Perpetua Collins. I'm Mr. Earthenhouse's assistant. He asked me to look in and make sure that you're satisfied with your . . . hired help." Her mind raced forward into the projected conversation: *Why didn't I call to make an appointment? he'll ask. Oh, but I did, I'll reply, and hope he doesn't call Earthenhouse to check.*

But Thompson pumped her hand as if he expected her to spit water. "Absolutely, we're satisfied! Best workers I've had the pleasure of dealing with. Always on time. Never ask for bathroom breaks. And are they ever efficient! Machines couldn't do any better. Sure, they look a little odd, but when you come right down to it, who doesn't? I assume you want the full tour?"

"Yes, thank you." Perpetua pulled her hand free and rubbed her sore knuckles. Full tour. Drawn deeper into the construction site, where every step made a quiet escape less likely and increased the chance she'd be spotted by someone who'd recognize her and rat her out to Earthenhouse. *This could be my last chance to get out of here and still keep my job!* "So long as I'm not disturbing anything important . . ." She took a step back toward the door.

"Oh, they'll hardly notice us." Thompson put a hand on her elbow and drew her down the corridor. "It's like digging dirt is the greatest thrill of their lives. Come on, I'll show you."

The corridor ended at the top of a flight of stairs built of metal scaffolding and enclosed in plywood. Perpetua could hear a distant, constant rumble, rising up through the metal struts and making her chest tremble. It didn't sound like machinery, but what else could it be?

They stopped at Thompson's office, a temporary drywall cube at the top of the steps. Perpetua fidgeted as he went through a locker to find her a hard hat. He frowned at her shoes, then simply told her to be careful and led her from the office and down the metal steps.

"They dug this whole corridor in half a day, would you believe?" said Thompson. "We just pointed to the wall, and they clawed it out. We could barely keep up, trucking the dirt away. Amazing! And they didn't stop there."

The rumbling increased the farther down the steps they went. They came to a wall of plywood between flights; this one, too, had a door in the centre. Thompson took out a set of keys and then glanced at her. "You're not afraid of heights, are you?"

Perpetua shook her head.

"Good." He put his key in the lock. "Welcome to the worksite!"

He opened the door. Perpetua's eyes widened.

They stood at the top of a cavern as big as an aircraft hangar. Spotlights flooded the area, revealing the grey, rough-hewn walls and ceiling. The place buzzed with activity. Trolls gathered at the far wall with their heads down, digging into a hole so vigorously that dirt was kicked back thirty feet onto huge piles. More trolls swarmed the mounds like bees on honey, grabbing up huge clods of earth and dumping them into carts, which other trolls pushed on their way.

Thompson tapped the wall beside them. "This stuff is amazing. We brought in an engineer to look at it, and, d'you know, he actually wept? No need for concrete reinforcement, because it's harder than concrete!"

Perpetua ran her hand along the wall. It looked like dirt, but when she touched it, there was a sheen to it that reminded her of glass. "This is—"

"Yup, troll spit," said Thompson. "People have to be careful not to get licked, and showers are standing by, but there are no accidents to report. C'mon, I'll introduce you to the guys." He clattered downstairs. Perpetua followed.

There were goblins at the worksite, too, gazing critically at the growing and shrinking mounds of dirt, peering at clip pads, and directing traffic. The only humans Perpetua could see were a cluster of men standing around a rickety table at the centre of a floodlit area, holding coffee cups and biting into cinnamon buns. They gazed at the activity as one would at a robot dog that also knew how to clean your living room and cook your dinner: amazed and amused.

Thompson led Perpetua to this group. "Look alive, guys! We got a visitor."

Most of the men jerked to attention at the sight of Perpetua. To their credit, no one whistled at her.

"What's this about?" one of them asked.

"Gentlemen, I'd like you to meet Miss Collins, who represents our TBL supplier." He smiled at Perpetua and pointed at the first man. "Miss Collins, meet Moe . . ."

Moe nodded. "Yo."

"And Joe . . ."

Joe gave her a polite smile. "Yo!"

"Flo . . ."

The woman Perpetua had taken for a man grinned at her. "Pleased to meet ya!"

"And Sto . . ."

"It's Stu, actually," said the last man, shaking Perpetua's hand. "But, you know, why mess up a good thing?"

"Um," said Perpetua. "Yeah."

"And this is Phil." Thompson waved a hand at a short, stocky man standing off to one side, wearing a white shirt and a black tie beneath his orange safety vest. He had his arm up and was bending away with a cell phone to his ear.

"Yup," he said. "Yup. That's right. Eglinton and Bayview. Yeah, well, you know, something tells me that's a good property to buy." He perked up when he saw Thompson leading Perpetua toward him. "Gotta go!" He hung up. "Hey, Gary! What's up?" Then he winked at Perpetua and whistled. "Well, hello there, lady!"

Perpetua crossed her arms and opened her mouth. Thompson quickly stepped between them. "Phil! Miss Collins is a representative from the labour supplier. She's here to inspect the site."

"Ah!" Phil shook Perpetua's hand. His own was pudgy and sweaty. "Well, I gotta say, you're the best looking of the company, by far!"

"Anyway!" Thompson again slipped between Perpetua and Phil. "Shall we continue the tour, Miss Collins?"

Perpetua turned and got a foreman's-eye view of the worksite. Again, she stared in disbelief.

Thompson led her across the cavern floor, Phil tagging along behind. They paused as two trolls ambled past, big as bulldozers. One had a sandwich board draped around his neck, with the words "TRAINING VEHICLE" printed on it in big black letters.

She couldn't take it all in. How could Earthenhouse keep all this activity secret? *Why* keep it secret?

Goblins looked up at her as she passed. Some frowned.

"As you can see," said Thompson, "We're a hive of activity. They're happy, and we're happy. I hope your boss is happy."

"He is, he is." Perpetua tried to keep her breathing under control. *Any minute now, I'm going to be recognized!*

Phil laughed. "We're definitely happy, especially that we still have our jobs." If he saw Thompson's disapproving frown, he ignored it. "I mean, some new technology comes along, and people start to worry. How many are going to be thrown out by these machines, they wonder. But then we saw what the heavies could do, and we realized: these guys don't replace workers, they replace *equipment*! Think of the reduced fuel costs! The reduced capital costs! And then your boss was kind enough to give us a cut of the savings? Well, he had the boys eating right out of his hand."

A goblin came forward, waving a clipboard. "Sirs? Your signatures are needed."

"Oh, yeah." Phil took up the clipboard and stepped a couple of paces away.

"The trickiest thing was changing the acronym from TBM to TBL," said Thompson. He gave a little laugh. Then, seeing Perpetua not get the joke, he added, "You know: tunnel boring machine to tunnel boring *labour*? A few people kept on using the old initials"—his smile faded, and he fixed Phil's back with a glare—"until I pointed out that they were workers, not machines. Excuse me a second." He stepped away to take up the clipboard.

Perpetua took two steps back. Maybe this would be a good

time to beat a retreat. She took another step back. Neither man looked up. She turned to run.

And thumped into the chest of Howard.

Howard gave a startled grunt. Then he looked at her, and his grunt deepened. He folded his arms across his chest and fixed her with an accusing stare.

Slowly, carefully, Perpetua brought a finger to her lips and mimed a shushing sound. Howard's thornbush eyebrows lifted, but he put his gigantic finger to his lips and held it there.

Another troll ambled up. He stared at Howard, who was still holding his finger to his lips. Howard looked at the troll, and then flicked his lips, making a deep "*blup!blup!blup!blup!blup!*" sound. The other troll stared back, grunted, and then brought his own finger to his lips, mimicking the gesture and the sound.

Perpetua left them to it and backed away, bumping smack into Thompson. He caught her as she staggered. "Whoa, there! I know this place can get a little disorienting." He waved a hand at the worksite. "Even with the redesign, we're ahead of schedule. The precision work will take a couple of years, of course, but we'll have the Eglinton line up and running before the decade is out."

Silence stretched as Perpetua struggled to take it all in. Then she saw Thompson looking at her, curious. Was this something she was supposed to know? She racked her brain for something intelligent to say. "Um . . . the redesign?"

He frowned at her. "You know, your boss's suggestion?"

Her stomach clenched, but she gave him a quick smile. "He doesn't always give me every detail."

Phil, beside him, laughed. "Yeah, he suggested we dig deeper. He said something about the shale in the area, easier for his guys to dig through than the strata higher up. I guess he wants to save his boys' knuckles, but the stoners know their rocks, so we took his advice."

She gave him a shocked look. He'd called them "stoners." She knew a racial slur when she heard one. Thompson glared at Phil, but Phil was oblivious. Which made it worse.

But as they headed across the cavern floor, Phil stopped and peered at a spot in front of the tunnel the trolls were digging. Goblins were there, digging a long trench. He flipped through the sheets on his clipboard, then strode forward. "Hey! That trench isn't on the plans. You sure you guys should be digging here?"

The goblins overseeing the shifting mounds of earth looked up sharply. Then another goblin ran over and tugged at Thompson's sleeve. "Mr. Thompson, sir? Ernest the troll is eating all the cinnamon buns again!"

Phil whipped around. "*What*?"

Thompson huffed. "I told him specifically to save me one!" He turned to Perpetua. "Sorry, Miss Collins. Please wait here!" He ran off. Phil passed his clipboard to the goblin and ran after him.

The goblin watched them go, then pulled a Post-it Note from inside his utility vest and stuck it to the top of Phil's clipboard.

Perpetua looked at him. "What are you doing?"

"Revised plans. His were out of date."

He stopped, then. So did every goblin in the vicinity. All eyes turned to Perpetua.

She cleared her throat. This was it. She was in trouble now.

A rumble echoed in Perpetua's chest; a low growl, like a passing train, but much closer. The ground shook, and her vision wobbled. The human overseers staggered and clutched at the table, the walls, each other.

Across the cavern, above the new tunnel the trolls were digging, a section of wall broke off and crumbled. The trolls looked up and then turned, herding the goblins ahead of them, but they were too late. Boulders crashed down. Even on the far side of the cavern, the impact of the rockfall knocked Perpetua off her feet. The air was alive with the crash and crush of stone. The uproar died in choking dust.

The goblin with Phil's clipboard helped Perpetua sit up. The clipboard lay discarded on the ground. "Are you all right?"

Perpetua blinked grit from her eyes and tried to wave the dust away. "Yeah," she choked. "What happened?"

Thompson stumbled over and hauled Perpetua to her feet. "Miss Collins! Are you hurt?"

"No." She pulled free of his grip and found her footing. Then she looked out across the cavern, and her hands went to her mouth.

The tunnel entrance was blocked by a mound of stones, some as big as trolls. Already, the trolls were circling, pulling boulders loose and chucking them aside. Each stone made an echoing boom as it landed. When Perpetua looked over at the men, she saw them holding cloths and dust masks to their faces, dusting themselves off, but looking . . .

Looking annoyed. Not alarmed.

Phil ambled up, hands in his pockets. He shook his head. "Damn it, not again!"

She rounded on him. "*Again*?"

"Yeah. Third one this week. Something about this site makes that wall unstable. Everywhere else, the tunnelling's proceeding smoothly, but here . . ." He pointed at the rockfall. "That wall just wants to cave in." He sighed. "So much for being ahead of schedule."

Perpetua looked back at the mound of fallen stone. Goblins were edging forward. Suddenly, there was a flurry of activity as some of the goblins lifted a smaller stone and revealed a protruding arm.

"There are people under there!" She surged forward, shouting, only to be grabbed and held by Thompson.

"Careful," he said in her ear. "It's not stable. You might get caught in another slide. Leave it to the workers. They know what they're doing."

"But—"

Nearby goblins stared at her. They looked startled.

"Yeah, don't worry about it," Phil soothed. "They'll be okay. It's just stoners under there." He laughed, and Perpetua wanted to punch him in the face. "It startled us the first time, too, but I guess that's why we pay them the big bucks." He looked at Thompson. "Hey, we've got to go work out the new schedule."

Thompson looked grim. "Excuse me a second." He stormed off after Phil.

Something tugged at Perpetua's dress. She looked down.

The goblin who'd revised Phil's clipboard looked up at her with beady eyes and lots of teeth. "Come."

She took a deep breath, then decided that honesty was the best policy. "I'm . . . I'm not supposed to be here. And I don't know—"

The goblin's smile vanished for a second. Then it reappeared, less wide, yet more encouraging than before. He beckoned. "You work for Earthenhouse. You speak for Earthenhouse. You need to see this."

"Okay." She took his dusty hand. "But don't tell Earthenhouse I was here, okay?"

"Whatever you say." The goblin led her across the cavern to a knot of goblins gathered around the base of the rockfall. They were carefully picking away the smaller stones. Carefully, and slowly. *Too slowly*, she thought. Anybody buried there must have suffocated by now. Her goblin brought her near enough to see that limp arm.

She jumped when the arm jerked. A battered-looking figure sat up, shedding dirt. She stared down at an undersized goblin with an irrepressibly impish, yet oddly vacant face.

"Card," demanded her goblin guide, whose hand she was still holding.

"Huh?"

"Business card. You got one?"

Did he mean Earthenhouse's business cards? Numbly, she pulled her hand free and felt around in her backpack. She pulled out the small case she'd filled on her first day and picked out a card bearing the office address and phone number, and that strange extra phone number "in case of amnesia" on the back. Then she looked at the little goblin, blinking and looking around as if all of this was new and wonderful to him. *Brain injury*, she thought. She tossed the card away and knelt before him. "Hey."

The imp's head jerked up with the sound of two stones clicking together.

She looked into those eyes and wondered how you checked a goblin for brain damage. It was hard to look for dilated pupils in eyes that were all pupil.

"Can you hear me?" she asked. "Do you understand me?"

The little goblin nodded cheerfully.

"Do you know where you are?"

The goblin blinked several times. "I just woke up."

Perpetua groaned silently. "What was the last thing you remember?"

"I just woke up."

"He won't remember," said the goblin beside her.

Perpetua's voice rose in panic. "I'm not a medical doctor. I don't know what to do!"

"Give him the business card."

"How's *that* going to help?"

The clipboard goblin patted her arm. "He just woke up."

"But—"

"He went underground. When you go underground, you forget who you are, and you come out somebody else, somebody new. Amnesia reset."

Still on her knees, Perpetua remembered the phrase from the folders in Earthenhouse's office. *This is what I was looking for?*

"He needs retraining," the goblin went on. "The hotline people know how to help."

The impish goblin smiled up at her. "What's my name?"

Perpetua gazed at him, helpless, for a long moment. Then she pulled herself together and fished through her backpack again. She handed over another business card. "Phone the number on the back of this card. They'll help you."

The small goblin looked at the goblin beside Perpetua, who

nodded. "Go ahead. Take it." Plucking the card from Perpetua's fingers, the small goblin stood up, shedding stones and dust, and ambled away across the cavern. Perpetua noticed that two other goblins followed him, while the rest stayed to pick away stones, looking for others still trapped.

She got to her feet, whacking dust from her skirt, and struggled to process this. She remembered fairy tales about goblins sleeping underground, in the hollows of the hills, under the mountains. They lived underground, so being buried under a rockslide meant nothing to them. Or did it?

As her gaze followed the newly awakened goblin ambling away, she noticed another goblin watching, his shoulders slumped. An old friend, perhaps, who now had to start again.

Stones rattled behind her as another goblin shook off the covering dirt and sat up.

She gave her business cards to her goblin guide. Then she retraced her steps out of the cavern, up the makeshift staircase, along the hallway, and out into the ordinary world of the subway station.

## Chapter 26
# Amnesia House

Perpetua got off the subway at King Street. She wasn't ready to go back to her apartment. It would feel too empty, and she wanted to be surrounded by people—people who weren't construction workers—while she thought things through.

It was Sunday, and families crowded the sidewalks. In the square with the fountain, tourists snapped pictures of Gunther.

Perpetua spotted another plywood construction fence, just like the one that blocked off the Eglinton station worksite. It even had a similar sign and map. When the light changed, she walked up to it.

The sign shouted in bold letters, "GROWING TO SERVE YOU!" It promised that a King-Yonge station on the Don River line would open in the near future.

Perpetua ran her fingers along the lines of the map. It took her a moment to recognize the Toronto subway network she'd seen on all the maps in the subway cars. The basic network was hard to see, what with all the extensions.

Three new lines stretched across the city: two running east-west across the middle and the top, while a third snaked down from them and through the downtown in a gigantic *U*. There were more miles of tracks under construction than the subway currently held. Beneath the map blared the words, "YOUR TAX DOLLARS AT WORK!" and "TECHNOLOGICAL BREAK-THROUGH!"

She looked at the map again and remembered the descriptions on the EM files. *Eglinton-Yonge. Eglinton-Bayview, Thorncliffe Park, Jane-Finch.*

They were all stations on the map.

"Miss Collins?"

She whirled around. The voice behind her belonged to a hunched, scruffy homeless man with a tangled beard, pushing a greasy, garbage-laden shopping cart. It took her a second to realize he was the man she'd pulled to safety her first night in Toronto. She'd also seen him feeding Gunther the night of her job interview with Earthenhouse. Now, here he was, standing less than six feet away, upright, and focused, and literally smelling like roses.

She almost felt like they were acquainted, but she didn't know his name, though he apparently knew hers. "Who are you?"

He flipped a hand carelessly. "Adamant."

"Is that a name, or a feeling?"

"Both."

"What do you want?"

"Well, that's direct." He sounded critical.

"I find that's the best way, don't you?"

"Not always." His grim face relaxed slightly. "But sometimes, yeah. Like now." He turned away, beckoning for her to follow. "Come on."

She planted her feet. "Where and why?"

"There's something you need to see. Four things, actually."

"What? And again, why?"

He paused, then turned back. "Because you work for Earthenhouse."

*Uh-oh.* "How do you know?"

He cast his eyes heavenward. "Girl, the whole goblin world

knows—or, at least, the Toronto goblins know. You're the talk of the town! You've seen us on top of the buildings? Our eyes are everywhere. Word gets around. We're better than email. I guess you'd call us gmail."

"Gmail's taken."

"Okay, maybe not. But we know who you work for and, more importantly, we know you were at the worksite."

Her mouth opened in horror. He cut her off. "We also know that you were the only human to run toward the goblins when they got buried. You didn't need to, but you did it, anyway."

She frowned at him. "So . . .?"

"So, the world needs more people like you." He turned away, motioning again for her to follow.

She didn't move. "Thanks. But still, what do you need to show me?"

He stopped and looked back. "The truth."

She hesitated. Then she gave herself a shake and followed. "Fine. Be Mr. Cryptic."

"I told you," he grumbled. "I'm Adamant."

She ignored the stares of passersby as they crossed Yonge Street. People were looking up from their cell phones to gape at her. Adamant grunted and sifted through his shopping cart. He pulled out a clipboard and pen and held them out to her.

She held her hands away. "What's this?"

"What's it look like? It's a clipboard. Take it and hold it."

"Why?"

"You know," he said with a humourless smile, "it's lucky for you that most humans are so bloody oblivious. You don't know the first thing about keeping attention off yourself."

"What are you talking about?"

Adamant tilted his shaggy head toward the baffled-looking passersby, all of whom were keeping their distance. "What's a nice young lady like you talking to an ugly old bum like me for? If I was to beg a couple of quarters off you, nobody would notice, but if you stop and *have a conversation* with me, well, that catapults you into weirdo territory, and it makes people look at *me* a lot sharper than I'd like. So, take this goddamn clipboard, hold this damn pen, and try to look like a blankety-blank social worker. *Okay*?"

"Well. Since you've explained so nicely . . ." She grabbed the clipboard and poised the pen over the paper. The puzzled frowns dissolved from the faces of the passersby. They turned back to their cell phones. Perpetua raised her eyebrows. The clipboard was like invisible armour.

Adamant's glare softened. "I'm taking a risk showing you this. But I think you've earned it."

They walked east along King Street, out of the downtown core. Perpetua soon recognized the neighbourhood, the cathedral where she'd thought she'd seen a stone gargoyle move, pointing the way to—

She saw the gargoyle again and recognized it as a goblin. She pointed. "That's—"

Adamant slapped her hand down. "Yup. That's Karl. That's been his space for years. Show some respect by not pointing him out to the tourists, eh?"

He led her across the street to the alleyway where Karl had pointed out the boarding house, and Perpetua did a double-take. The boarding house was there, plain as day. How could she have missed it that night? Adamant opened the door for her and waved her inside.

The desk manager was at his station, excitable as ever. He stared to see her, but relaxed when Adamant entered after her. "So, you decided to bring her?"

"Yup," Adamant drawled.

Perpetua looked from the desk manager to Adamant, and back again. She pointed at the desk manager. "You're a goblin!"

She could see it now, having worked with more obviously goblin-like goblins for so long. Then the other shoe dropped, and she stabbed a finger at the floor. "This is a goblin hostel!"

Adamant chuckled. "Did you think we'd point you to a Hilton?"

"But why—?"

"Payback," Adamant replied. "You saved me from a bit of trouble—"

"From a truck."

"—and you looked like you could use some help yourself."

"We know what it's like, not having a place to rest your head," said the desk manager.

"And then you disappeared on me, throwing me out on the street." She scowled at him.

The desk manager spread his hands. "I said you could stay two weeks. We didn't know you back then, and there were plenty of goblins needing the space. Now that you've worked with us a while, you know what it's like."

She nodded reluctantly. To Adamant, she said: "You didn't bring me here just to show me I'd been staying at a goblin hostel without knowing it, did you?"

The desk manager looked thoughtful. "She's right. Why *is* she here, Adamant?"

"She needs to see the operation."

The manager gasped. "A human? Down there?"

"She's already seen what Earthenhouse is doing," Adamant replied. "She's a human who actually cares."

"But we've never done this!"

"She needs to see."

"She also hates people talking about her in the third person when she's standing right here!" Perpetua cut in. "See what?"

Adamant looked at her. "You need to see what amnesia reset looks like, after we get a hold of the patient."

"But why here?"

"You may have noticed our phone number." The desk

manager flipped the phone around. Perpetua looked, then peered closer. The number below the buttons read 416-594-6264, which seemed strangely familiar. Then she glanced at the letters that went below the numbers on the button, and put it together: 416-5WHO-AM-I.

She looked up. "That's *your* number on the back of Earthenhouse's business cards!"

Adamant nodded. "Item one: welcome to Amnesia House."

The desk manager rummaged out a set of keys and electronic key cards and led Perpetua and Adamant down the hall. They passed the room she'd slept in during her first two weeks in Toronto. The door creaked open, and Perpetua caught a glimpse of dark eyes peering out before it slammed shut.

"I'm sensing a bit of paranoia," she muttered.

"Nobody likes to see our ugly mugs," said the desk manager. "We're used to not showing them."

Perpetua wrinkled her nose at the word "ugly," but said nothing. They headed to the basement, where a flickering bulb drenched the stairwell in shifting shadows. The desk manager passed a card before a reader, and a light flipped from red to green. The door clicked, and he opened it.

Perpetua wasn't sure what she'd expected. Stone-walled dungeons? Dank corridors? What she didn't expect was bright lights, clean, dark green carpeting, or a reception desk set amid the quiet chatter she would associate with a busy library.

The receptionist was a goblin, wearing a neat grey dress with white trim. She tapped away at a keyboard with thimbles on all her fingers. *That's clever*, Perpetua thought. *Why didn't I think of that for my clerical division idea? Would've saved a few keyboards.*

The receptionist looked up at Perpetua, and the *takka-takka-takka* checked. She flipped her gaze up and down, then inclined her head briefly. "Welcome, fellow secretary," she rasped.

"Hello, Phillipa," Adamant said. "Is the meeting room free?

"Yes, sir. Quiet night, for once." The *takka-takka-takka* resumed.

It didn't seem so quiet. The waiting room was busy. Goblins sat on seats along the wall; she didn't recognize most of these from Earthenhouse's office, but they chattered amongst themselves the way her goblins did. There were even one or two trolls.

"I'll leave you to it," said the desk manager, and he retreated out the door. It swung shut, the crash bar clicking into place.

"C'mon." Adamant led her forward. "I'll show you around."

As she followed Adamant, some of the goblins looked up at her. They leaned in and started whispering to their friends. She heard snatches of "Is that her?" and "It is, isn't it?" She ducked her head and hurried along.

"It *is* a quiet night," said Adamant. "Comparatively. We've been dealing with three times this volume from about a year ago."

They walked down a long hallway. Perpetua wasn't sure, but she felt this basement was longer than the building above it. Room after room opened up to the left as she passed. She saw goblins sitting around tables, playing games. Trivial Pursuit appeared to be popular.

One goblin picked up a card and peered at the writing. "What Central American country boasts Queen Elizabeth the Second as its head of state?"

His partner thought a moment, then shot up a hand. "Ooo! Ooo! Belize!"

"Correct!"

"My turn!"

There was a television room, the TV tuned to the Discovery Channel, which was airing a documentary about the building of a long tunnel beneath the Swiss Alps. A troll sat watching it, taking up an entire couch. He looked eagerly at his hands, then up at a sign on the wall, which said, "Please do NOT dig here." His shoulders sagged, and he turned back to the TV.

Perpetua hurried after Adamant. He stepped into a room at

the end of the hall. The centre was occupied by a long table with a dozen chairs.

At one end of the table sat a small goblin. He was twiddling his thumbs in a Dr. Seussian manner.

"Ah, here's who I wanted you to see," said Adamant. "Say hello, Xerx Metalmurder."

The goblin looked up and grinned impishly. "Hello, Xerx Metalmurder!"

Perpetua pointed. "You're . . . you were at the worksite!" *He was the first goblin rescued, the one I gave the business card to.*

Xerx shrugged, untroubled. "If you say so."

"Thank you for sending him to us," said Adamant. "And the others. I thought you'd want to see that he was okay, relatively speaking."

She looked at Xerx. "Are you okay?"

He looked thoughtful. "I *feel* okay. Don't remember feeling anything other than okay. Maybe a bit hungry. Is that okay?"

Adamant showed Perpetua a plastic bag containing a leather pouch and a wad of papers. "Here's where we found out his name is Xerx Metalmurder. Seems he was bright enough to keep an emergency kit on him."

"So, what happens now?"

"Well, we gather what information we can from him. Whatever pieces of ID he's been able to acquire." He opened the leather pouch and slid out its contents. "No driver's licence. No health card. He managed to get a library card, though! Clever boy!" He set this aside and unfolded a large sheet of paper. "Ah! A list of phone numbers! It's not the recommended journal, but it's information written down, and that's what matters." He peered at them. "He has family in Montreal. That's good."

"Is it?" Perpetua was still running over "no driver's licence, no health card" in her mind.

"Sometimes, family is all we've got," said Adamant. "And if you can't remember your family, we try to provide the next best thing." He nodded at the goblin. "Thank you, Xerx. Wait in the waiting room, please. Somebody will be along to help."

Xerx slipped off the chair and ambled away.

Perpetua watched him go. "What's going to happen to him?"

"We will help rebuild his life," Adamant replied. At Perpetua's wondering look, he added, "It's easier than you think. Amnesia reset wipes the personality, but leaves the skills and facts intact. We can get him back to his old place, and he'll remember where everything is, though it will be like finding those things for the first time when he looks at them. Put him back at his old job, and he'll know what to do. Get him back to his family, and they'll help him, but he won't remember who they are."

That hurt. "Can't you do something about that? Like, hit him on the head again?"

He let out a bark of laughter. "Hitting people on the head doesn't cure amnesia outside of the movies." Then he sighed. "The *human* brain is as much a mystery as anything else, and nobody's bothered to look inside a goblin's head. I'm not even sure they can, what with our thick skulls." He looked at Perpetua, and his eyes were sad. "He's with friends, now. He'll be safe. He's already happy."

"Thank you for showing me this."

"Well, you see? You didn't have to run to help. It was appreciated, though."

She looked away. "It was noth—" She stopped. The words sounded trite in her mouth. "It was what I had to do," she said. "Nobody else ran to help! I couldn't believe how callous those people were!"

Adamant laughed under his breath. "*I* can. They see with their own eyes goblins and trolls emerging from the ground and dusting themselves off like nothing happened. Of course, they'd think we'd survive a cave-in without problem. Why should they run to help? That's why what you did made such an impression on the goblins at the worksite. Those that remembered you, anyway."

“How many were buried?”

“A dozen will have to reestablish who they are.” He shoved himself off his chair. “Come with me.”

She stood up. “Again? Where to now?”

“To the second thing I need to show you.”

# Chapter 27
# Remember the Klondike

They emerged from Amnesia House into a cloudy late afternoon. Adamant handed Perpetua his clipboard, and she held on to it as they walked. She wasn't sure she needed it. A light drizzle fell, enough to have passersby ducking their heads and hurrying past.

The sidewalk and pavement glistened. Lonely cars whished past. A streetcar rang its bell and sounded its horn as it glided through an intersection. One wheel of the shopping cart rattled persistently as Adamant shoved it along.

Perpetua wondered why he never fixed it. *Part of his image as a street person, maybe.*

*Speaking of street people* . . . "Why are you feeding our clients stuff from a dumpster?"

Adamant jerked his head up. "Dumpster?"

"When I saw you feeding Gunther, you said you were feeding him lettuce that the stores had thrown out."

He looked offended. "I didn't get that from a dumpster! The key is getting it just *before* it goes in."

"But why that stuff?"

"Can't afford the posh stuff." He glanced at her. "Anyway, we're not picky. And we have the constitution of a stone."

"But—"

He laughed shortly. "You want us to line up at a food bank? Girl, use your head. We've spent centuries trying to keep out of sight of humans. How d'you think they'd react if a big chunk of their food supply suddenly started disappearing? People used to chase us down over chickens, y'know. With pitchforks."

"But . . ." She struggled to think this through. "You run hostels, but I still see goblins on the rooftops."

"There are hostels like Amnesia House in every city with a good-sized goblin population. Hamilton. Detroit. Montreal. Still, not everybody can find a bed. Not everybody wants one."

"But what kind of a way is that to live?" she burst out. "Eating food that humans throw out, sitting all day on roofs, pretending to be gargoyles—"

"And sleeping under bridges. There's a good reason all the stories mention that." He pushed the cart on at top speed.

Perpetua trotted to keep up. "Why can't you ask people for help?"

"We don't want charity," Adamant snarled, not at all out of breath despite his pace. "We'll *take* charity, but that's different. What we want is to matter. And that's hard to do in the human economy. The humans have written the rules so that mattering means having or earning money. Money isn't something you can just take. Just like the chickens."

"The faeries seem to be doing just fine."

"Is it any wonder? Hard to say 'no' to those faces. We don't have that advantage. So, we make what money we can in secret. That's how it's been for centuries. And it's better than being chased with torches and pitchforks."

"But we wouldn't—"

"Oh, yes, you would!" He stopped and turned on her. "Maybe not you, yourself, or the homeless who've sat beside us under the bridges all this time. Maybe fewer people these days, compared to centuries past. But still, some of you, once you get done running around in circles, waving your arms in the air, some of you would pick up pitchforks. You know the people I'm talking about."

She looked away, grimacing. He was right.

"So, we get by." He pushed the cart ahead. "Then Earthenhouse comes along, full of energy and bright ideas and hope. He finds a way around the Mores, negotiates deals and makes use of the trolls' powerful ability that we should probably have thought of earlier. Suddenly, there's money. Suddenly, there are jobs. And you had to admire his enthusiasm."

She heard an unspoken "but" dangling in the past-tense wording of his statement. "So, what went wrong?"

Adamant stopped and thought for a long moment. "Goblins: we were proud creatures, once. Still are. If we can't earn our way, then we might as well just go to sleep."

*Sleep*. She was getting a bad feeling about that word.

He nodded across the street. "Here's the second thing I needed to show you."

They were standing across from the bus station where Perpetua had arrived weeks ago. Intercity buses poked out from the concrete shell of the building, like cautious turtles.

A bus pulled in. The PA system crackled. "Now arriving: Greyhound express service from Montreal, at platform one." The bus stopped with a chuff of brakes. The driver got out and unloaded luggage. Passengers grabbed their bags; some hugged waiting loved ones, while others ducked their heads and slipped away. The platform emptied. The driver leaned against the front of his bus and sipped from a cardboard cup of coffee.

Perpetua glanced at Adamant. "So, a bus. Well?"

He pointed. "Look, would you!"

She looked again. She'd thought the bus was empty, but movement caught her eye. A mountainous shadow detached from the back and squeezed its way up the aisle, off the bus, and onto the platform. The driver took no notice.

Perpetua's breath caught. It was a troll, seven feet tall and about as big around. How did he even get a bus ticket?

Looking around stealthily, the troll ambled over to the stack of unclaimed luggage. He pulled a large, zippered suitcase from the pile, set it on the sidewalk, and then tapped the side sharply, twice.

The suitcase unzipped itself and flopped open. Five goblins stood up and stretched.

Perpetua gaped. "What the hell?"

"Immigration," said Adamant. "These are your tired, your poor, your huddled masses, come to the big city where, if the streets aren't paved with gold, at least the grass is always greener."

"They're *smuggled* here. And they need work, right? They're homeless?" She stepped onto the road and waved at the departing group. "Hey!"

Adamant caught her by the arm. "What are you going to do? Buy them a pizza?"

"I have to do something!"

"Tonight? Don't bother. They'll have enough money for pizza. And they know where to stay. If there's no room at Amnesia House, there's room under the Gardiner Expressway. You may even meet one or two of them at your office tomorrow."

She confronted him, hands on hips. "Why are you showing me this, if you don't expect me to help?"

"I'm trying to give you the big picture. Think about it! That was just one bus. You can bet there are others. We goblins are perennially down on our luck; then, all of a sudden, one city opens up with the promise of jobs. You've seen it in your own history. Remember the Klondike?"

Perpetua digested this. "Earthenhouse has started a gold rush?"

"That's one name for it."

Perpetua watched the troll and the goblins disappear around a corner. She remembered that TV interview with the city councillor. "Thirty-five thousand new goblins in Toronto," she muttered.

"We think there are many we haven't seen," said Adamant quietly. "You could ask Earthenhouse about that."

She waved the clipboard. "This is impossible! I came here with $500 in my pocket, but I also had a driver's licence and a health card. Xerx had neither. I could have gotten help if I needed it. He can't. He just has you."

"That about sums it up."

"This would be a lot easier if you didn't have to keep your presence a secret."

Adamant laughed. "And I thought Earthenhouse was naive."

"You're working so hard trying to feed yourselves because you're working even harder trying to stay hidden. Screw the Mores! If you stood up for your rights, you could get help!"

Adamant looked at her, then at the bus station. "You may be right. Some might say that it's better to get the short end of the stick than get beaten by it, but some days . . . you gotta wonder."

"No kidding!" she snapped. "And more than thirty-five thousand goblins and trolls all at once? Whatever 'ignore us' mojo you've got going can only stretch so far. Something that big can't stay hidden forever. People are going to notice."

"Some already have." Adamant jerked a thumb behind them. "That's the *third* thing I wanted to show you tonight."

She turned. The entrance to an alleyway opened up behind them. The ground was filthy and littered, the brick and concrete walls covered with graffiti. Nothing there seemed worth looking at until she took note of one particular patch of wall.

*We must not look at goblin men,*
*We must not buy their fruits:*
*Who knows upon what soil they fed*
*Their hungry thirsty roots?*

She stared at the scrawled words. They were sprayed in black, without any attempt at colour or design, but they were perfectly spelled and punctuated, unlike the other efforts. That made this verse more worrisome. The wind chilled the drizzle on the back of her neck.

"And the fourth thing?" she asked.

Adamant rummaged in his shopping cart and pulled out a piece of stiff paper that rattled in the wind. "Your boyfriend has been looking at us funny." He handed her the photograph.

"Huh?" She looked at it. Then did a double-take. It showed Fergus in his parked cab. He was looking straight at the camera, and he held his own camera in his hands.

"What—?" she began.

"We've seen him around a lot."

"Well, he is a cabbie. They drive around."

"Yeah, but he's been seen near a lot of our places. And always with a camera."

She remembered the camera in the passenger seat when she'd woken up in his cab.

She flapped the photo. "What am I supposed to do with this?"

Adamant didn't answer. She turned to face him, only to find herself alone. She heard the squeak and rattle of a wobbly wheel farther up Bay Street.

He'd left her holding the clipboard. She set it on top of a newspaper vending box. She stood a moment shivering on the wet sidewalk before she wrapped her arms around herself and walked away.

# Chapter 28
# We Must Not Look at Goblin Men

Perpetua wandered through the rain until her wanderings brought her to Corned Beef House, and her stomach rumbled. She ordered a sandwich and coffee, and then sat and ate and thought.

*Cabbies*, Fergus had said. *The eyes of the city*.

Adamant thought Fergus was spying on the goblins. Perpetua didn't want to believe it, but . . . it would be a dark, but reasonable explanation as to why Fergus had encouraged her to spy on her boss in the first place. And there was something else; something she thought must be staring her in the face.

*Maybe not in the face. Maybe in my backpack*.

She hoisted her backpack onto her lap and fished out the toy taxicab Fergus had given her. He'd paid a lot of attention to it when it had rolled underneath the futon.

Pulling a jeweller's screwdriver from her ponytail, she found the central screw and twisted at it. The car came apart in her hands, and she was left holding a mess of plastic, die-cast metal, and wire. A light blinked in her face.

She drew a sharp intake of breath. "You son of a—"

She paid her bill, fired the remains of the toy into her backpack, and swept from the restaurant.

"Fergus!" Perpetua pounded on Fergus's door. "Open up! I know you're in there!"

"Sure thing!" cried Fergus from within. "Yes! Wait right there! Only be a minute!" Then came a sound like a plate crashing. "Oh, damn!"

Perpetua remembered suddenly that she still had a key to his apartment. She grabbed it from her backpack and unlocked the door. She barreled in to find Fergus struggling to pull himself through one of his apartment's small, high windows.

Perpetua bared her teeth at his retreating foot. After listening to him struggle and swear for a few seconds, she walked through the kitchen, opened the back door beside the stove, and strode up the alley. She was standing over him just as he pulled his foot free and scrambled up. He jerked to a stop at the sight of her, eyes fixed on him, fists clenched and ready.

"Oh!" He broke into a grin of relief. "Thank God! I thought you were—"

She plowed him up against the wall, pressing a forearm to his Adam's apple.

"You used me!" she yelled. "All this time we were seeing each other, you were using me!"

"Per—" He gagged. "What are you talking about? How—?"

"You're spying on the goblins! You wanted me to plant a bug in my own office!"

The colour drained from his cheeks. "What? No! How—?"

With her free hand, she held up the disassembled toy taxicab. The wires poking out from the small (now smashed) camera were clearly visible. "This broadcasts over Wi-Fi, doesn't it?"

He choked. "Ack—actually . . . 3G. Makes sure the signal doesn't drop out—"

She threw the broken toy aside and leaned in close, her eyes blazing. "The only reason I'm not choking you to death right now is because you only asked me to put this on my desk at work and not, for instance, *in my bedroom*! Because of that, I'm giving you ten seconds before I start to kill you. Use them to explain! One!"

"I-I-I—"

"Two!"

"Oh, God! I don't even know where to begin!"

"Are you working for Christina Bell?"

"No!" he shouted, too quickly. Then, "Yes! I mean, I was! I mean, I'm not anymore. I quit yesterday! I don't work for her anymore!"

She glared into his eyes, looking for the truth. Then she released him and took a step back. "That buys you a few seconds." Before he could relax, she poked him in the chest. "Explain more! Why were you working for Christina? Why are you taking pictures of the goblins?" She yanked the photograph from her backpack, miraculously managing not to rip it. "They know! They saw you! They gave me this! So, tell me the truth!"

Fergus breathed deeply for a minute. Then he pushed away from the wall and looked her in the eye. "You want the truth? The whole truth? I can give you that. But . . . can we go back inside? There's something I need to show you."

*I've heard* that *line in many a horror movie*. "If you try anything funny, I will *hurt* you! You can show me out here."

He raised his hands, palms out. "No. It's private. I have to take off my shirt."

"Remember what I said about me hurting you?"

"Perpetua, please."

He stood there, looking plaintive. In spite of her anger, Perpetua began to feel uncomfortable and strangely guilty. She waved him forward. "Fine. But stay where I can see you, and no funny business!"

He walked back into his apartment with the stoop of a man condemned. Perpetua faced him in the middle of his living room.

"Well?"

He took a deep breath. Then, turning his back on her, he

unbuttoned his shirt. He hesitated a moment and then shrugged it off, letting it drop to the floor.

Perpetua's eyebrows knotted. Why was he wearing suspenders *under* his shirt?

Only . . . they weren't suspenders. There was a sheet of fabric between them. He unhooked these "suspenders" from his belt, and the fabric slid off like a sock.

He still had his back to her. He was painfully thin, she noticed, and his shoulders were drawn up as if bracing for a blow. For a moment, Perpetua wasn't sure what she was seeing.

Then her hand went to her mouth. "O-Oh. Oh my God!"

"Yes," he said dully.

"You have a, a . . ." Her hand went out by itself, pointing. "A tail!"

A long, leathery and pointed tail poked up from his pants and curled in the air by his shoulder blades.

"Yes. I have a tail."

"You're a goblin!"

"What, did my tail give it away?"

Her hands went back to her mouth. "This can't be happening!"

His shoulder blades—they had little ridges on them, like pinched clay—drew together, as if in pain.

She threw up her hands. "I don't believe—I—I *kissed* you!"

Fergus turned around. She stared at him, open-mouthed.

"All this time, you were my boyfriend," she continued, "and instead, you're a goblin—I—we—we were even thinking of—" She stopped, spinning her fingers. "Is that even *possible*? Do we even—?"

"It's happened," he said quietly. "Goblins and humans aren't all that . . ." He stopped. "Yes. We could have."

His eyes, she noticed now, were darker than most humans'. They were almost like Earthenhouse's. Alien.

"Perpetua . . .?" He reached out.

Her hands curled into fists. "Why didn't you tell me?"

"I just did!"

"Earlier!"

"I wanted to." He let his hand drop. "I tried."

"You failed!"

"You think it's easy?" The intensity in his eyes now made her take a step back. "With how you're looking at me, as if I'm some kind of monster, you think it's easy?" He drew a shaky breath. "I loved you! I still do! And I thought that, if I had more time, I could ease you into things. But no, you had to know everything right away. So, I told you. And you're just like all the rest. Ready to invoke your screaming clause. Well, go ahead." His voice cracked before he could wrench it back to deadpan. "Go ahead! Get your screams out. I've seen it all before."

She gaped at him.

His voice edged up. "Just... just go!" The deadpan cracked. "Go!" he hollered.

She turned and ran.

Perpetua ran for several blocks until a streetlight stopped her. She clutched at the lamppost and caught her breath. What had just happened?

She knew what, but she couldn't process it. She needed time, and she needed space. She was too dazed to even take in where she was. So she picked a direction and followed the roar of traffic, walking faster, her stride lengthening, while her mind put it all together.

He'd lied to her about who he was and what he was doing. Her hands balled into fists. He lied! And *he* was the one screaming at *her*? She knuckled off a tear. She'd show him! She'd tell the goblins everything about the traitor in their midst. She'd destroy his spying game right here, right now! Let him try to show his face on the street ever again. See if she cared!

Yes, that's what she would do. That felt good.

Well, no. Not good. Satisfying.

Well, no. Not satisfying, exactly.

Her stride slowed. She stopped in the middle of the sidewalk. This late at night, no one pushed past her. Isolated cars breezed past. In the distance, the towers of Toronto's financial district glittered like Christmas trees.

She took a deep breath, then another. The ache in her heart was getting harder to ignore. He'd said that he loved her, and she'd believed him. Possibly because he'd meant it. Seemed to mean it. And to see him so angry, so hurt . . .

Hurt. She'd hurt him. With the way she'd reacted when she saw his tail, she'd hurt him. More, even, than when she was shoving him against a wall.

*Why should I feel guilty about that? He's been hiding this from me the whole time. This is his fault, not mine.*

She looked around and realized she'd walked all the way to Corned Beef House. The lights were on inside, people were eating. Perpetua remembered taking Fergus to breakfast there. It was a good memory. But he'd spoiled it.

*Somebody* had spoiled it.

For no obvious reason, Perpetua suddenly remembered a conversation she'd had with her best friend, Betsy, just before they graduated high school. Betsy had finally gotten up the courage to confide something important. No, something shattering. *I love you*, she'd said, and had held her breath.

Perpetua had reacted with shock. How could somebody she'd thought she'd known her whole life turn out to be so completely different? She remembered the look Betsy had given her that night, before quietly excusing herself and leaving. Sure, they'd patched things up eventually, but Perpetua could never forget that look, its mixture of shame, anger, and misery, before Betsy walked away.

That look had been on Fergus's face when he'd ordered her out of his apartment.

Perpetua unclenched her fists. She turned and walked back to Fergus's place.

She didn't use her key this time. She tapped quietly and kept tapping until Fergus opened his door. Then she took one step into the doorway and stood there, one hand on the panel, in case he tried to slam it in her face. She needn't have bothered; he looked at her as if at a ghost.

"I'm sorry," she said, getting the important stuff out of the way. "I'm really sorry. I shouldn't have freaked out like that. You tried to warn me, and I should have seen the clues, but you're no monster. I don't think that at all. And I want to take back my reaction, what I said, all of it, but I can't. All I can be is sorry, and I am. Okay?"

He stood there a long moment, expressionless. "Okay," he said at last. "I guess." He didn't step aside.

"Ask me inside," she prompted.

"Why?" His voice was noncommittal, his eyes wary.

*So I can repair what I broke. If that's possible.* "We have to talk."

"You said you were sorry."

"About Christina and the spy camera."

"Oh. Yeah." He stepped back from the door. "You'd better come in."

She stepped inside. Was it her imagination, or had the apartment gotten more cluttered since she'd left an hour ago? Then she saw the plastic tubs stacked by the sink. Several were open.

He glanced that way. "I . . . er . . . needed something to drown my sorrows in."

She picked up a tub at random. Chocolate chip cookie dough, said one. Rocky Road, said another. She looked at Fergus, eyebrows rising.

He tried to frown, but it turned into a smile. "What? Did you think I'd be downing shots of bourbon?"

She grinned, fished a spoon from a drawer, and grabbed one of the tubs.

Perpetua swallowed her mouthful of mint chip. *Mmm*. "So, why did you try to run away from me? When I first arrived, I mean."

They sat across from each other at the kitchen table, two tubs of ice cream between them, each with a long spoon in hand.

"I wasn't running from you. I thought you were Christina."

"Okay, I can see that. But . . ." She pointed with her spoon. "Why the window? You could have been out the back door and away the moment I banged at the front."

"Well, I—" He looked at the door that was right beside the stove. Then he looked at the window he'd almost gotten stuck in. He sighed, then laughed softly. "Come on. You've met Christina. You're surprised I panicked?"

She poised the spoon over the waiting ice cream, but didn't let it dig in. "Fergus, are you in danger? Are *we* in danger? Why are we eating ice cream when we're in danger?"

"We're not. I mean, I think we're not. The St. Brigid Social Club exists to keep the peace and maintain the veil, to keep the secret of the Mores. It's just, you know . . . I sent her a nasty resignation letter, and Christina's kind of scary. I've probably mortally offended her."

"So why work for her—them—in the first place?" She dug into her ice cream.

"They found me." He held her eyes, willing her to understand. "They told me who I was. They said it was some kind of car accident, that I was buried under a piece of the Gardiner Expressway that broke off and fell on me. They gave me my wallet. Phone numbers of my friends. My ID. They could have sent me to Amnesia House, but I think Christina had a plan for me from the start. I didn't question it at the time; I was confused, and afraid, and they were kind and polite. They got me my old job back. At least, they said it was my old job."

She rested her chin on her hand without the spoon. "You don't remember anything from before?"

"Not really. Don't remember my parents. Friends' faces are unfamiliar to me. But I get flashes, you know? I step into a room, and suddenly, I know where everything is. I don't remember learning to drive; I just put my hands on the wheel, and the knowledge is there. I get déjà vu so often that . . . well, it's weird when I *don't* get déjà vu."

She remembered the picture of his mother. "*Cancer, I'm told,*" he'd said. *He doesn't even know his mother, except in pictures.* Then a thought struck her. "Your mom . . . she was human."

"Apparently, I'm half goblin."

"How—?" She caught herself. She was being stupid. Of course, she knew how.

Fergus got up and fetched the picture. He popped it out of the frame and held it out. She took it and studied it.

Fergus's mother was a museum-standard specimen of "human, 1990s" (plain flannel, bad hair). She was grinning at the camera, her teeth white, but slightly crooked. An arm was draped around her shoulders, belonging to someone off-frame.

Perpetua unfolded the picture. What was off-frame came into frame.

He was obviously a goblin. The ears were pointed, the eyes were night-dark. The grin on his face showed pointy teeth, but this only emerged after some staring. Perpetua rubbed her eyes and looked again. The more she looked, the more goblin-like Fergus's father appeared, but his McGill University sweater didn't change.

The two of them looked cute together. That didn't change, either.

She handed the picture back. "So, Christina asked you to spy on Earthenhouse."

"Yeah." Fergus carefully refolded the picture and fitted it back into its frame. "They were noticing more goblins about. More money flowing. They wanted to know if he was violating the Mores. They asked me to look around, listen. Goblins are a suspicious bunch, but they let their guard down a little if you're a cabbie, especially if they see you're a goblin."

"Are a lot of cabbies goblins?"

"You'd be surprised."

She fixed him with a hard stare. "Okay, so then tell me this: when you told me that Earthenhouse was hiring, was that under orders from Christina?"

He met her stare. "No. But she'd heard about it, and she must have made note of it, because soon after you moved into your apartment, she showed up, gave me the bug, and told me to find some way to get it into Earthenhouse's office. She suggested you'd be good for that. I didn't want to do it, but . . . well, it's hard to say 'no' to her."

She knew what he meant. And she remembered how Fergus had struck her when they'd first met: incredibly nice, gentle, almost childlike. *Like Xerx, after he woke up.* How easy would it be to dominate and exploit a person in that state of mind?

*I'm guessing really, really easy.*

She also wondered how long it took for a person to regain his individuality and maturity after amnesia reset. How much was Fergus going to change?

"The thing is, I don't think I'm the only agent," he was saying. "The St. Brigid faeries . . . they're getting nervous. They keep talking about the state of the veil. The time you told me she showed up at Earthenhouse's office, that must have been just hours after she handed me the bug. Something spooked her and made her confront Earthenhouse directly."

"And you quit after you heard about that?" she asked.

His eyes met hers with an intensity she hadn't seen before. "Yes. I didn't like the way she treated you. She scared you. She hurt you. I don't work for people who do that."

She tried to keep her expression stern, but failed. Instead, she tucked her head and blushed. It occurred to her that Fergus hadn't sounded the least bit gentle just then. She liked that.

"The thing is . . ." He fingered the photograph Adamant had given her. It lay on the table between them. "You're probably going to notice this eventually, so here goes. This photo was taken earlier today."

She frowned at the photo. "But . . . when did you resign?"

"Last night."

Her hand hit the table with a thump. "Explain!"

He winced, got up, and started walking around his apartment. Perpetua sat, watching, puzzled as he pulled folders and sheaves of paper from bookshelves and cupboards, and gathered them into a thickening pile. She realized that he was raiding all his hiding places. But hiding what?

When he was finished, he put everything into a red folder and then placed this in front of her. He sat down opposite and watched her guardedly.

Perpetua opened the folder and flipped through the contents. There were photographs of goblins sitting on cornices, or grouped in public squares, sharing a single sandwich while people walked blindly past them.

There were papers with charts and tables full of heights and weights. There were documents, medical records—including somebody's immunization record. Then she saw the name. *Fergus's medical records.*

She looked up at him. "What is this?"

"It's a plan," he said, carefully. "I started working on it months ago. I haven't told anybody about it, not even Christina. Especially not Christina. The medical records are part of a biological treatise."

She picked up a paper and goggled at it. "You took a DNA test? When?"

"Last Friday. Company insurance covered it, amazingly enough."

She flipped the folder closed. "Fergus! Why are you writing a biological treatise on your own people?"

He flipped a hand. "If I do a good enough job, I might get a Nobel Prize."

"*Will you be serious*?"

"I *am* sort of serious," he said. "It could give this project a lot of media attention, and that's what I think the goblins could use: the right sort of media attention."

She looked at him, bewildered, so he went on: "After working with Christina, after seeing how the goblins and trolls live, after living this life myself, I've decided . . . well, I've decided I can't do it anymore. The secrecy between humans and goblins isn't a good thing. It's wrong that I have to hide my tail all the time, or think about surgery to lop it off. I shouldn't have to pretend to be someone I'm not, just to avoid some ignorant person's fear response. No one should. We have a right to stand up and be who we are!" He thumped the table with a fist.

"Yes!" Perpetua couldn't help applauding. Fergus flushed. She laughed. "No, I'm not making fun of you. I'm with you, one hundred percent!"

"Really?" His flush subsided.

"Really. I said something similar to Earthenhouse when I tried to sell him on the idea of setting up a clerical division. But I talked about how the secrecy was harming the goblins' job prospects. You"—she pointed at him—"just nailed the personal reasons. But what about the Mores?"

"I know," he said bitterly. "I'm not sure how much longer Earthenhouse can keep doing what he's doing and still stay on the secret side of the Mores. And what about the rest of the goblin race, those who can hide what they are well enough to pass as human, and the others that simply hide? Is that the best we can hope for? Yes, the Mores are there to make sure humans don't see us and freak out, but there's another way to calm humans down, and that's with information. Lots of it! Flood the world with so much information about who we are and how we live that we stop being mythological and become simply mundane."

He flipped through the folder to the files at the back. "So, I took courses in marketing. I've gathered contacts, the best people to phone or send press releases to. I've even gotten access to a couple of celebrities." He tapped a page.

Perpetua leaned over to look. She did a double-take. "Wait. Is that . . . Bono?"

Fergus nodded.

She looked at him in awe. "U2? 'Where the Streets Have No Name'? *Him*?"

Fergus nodded, smiling.

Perpetua picked up the letter. It was on U2 stationery, with a handwritten note beneath the signature that said, "Looking forward to working with you, Fergus!"

"How did you get Bono?"

"He does this sort of work a lot." He avoided her gaze. "Right now, he thinks we're talking about refugees."

"You lied to Bono?"

"Only temporarily."

"That's not—" She cut herself off and pinched the bridge of her nose. "Fergus, why?"

He flexed his fingers, then looked her in the eye. "Because of Dad. No, I don't remember him, but I know of him. While he looks like a goblin in the picture you saw, I think he played that up for the camera. Goblins can do that, you know. He was a tax accountant, so I'm guessing that most people didn't know about his tail. Or his tale.

"Then, there are the people I work with at the taxi company," he went on. "Shelly at dispatch got her ears bobbed. We never talk about it. We just see it in each other's eyes and nod as we pass. Goblins are everywhere, living as humans, working and raising families in places where humans don't take notice of the little differences."

He closed the file and tapped it on the table to straighten the papers inside. “What Earthenhouse has done has given a lifeline to those goblins who couldn’t possibly pass as human, who had no hope of participating in the human economy. But we’re all still goblins. We’re all still at the bottom of the ladder, and the faeries are at the top.” He put his hand on hers. “Perpetua, I’m sick of hiding. I’m sick of being afraid of what humans might say.”

She looked at his hand, then turned hers so that they intertwined. She couldn’t meet his eyes. “Even after I activated my screaming clause?”

“Yeah. Because you came back.”

Their eyes met, and he was smiling. She matched his smile. “So,” Fergus said, “what happens now?”

Perpetua thought a moment. “You have to tell the goblins.”

He looked nervous. “I will. I was planning to. I just need to feel ready.”

“No,” she said firmly. “You need to do it now. Tomorrow, at the latest. The goblins know you’re watching them. They’re going to come up with their own ideas about why unless you tell them the truth. And you need to get them behind your plan before you act on it.”

“Um . . .”

“C’mon. You worked hard putting this plan together, but you’re not going to be able to put it into action all by yourself.”

“Argh.” He pulled at his hair. Then nodded. “You’re right.”

“Tomorrow, okay? You’ll tell Earthenhouse everything.”

“Will you be there?”

She squeezed his hand with both of hers. “Right beside you.”

After a minute, Fergus let go of her hand and sat back. “Perpetua. Are we okay?”

“What do you mean?”

“Well . . . I didn’t tell you the truth. I went behind your back, and . . .”

“You used me,” she said.

He looked at his hands, open on the folder.

She looked him over. It was strange. She’d never seen anyone more stalwart than when he'd talked about why he was doing what he was doing. At the same time, he looked small: small in a way she understood, having come to this big city with just five hundred dollars in her bra, and no place to live.

"I get why you did what you did," she said. "I . . . I don't like that you kept this from me until now, but now you've told me, and now, you've promised to do this thing right . . ." She reached for his hands. "So yeah, we're okay."

He laughed, relieved. "I swear, I am the luckiest guy in the city. I couldn't imagine someone as beautiful as you ever giving me the time of day."

She smiled at the first part of that sentence, but her brow furrowed at the second. "What are you talking about?"

"Well, you know." He looked perplexed. "You. Me. Us. The fact I'm a goblin."

"Yeah," she said with a chuckle. "Your tail gave that away."

His hands pulled away. "I'm ugly, Perpetua."

She slammed her palms against the table so hard, he jumped. "What—?"

"Why do you say that?" She stood up, knocking her chair back. "How can you *think* that? Four times, I've heard that word from goblin mouths! You! Earthenhouse! Adamant! The desk manager guy! Does *every* goblin in this city think they're ugly?"

He struggled for words. "I—But—Well, probably."

"Seriously? After all that talk about wanting to be yourself as a goblin, you can't imagine that I'd want to *be* with a goblin?"

He looked away. "It's one thing to want to stand up. It's another thing to . . ." He bit his lip, then let it go. "Well, to believe."

She came around the table, and he stood to face her. She touched his cheek. "Fergus, I don't think you're ugly. I never have. Not even when you showed me your tail."

He blinked at her. "You mean it?"

She looked at him a long moment, then she slipped her arms around his neck. His arms rose in answer. Their lips met. They kissed, and then kissed again. Perpetua kissed him harder, hungrier, then gripped his arms and guided him backward.

He lurched. “Um . . . w-what are you doing?”

She touched her nose to his and looked him in the eye. “Proving it,” she whispered, and shuffled him through the open bedroom door.

## Chapter 29
# Fergus Journal Entries VII

*Monday, August 26*

*I need to remember this. I need to write this down.*

*She is beautiful. She is determined. And, clearly, she knows what she's doing. I didn't, but she was patient, and she showed me. And for that, I will always be grateful.*

*Her kisses are powerful, warm, but also small and sweet. I could get drunk on them. And, while she's strong, she didn't push me around. She guided me, easing me backward with the touch of her hands and the brush of her body, until I bumped against the foot of the bed and fell over backward, taking her with me. There was a brief struggle as we figured out what was what, and her soft, giggly laughter.*

*Laughter. I've heard her laugh before, but never giggle. And I think she realized that. For all of a sudden, we were face-to-face, and she was staring at* me. My heart was pounding, my breathing ragged, but she was still and calm. Her breath brushed over my face. She looked certain, except . . . I saw a look in her eyes I didn't recognize. It was followed by a smile that was small, just barely peeking out. A smile that made her look . . . shy.

Shy? After all this? Me, with no experience, and her on top of me; she, who'd made the decision and told me she would "prove it"? She was shy?

But she was. And seeing that smile took my breath away.

She kissed me once, lightly, on the lips. Then she pushed herself upright. I sat up, staring, afraid for a moment that she was going to get up and leave.

But she wasn't leaving. She was pulling out the things that were tying back her hair, letting the length of it drop down to her shoulders. Then she stepped back to look at me.

And started to undress.

She is truly ~~gorgious~~ gorgeous . . .

I think I'm going to stop here, because I don't want this journal read by strangers. And if you have forgotten about this moment, Future Self, then you, too, are a stranger. If you want to remember this again, I can only tell you to find things out for yourself. You won't regret it.

## Chapter 30
# Détente

Perpetua breathed deep and opened her eyes. She looked around.

Sun shone through gaps in the curtains, lighting beams in the dusty air. The windows muffled the sound of traffic outside. And beside her, someone was snoring softly.

She remembered last night and smiled. Hugging the covers around herself, she turned and looked down on Fergus as he slept.

He had his head on his hand on the pillow, his lips parted. She resisted the urge to kiss him awake, then spotted the tip of his tail poking out from the covers behind his shoulders. Pointed and greyish, it was almost camouflaged among the pale blue sheets.

She propped herself up and ran her fingers along the tail. She cocked her head, curious. It felt warm and smooth, like a beach stone in summer.

Fergus giggled and shifted in his sleep. Perpetua drew her hand away as he turned and snuggled deeper beneath the covers. Spotting her clothes at the foot of the bed, she leaned forward and sorted through them for her cell phone, then lay back again, well tucked in.

A low rumble started up, like a truck passing nearby, or a subway train below. It rippled the water in a glass left on the bedside table and set a bookcase swaying gently, before gradually fading away. Perpetua frowned at that, but continued to peer and poke at her cell phone.

After a few minutes, Fergus shifted and rolled over. His breath caught. "Hey, you."

Grinning, Perpetua set her phone aside and rolled to face him. She nuzzled her nose to his. "Hey." She kissed him.

"Been awake long?"

"A little while."

He let out a squawk of surprise as she pushed him onto his back and draped herself across him, resting her head on his shoulder and putting an arm around his chest.

She let out a satisfied sigh. "This is nice."

Fergus swallowed. "Yeah. Very nice!"

"I can hear your heart."

He focused on the ceiling. "So you can."

"It's beating rather fast."

"You don't say!"

She looked up at him. "You don't mind?"

"Well . . . no, not at all, but . . ." He glanced down at her, sheepish. "It's just that . . . I've never done anything like this before. I don't know what I should do, and—"

She nestled closer. "You're doing fine. Just hold me."

He hesitated only a moment, then his arms went around her and pulled her close. He ran a hand tentatively up her side and, with more confidence, traced a finger over her shoulder blades. "Yeah. I can do that."

She giggled and shifted her leg over his. "You're getting the hang of it."

She could feel him tense beneath her, but she lay quietly, breathing him in, and the moment lengthened and became soft. "Nice," he whispered.

She kissed his shoulder. "Care to guess what I was doing while you slept?"

"I can't imagine."

"Doing research on my cell phone."

"What for?"

"Did you know that you can buy a tunnel boring machine for around $50 million?"

She could almost hear him raising his eyebrows. "Be a bit big to put in the garden," he said.

She nodded. "And typically, four machines are used on any given project. Then, there are the tunnel liners: precast, concrete things the machines stick onto the sides of the tunnel. Those cost about $5,000 per metre."

He pulled his head back to see her face. "Where are you going with all this . . . sexy subway talk?"

She smiled up at him. "Just adding a few things up. There are four subway projects under construction right now. The Eglinton line is thirty-two kilometres long. The Don River line is forty kilometres long. The McCowan extension adds eleven kilometres, and the Sheppard-Finch line is as long as Eglinton. Add the cost of concrete and the tunnel boring machines together . . ."

"And?"

She looked serious. "You get a number with a lot of zeros at the end of it. Divide that number by $35,000—the average salary a unionized construction worker gets—and you get . . ."

His brow furrowed. "A whole lot of construction workers?"

"A whole lot of trolls."

"Oh!"

"Yeah."

She rested her head on his shoulder again. They were silent for a moment. Then Fergus said, "Tell me something. Why Toronto?" He looked down at her. "Why come here?"

She raised an eyebrow at him. "Other than the jobs being here?"

"Well, yeah . . ." He brushed his hand up her side. "But there are other cities with jobs between here and North Bay."

"I was born here."

His eyes widened. She nodded. "Mom took us away when I

was two. I have vague memories of Toronto. When I left North Bay, it just seemed right. Leaving home to come home."

"Cool."

She chuckled. "Glad you think so."

The soft silence returned. Perpetua hugged the moment, but her mind ran ahead. They had to tell Earthenhouse. But what was he going to say when he found out?

Something about her must have told Fergus enough, because he gave her a squeeze. "You nervous?"

She gave him a sheepish smile. "Yeah. Aren't you?"

"Of course," he said with a deadpan smile. "But you know me. I hide my feelings so well."

"Except when I shove you against a wall and threaten you, right?"

He grinned. "Yeah." He shifted uncomfortably. "But . . . when do we need to be there? Not that I want this to end, you understand."

She propped her chin on her hand and thought about the time. "Not for a few hours yet. The office will be empty until this evening, and I don't know how to contact Earthenhouse this early."

"Oh," said Fergus. "So . . . what do we do in the meantime?"

She looked at him with a raised eyebrow. Her smile widened when he looked back at her, completely innocent.

"What?" he asked.

She shifted beneath the covers, sliding herself atop him, pressing closer until she was nose to nose, staring into his eyes.

The light dawned. "Oh," he said.

"Yeah," she whispered, and she kissed him deep.

Sometime later, when they were dressed, Perpetua came from the kitchen holding two mugs of coffee. She saw Fergus on the couch, writing busily in a notebook.

"What'cha doing?" She set his cup on the table beside him.

"Just writing things down." He gave her a glowing look. "I don't want to ever forget last night."

"Ah." She glanced at the page. "'Gorgeous' is spelled with an *e*, not an *i*." She kissed the top of his head.

He crossed the word out and started again.

The intersection of King and Bay was choked with people. The cars honked and growled. Perpetua spotted parts of Gunther's bulk through gaps in the crowd. The rooftop tenor sang above the street noise. Perpetua smiled at this blast of normality—and laughed to herself at the thought that this could be considered normal.

But something wasn't right. There was a commotion in the intersection. People looked up from their cell phones, which was abnormal in itself.

"They're all around us! They're everywhere!"

Perpetua jerked to a stop, and Fergus bumped into her. The voice was hoarse and ragged, edged with madness.

"Look up, all of you! Look around! Are you blind?"

A man staggered in the middle of the streetcar tracks, his grizzled beard ragged, his dirty coat too warm for the weather. He stabbed a hand at the rooflines.

"They're watching every move you make!" His voice slurred. "They stare at us with their teeth and claws, and their big, big ears! They're making their lists! They're reporting to their masters! Everyone, look! Look! The goblins are everywhere!"

The people on the sidewalk, sensing the street drama, were starting to pay attention. The tenor had stopped singing. Cars backed up on either side of the staggering man. Drivers leaned on their horns. A streetcar slammed on its brakes and rang its bell.

"Look!" He jerked his finger at the rooftops. "For God's sake, look!"

Perpetua looked up and felt a chill. She nudged Fergus, and he looked up, as well. "Oh, dear."

Along the rooflines, the silhouettes looked back.

Perpetua quickly lowered her gaze. "Keep your eyes down!"

Two other homeless men stood on the sidewalk, looking embarrassed. One stepped out into the street. "Jeff, come on! Come back!" The other cast a furtive glance up at the rooflines and shrugged apologetically.

Perpetua leaned toward Fergus and whispered, "This is going to get awkward unless somebody does something."

"Hand signals."

"What?"

"It's something goblins know. Earthenhouse should have taught you."

"Well, I may have mislaid that Post-it Note—"

"Do this." He swiped his hands down from his chin and out to his sides. "That's 'clear out.' Except for the troll." He nodded at Gunther. "He'll be missed, so he's got to stay."

She spluttered. "Wait—why don't you do this?"

"Because the goblins are looking at you."

Perpetua looked up. Though she saw only silhouettes, she sensed that, yes, all eyes were indeed on her. Gunther sat as still as statues should, but she could feel his eyes on her, too.

"What's the gesture for 'stay there'?" she asked.

"What you'd expect. Palm down."

Careful not to draw attention to herself, Perpetua extended her hand toward Gunther, palm down. *Stay where you are*, she thought.

Then she looked up at the cornices, too ragged with shadows and shapes. As more people looked at each other, their bewildered smiles gave way to nervous frowns, and their eyes tracked up. Perpetua made the signal Fergus had shown her, swiping her hands down and out. *Get away. Now!*

She blinked, and in that blink, the rooflines became crisp.

People looked up. They grinned to see nothing there. They turned away, chuckling.

The ragged man stared upward. "What the—But—But where—?"

Traffic lights changed. Cell phones went to ears. People walked on.

The man looked around, wild, and his gaze fell on Perpetua, suddenly left at the centre of an empty patch of pavement as the streams of people flowed away. He pointed a shaking forefinger. "You! You're working for them! You're bringing them down on us!"

A police cruiser pulled up. The two homeless men grabbed their friend and hauled him, struggling and shouting, off the road and into an alleyway.

Perpetua let out the breath she was holding. "What almost happened?"

Fergus looked grim. "About what you think."

They made their way into the Underground City and waited in the food court while the crowd flow ebbed. When the corridor was nearly empty, they headed down.

Perpetua's footsteps echoed, while Fergus's squeaked. The distant warble of the soprano reached their ears.

Fergus turned around. "What the heck?"

Perpetua didn't slow. "Busker."

"At this hour?"

"I didn't say she was a rich busker."

As they entered Subbasement Three, Fergus stopped to stare at the sign for the House of Limericks. He poked his head inside.

"There once was a woman named Venus—"

Fergus let the door slam and hurried along. "So," he said, "is this . . .?"

"Another Monday at the office? Oh yeah." Then, looking ahead, she stopped short. "This, however, is new. Howard?"

Howard pushed away from the wall he'd been leaning on.

Perpetua frowned. "What are you doing here?"

Howard stopped a few feet away and tucked his head low. "Want new job," he rumbled. He looked sad and guilty.

"What happened?"

"No dig job. Dig job done."

"Did you quit?"

He shook his head slowly. "No. Want to."

"But—" Objections filled Perpetua's mind, reasons why Howard shouldn't quit: the money, and the fact that he had a job others wanted. Then she realized she hadn't asked an important question. She touched the troll's arm. "Why do you want to quit, Howard?"

"Dig boring. Want bounce."

"You want to be a bouncer?"

Howard nodded.

"But, Howard, the person you threw out at your last job only just checked out of hospital."

Howard lowered his head in shame.

"Look, Howard, you're a great digger . . ."

He drooped. "Dad dig. Ma dig. Grandpa dig. So I dig. No want to dig. Want to bounce."

Perpetua couldn't think of anything to say.

"Make mistakes," Howard went on. "I fix. I learn. Want bounce."

"Well, um . . ." She patted Howard's mountainous arm. "I'll see what I can do, okay? You're not skipping work, are you?"

He shook his head.

"Good. Come inside." She unlocked the office door and waved them inside. "Why don't you . . .?" She liked Howard, but the thought of him looming about, depressed, while she and Fergus waited for Earthenhouse made her uncomfortable. Then she spotted an envelope on her desk and recognized the return address. "Oh, good, the new DVDs arrived! Can I put on a movie for you?"

Howard perked up and rumbled happily.

She set up the movie—*Casino Royale*—while Fergus waited by the front door. He jerked back as the door swung open and Chim and Chum bounced in. They saw Perpetua by the DVD player and bolted to the training room door. "Movie?" said Chim. "Movie!" said Chum.

She frowned at them. "You guys are early."

"We know," said Chim.

"Want to beat the crowds!" said Chum.

The door opened again, and Trixie sidled through. She looked into the training room and saw Howard. Howard looked back. Their eyes met. Trixie rumbled. Howard rumbled. Trixie lumbered into the training room, and Perpetua retreated to her desk.

More goblins entered and, spotting the movie, headed into the training room.

Perpetua nudged Fergus. "Let's wait in Earthenhouse's office." She scribbled the words, "MOVIE, THIS WAY," onto a piece of paper, with an arrow that pointed to the training room, and taped it to the front of her desk. Then she ghosted into Earthenhouse's office, followed by Fergus and Scooter, and closed the door.

"Have a seat." Perpetua gestured at Scooter.

Fergus and Scooter stared at each other. Fergus drew back. "I think I'll stand. Why aren't we waiting outside?"

Perpetua leaned against the desk. "Sometimes, Earthenhouse appears in his office without using the front door. If we want to talk to him right away, and we do, we need to wait here."

"Because of that homeless man?" Fergus said.

"That, and the fact that the office is filling up fast and early."

"Something's about to break."

She nodded.

"So, where is he?"

Just then, the door to the bathroom opened and Earthenhouse loped in, hands in his pockets. He kicked the door shut behind him and sighed. "Subways, subways, subways," he muttered. "That's not a mayor, that's a broken record."

He turned to his desk and checked his stride when he saw Perpetua and Fergus waiting for him. "Good evening, Miss Collins."

"Hello, sir," said Perpetua.

Fergus waved.

"Why did you bring a guest?" Earthenhouse took a second look at Fergus, and his brow furrowed. "Are you one of our clients?"

"No, sir. I already have a job. I drive a cab."

Earthenhouse looked impressed. "Oh! Congratulations."

"Thank you, sir."

Perpetua looked from one to the other. She pointed at Fergus. "Sir? Did you just—? How could you see he was a goblin?"

Earthenhouse didn't answer. Fergus cleared his throat. "He recognizes the air of self-loathing," he said quietly.

Perpetua gaped.

Earthenhouse turned away. "I assume you have important business to discuss, Miss Collins." He loped over to his side of the desk and sat, polished shoes on the edge of the chair, pinstriped knees up by his ears. "Is it, by chance, about your unauthorized visit to our client's worksite yesterday?"

She winced. She wasn't surprised the news had gotten back to him already, but it was still an unwelcome development. "Kind of, yeah."

"I'm sorry." He straightened in his chair, without unbending his knees.

That was all he said. Perpetua waited for the sentence to complete itself with "... but you've crossed the line, and I'm going to have to fire you." But it never did.

"You're . . . sorry?"

Earthenhouse looked at his hands, clasped together on the

desk's shiny surface. "We have both been lax in trusting each other, Miss Collins. I should have been more forthcoming after Ms. Bell's visit. I admit, I was disturbed by your after-hours visit to the worksite, but you came back. That shows how much you value this job and the people you've agreed to work for." He raised his head and narrowed his eyes at Fergus. "I'm not sure why this young fellow is here, though. I'm waiting for an explanation."

"He worked for Ms. Bell."

Earthenhouse's knuckles whitened. "Oh?"

"He quit."

The knuckles relaxed. "Oh."

"I trust him."

He looked from Fergus to Perpetua, and back again. He sat back, eyebrows rising. "Ah."

"Why didn't you tell me about the earth movers division, sir?" she asked. "Or amnesia reset?"

Earthenhouse glanced warily at Fergus before looking back at her. "I didn't know how you'd react. I had to be sure of your loyalty. I am sure, now, but . . ." He looked again at Fergus.

She raised her hand. "Sir, please, let me see if I have something right, okay? The earth movers division: it's the bulk of this company, isn't it?"

He took a deep breath. "Yes."

"This city went for forty years hardly building any new subways. Then suddenly, just a little while ago, they started building again. They don't talk about what changed, only mention some vague, technological breakthrough." She nodded over her shoulder at the door. "Howard's the technological breakthrough, isn't he? Him and the other trolls?"

Earthenhouse nodded, eyes moving warily between her and Fergus.

"In fact, the trolls are subsidizing the rest of the business," she went on. "There can't be much demand for gargoyles in this city."

Earthenhouse looked away. "I had to start small. I'd hoped

that, given time, I could expand my operation to other cities, like Montreal, New York, London."

Perpetua leaned on Earthenhouse's desk. "A report just leaked from the City of Toronto states that the homeless population jumped from five thousand to fifty thousand in the past year alone. Most of those are goblins and trolls, am I right?"

Earthenhouse nodded.

*So, thirty-five thousand new goblins. But Adamant is certain there are more than that.*

*Where are the missing goblins?*

She straightened up. "Then there's the amnesia cases. There were generally one of two reasons listed. One was accident, with most of those related to the worksite at Eglinton and Yonge."

Earthenhouse tensed at that, but she went on. "The others, though—practically all the others were said to be 'voluntary due to depression.'" She frowned at him. "How do you voluntarily accept amnesia?"

He sat still for a long moment before answering. "It's clear that very little escapes you, Miss Collins." He looked up at her. "You're right, almost all the real jobs go to the trolls. I can't find jobs for all the goblins. I've had to disappoint many, and I've been swamped." He unfolded from his chair. "I have only one thing left to offer them. Come with me."

He ambled over to the bathroom, opened the door, and looked back. "Coming?"

Fergus stepped forward, but Perpetua grabbed his arm. "To where?"

"Subbasement Four," said Earthenhouse.

# Chapter 31
# Subbasement Four

Perpetua had wondered how Earthenhouse could disappear into a bathroom and never come back out. There didn't appear to be a secret door. The place looked exactly like a bathroom, with white marble countertops and a fine porcelain toilet and sink. Brass fixtures gleamed.

Then Earthenhouse shut the door behind them and flipped one of three switches beside it.

Hydraulics whined. The floor jerked. Fergus said, "Whoa!"

Perpetua grabbed the countertop as she felt her body drop ahead of her stomach. The bathroom was an elevator, descending fast. She swallowed, and her ears popped.

Fergus leaned close to Perpetua. "Are you sure about this?"

"Of course," she said airily. But she kept one eye on Earthenhouse.

The floor juddered, and Earthenhouse opened the door. Darkness yawned.

He reached around the doorframe. Something clicked, and a fluorescent tube flickered on. He stepped out, and Perpetua and Fergus followed him.

They couldn't see anything beyond the small pool of light shed by the single bulb in the ceiling. But there was a spacious quality in the way sound moved, and the air smelled cool and musty, like the inside of a cave. The floor was compacted dirt.

Perpetua hung close to the bathroom door. "What is this place?"

Earthenhouse walked over to a fuse box, pulled a key from his pocket, and opened it. He flicked on an array of switches inside.

There was a click and a hum, and a click and a hum, and more clicks and hums as long fluorescent lights flicked on, pushing back the darkness to show a concrete ceiling.

Perpetua felt the weight of the skyscraper above pressing down on her. Her throat tightened with claustrophobia.

She stared out at the long, low cavern. The ground was shaped into mounds: long ranks and files of them, each marked with a clipboard on a metal pole. These stretched in every direction, reminding her of the white crosses in the military cemeteries of Europe.

"Holy crap," Fergus breathed.

"What am I looking at?" She gazed around in awe.

"These are the goblins who decided that waiting for employment was a waste of their waking hours," said Earthenhouse. "These are the goblins who have gone underground and voluntarily accepted amnesia reset."

Perpetua started forward, stumbling on the uneven ground. She snatched up the closest clipboard and flipped through the papers.

The first line of text was a jovial, black-on-white square that said, "Hello, your name is . . ." followed by a line on which someone had written, "Olaf Radiwanson."

She knew that name. She'd seen him around the office a couple of times, but he'd had bad luck finding assignments. She'd suspected this lack of progress was getting him down. Before she could do anything, however, he'd stopped showing up. She'd assumed he'd found a job somewhere, and she'd been too busy to check.

On the clipboard, the name was followed by, "You have been

asleep since," followed by a date from a week ago. His list of skills included tap dancing, fencing, and tightrope walking. Under the "Office Use Only" section, Olaf's marketability was rated as "low," and the wake-up date was listed as "indefinite."

She hooked the clipboard back on its pole and looked again at the rows of mounds stretching in every direction, too many to count. "Why?"

Earthenhouse took a deep breath. "Many of us have been destitute, sleeping under bridges, for generations." He chuckled softly. "Isn't that how the legends go? But just because we're used to it doesn't mean we like it. I opened up as many positions as I could for goblins who could fill them. Failing that, I offered this, as a last resort: a place where goblins and trolls can rest in peace."

"They're not dead?" Her voice shook.

Fergus shook his head, speechless.

"No," said Earthenhouse. "Only sleeping. Until conditions change."

"So, this is our choice?" said Fergus. "Work underpaid, live destitute, and in hiding . . . or go under the ground?" He waved at the lines of poles. "They might as well be dead!"

Perpetua struggled to find the right words. In the end, all she could say was, "There has to be another way."

"I've spent this waking life looking for another way," said Earthenhouse

"But this is wrong. Can't you see?" She pointed at the ceiling. "How can you expect me to live comfortably up there with all of this down here? It's just wrong!"

Her voice echoed back at her. Seeing Fergus and Earthenhouse looking strangely at her, she realized that she'd been shouting. She touched her cheeks. Her fingers came away wet.

Fergus reached out. Perpetua wiped her face, clasped his hand for a moment, and then turned to Earthenhouse. With a shuddering breath, she said, "I'd like to go back up now, please."

"As you wish."

He went to the fuse box and flicked the switches off. Darkness swept back in.

The ride up was slower than the ride down. Perpetua broke the silence. "Sir? You said, 'this waking life.' Did you have amnesia reset, too?"

He smiled faintly. "My memories stretch back twenty years, but I must have had a head for business in my previous life. My work here came easily, at first."

"You don't remember anything from before?"

He shook his head. "Not even my own name."

"So, how did you pick the one you have?"

"A woman picked it for me," he replied. "She said it was the name I had before."

"A woman. A human woman?"

"Yes," he said distantly.

Perpetua exchanged a surprised glance with Fergus. She was brimming with curiosity, but after a look at her boss's closed expression, she limited herself to, "Thorsen P. Earthenhouse. What does the P stand for?"

"Phileas."

"Phileas?"

"It seemed to fit."

Fergus cleared his throat. "Mr. Earthenhouse? How many goblins are buried down there?"

Earthenhouse sighed. "Around ten thousand."

Fergus swore.

The floor shuddered. A moment later, they were back in the office.

"How did this get started?" Fergus sounded bewildered. "How did the St. Brigid faeries not throw a fit at the first sign of what you were doing?"

"It was tricky." Earthenhouse sat down at his desk. "But I found a loophole. The Mores govern the use of goblin and faerie magic in the human world. Trolls aren't magical. They just know how to dig."

"And you found a city that needed to dig," said Perpetua.

Earthenhouse looked weary. "It has been difficult, but I've managed so far. If I had just a little more time . . ."

*But we're running out of time.* She hated to break this news, but knew she had no choice. "Sir, coming here, we saw a homeless person yelling and pointing at the rooftops. If we hadn't warned the goblins away, some of them might have been seen by the wrong people. There are too many goblins here. Never mind the unemployment, we're running out of room on the rooftops. All it's going to take is one wrong person looking up at just the wrong time, and the whole thing will come crashing down."

She remembered the graffiti in the alleyway. *We must not look at goblin men . . .* "People are beginning to notice, already."

Earthenhouse sat silent. He didn't look at her.

"The goblins can do good work," she went on. "They can do office work, computer work, and engineering work. I know this because I've seen them do it. They just need a chance to shine, and you can't shine if you hide. You negotiated your contract with the City of Toronto in secret. I'm guessing you didn't contact Montreal, Ottawa, New York, or any other city. If you had, you could have negotiated a better deal, got competition."

"I understand what you are saying, Miss Collins," said Earthenhouse. "But I don't think you understand how my hands are tied. I had to negotiate my contract with Toronto's city council in secret. It was a precondition of the Mores. How do you think humans would react if they learned we were here? You said you saw a homeless man almost give away our presence to a crowd. Ask yourself, Miss Collins, why was that a problem? You were afraid. I think you know why."

"Sir—"

Earthenhouse sat forward, resting his face in his hands. "Even though the faeries left us behind, they did us one good service: they made humans forget about us. Centuries of whispering in humanity's ear, and they've turned us into myths and legends and so many bad dreams. They put humanity to sleep. Nobody chases us with pitchforks anymore." He dropped his hands. "How can you ask me to reverse that?"

Perpetua glanced at Fergus. "Sir, we may have a plan."

Fergus looked nervous. Perpetua clasped his hand. "This is why I brought Fergus here. He's been working on a plan on how to make the human race aware of the goblins—without the torches and pitchforks. You two should talk."

Earthenhouse sat back, interlaced his fingers and gave Fergus a skeptical look. Fergus straightened his spine and attempted a look of cheerful confidence. "Well, sir . . . it's like this." He set his folder on Earthenhouse's desk, cleared his throat, and talked.

Perpetua settled on Scooter while Fergus outlined the main ideas of his plan, the people he could contact, the types and intensity of marketing campaigns he could put in place, even a timeline of when they could go public. His voice shook a bit at the beginning, but he kept going, and Earthenhouse listened in silence all the way through to the end. Fergus caught his breath and stood waiting, a hopeful look on his face.

Earthenhouse picked up the folder, flipped through the photographs and charts, and raised his eyebrows at Bono's cell phone number. Then he closed it and slapped it down on his desk. An autographed photo of Bono slid from the folder and fluttered to the floor. "This is the most naive thing I have ever heard!"

"Hey!" Perpetua stood up so fast, Scooter squeaked and rolled back a few feet.

"Never mind how the average human would react to this," Earthenhouse went on. "If you think, for a second, the St. Brigid faeries would stand for social media campaigns . . ." He flapped his hands at the folder.

Fergus, looking gloomy, knelt to pick up the fallen photograph.

Perpetua folded her arms. "So, what's the alternative?"

Silence stretched in the office, broken only by Scooter's squeak as it repositioned itself behind Perpetua.

"I have been drafting contingencies," Earthenhouse said at last. "I have some ideas . . . on what we can do." He avoided her gaze. "I'm not sure you would entirely approve."

Perpetua tilted her head. "Sir . . .?" *Why should he care if I approve?*

"Um, sir?" Fergus cut in. He was still on his knees, the photograph forgotten in his hand. He was staring at the base of Earthenhouse's desk. "What were you saying about how the St. Brigid faeries would react if they found out about my plans?"

Earthenhouse stood up to look over his desk at Fergus.

"It's just that . . ." Fergus reached under the desk. "I can't think of many things attached to a desk leg that would have a blinking red light."

He pulled something free and held it up. It was a small, electronic device that Perpetua recognized. It looked like what she'd found inside the toy taxicab.

Earthenhouse reached for it. "What is that?"

"It's a bug," said Perpetua. "A listening device." She grabbed it from Fergus. "But I don't understand—you didn't put this here. You couldn't have." Fergus shook his head. He looked white enough to faint. "How did they get the bug in here? We haven't had any visitors—"

Then she remembered: that human client who had wandered in and talked to her about the statues. What if he hadn't been as stupid as he'd appeared? "Dammit!"

"You need to get out." Earthenhouse looked at Fergus. "Leave this city. If the St. Brigid faeries know about this, your life is forfeit. They have spent centuries protecting the veil. They won't let you threaten that."

Fergus shifted from foot to foot. "They wouldn't go that far, would they? I mean, people would notice a body? Right?"

"They don't have to kill you to silence you," Earthenhouse said.

A chirpy little voice suddenly spoke up outside the door, in the reception area. It was the coffee maker, talking loudly.

"You look like you could use a nice cup of coffee!"

Someone shushed it.

"But you do!" the coffee maker piped, louder. "Maybe you'd like an espresso! Or a mocha! I also do cinnamon dolces!"

Perpetua's stomach dropped. "There are no client appointments scheduled for right now."

Earthenhouse bounded from his chair. "They've come for us. Or rather"—he nodded at Fergus—"for him."

Perpetua stepped past Fergus and toward the office door.

He grabbed her arm. "What are you doing?"

She shook him off. "I have to go out there. I'm the receptionist. I can delay them, maybe talk them away."

"It's too dangerous!"

She squeezed his hand. "So are the alternatives." She looked hard at Earthenhouse. "Get him to Subbasement Four, now!"

Earthenhouse gripped Fergus's bicep and dragged him away.

She waited until they were inside the bathroom before she smoothed her skirt and her expression, and opened the door to the reception area.

She jerked back when she found herself face to face with one of Christina's black-clad agents, so close she saw herself reflected in his mirrored sunglasses. She held her ground and closed the door behind her.

"Hey!" she snapped. "Personal space." She made shooing motions with her fingers. "Step back, please! Back!"

The faerie surprised her by taking two precise steps back, until he was standing beside his partner. Perpetua glanced from one to the other. *Two against one. I'm not liking these odds.*

She put on a professional smile. "How can I help you, gentlemen?"

"We wish to speak with your boss," said the faerie on the left. His voice was a reedy tenor, like the sound of wind through dry sedge.

"He's unavailable. I can make you an appointment for next Saturday. Will 2 a.m. do?"

The faerie on the right shook himself—vibrated, actually. He moved so fast, he buzzed like a hummingbird. And then he disappeared.

Perpetua stared. Where there had been two faeries in front of her, now there was only one, staring at her through his sunglasses.

And reflected in those sunglasses . . .

She ducked. From behind, a fist swung through where her head had been. She threw up a hand, grabbed his arm, and then lunged back. He grunted, then hissed as she pitched him over onto his back. He landed hard. A quick punch to the throat left him choking.

Before she could straighten up, a hand grabbed her shoulder. She turned, punching, but her fist jabbed the air. The second faerie grabbed her wrist with a grip so tight, she yelled in pain. She shoved her shoulder into her attacker, only to have him neatly step around her, his long, thin fingers like steel around her wrist. He twisted her arm up behind her, grabbed her other arm by the elbow, and pulled back. She kicked back viciously. The faerie pulled her arm and elbow back, back, until she gritted her teeth and struggled for breath.

The other faerie got to his feet, apparently barely ruffled. He positioned himself in front of her. "Where is Aloysius Fergus?"

"I . . . don't . . . know . . ." she grunted.

"That is a lie." The faerie's pale, perfect lips curved upward. "We can tell."

"Fuck off, Elrond!" The faerie behind her pulled on her elbow so hard, she thought her shoulder might dislocate. She screamed.

The faerie in front stood almost nose-to-nose with her. He did look and sound like Elrond in the movies. Any other time and situation, she might have been impressed. "We know you know where he has gone. Tell me!"

She spat in his face.

He reared back, his expressionless mask cracking into a snarl. His hands rose, curved like claws. The next moment, a massive hand crashed down on his shoulder. Another hand crashed down on the other faerie. Perpetua fell to the floor as both faeries rose into the air, kicking.

Howard glared at his catch. "Who make noise during movie?" he bellowed.

Then he looked down, saw Perpetua struggling to sit up, grimacing in pain. He looked from her to the faeries twisting in his grip. Silence fell, punctuated by the James Bond musical sting from the movie in the next room.

A deep, menacing rumble rose up in Howard. He grinned, showing an array of stony teeth. "Bounce, bounce!"

Both faeries flicked up their hands like knives. Perpetua struggled to her feet. "Howard! Watch out!"

Howard turned, fast. The glass of the front window shattered as the two faeries sailed through it.

The shattered glass revealed two more faeries-in-black with mirrored sunglasses. They glanced at their fallen comrades, then up at Howard. Eyebrows rose. One touched his hand to his ear. "Backup."

Howard lumbered forward. The fallen faeries scrambled up and backed away.

The faerie's voice edged up. "We need that backup, *now*!" The faeries retreated toward the stairwell with swift, flickering movements that made Perpetua think of strobe lights.

Silence descended. Howard stood guard at the wider-open entrance. Curious goblins filed in from the training room, *Casino Royale* forgotten. Perpetua stood, breathing heavily, rubbing at her shoulder. She jerked when a hand touched her arm, but relaxed when she saw that it was Fergus. She hugged him close.

Then she pulled away and slugged him in the shoulder.

"Ow!" he cried.

"I told you to hide in the subbasement!"

"He refused to go without you," said Earthenhouse behind him. "I'm inclined to agree with him. You *both* need to get out of here. The St. Brigid faeries will be back with reinforcements.

There's not much they can do to a troll, but we goblins are another matter. We will not be able to hold them off for long."

Perpetua glanced from Fergus to Earthenhouse. "Then how can we leave you here?"

"Don't worry about me or the others. We're goblins." He smiled briefly. "We know how to disappear. Go!"

She hesitated, then grabbed up her backpack and took Fergus's hand. "Let's go!" She started for the front door.

"Not that way!" Earthenhouse called. "They'll have that route guarded. You have to go out the back." He handed Perpetua the key to the fuse box. "Through the subbasement. Get off the elevator, turn right, and follow the line on the ceiling to the emergency exit."

"Emergency exit?"

"I had to build the chamber to code, of course."

"Thank goodness for Toronto's Fire Safety Regulations," Perpetua muttered. "Fergus?"

"I'm right behind you!"

Hand-in-hand, they ran for the bathroom elevator.

## Chapter 32
# Under and Over

A grey door opened onto a corridor of pink-painted drywall. Perpetua and Fergus stepped out.

The corridor ran for several metres in both directions, with glass doors at either end. Only one set of doors had an "EXIT" sign in front of it. Fergus pointed. "I guess that's the way out."

But Perpetua was looking back the way they'd come. The grey door had a simple handle and a lock. There'd been a crash bar at the other end. Without a key, it could only be opened from the other side. Thousands would pass by without noticing. "That cavern is huge," she said. "Where are we?"

Fergus glanced at a map of the Underground City posted on the opposite wall. "We're right near City Hall."

"I guess this was Earthenhouse's direct line. I wonder how many of these doors he has around the city."

Fergus took her hand. "We'd better get going." He shoved open the door marked "EXIT," and they started up a flight of concrete steps. They could hear the traffic outside and the bell of a passing streetcar.

Fergus froze, listening. Then he grabbed Perpetua and urged her back through the door. "Come on!" He walked quickly in the opposite direction, trying to look nonchalant.

"What?" Perpetua trotted to keep up. "Fergus, what?"

"You remember what Earthenhouse said about the faeries sending reinforcements?"

The exit door swung open behind them, and the corridor came alive with marching footfalls.

"Seriously?" she muttered. "They pick *that* exit to enter the Underground City? Remind me never to buy a lottery ticket, ever!"

"Come on. Hurry up!"

They burst from the pink corridor and into a shopping concourse. The stores were all shuttered, the lights dim. Fergus sucked his teeth. "Not many places to hide."

Over the hum of the ventilation ducts, Perpetua heard a familiar sound from the direction of the food court. She clasped his hand. "I've got an idea. Come on!"

The clatter and slap sounds stopped as Perpetua and Fergus ran over. The food court looked empty. "Hey! I know you're here!" she called. "We need your help."

A listening silence answered.

"The guards!" She raised her voice. "They're coming for us!"

With a scrabble of wheels, a tall, spiky-haired skater about Perpetua's age glided out from behind a vending machine. "Where?"

Perpetua pointed over her shoulder. "They're covering the northern exits. We need to get to the south end of the Underground City, fast."

With another rattle of wheels, a girl who looked maybe fourteen glided into view. "How fast?"

Perpetua tipped her head at their feet. "Can we borrow a run on your boards?"

Fergus took a step back. "Wait, what? I've never skated before!"

"First time for everything," said the spiky-haired skater.

Other skaters rolled into view. One plunked a board at Perpetua's feet, another at Fergus's. Spiky Hair looked Perpetua up and down. "You know the boards?"

She grinned. "Misspent youth."

"Well, I'm too young to die!" Fergus's voice edged up. "Will you listen to me? I don't know how to skate!"

"Do you know how to stand up?" The young skater girl shoved him onto his board, then nodded at Perpetua. "Hold the newbie."

Perpetua shifted her board next to the one Fergus was standing on, stood on it, and wrapped her arms around Fergus's chest. "Got it."

Behind them, the doors swung open. Somebody called: "Found them!"

"Go!" the girl shouted.

The skaters scattered, shouting at the pursuers to draw them away. Perpetua kicked off. Spiky Hair kicked with them. Bracing Fergus between them, they rolled down a wheelchair ramp, gathering speed. Skater Girl followed. Feet pounded right behind.

Leaning in tandem, Perpetua and Spiky Hair guided Fergus along the marble walkways, zipping past benches and wayfinding boards. Skater Girl kicked on ahead, jumping off and kicking up her board as they reached the doors between buildings. Fergus shouted and covered his head.

"It's okay!" Perpetua hissed in his ear. Her heart pounded. They hit another ramp alongside a flight of stairs and reached frantic speed.

The building doors smashed open behind them, and the pursuing footfalls multiplied.

"They're not giving up," Fergus muttered.

"I know!"

The mall security guards ambled out of a side corridor as Perpetua and the skaters shot past. Two of them glowered and lunged, only to have Patrick pull them back. He stared nervously as the faerie agents charged past.

Skater Girl kicked frantically to keep ahead. She met the next set of doors at full force, crashing them open. Perpetua, Fergus, and Spiky Hair crammed together as they shot through, then went into a lean and a sharp turn to make the next wheelchair ramp. They shot past signs pointing the way to Union Station. The storm of pursuing feet stayed close on their heels.

The girl skater was beside them now, kicking constantly. "These guys are fast!"

"And we have a problem," said Spiky Hair.

"A problem!" Fergus yelled. "*Now*, we have a problem?"

"The next set of stairs is a full flight," Spiky Hair gasped. "Twenty steps. No wheelchair ramp."

Perpetua swore. "We can't make that."

"*I* can. I don't know about you, and the newbie certainly can't. You're going to have to bail."

"You're kidding me! You'd never make it!"

Spiky Hair shot them a grin that made Fergus tense in her arms. "Maybe. But it's going to be awesome!"

Perpetua saluted him with her free hand.

They zipped past another side corridor and veered around a bench.

"Okay!" Spiky Hair snapped. "Emergency exit on the right, by the stairs. It's going to be sketchy, but . . . veer off at my signal, and then run. We'll try to lead them away."

"Okay."

"On three, got it?"

"Yeah."

"Guys," yelled Fergus. "I don't think this is a good idea!"

They shot past another wayfinding map.

"One," said Spiky Hair.

A set of glass doors came into view, leading to a landing and a flight of stairs. The red-lettered sign above it said, "UNION STATION."

"Really, *really* not a good idea!" Fergus yelled.

"Two!"

Behind them, the last set of doors crashed open.

"Three!"

The skaters pushed. Perpetua leaned. She and Fergus swung right, making straight for a utility door marked: "EMERGENCY EXIT. ALARM WILL SOUND." Perpetua braced herself, twisted, and smashed back-first into the crash bar.

Klaxons buzzed. Their skateboards crashed into the first step of a flight of stairs, dumping them into a heap. Perpetua struggled up, clutching at her elbow and hauling at Fergus. They charged up the stairs. On the landing, Perpetua looked back and saw a faerie agent looking up at them. He put a finger to his ear. "They're exiting onto Wellington Street."

Then they were out the fire door and on the street. Traffic rumbled slowly under the streetlights. Crowds clogged the sidewalks, many wearing baseball hats and waving foam rubber hands.

"The Jays game must have ended." Fergus led Perpetua through the crowd. "This is good. Maybe we can hide amongst all these people."

A voice spoke, disturbingly close. "Got them!"

Perpetua leaped back as a black-clad faerie lunged at her. Grabbing Fergus by the hand, she stumbled off the sidewalk and onto the road.

Horns blared. Truck headlights bored down on them. Perpetua yelled and covered her head. There was a horrifying screech—

And then nothing. She opened her eyes. The truck had stopped an inch away. When she breathed out, her stomach brushed against the grill. She backed up. Brakes screeched again, and she found herself in the next lane of traffic. A taxi driver stared at her, then leaned on the horn.

The truck in the lane that Perpetua and Fergus had just left pulled forward. The cars behind it picked up speed.

The black-clad faerie stared at them from the sidewalk. Perpetua stepped back once more, pulling Fergus with her, and another lane of traffic screeched to a halt, while the one they had left moved faster than ever, as impenetrable as a moat.

The faerie agent stepped off the curb, then leaped back as a bus rolled past. Perpetua and Fergus stepped into the last lane of traffic.

"How are you doing this?" Fergus shouted.

"I don't know!" They leaped onto the sidewalk.

Across the street, more faeries were striding up the sidewalk, emerging from doorways or stairwells. Many were speaking, their hands on their ears. None, Perpetua realized, were wearing earphones.

Fergus wheezed. "They've got us in a net."

"Keep going," she gasped. "There's got to be a way out!" They rushed for the next intersection and then skidded to a stop. More agents were approaching from up ahead. Perpetua turned and stopped again. More agents in that direction, too.

The only opening was an alleyway between two buildings. Fergus grabbed her hand, and they dashed. Their footfalls echoed off the sheer concrete walls. They charged around a corner and stumbled to a stop. Dead-end. Perpetua looked around, frantic. There were no doors, no fire escapes. The nearest windows were all well above leaping height.

"Back!" Fergus grabbed her arm, then gasped and pointed. Shadows cast by the streetlights writhed along the concrete walls toward them. They were trapped.

Fergus put a hand on Perpetua's shoulder and turned her to face him. "Look . . . just in case . . . whatever happens, I—"

She recoiled. "No! Don't say, 'whatever happens'! Only one thing ever happens when you say that, and it's bad!"

"Okay. But—" They were at the end of an alley. No way out.

"But what?"

"But I love you."

"Oh." She panted. "Okay."

The shadows of the faerie agents shrank and grew more solid as they approached. "I love you, too. Whatever happens." She threw herself into his arms, and their lips met.

Someone tapped Perpetua on the shoulder. She whirled around, raising her fists.

It was a goblin. He grinned at her. Only, his grin was upside-down. His face was at eye level. The rest of him clung to the wall above her head.

"What—?" she began.

"Earthenhouse sent us." His voice was like a gravel road. "Said you and your boyfriend needed help."

"And . . .?"

He grabbed her under her arms. "Hold on."

"Wait, what—?" She yelled as the goblin lifted her off her feet. He clawed his way up the sheer concrete wall, rising as fast as an elevator.

Perpetua stopped yelling and hung on. Below, another goblin hauled Fergus up after her.

Despite her stomach telling her not to, she looked down. Five faerie agents stood in the alleyway below, dark glasses turned upward. Perpetua couldn't help thumbing her nose.

One of the faeries backed up and took a running leap at the wall. One foot had barely scuffed the surface before he twisted in midair and kicked at the other wall of the corner, then flipped back around to the first wall. Leaping from side to side, he rose like a grasshopper.

"Showy bastards," said the goblin.

Reaching the roof, the goblins dumped their cargo. Perpetua and Fergus rolled over the gravel surface and scrambled up. "What now?"

The goblin looked down at the rising faerie. He looked grim.

Fergus grabbed her hand. "I don't think we should wait for the answer."

"What can we do? We're trapped! On top of the"—she glanced at the huge roof sign beside her—"Royal York Hotel!"

He pulled at her hand. "Come on!"

She staggered after him. "To where?"

The goblins were leading the way. Fergus ran after them, pulling Perpetua along.

"Where are we going?" she shouted. "Where are the stairs?"

"We're not taking the stairs," the goblin called back. "We've got a shortcut."

They were racing straight for the edge of the roof. It was a thirty-story drop to the street below.

"You're kidding me!" she yelled. The bottom stories of the building across the street came into view, followed by the sidewalk and lanes of cars. The cars were honking madly. "Are you freaking kidding me?" She tried to hit the brakes.

Fergus yanked her forward. "Come on! Keep going!"

"No! *No*!"

Then, in front of and beneath her, she saw goblins swarming up the side of the building. When they reached the roof, they clambered over each other, linking hands and bracing legs and stretching across the hundred-foot gap, forming a bridge like a barrel of monkeys.

*They want me to run across* that? *Are they crazy?*

But she didn't stop. She closed her eyes. Her foot swung out over air. She felt it land on a cupped hand, which lifted her up and propelled her forward. When she made the mistake of looking down, she was halfway between the two buildings. Goblin hands reached up for her next step. She closed her eyes, widened her stride, and, for the first time in seven years, prayed.

Gravel crunched beneath her. She sprawled. Fergus landed beside her, rolled onto his feet, and hauled her up. "Are you okay?"

She trembled and gasped, her heart going a mile a minute. "That was insane!"

He grinned at her wildly. "We're still alive! And look!"

He pointed across the gap. On the roof of the Royal York Hotel, one faerie-in-black stood on the precipice, looking down. Another gazed at them through his sunglasses. The goblin bridge was nowhere to be seen.

The faerie-in-black took several steps back, eyes fixed on them. He crouched low.

Perpetua straightened up. "Faeries can't fly, can they?"

Fergus swore. "No, but they can jump. Come on!"

They ran again. Ahead, another goblin bridge rose up. Perpetua put her head down and pelted across. She only opened her eyes when gravel again crunched beneath her.

Hand in hand with Fergus, she raced to the next gap. This one was narrower, spanning over an alleyway. Another group of goblins was already linking arms and bracing legs.

Halfway across, something that sizzled and flared like lightning caught her under the shoulder, hard as a baseball bat. She pitched sideways. Fergus pitched with her. They fell. A goblin grabbed at their heels, but another lightning bolt knocked him back.

Perpetua felt the wind hit. Windows whipped by.

The only thing not moving in her frame of reference was Fergus. He fell with her, hand clutching hers, eyes black with terror.

Her hair streamed upward, and her skirt plastered against her body. The wind howled in her ears. Perpetua screamed, and the air was sucked from her lungs. She fell and fell and—

A force pressed into her from below. She turned in midair. Fergus was below her now, still clinging to her hand. *I'm . . . I'm slowing down! How . . .?*

Fergus was getting heavier. She was having trouble holding him. Her arm felt like it was about to rip free from its socket. He shouted something that the wind blew away.

Then she saw, fifteen stories below them, Christina and her faerie agents standing in the alleyway beside a low, square roof that jutted out over a loading dock. The roof was growing larger and more distinct with every frozen moment. Christina was pointing at her, and Perpetua could see a lance of blue light running from Christina's finger to her chest. Her, and not Fergus. The pull of his weight on her arm intensified.

She clutched desperately at his hand, but her fingers slipped. She screamed as he fell away. He hit the roof waiting below. It collapsed onto the loading dock with a spray of stones and a cloud of dust that billowed up to meet her.

Perpetua clapped her hands to her face.

The force that was slowing her pushed her to a stop. Coughing, she opened an eye and found herself suspended in midair, staring at the gravel one foot below.

The beam cut out, and she fell the rest of the way, landing on the rubble with a bone-jarring crunch.

"Fergus!" She was up on her knees in an instant, digging out gravel, throwing stone and broken concrete aside. "Fergus!"

"Miss Collins," Christina called. "We need to talk."

When a faerie grabbed her by the shoulder, she jabbed back with an elbow. "*Fergus*!" Tears streaming down her face, she scrabbled frantically at the debris.

"Calm down." Christina's voice was a baseline of disdain. "He has the constitution of a stone."

Perpetua's bleeding hands dug and tossed aside. She uncovered an arm, a shoulder—

Fergus sat up, choking and retching, hair and skin and clothes grey with dust, debris falling away. Perpetua jerked back then, sobbing with relief, and threw her arms around him. "You're alive!"

Crisp footsteps halted behind her.

Fergus leaned into her, and she held him while the choking spasm ebbed. Then he blinked away dust and looked into her eyes. "I . . . I am alive, aren't I?"

"Of course, you're alive!" Perpetua laughed between her sobs. She hugged him. "I thought I'd lost you!"

"Um . . . oh?"

She leaned back, her hands on his shoulders, and looked him in the eye. "Are you . . . okay?"

"I think so." He looked down at himself, dust-whitened and

battered. He glanced at her hands on his shoulders. "But . . . there is one thing." He looked at her.

Her heart clenched. "What?"

"What's my name?" He smiled expectantly.

She sat back on her heels and pressed her hands to her mouth. "*No.*"

Behind her, Christina snapped her fingers. "We've waited long enough. Bring them both. We need to be away from here."

Perpetua gripped his hands. "Your name is Fergus," she said, quickly, urgently. "Aloysius Fergus. You drive a taxi."

His brow furrowed. "I do?"

Long-fingered hands clamped down on Perpetua's arms. She struggled and shouted, but they hauled her to her feet. Two other agents picked up Fergus, each to an arm. They dragged him, looking up and around quizzically, to a black van that waited at the mouth of the alley. He caught Perpetua's eye and smiled sweetly. "Are these guys my fares?"

"Don't trust them!" she yelled. "Whatever you do, don't believe a word they tell you!"

The faerie agents tossed Fergus inside like a sack of potatoes. Perpetua's agents shoved her simply forward. She rolled over the metal floor, crowding into Fergus.

The doors slammed shut, and the van took off with a screech of tires.

# Part Five
# Drop the Veil

*All* ~~*human*~~ (*sentient*) *beings are born free and equal in dignity and rights. They are endowed with reason and conscience and should act toward one another in a spirit of brotherhood.*

— The Universal Declaration of Human Rights

## Chapter 33
# Confronting Christina Bell

As Fergus helped Perpetua up, the van took off and turned right, pitching them into the wall and landing them on the metal bench that ran along it. Perpetua clutched her head.

Fergus stared at her. "Are you okay?"

She gave him a strained look. "Just peachy."

"Do I know you?"

She looked at him, and her heart twisted. She couldn't tell him. Not right now. "I'm a . . . I'm a friend."

"Oh." He smiled and waved. "Hello, friend."

The van accelerated and turned, hard, shoving them together. When the pressure lifted, Perpetua pulled away.

"So, where are they taking us?" asked Fergus, not as if he were much worried.

"Darned if I know." The windows in the back of the van were blacked out. She knew where they'd started from, and she knew the van had taken a sharp right turn, and then a left, and was moving fast. "Back to their headquarters, perhaps? Back to their lair? I'm pretty sure Christina has a lair."

"Um," said Fergus. "Can you explain something to me?"

"I'll try. What is it?"

"Why are we here? Who are these people, and why are they taking us to their lair?"

She met his eyes. It was hard, but she made herself do it. He deserved nothing less, precisely because he didn't know it.

His eyes were gentle and dark brown, the same as before. And yet, they had changed completely.

"Your name is Aloysius Fergus," she said at last. "You're a goblin. And you have a plan to help the goblins stand up for themselves against the faeries and the humans."

He blinked at her. "I do? Gosh. Is it a good plan?"

She smiled to force back tears. "I'm sure of it." She took his hand. "Now, I need to figure out where they're taking us."

She leaned against the wall and composed herself. The last thing she needed was for Fergus to see her cry. Instead, she tried to remember the turns the van was taking. "Right, then left, then left, now right."

"We just got on a highway," said Fergus.

"How do you know?"

His brow furrowed. "I just . . . know. We're picking up speed, and we're not jerking about like before. I think it's the Gardiner Expressway."

She jerked up. Then she remembered what Adamant had said. "*Amnesia reset wipes the personality, but leaves the skills and facts intact. We can get him back to his old place, and he'll remember where everything is.*"

"Huh. Good. Keep, um . . . monitoring." She moved to the bench on the other side of the van and slid close to the door. It was locked, of course, but maybe she could grab the element of surprise when the door opened. When the faeries came for her, she wouldn't go without a fight.

Fergus watched her, brow still furrowed, as she sat poised by the door, but he continued to listen to the noise of the van. He told her when the van hit an on-ramp to another highway, heading north. They were in the west end of the city, now, approaching the airport. She frowned. *They aren't taking us out of the country, are they?*

Finally, the van came to a halt, and Perpetua heard doors open and slam. "This is it," she said to Fergus, keeping her voice low. "Get ready."

"For what?"

"For—"

The back doors opened then, and Perpetua wondered that herself. Four faerie agents stood there, hands poised, ready for her attack. Behind them, Christina watched, arms folded. No hope; no chance. Yet. Perpetua lowered her hands.

Christina tilted her head in mocking invitation. "Coming?"

The faerie agents stepped back and gave Perpetua and Fergus room to jump down. They flanked them as they strode through a cracked and empty parking lot.

Their destination was a two-story motel built of yellow brick. The central area was a squat, low outcrop with floor-to-ceiling glass, topped by a sign reading, "FAIR WAY INN." The place was either badly dated or cleverly retro, but it was at least kept up. The sign shone bright, and the topiaries by the door were well trimmed. Christina led the way to the front door.

Perpetua stared up at the building. "Seriously? This is your lair?"

Christina smirked. "What were you expecting? A Disney castle?"

"Kind of, yeah."

Doors opened ahead of them as Christina led them through the empty reception area and into a hallway, past a deserted but filled swimming pool, through a restaurant where nobody ate at the fully set tables, and through a kitchen where there was not even a smell of cooking, past or present. Each door moved automatically, untouched, and it took a minute for Perpetua to realize that these weren't automatic doors, and to catch Christina swiping her hand to one side before each one opened.

"We can't afford to be showy," said Christina. "That's more than a condition of the Mores; it's a matter of survival. Let the billionaires and the Hollywood celebrities command human attention. If we advertised ourselves as a group, the veil would drop."

Another door swung open.

"And yet, you can't help yourselves," Perpetua said.

She glanced at Fergus and saw him staring, puzzled, at their clasped hands. He looked up at her, and she gave him a smile. "It's going to be okay."

She glanced back. The four faerie agents strolled in the rear. No escape that way.

The final door opened into a small office with a plain metal desk, a leather-backed swivel chair, and two leather-and-metal chairs positioned in front. A table in the corner held a cheap plastic coffee maker, a stack of Styrofoam cups, and small bins of sugar packets and artificial creamer. It was as depressing an office space as Perpetua had ever seen.

Christina flicked a hand at the two chairs as she passed between them. "Sit, please."

Perpetua took hold of the left chair, but didn't sit down. Fergus sat, then looked up at Perpetua. Christina walked around her desk, turned, and looked at the agents. "You can go. Make sure this place is secure. Under no circumstances are we to be disturbed."

They bowed, turned gracefully, and followed each other out.

Perpetua stared. *Are they really going to leave me alone with her? Oh, I sure hope so!* Her muscles tensed.

The door closed. "I told you to sit," Christina said to Perpetua. She sat down herself and flipped through some papers on her desk. "A nice trick, stopping traffic like that. It makes me wonder if you have some faerie blood in you. I—"

Perpetua got as far as lunging across the desk and clawing at Christina's face. Then Christina threw up a hand, and Perpetua flew backward.

When Perpetua came to her senses, she was staring down

from an unexpected height. Her neck was crooked painfully against the ceiling, and her arms and legs were splayed out on the wall. She tried to struggle, and found she couldn't. She tried to speak, but her mouth wouldn't move. It was as though the air around her had turned to glass. She could only blink and breathe.

Fergus sat in his chair, eyes wide, mouth clamped shut. His hands gripped the armrests, but stayed locked in that position. Perpetua could see the muscles of his jaw straining, but his mouth wouldn't open, and no sound came out.

Christina touched the scratch marks marring her otherwise flawless left cheek. Her fingertips came away with blood. She pulled a Kleenex from a box on her desk and dabbed at the marks. Without looking at Perpetua, she said, "I hope you'll take this moment to consider your predicament, my dear."

Still holding the Kleenex to her cheek, she looked up. "I've stopped all your motor functions, save for those you need to live. I'm also holding your friend in his seat, in case he feels the impulse to do something similarly stupid and gallant. I'll be honest, this does take some effort. I can't keep it up forever. But you can see how futile it is to attack me. I could hold you there for a while." Her gaze darkened. "Or I could stop the remaining motor functions altogether."

She looked at the Kleenex, frowned at it, and sighed. "I don't want to kill you. I just want to talk. We can do that now, or we can do that an hour from now, after you've had some time to 'hang around.'" Perpetua could practically see the quotation marks around the phrase. "So, your choice," said Christina. "If I let you down, will you play nice?"

She dropped the tissue into a wastebasket, sat back, and folded her arms. The scratch marks on her cheek were visibly fading.

Perpetua strained to speak, but not even her tongue would work.

Christina smiled. "Blink twice for yes."

Perpetua blinked twice.

Christina swept up a hand, and Perpetua fell from the ceiling. She landed with a yell.

Fergus leaped out of his chair and knelt by Perpetua's side. As he helped her up, he whispered in her ear. "Why are you doing this?"

"Because it's important. You're important," she murmured back. She eased him away and sat down heavily in one of the two chairs. Fergus, looking worried, sat down in the other.

"All right." She fixed Christina with a glare. "What do you want?"

"I wanted to talk to you, Miss Collins."

"Why me?" Perpetua snapped. "I'm just a secretary."

Christina shook her head. "You're more than just a secretary. We know of Mr. Fergus's plan to reveal the goblins to humanity, and, yes, that threat cannot stand. But I can also see that he is showing all the symptoms of amnesia reset. That means that he's no longer a threat. Earthenhouse, for all that he has done, is a businessman. He has tried to remain on the right side of the law when it comes to the Mores. An order to shut his company down may anger him, but he will abide." She leaned forward, resting her chin on her folded hands. Her gaze was cool and searching. "That just leaves you."

"Me," Perpetua deadpanned.

"Though you work for Earthenhouse, something tells me that you might not respect a direct order from him to not go public with what you know. That's where I come in."

Perpetua let out a short, bitter laugh. Her knuckles whitened on the armrests. "So, is this where we bring out the thumbscrews? Is there a rack in the basement next to the high-efficiency furnace?"

The phone on Christina's desk rang. She stabbed a look at it. It stopped ringing. She looked again at Perpetua. "I intend you to sign a nondisclosure contract."

"That's optimistic."

Christina pulled a folder from the pile and held it up. "You will do so willingly. And when you do, it will be in blood, not with spit, as Earthenhouse does it." Her lip curled. "I am a traditionalist when it comes to such things."

"Why?" Perpetua snapped.

Christina's fine eyebrows drew together. "Why, what?"

"Why do you expect me to sign? Unless you're going to use magic—which I expect would be illegal, or else you'd have put the whammy on me already—you intend to talk me through this. So, just cut the crap and tell me why!"

Christina stood up, looked down at her desk, and flexed her fingers, as if contemplating putting a particularly mean hex on Perpetua. Then she dropped her hands and looked Perpetua in the eyes. "The Mores were put in place for good reasons," she said crisply. "No, they were not popular reasons, but surrender never is. The Celts had us beaten in every way: technologically, strategically, by the numbers. We had to find a different way to survive. And that way was making sure the Celts—all of humanity—had no reason to hate us." She gestured at herself. "*We* could talk the warriors down. Some of the trolls could make themselves useful. Some of the goblins were not too ugly. But the rest? We had to make the humans forget about us, about our magic. Only when the humans thought they were safe from us could we be safe from them."

Her eyes, Perpetua thought, were both fiercer and more vulnerable than her voice. *You could almost start to feel sympathetic* —Perpetua choked that off.

"That's what we created," Christina went on. "It hasn't been easy, and I know it hasn't been fair, but it allowed us to survive. Earthenhouse knows this. What was it he said to you? 'Nobody chases us with pitchforks anymore'? *We* created that reality."

The phone on Christina's desk rang once again. She glared at it. It let out two more rings, and then a contrite-sounding partial ring.

She looked again at Perpetua. "I know you came to this city less than two months ago and with not much money, Miss

Collins. You've worked hard. After just two months, the goblins look up to you almost as much as they do to Earthenhouse. I know that you can understand why Earthenhouse has had to take the extraordinary measures he has. I know you've seen the work of Adamant and Amnesia House. The world we have created isn't perfect, but it has been built with great care, because the alternative is worse. Everybody knows this except"—she jerked her head at Fergus—"except for some idealistic young fools who haven't truly experienced the full range of human hostility. This world of ours cannot be thrown away. I know this. Adamant knows this, though he's loath to say it. I daresay even Earthenhouse would admit it, too.

"And you, Miss Collins." She turned the folder around and opened it. She pulled an X-Acto knife from her hair and dropped it on the paper. "Don't threaten this hard-won reality for some seductive, illusionary ideal. Sign the nondisclosure contract and walk away. Please."

Perpetua stood up. She took the contract and picked up the X-Acto knife. She read through the document carefully. She looked at Fergus and saw him looking back at her, bewildered, and innocent as a newborn baby. She looked at the contract again, then at the X-Acto knife. She brushed her thumb lightly on the blade. Christina grew still.

Perpetua set the contract down and placed the X-Acto knife on top of it. Then she looked Christina in the eye, and said: "No."

The blood rushed to Christina's cheeks. "What did you say?"

"I said, no! You want me to keep quiet like a good little girl? You want me to keep this lie going? After all you've done? After all the suffering I've seen? The answer is no! *N. O.* So, what are you going to do about that, eh?" She set her hands on her hips. "Kill me? If that were an option, I'd be dead by now. So, the answer's no!"

Christina leaned forward. And as she leaned forward, Perpetua felt the pressure to sit down increase until it was like an elephant was trying to get on her lap. She fought it, gripped the edge of Christina's desk, but her fingers slipped. She fell back into her chair with a thud and a grunt, while Christina stood up to her full height. She seemed taller now.

"In this situation, when the Mores are threatened, the use of magic is *not* illegal." Christina showed her sharp, white teeth. "There are spells we can use."

With an effort, Perpetua kept her breathing steady. "Spells?"

"To make you forget. I don't want to use them, because it's hard to control where they stop." She took a deep breath. "But I will, if I have to. Will this change your answer? Just nod if it does."

Silence stretched. Perpetua looked at Fergus and saw him watching her with wondering eyes. She looked up at Christina. Then she shook her head, hard.

Christina clapped a hand to her face. "Dammit! You are the most stubborn human being I've ever met! And, trust me, that is saying a lot!" Her hand dropped. "But if that is your choice, then so be it."

She walked slowly around the desk. Perpetua couldn't move. She couldn't speak. She could only stare, wide-eyed.

Christina stood over her, reached down, and tilted Perpetua's chin up. "I'm sorry."

On her desk, the phone rang again. Christina let go of Perpetua and snatched up the receiver. "I said, I was not to be disturbed!"

She froze. On the other end of the line, Perpetua could hear an agent shouting. "Ms. Bell. We've been trying to tell you, Earthenhouse is here. And he's not taking no for an answer."

Footsteps were coming down the hall. Heavy footsteps. Suddenly, Christina's enchantment lifted. Heart racing, Perpetua jumped up and pulled Fergus to his feet as the door crashed open behind them. A faerie agent sailed through, smacking headfirst into the desk, where he crumpled and lay still.

Howard ambled in. "Deliver message from Earthenhouse!" he rumbled.

Christina jumped back, her hands curled into claws. "What is the meaning of this?"

Perpetua grinned. "This would be the cavalry." She looked at Howard and nodded at the faerie sprawled on the floor. "Was that the message?"

Howard shook his massive head. "That message from me." His grin showed all his teeth. "Troll diplomacy."

Perpetua laughed happily. "Fergus, come on, let's—"

A throat-clearing sound in the doorway snapped her head around. Earthenhouse stood there. "You're an idiot," he said, with grim deliberation.

Perpetua shot him a look of protest. "But—"

"Because of you, humanity knows."

## Chapter 34
# The Veil Drops

Earthenhouse pushed past Perpetua, his gaze fixed on Christina.

"Humanity knows, Ms. Bell," said Earthenhouse. "Because of that stunt of yours on the rooftops."

"That 'stunt' would not have been necessary if you had handed Mr. Fergus and Miss Collins over to us, as we had asked," Christina cut in.

Earthenhouse splayed both his long-fingered hands on her desk. "Miss Collins and Mr. Fergus are under my protection! If you think I'd tolerate you laying a hand on either of them, then you are a bigger fool than I've taken you for! Still, that does not compare to what you've just done!"

Behind Earthenhouse, Perpetua folded her arms across her chest and smirked at Christina.

Christina leaned forward. Her teeth looked suddenly sharper. "Are you threatening me?"

"Madam Bell . . ." A faerie agent stood in the doorway, casting a wary eye at Howard. "Earthenhouse and his troll did not come alone." He took a step back and crouched, hands ready, as Howard half-turned toward him and growled.

Christina frowned at Earthenhouse. "What does he mean?"

Earthenhouse extended a hand past the broken door. "Have a look for yourself."

Christina stepped around the desk and over the fallen door. Perpetua grabbed Fergus's hand and followed. Earthenhouse loped behind them.

In the lobby, the two remaining faerie agents were staring warily out the big windows. At the edge of the parking lot, silhouetted among the topiaries, goblins stood, their arms crossed.

One of the agents leaned in close to Christina, but Perpetua could hear him as he whispered. "We've counted two dozen around the perimeter, plus one more troll. They have us surrounded."

Perpetua smiled. Twenty-four goblins and one troll, plus her, plus Fergus, plus Earthenhouse, plus Howard, versus five faeries. *I'm liking these odds.*

Christina gnawed her upper lip, thoughtfully. "Reinforcements?" she murmured. The agent nodded.

Christina turned to Earthenhouse, chin rising, all confidence. "Reinforcements are on the way, Thorsen. Are you sure you're on the right path?"

Earthenhouse was impassive. "I have reinforcements, too, Christina."

Perpetua felt the tension rising in the room like the air before a thunderstorm.

"Do you honestly want to start a war, Earthenhouse?" Christina asked.

"Is there any reason left to keep the peace?" Earthenhouse growled. "We have given the faeries so much for so long for one reason only: to keep the humans unaware of us. For that, we eke out what life we can at the edges of things, while you live in comfort. With that one reason gone, what does peace between us matter?"

Christina's hands clenched. "What are you talking about?"

Earthenhouse glared. He pointed behind him at a television set suspended from the ceiling. "Check the news."

Christina stared at him. Then she looked up at the lobby's television screen. At her nod, the blank screen flickered on.

Still holding Fergus by the hand, Perpetua stepped forward for a better view. The local news channel showed a dark and grainy scene that looked like video taken on a cheap smartphone. The crowd noise surged like surf. Horns honked. Voices yelled. It was hard to see what was going on until Perpetua picked out the image of the Royal York Hotel. The camera panned up.

"What are they?" gasped a voice on the film. "What are they doing?"

Then she saw it: the shimmering on the building that revealed itself to be goblins clambering their way up the stonework, hopping over windows, racing for the roof, then linking up to provide the bridge across University Avenue.

"I think those are gargoyles!" said another voice. "You know, the statues."

"What?"

"I saw them! They came alive and just swarmed up the side of the building. I couldn't believe it!"

Somebody laughed. "No!"

Someone else shouted, "Are you getting this?"

The crowd shouted as Fergus and Perpetua ran across the goblin bridge.

"Did you see that? What the heck was that?"

The bridge came apart, goblins swarming back away across the face of the building. The people's chatter ebbed a moment, until . . .

"Hey! Look at that!"

A slim figure leaped across the gap, arms outflung, soaring like a bird.

The camera juddered. The video stopped.

"This video," said the news announcer, "uploaded to YouTube an hour ago, already has over a hundred thousand views, since links to it raced throughout Twitter and other social media outlets. We have received other cell phone videos from people at the scene, including this one, which we believe was shot moments earlier."

Another clip, this one of a downtown street, caught Perpetua and Fergus miraculously avoiding traffic. "What the heck?" said a voice on the clip. "How did they not get hit?"

"Hey, look at that!" The lens jerked around. It caught a faerie agent in mid-leap, landing lightly on the hood of a speeding car, then running across a series of moving car and truck roofs and hoods before leaping off into the shadow of a building.

Christina's mouth tightened. Perpetua chuckled. Then she caught Earthenhouse's eye and stopped laughing.

Christina changed the channel with a flick of her hand.

The screen showed a bearded man who was, according to the caption, a professor of architecture. "Look at this," he said. He held up a large photograph. "This picture of the Gooderham building behind me was shot just months ago." He pointed. "You see the bumps on the roofline? Statuary, the lot of them. But look now!" He waved at the camera, and it swung up to focus on the now unbroken roofline. "All gone! Where did they go?"

Christina flexed her fingers. "These are your people, Thorsen. Where *did* they go?"

"Where do you think?" Earthenhouse snapped. "They know Toronto is no longer safe for them."

Christina changed the channel again. The screen showed a female news anchor. Behind her was a shot of crowds in the public square Perpetua had walked through weeks ago, then studded with statues that she now realized had been goblins: goblins allergic to lavender. Now, the plinths were empty.

"Many of these installations were created through contracts with the City of Toronto," said the anchor. "Contracts which our news team has found did not follow the standard tendering process and had minimal public consultation. This revelation has led to questions for the mayor's office. What exactly were the artworks installed on the rooftops throughout the city, and does this have anything to do with the unbelievable footage now going viral?"

The scene changed again, to the lobby of City Hall. "The mayor was not prepared for this news when questioned about the contracts," the anchor added.

The mayor, flanked by advisers, gripped the podium in both hands. "I can't comment on a bunch of videos that I have not seen, and which may not exist!"

Reporters started holding up cell phones, screens forward. A dozen recorded shouts of "Hey, look at that!" echoed through the room.

The mayor winced. "Aw, damn!"

The channel flipped. An American reporter stood in front of crowds in Times Square. "Officials are at a loss to explain why so many statues in Central Park have suddenly disappeared. They say that these installations were not made through city contracts, unlike what has been reported in Toronto. Indeed, city officials reacted with surprise on learning that the installations had been there at all."

On another channel: "Crowds have gathered in Leicester Square. Ever since the incidents in Toronto, Canada, people are watching the statues, looking for them to move."

A phone on the front desk rang. One of the agents got it. "Hello?"

Christina pinched the bridge of her nose and shook her head. "You've ruined everything!" she snapped. Perpetua wasn't sure if Christina was talking to her or Earthenhouse. Possibly both.

"I told you," Earthenhouse growled. "You attacked the people under my protection. You showed off. We did nothing but protect ourselves."

On the television screen, a reporter stood on a downtown street thronged with people. "It's late, but crowds have stayed downtown. Others are coming in from the suburbs. Many are watching the remaining statues to see if they'll move. The police are encouraging people to go home, but haven't yet called for a curfew."

Behind the reporter, Perpetua saw security guards she recognized in the crowd, helping the police to ease people back. Patrick was among them. He looked worried.

"No," said the faerie agent into the phone. "No, you cannot. You will not be welcome!" The agent hung up the phone, looking grim. "Madam Bell? That was a reporter from the *Toronto Star*. She wanted directions to this place. I think the media are converging on our location."

Christina spluttered. "What? How do they even know where we are?"

"Because I supplied them with the address," said Earthenhouse. He smiled minimally. "They're my reinforcements."

Her eyes flared. "Why would you *do* that?"

"If humans can see us now, they should also see you." His smile sharpened. "Why should we hog the attention?"

An agent turned from the window. "News trucks arriving!" Outside, a convoy of trucks, all sprouting satellite dishes, turned into the parking lot.

Christina went white as ice. Perpetua almost felt sorry for her. Almost. "You could sneak out the back way," she said.

"There is no back way," Christina snapped. "There's a fence behind this place, and a creek!"

Outside, van doors slammed. Feet crunched the asphalt.

"Shall we go?" asked Earthenhouse. "Shall we see how you manage this crisis you created?" He loped out the door.

"Where are you going?" Christina yelled. "Stop him!"

The faerie agents tensed. Howard growled low. Earthenhouse turned in the doorway, tilting his head. "Come, now, Ms. Bell. Do you really want to start a war when the whole world is watching?"

He stepped out the door.

# Chapter 35
# Meet the Press

Camera lights flooded on when Earthenhouse stepped out of the front door, leading the others behind him. Christina winced and threw up a hand against the glare.

The crowd gasped. It struck Perpetua that he must no longer be veiling the full goblinness of his build and features. He was letting people see him the way she saw him.

She stared in wonder. *Is this being broadcast live? It's probably breaking news. Is Mom watching? What would she say if she could see me now?*

Her cell phone buzzed. She pressed the button to shut it off, but it buzzed again.

*Not now!* She pressed and held the button until the phone powered off.

Earthenhouse cleared his throat. "Good evening. My name is Thorsen Phileas Earthenhouse. I believe you have some questions for me."

For a long moment, the reporters said nothing—something Perpetua had never seen reporters do. They just stared. Finally, a balding, dark-haired, bearded man in his thirties stepped forward hesitantly. He handed Earthenhouse a microphone and quickly stepped back.

"Who are you?" shouted somebody in the back.

Earthenhouse cleared his throat again. "My name, as I said, is Thorsen Phileas Earthenhouse. I am the founder and CEO of T.P. Earthenhouse: Bouncers, Rare Coins, and Art Installations, and holder of a number of art installation contracts with the City of Toronto." He tipped his head sideways. "The lady behind me and to my left, attempting to hide in my shadow, is Ms. Christina Bell, president of the Toronto branch of the St. Brigid Society and Cultural Association. Neither of us is human. The young woman on my right is Miss Perpetua Collins, my secretary—" He coughed. "Ah—I should say, my administrative assistant. You may have heard our names recently."

Standing beside Earthenhouse, Perpetua gave an embarrassed grin and waved at the people behind the lights.

The reporter who'd handed Earthenhouse a microphone picked up another one. "We've seen gargoyles leaving their places and climbing buildings. They're clearly alive." He cleared his throat. "They look like you. We have been hearing names from Celtic mythology." He took a deep breath. "Mr. Earthenhouse, are you a goblin? Ms. Bell, are you a faerie?"

Christina reddened. She grabbed the microphone from Earthenhouse's hand. "Don't be absurd!"

Earthenhouse snatched the microphone back. "It's all true."

Perpetua shot up her hand. "Tie-breaking vote!"

"Of course, I'm a goblin," said Earthenhouse. "Look at me. How could I possibly be human?"

The reporter gaped. Still, Perpetua had to give him points for being willing to contemplate the impossible. "How long have you been in this city? How is it that we haven't noticed you until now?"

"We have always been here," said Earthenhouse. "You haven't noticed us, because we didn't want you to."

Somebody else in the back shouted. "All those fairy tales? They're all true?"

"Some of them," said Earthenhouse. "The question is—what are you going to do about it?"

More shouts from reporters. "There are stories of human babies being stolen and changelings put in their place," a mop-haired, forty-something woman in the back shouted. "Are faerie secret societies holding humans hostage?"

Christina stood ramrod-straight. "That is a ridiculous question! Of course, we do not hold humans hostage!"

Perpetua waved a hand to get attention. "Actually, you are kind of holding me hostage—"

"Shut up!" Christina snapped.

The female reporter pointed at Earthenhouse. "Have you, or any of your kind, signed contracts with people, promising gold in exchange for their first-born children?"

Perpetua frowned at the reporter. "*Your kind*"? *What the hell?*

Earthenhouse rocked back on his heels. His smile was tight and tense. "Such stories are typically embellishments by individuals who reneged on the terms of their contract."

More reporters shouted questions; Perpetua could hardly hear the words through the babble. Earthenhouse tilted further back, and Perpetua remembered the look he'd put on when Christina confronted them in his office. Christina stood proudly straight, but apparently relaxed, arms folded. The glance she shot at Earthenhouse said, "*I told you so.*"

"How can we trust you?" said the mop-haired reporter. "You've been hiding for years, masquerading as humans. How do we know you aren't secretly plotting against us?"

"Hey!" Perpetua snatched the microphone from Earthenhouse's hand. The cameras and their spotlights swung to focus on her, and for a moment, she squinted against the light. But the hostility behind the question itched at her feet and sent shocks up her spine. "Would you ask these questions if these were refugees seeking asylum?"

*Yes, some would.*

She tightened her grip on the microphone. *It would still be wrong.*

"Look." She took a breath to stop her voice from shaking. "Goblins, faeries, and trolls are people. They're just . . . different kinds of people. So, you haven't noticed them. They've just been living their lives, not bothering anybody. So, what? That's their choice. We all have a right to stand up and be who we are!"

She ran out of words and stood there, blinking at the lights. For a moment, she had forgotten that the cameras were there. One or two reporters were nodding their heads. Some were shaking their heads. And she suddenly realized where she was, just how many people were probably watching. She felt the heat rise in her cheeks. She ducked her head and turned away, and there was Fergus, gazing at her with awed brown eyes.

Suddenly, the back door to a news truck popped open. A young man hopped out. "Hey! Something's happening downtown. Something big. The crowd's turning nasty."

Earthenhouse tensed. Christina narrowed her eyes. Perpetua looked from one to the other. The way back to the motel lobby, with its TV set, was blocked by faerie agents, so she jumped off the front steps and ran to the reporter. "Show me!"

He hesitated only a moment, then opened the back doors wide, tilted a screen forward, and turned the volume up.

The screen showed the King-Bay intersection, full of shouting people. Police officers yelled and struggled to push the crowds back.

"We're not sure who threw the first stone," a reporter on site shouted. He ducked. The picture jerked as something almost hit the camera. "A youth, who appeared to be drunk, probably. One of the statues caught the stone and threw it back. The young man was taken to the hospital. He may need stitches. The violence then escalated."

Behind the reporter, Perpetua spotted a young man with a studded leather jacket, his fingers curled around a fist-sized stone. On the building wall in front of him, a goblin stood, glaring.

A young woman grabbed the punk's arm. "Stop it! They're not doing anything to you!"

The punk shoved her back and took aim.

From his position in the fountain in the centre of the square, Gunther stood up. He was gigantic, radiating menace: a monster. He fixed his eyes on the punk and roared, showing teeth the size of granite slabs.

The crowd screamed.

Gunther jumped off the fountain. The sidewalk beneath him cracked. The crowd scattered, and the punk turned pasty white. He hurled the stone. It crashed into Gunther's head, rebounded into the air, and then landed on the sidewalk beside him.

Gunther's deep growl shook the camera. He put his head down and charged.

Perpetua gasped. "Gunther! No!"

"Gunther?" said the reporter who had opened the truck. "That thing has a name?"

"Of course, he does!" she snapped. "He's the sweetest, gentlest troll you could possibly meet. He wouldn't hurt—"

On the screen, Gunther swung his arm wide. Three teenagers sailed over the heads of the crowd.

"—anyone who didn't deserve it . . ."

Two more punks flew into the air, screaming.

Perpetua's hands flew to her mouth. "Gunther!"

People yelled. Rocks showered. Gunther roared and swung.

"Stand down!"

The camera jerked, trying to find the source of the shout. It focused on a police officer. Compared to Gunther, he looked small. But he had his gun drawn.

"Stand down!" the officer repeated. "Hands where I can see them! Stand down!"

In the crowd behind the police officer, Patrick rushed forward. "Officer! Back off! Please! You don't know what you're dealing with!" Another policeman pulled him back.

Gunther roared.

There was a gunshot. Perpetua flinched and cried out.

On the screen, Gunther looked down, puzzled, as a trickle of dark liquid ran down his chest. He looked up, growled again, and lunged forward.

"No!" Perpetua screamed.

The officer fired five more shots.

Gunther stopped and stood, swaying. His stony chest was striped with dark trickles. He took a step, staggered. The crowd scrambled back as he fell forward, slow and terrifying, like a collapsing building. He landed with a jarring crash.

Perpetua struggled to breathe. Around her, no one said anything.

Earthenhouse bounded down the steps, marched up to one of the reporters, and snatched the woman's microphone.

He looked at Christina with his shark-black eyes. "His blood is on your hands." Then he rounded on the reporters. His voice shook. "His blood is on *all* your hands."

"Thorsen . . ." Christina said softly, in a voice that hardly sounded like hers. She was pleading. "Thorsen, stop."

"Now you see why we hide," said Earthenhouse. "Now you see the need for secrets! And now that those secrets are out, we have no choice but to defend ourselves."

"Thorsen, please!" Christina shouted.

Earthenhouse faced the cameras, stony-faced, his eyes glittering. "What happens next is up to you, humans. Unless you get your people under control within the next two hours, I will be forced to take the strongest possible measures."

Christina paled. "Earthenhouse, you wouldn't dare—"

"We have the means to fight back," said Earthenhouse, still speaking to the cameras.

Every faerie went stiff as steel. *They're appalled*, Perpetua thought. *No: terrified*.

"I am a goblin," Earthenhouse went on. He cracked a ferocious grin. "We plan for every contingency. If I can no longer help my people live in peace among the humans, then we goblins will make do."

Perpetua stepped closer to Earthenhouse. "Sir? What are you doing?"

Earthenhouse paused, then put a long-boned hand over the microphone. He looked her in the eyes. "Miss Collins," he said. "Howard will ensure that you and Mr. Fergus reach safety. After he does, please go back to North Bay."

"Sir?" Her voice rose. "Sir, what are you going to do?"

He turned back to the cameras and took his hand off the microphone. "Humanity has two hours," he growled. "If they want monsters, then I'll give them one."

He opened his hand and let the mike drop to the pavement.

And then, in a blink, he wasn't there. The goblins that were with him were gone. Even Trixie the troll. But not Howard.

The reporters gaped and milled around. "Hey, what?"

Christina backed up, waving her agents toward the motel door. "Get back inside. We need to regroup."

"What about them?" An agent aimed his dark glasses at Perpetua and Fergus. Howard, standing behind them, crossed his arms and rumbled.

Christina's eyes flicked to Perpetua, then Howard. "Let them go. The damage they could do pales in comparison to what's being done right now."

The reporters were still looking for answers. "Hey!" shouted one. "What did he mean, 'humanity has two hours'? Two hours for what?"

The door swung shut behind her with a final slam. One of the reporters pounded on it, then pulled on it, before backing up. "Where's the back door to this place?"

Perpetua, Fergus, and Howard stood at the edge of the parking lot, watching the reporters mill about and babble.

"Are we still live?"

"No. All the stations are focused downtown."

"We're just staring at a locked door. Waste of time!"

Reaching out behind her, Perpetua guided Fergus and Howard backward.

Fergus stepped on a discarded plastic juice bottle that crumpled with a crackling sound.

The camera spotlights swung on them like laser-guided missiles. "Hey! What did that goblin mean, 'humanity has two hours'?" the reporters shouted, surging forward.

Perpetua grabbed Fergus by the hand, wheeled, and started running. "Come on! Out the back way!"

"Uh . . ." Fergus stumbled. "Didn't Ms. Bell say there wasn't a back way?"

"We have a troll!"

Howard grinned. He loped on ahead, toward the chain link fence. One good kick, and the fence lay flat. They hopped over a set of abandoned railroad tracks and into a wooded field, then stumbled down an embankment to a narrow creek.

There were no electric lights out here, but the moonlight was bright enough to show a heavy branch lying across the creek. Perpetua and Fergus crossed, one after the other, teetering. Howard sloshed across in two strides. The shouts of pursuing reporters faded behind them.

They climbed up a hill and came to a scrubby field bordered by a roadway that ran a short distance before diving beneath an elevated highway. Perpetua and Fergus stood, breathing heavily.

Fergus turned and gave Perpetua's hand a playful shake. "So, what are we?" he said, smiling. "Cousins? Brother and sister? We must be awfully close for you to go out of your way like this to help me."

Perpetua bit her lip. "Look, we're just friends, okay?" She swung his hand, but couldn't meet his eyes. "Just friends. And I'm going to get us out of this mess."

"How?"

She opened her mouth to answer, but found nothing to say. "I'll think of something."

She turned and bumped into the mop-haired reporter. The

woman was breathing heavily, and her pant legs were splattered with mud, but her grin was triumphant.

"Hi there!" She grabbed Perpetua's arm. "Now, Miss Perpetua Collins, you're going to answer a question. What did that goblin mean by giving humanity an ultimatum? Two hours until what? Is this a terrorist threat?"

Howard grunted.

"No!" Perpetua wrenched her arm free. "I don't know what he meant—"

Howard grunted again. His nose wrinkled.

Perpetua froze. "Um . . . that perfume you're wearing. It wouldn't happen to have lavender in it, would it?"

"Yeah. So?"

Perpetua threw herself to the ground, pulling Fergus down with her.

"ACHOO!"

Howard's sneeze blew over Perpetua's head and picked up a cloud of dust that settled on them gently.

Perpetua and Fergus climbed to their feet. "So, trolls are allergic to lavender, too," said Perpetua. "Good to know."

Howard sniffed and rubbed his nose.

"Uh . . ." Fergus pointed. "That reporter is on her back across the road. Should we go and help her?"

As they looked, the mop-haired reporter struggled to her feet. Casting a fearful glance at Howard, she took off at a stumbling run.

Perpetua shrugged. "She'll be fine."

"That's good." Fergus looked at her expectantly. "So, what do we do now?"

Perpetua opened her mouth, then closed it again. Finally, she said, "I don't know."

All she had to guide her was Earthenhouse's warning to leave the city.

*I can't do that, though. I just can't. It's going to get really bad for some really good people, and I can't just run away and leave them.*

*But where do I go?*

An engine roared. Wheels squealed around a curve. Perpetua flinched as headlights flashed in her eyes.

A taxi screeched to a halt beside them. "What the heck?" said Perpetua.

Adamant rolled down the passenger-side window. "So, you getting in, or what?"

## Chapter 36
# Job Action

Perpetua gaped at Adamant. "What are you doing here?"

Adamant opened the door and hopped out of the cab. "Thought you needed a ride."

"I do, but . . ." Perpetua waved her hands. "How did you know?"

"Saw you on television. I liked what you had to say in front of the media. I've also heard rumours about what you and this Fergus kid talked to Earthenhouse about before the faeries crashed your office." He nodded at Fergus. "Is it true? Do you have a plan to make contact between humanity and the goblins work?"

Fergus looked at him blankly. "Do I what?"

Adamant's eyes narrowed. "What's your name, son?"

"Aloysius Fergus, sir." He nodded at Perpetua. "At least, that's what she told me."

Adamant leaned back. "Oh, dear."

"Yeah," said Perpetua. "Things are kind of a mess right now."

"You don't know the half of it," said Adamant. "I think Earthenhouse is about to do something we'll all regret."

Perpetua's heart sank. "What are you hearing?"

"Feeling, mostly," said Adamant. "Earthenhouse's supporters

have disappeared from the rooftops. Our goblins know something is up. And that ultimatum? Goblins keep their promises. That's why we're so good with contracts; just ask Rumpelstiltskin."

"Rumpel—"

"Not important," he snapped. "I think you're the only one left who can stop Earthenhouse from doing something stupid, but first, I have to ask you something serious." He jerked his head at Fergus. "Do you think his crazy plan could work?"

Perpetua sputtered. "But—I-I don't know the details of his plan. He designed it. He wrote it down. It's back at Earthenhouse's office!"

"I'm not asking if you know the details, girl," said Adamant. "Only if you think it's possible for humans and goblins to get along. Do you?"

"Yes!" she said, and blinked in surprise. "Yes," she said again. She looked at Fergus and took his hand. He looked at it, then at her. "Yes, I do. Because it's been done." She looked at Adamant. "And because, right now, I don't think we have a choice."

Adamant nodded. "Okay, then. We'd better get into the city." He motioned them toward the cab.

"Where'd you get a cab?" asked Perpetua.

Adamant nodded at Fergus. "It's his cab."

Her eyes widened. "You stole it?"

Adamant's brow furrowed. "Nah. Giving it back."

Fergus pointed. "That's my cab? I don't remember it."

"You will." Adamant pulled him forward. "Just get behind the wheel."

Fergus looked nervous. "But I've never seen this thing before in my life! I don't remember learning to drive! I don't know a thing about this city!"

"Fergus, please, you can do this," said Perpetua. "Just do as he says."

"C'mon!" Adamant shoved Fergus into the driver's seat.

Fergus sat, then straightened up. "Oh."

Perpetua slipped in beside him. "Oh, what?"

"I know how to drive a cab." He rubbed his hands along the steering wheel. "How did I learn this, all of a sudden?"

Adamant hopped into the back seat and slammed the door. "It's how amnesia reset works. The facts and knowledge remain; only the personality gets wiped."

"*All* of the personality?" Perpetua stared at Fergus. She bit her lip.

"Yup," said Adamant. "What develops is an entirely new person." Looking from Perpetua to Fergus, and back again, he added softly, "Sorry."

She looked away, then looked around to make sure everybody was aboard. "Come on, Howard," she called out the window.

Howard looked dubiously at the remaining back door. At Perpetua's command, he shrugged, crammed himself in, and then pulled the door shut.

"Comfortable back there?" asked Perpetua.

"Kinda," Adamant grunted. Perpetua looked back. Howard was taking up seven-eighths of the back seat, with Adamant pressed up against the window.

Fergus turned the key in the ignition, then looked at his fingers in surprise. "I know everything about this vehicle. This is the weirdest feeling of . . ." He snapped his fingers.

"Déjà vu?" asked Adamant.

"Yeah! That's it!"

"So, you've got your ride," Adamant said to Perpetua. He shifted and prodded Howard to give himself some breathing space. "What now? I've done what I can. You've got to take the next step."

Perpetua drew a shaky breath. "I don't know. I mean, what have you heard from your friends?"

"Everything I told you," Adamant snapped. "We know Earthenhouse is planning something big—he just said so! But we have no idea where. Think, girl! If he has something to threaten humanity with, it's not something he can produce in just two hours. He has to have prepared for it."

"He wouldn't tell me!" she said defensively.

"Of course not. But surely you got some sort of hint? You investigated him, right?"

"Adelaide Street?" Fergus said suddenly. He looked at her. "That sounds like a place I'm supposed to go. Is that important?"

*Where he used to pick me up at the end of every day.* That stung. It stung even more when she looked at him sharply and saw only a blank slate of innocence and wonder. She looked ahead and clenched her jaw against the tears. "No," she said. "Not Adelaide. I don't—"

Then, suddenly, she had it. "Eglinton subway station!"

"Why there?"

"Because the goblins were digging something there that wasn't on the foreman's plans," she replied. "When the foreman asked about it, they distracted him and changed the blueprints." She turned. "Fergus, can you get us to Eglinton Station?"

"In this city?" he protested. "I only just—" He froze. "Oh."

"What?" she asked.

"I *do* know how to get to Eglinton Station." He put the car in gear, and they sped off into the night.

The sky lightened toward dawn as they drove into the city. The rising sun turned the skyscrapers a burning orange.

Perpetua turned on the radio and instantly regretted it. There was nothing new to report, so the anchors went on and on about what had happened earlier that night, and the threat Earthenhouse had made. All she learned was that the gargoyles had vanished from every downtown building. The police had broken up the big crowd in the square, but people still milled about. There were no human casualties, the reports said, only injuries. There was no report on Gunther.

She switched the radio off.

"The world is changed," said Adamant, softly.

She looked over her shoulder at him. "What do you mean?"

"You know what I mean. And though you're young, you're old enough to have some idea. It's the end of the world as you know it. Everybody will remember where they were when they heard this piece of news. Because, from here on in, nothing will ever be the same again."

"Not me," said Fergus. "All I see is . . . new."

"You're lucky." Adamant shook his head. "It's all opportunity for you. It's all going forward. And there is that. But the rest of us still have to remember the world we left behind. We're going to miss parts of it."

"Yeah," Perpetua whispered.

Fergus pulled up to the curb. "We're here."

They were at the corner of Yonge and Eglinton. Skyscrapers stretched above them. Grumbling buses were turning off the street and heading into the station's terminal. At one of the station entrances, early morning commuters filed inside. Perpetua scanned them for signs of anxiety or excitement.

*They're acting like it's a normal Tuesday. You'd think nothing happened last night.*

She started forward. Adamant caught her arm. "Be careful," he said. "Remember, the veil is gone. I think the last thing we need right now is more cameras."

She glanced at him. He looked every inch your average homeless person, even without his cart. Fergus looked like a slightly scruffy young man. Howard . . .

*Oh, right.* "Let's move fast, then."

They entered the station as if there was nothing unusual. Then, Howard politely held the door for the man entering after him. The man stopped and stared. Other commuters plowed in behind him. A crowd piled up.

"Howard, hurry up!" Perpetua called. Howard let go of the door and lumbered after her.

The station was full of the sound of rushing feet. From the platform below came the roar of an arriving train. On the plasma screens, a morning talk show host beamed at the camera. "Next on Coffee Television: Do you think your coworker might secretly be a faerie? We offer tips on how you can find out!"

At the mezzanine level, they found the hoarding mobbed by construction workers. Perpetua spotted Flo, Jo, and Stu off to one side, looking sheepish. Moe jiggled the doorknob while Phil banged on the door and shouted.

Perpetua and Mr. Thompson spotted each other at the same time. "What happened?" she demanded.

"They locked us out," Phil cut in. "They sent us up here and then locked the door. It's just stoners down in the worksite, digging their big hole."

"What? How—?"

"They told us the cinnamon rolls were on sale, a dollar a dozen," said Thompson. "I know I should have been suspicious, but if you've ever had their frosted—"

"Never mind that!" Perpetua snapped. "What big hole?"

"Right in the middle of the bore area," Thompson replied. "Way bigger and way deeper than what was on the plans. I don't know how they kept it hidden for so long. What's going on?"

"I'm going to find out." Perpetua shouldered through the crowd of workers and pulled at the door. It wouldn't budge.

"Howard?" she called. The troll ambled up, the sea of people parting before him. "Open this, please?"

Howard tried the handle, shook it, then turned back to her. "Locked," he rumbled.

Perpetua slapped her forehead. She'd never realized a troll could be so gentle. Then, an idea came to her, and she stepped back a few paces. "Howard, get the door, please?"

He gripped the handle and pulled. The door came off its hinges. He meandered over, holding his trophy, looking proud.

"Thanks, Howard. Now, put the door down."

He set it down with a clatter. Passing commuters faltered,

stopped, and stared. The construction workers stood around with hands shoved in their pockets, avoiding everybody's gaze.

Perpetua saw one man pull a cell phone from his pocket and aim it. *Crap! Camera!*

"Let's go!" She charged, batting the cell phone out of the man's hand as she passed, sending it on an arching curve down the stairs.

"Hey!" the man shouted.

"Sorry!" she called back, hopping over the fallen door. As she passed Thompson, she looked him in the eye. "Post guards." Then she dashed through the opening in the plywood barrier.

Thompson shouted at his workers to follow, and Perpetua led the charge toward the scaffolding stairs.

She didn't notice Phil falling behind and slipping into an office, but as she approached the door in the middle of the stairs, he was beside her again, hoisting a pickaxe. She grabbed his arm. "What the hell are you doing?"

He looked at the axe, then at her. "Um . . ."

"Thought you'd do some digging, did you?"

His face set. "This is . . . you know . . . just in case."

"Give me that!" She grabbed the axe and staggered under the sudden weight. Hefting it in both hands, she rounded on the construction workers. "We are *not* going in waving axes and pitchforks. If anyone has any torches, please extinguish them now! We're here to *talk*, got it?"

"Who died and made you God?" shouted one of the workers.

"No one," she shouted back. "But if you pick a fight with the trolls, people *will* die."

She stabbed her forefinger at Howard. He looked around and blinked at suddenly being the centre of attention.

The men looked contrite. Or, at least, cowed. "All right, then." Perpetua shoved the door open and then stopped dead.

Before, she'd been hit by a wall of sound. This time, it was a wall of silence. The cavern yawned. The walls had been smoothed, and a tunnel made for subways gaped at one end.

What was new lay at the centre of the cavern: a deep hole, located directly in front of the subway tunnel, and wide enough to swallow a tractor-trailer. Light the colour of embers stained the sides of the hole.

Perpetua became aware of a new sound: a low rumble, felt more in the chest than heard in the ear. As she braced the pickaxe on the scaffolding rail, a vibration buzzed up through the pick and into her hands. It sounded just like a truck on the street outside, or a subway underneath, but much, much louder.

And Perpetua realized that she'd heard the sound before. She'd been hearing it for days, throughout the city, even in areas where there wasn't a subway nearby.

Hauling the pickaxe up with both hands, she thumped down the scaffolding stairs. The others clattered behind. She ran awkwardly across the construction site toward the hole. It was guarded by a circle of goblins, punctuated by trolls. The goblins looked this way and that, down the hole, or at the approaching humans. The trolls just stood around the edge, staring outward, arms folded, unmovable. Perpetua recognized Chim and Chum, and one of the trolls was Fred.

When she was near enough, she looked past the edge and down. The hole was perfectly round. Its walls were smooth, and a set of stairs had been cut into the side, running down from the rim in a shallow spiral that vanished from view into the depths.

Another rumble shook the cavern. A blast of hot air caught Perpetua in the face. She stumbled back and spat out the taste of ashes.

Thompson marched up to the troll nearest the stairs—Fred. "Guys, what's going on?" His voice echoed through the cavern. "Who told you to dig a big hole right where the tracks are supposed to go?"

Fred glanced at Thompson, then stared into the vacant space above the man's head.

"Hey!" Thompson shouted. "I'm talking to you!"

Chim and Chum stood beside Fred, bobbing like pistons. "Chim! Chum!" Perpetua said. "What are you doing?"

They grinned and kept bobbing up and down. "Work to rule! Work to rule!" The cavern walls picked up their sing-song voices and threw them back. *Work to rule! Work to rule!*

Fergus took a step toward the edge. He stared down the hole in wonder. "What the heck is down there, anyway?"

Fred stopped him with an arm like a steel beam. He eased him back. "You no go," he rumbled. "Unsafe."

"Unsafe! Unsafe!" Chim and Chum chanted.

Thompson stared with wide eyes. "That's not your call, guys." But he backed away from the hole. He looked at Perpetua. "What do we do now?"

"I knew something was wrong," said Phil. "The stoners were always looking at me funny. I think they were making fun of me behind my back. And they always thought they knew better about construction. Just because they know rocks, they think they can build better than us. Well, now we know what's what. They were planning something all along, just like I said!"

"Phil!" Flo yelled. "Shut up!"

Perpetua had been heading over to belt Phil, but Flo's shout stopped her in mid-stride. Some of the goblins were glaring at Phil, but others were looking at Flo in surprise, and at Moe, Joe, and Stu, who stood behind Flo, arms folded aggressively as they scowled at Phil.

Perpetua saw Adamant frowning at Fred. She stepped to his side. "Adamant? What's down there? What on earth do they want with a hole that big?"

Adamant looked grim. "Whatever it is, it's something that scares the faeries something fierce."

A crash from above made them turn. Faerie agents ran down the stairs. She recognized a green dress among them. "Speak of the devil," she whispered to Adamant. "How did you know she'd turn up?"

"There are two reasons Bell didn't start a war with Earthenhouse right at their headquarters," he replied. "One, he brought the media's cameras with him. That was a brilliant move. And two: she knew he had to have an ace up his sleeve."

The faeries marched across the cavern toward them. Perpetua pushed back through the crowd of construction workers and met Christina halfway. "What are you doing here?" Her voice echoed. "I thought you were holed up in your secret castle."

Christina looked down her perfect nose. "You think we'd stand idly by while Earthenhouse threatens us?" She spoke quietly, yet her voice was clearly audible. "We were gathering reinforcements. If he has anything more than an empty threat, we'll deal with it."

"This is complicated enough as it is! You're not helping!"

Moe, Joe, Stu, and Flo frowned at the newcomers. They started forward, and Thompson went pale. He darted in front of them and pushed them back. He reached for Flo's arm, but she'd moved too fast.

"Actually," said Christina, still in that quietly confident tone, "I think the situation is simple." She nodded past Perpetua. "Earthenhouse has dug a big, conspicuous hole in the middle of a major construction site. He did it as a deliberate, hostile act against the Mores. The appropriate response would be to fill in the hole and seal everything up."

"But there could be people down there!" Perpetua shouted.

Flo shoved forward and planted herself beside Perpetua. "Excuse *me*," she said to Christina. "But just who are you?" She didn't raise her voice, but everybody around her took a step back. "You're not in charge here. You can't give orders at this site."

Christina lifted her eyes to the distant ceiling. Then she smiled. "We'll make this a government matter, if we have to. Whatever Earthenhouse has planned, it stops now."

"Hold your horses there, sister," Flo snapped. Perpetua stared at her in awe. "There's a process to be followed."

"You've got bulldozers. Use them!" Christina waved a slim hand. "Fill in that hole!"

"First of all," Flo said, "the only 'bulldozers' we have here are *guarding* that hole. It would take hours to get the equipment needed to open a hole on the surface and lower mechanical earth-movers down, and that's assuming the big guys back there don't object. Second: we don't know who, if anybody, is down there. We've had more than enough people buried by rockfalls at this worksite; we're not gonna start doing that deliberately. Third—"

She never got to third because Christina rounded on Perpetua and grabbed her arm. "This is your fault!"

Perpetua laughed. "How? How is this my fault?"

"Working with the goblins, treating them as colleagues, allowing them to believe that humans could see them as equals and let them come out of hiding! You see the damage you've done?"

Perpetua gritted her teeth as Christina's fingernails dug into her arm. She pushed back, hard. "Shove off, Tinkerbell!"

*Tinkerbell*. The moment the word left her lips, she knew it was a mistake.

Christina reared back. The light in the cavern darkened, as if she'd sucked it all away. For a fraction of a second, Perpetua saw shark-black eyes and fangs in a bright porcelain face. Christina raised a sparking-blue fist and—

"No!" Thompson threw up a hand. The sparkling knot thrown by Christina bounced off his palm. It hit Christina square in the chest and sent her staggering into the arms of one of her agents. All the faeries stared at Thompson in shock.

"Is that the best we can hope for?" he yelled. "Pretending to be human if we're beautiful enough, hiding who we are, not telling anyone, not even the people we love? Well, I'm sick of it! I'm sick of hiding who I am!" He stood up straight and tall. His gaze travelled through the crowd. "My mother was a descendant of the Daoine Sidhe! My great-grandfather was a member of the Seelie Court! I am a faerie, goddamn it, and I'm proud!" He paused, then added, "Also, I'm gay."

He stood breathing heavily. Nobody spoke. The rumble of

the pit throbbed around them. Finally, Flo stepped forward and patted his shoulder. "Gary, dear? That second part? Wasn't a surprise."

Christina, her agents, and the goblins stared, while the humans slapped Thompson on the back and gave him hugs. Phil, Perpetua noticed, was leaving, walking up the scaffold stairs and shaking his head in disgust.

Perpetua marched up to the goblins and trolls guarding the place where the spiral stairs led down into the hole. "Chim? Chum? Fred? Look at me."

Chim and Chum stopped bobbing. Chum's tail curled. Fred looked down at her. *They look nervous*, she thought. And that was something they hadn't looked when they'd been talking to Thompson, or with Christina in the vicinity.

"Chim? Chum? Fred? Tell the others who I am."

Chim and Chum grinned nervously. "They know."

She looked around. All the other goblins were watching her. "Who am I?"

Every one of them snapped to attention. "Mr. Earthenhouse's secretary," said a few voices.

"That's right. And what does that make me to you?"

"Boss Lady," Fred rumbled.

"Okay, then. Did Mr. Earthenhouse tell you to stop me?"

Fred shook his head. She looked at Chim and Chum. They looked at each other, then back at her. They shook their heads.

"Good! My friends and I are going down, and you are not going to stop us. Is that clear?"

Chim and Chum saluted. Fred stepped out of the way.

"Thanks, guys," said Perpetua, trying to sound confident and upbeat.

The ground rumbled and shook, like a train arriving. The sides of the pit brightened. Perpetua thought she could see black shadows in the red light shaking on the cavern walls.

"Howard! Adamant!" They looked up. She waved. "Come on!"

"And me?" said Fergus, in his childlike way. She had nearly forgotten he was there. She hesitated. There was a good chance they were all going into harm's way. What right did she have to drag Fergus down there?

"And me," he said, unexpectedly firm.

She held his eyes a moment. "All right." Holding him tightly by the hand, she led the way down the spiral stairs.

## Chapter 37
# Fired

The low rumble grew louder with every step. The stairs circled the gigantic hole, narrowing the shaft as they descended until the hole was half as wide at the bottom as it had been at the top. Even so, when they reached the bottom, they stared across a wide expanse.

Cut into the opposite wall was another tunnel, wide enough for two trains to pass, stretching into the distance. The red light glowing from its near end made it plainly visible. She heard a distant grumble of digging trolls and breathed in the smell of ash and smoke.

"How deep are we?" Her voice echoed back at her.

"Bedrock." Adamant rapped the nearest wall with a rough knuckle. "About fifty metres."

"How do you know that?"

"We stoners know our rocks, apparently."

*Stoners*. "Sorry about that."

"You don't have to apologize for that asshole up there."

"Actually, I think I do." She took Fergus's hand and thought, *It's not just Phil.*

Fergus gave her hand a squeeze. Perpetua tucked her chin.

"Let's go." She marched across the cavern floor toward the luridly lit tunnel.

The brightness and redness increased as they walked. So did the noise. So did the heat. Perpetua wiped sweat from her forehead, and more trickled down the back of her neck. As they drew closer, she saw the silhouettes of trolls, black in the volcanic glow. Seeing a shorter shadow standing off to the side, she let go of Fergus's hand and ran forward, shouting, "Mr. Earthenhouse!"

He turned in her direction. But before she could reach him, Fergus caught up with her and grabbed her around the waist. "What the—?" She struggled a moment before she realized why he'd pulled her back. She froze.

She, Fergus, and Earthenhouse were standing by the edge of another cavern. The sides dropped away from them, fifty feet to the floor below. If it even was a floor. It was crisscrossed with cracks that glowed yellow and orange. The ground heaved.

She could tell that the trolls hadn't dug this place. They'd only cleared away the rocks from the tunnel opening. The clods of earth they shoved away steamed.

Earthenhouse wore red robes that covered him from neck to toes. The fabric was embroidered in black with intricate, occult-looking figures. He held a leather-bound book in his hands, open to a page full of colourful and ancient-looking drawings. He closed the book, holding one finger inside to keep his place. "Miss Collins!" He raised his voice over the roar that came from the pit below. "I wish you hadn't joined me."

She pulled herself free from Fergus and rounded on Earthenhouse. "Sir! Respectfully: what the *hell* are you doing?"

"Technically speaking, nothing illegal." He reopened the book.

"Oh, really?" she snapped. "Then why does the air smell of sulphur?"

He closed the book again, but didn't look at her. "The intent of the Mores is to maintain the peace between the goblins, the trolls, the faeries, and the humans. This means that goblins are allowed the expectation of peace if they choose to sleep, through amnesia reset. It also gives the goblins the right to unbury any goblin or troll who is buried. I am unburying one of our brethren. He is a relative of the trolls, so the Mores technically apply to him."

"Sir?" She staggered as a rumble shook the ledge they stood upon. "Sir, are you sure about this?"

"I have tried to live within the constraints of the Mores. My contracts were solid. I offered what I thought was a fair deal." He looked at her, his eyes midnight-dark. "The faeries wanted to stop me because they were afraid that if I went further, humanity would wake up and call us monsters. And they were right! No one ran to save them from the rockfall, Miss Collins, except you!" His grey hands tightened on the book, the knuckles whitening. "That policeman shot Gunther six times! If we are to survive in this new world where humanity can see us, I will need a new contract, a new set of Mores that enforces human respect. I need a bigger stick."

The ground shook. Perpetua clutched at Fergus to stay upright. The glare in the pit intensified. Cracks widened, and the surface heaved. There was a throaty growl in the rumble, like something waking up.

Adamant stepped forward. "Thorsen," he said, calmly, almost casually. "Don't you think you might have gone just a tad too far? Tell me you know better than to dig up something you can't control!"

Earthenhouse gave him a pleading look. "Adamant, it will give us the leverage we need!"

"You idiot!" Adamant shouted. "You'll kill us all!"

Perpetua grabbed Adamant's arm. "What's he done? What's he digging up?"

The look on Adamant's face raised the hairs on the back of her neck. "It's a balor." He rounded on Earthenhouse. "You know those things can't be controlled!"

She yanked Adamant back. "What's a balor?"

"A balor," said Fergus. "One of the great Fomorian giants of old Ireland." He shook his head. "Whoa, the facts just boil up, don't they? It's like Wikipedia's inside of me. I wonder if I know how tall Mount Everest is. Oh, yeah: 29,029 feet. Cool!"

"What are you talking about?"

"Look," said Adamant, speaking quickly. "You may have heard about the Battle of Magh Tuireadh, where the faeries, goblins, and trolls stood together against the Celtic invaders."

"And they lost. I heard this story."

"You may have heard that they lost, in spite of having some magical superweapons?" He glanced at the pit, then looked at her, meaningfully.

She looked at the pit. "The balor is a superweapon?"

He nodded. "A giant. A beast with magical powers. It should have been enough to carry the day, but one of the Celts got a lucky hit with a slingshot. One in a million. He brought it down."

"That doesn't tell me anything!" she yelled. "How big are we talking about? What the heck can it do?"

Fergus visibly searched his memory. "The Dungeons & Dragons people used the term 'Balor' interchangeably with 'Balrog,' until the Tolkien estate threatened to sue."

Perpetua looked down into the pit, just in time to see the ground split open and a fist the size of a rain barrel punch through. "Oh, crap!"

Earthenhouse shouted at the trolls around him. "All of you, you're done! Get out, now! Go!"

The trolls bolted down the tunnel. Perpetua dodged one, then grabbed Earthenhouse's arm. "Mr. Earthenhouse, you've got to stop this."

"Miss Collins." Earthenhouse pulled free. "With all due respect, this is none of your business. I know what I'm doing, and this is what my people need."

A roar from below shook them like violin strings. Perpetua clapped her hands over her ears. The floor of the pit split apart as another gigantic hand grappled at the edge. Sinewy arms tensed.

A head and shoulders emerged. The creature pulled itself onto the broken floor like a swimmer crawling onto shore.

Although it was hard to judge height when the creature was still on its hands and knees, Perpetua guessed it was over twenty feet tall. It had horns. Its skin was black as charcoal, except where it cracked. In those cracks, the skin glowed like fresh lava, a bright and glaring red.

Perpetua took two steps back on trembling legs and tapped Fergus on the arm. "Fergus?" She just managed to keep the squeak from her voice. "Get out. Now. Get back out of the tunnel and get somewhere safe, okay?"

He didn't move. "You don't seem to be leaving."

Adamant poked her in the shoulder. "He's right. It's too dangerous for both of you. You should get out."

"I can't!" She gestured at the creature on its hands and knees below them. "If that thing gets out . . ." She waved her hands, not finding the words. "I have to do something!"

"Then I'm not leaving, either," said Fergus. His gaze softened. "Look, I know I don't know you, but something tells me that if I lose you, my life will get a whole lot worse."

"Fergus! Please!"

Behind her came a gusty sound of inrushing air. The balor was drawing breath. Then, with a roar that would have sent Godzilla running for cover, the cavern filled with fire.

Perpetua and Fergus hit the ground together. Flames shot up the cavern walls and licked across the ceiling. The rising heat sucked at Perpetua's breath. She felt her skin tightening, paper-dry.

Then, as suddenly as they had come, the flames disappeared. Perpetua and Fergus scrambled up and checked each other for burns. Perpetua stared wide-eyed back at the pit, much too near. "This thing breathes *fire*?"

Adamant coughed as he picked himself up off the floor. "So they say. Seems it's true."

"Could be worse," said Fergus, considering. "Tolkien's Balrog had wings."

"Yeah, that will be a great comfort as it *kills us on the ground*!" Perpetua jumped up and grabbed Earthenhouse's arm. He alone had not ducked for cover. "You've got to stop this, sir, please! Right now!"

"I can't." Earthenhouse looked down at the creature, which was bending and flexing. He opened his book. "Now that the balor is awake, it won't sleep unless we bury it again. I have to make it acknowledge my authority. That's what this book is for."

He found his place and stepped to the brink of the ledge. "Balor of the Deep!" His voice rose over the cavern's rumble. "Attend to me. *I* have woken you from your slumber."

The balor stopped stretching and looked up. Perpetua saw its face properly for the first time, and her stomach clenched. The face was grotesquely misshapen, as though some larger creature had beaten it to a pulp. One eye opened and looked around, but the other was swollen to half the size of its head, and stayed closed. It snorted, and its nostrils shot out a cloud of embers.

Adamant grabbed Perpetua's arm and pulled. "Back up! Back up! We'd better hope that other eye stays closed."

"What are you talking about?"

"That's the superweapon. Not the fire-breathing. The eye. They say one look from that eye can strike twenty men dead."

Perpetua backed up.

"Balor of the Deep," Earthenhouse's voice echoed across the cavern. "You awaken in a new world! Attend to me. I am your guide and mentor! I have need of your service."

The balor focused on Earthenhouse with its smaller, open eye. It grunted and snarled.

"By the power of the Mores, I command you!" Earthenhouse boomed. "Stand tall and acknowledge me!"

The balor crouched down and bellowed.

The pages of Earthenhouse's book went up in smoke.

He gaped at it, then closed the charred leather-bound covers. “Well, damn!”

The balor turned away and examined the confines of its cavern. It stamped across the cavern floor, leaving glowing lava footprints in its heaving wake. It scrabbled at the cavern walls.

*Looking for a way out*, she thought.

Perpetua grabbed Earthenhouse again. “Sir! You can’t control this thing! It doesn’t sign contracts! It doesn’t obey laws! It’s just an animal! A twenty-foot-tall animal that breathes fire!”

“Oh?” He glared at her. “An animal like us goblins?”

She dropped her arms to her sides. “Sir, you don’t negotiate for equality with an atomic bomb!”

He looked at her, and she saw the desperation in his eyes. “Why not, when it’s all we have left?”

She took a deep breath and continued more slowly, though she could hear the balor’s feet stomping below. “If you do,” she said at last, “you might get what you want on the first day, but what about the next? What about the day after that?” She held his gaze. “People will only remember that the goblins and trolls materialized around them because you threatened everybody with a fire-breathing monster!”

“She’s right, Mr. Earthenhouse.” Fergus stepped forward. “You do this, and the humans will never forgive you. They’ll never trust you.”

Earthenhouse rounded on him. “You saw humanity through new eyes. You saw what they did to Gunther! Don’t you understand? We can’t trust them!”

“I trust Perpetua,” Fergus nodded at her. “I don’t know her, but she’s been with me from the moment I woke up. She stayed with me through the kidnapping, and all of this, and she’s standing here against you.” He gave her a shy smile. “It’s a big world; I can’t deal with it on my own. But she helped me, without asking for anything in return. If there are humans like her, even just a few, then there are people I can trust. And you’ve got to trust someone, too, sometime.”

Perpetua looked at Fergus and away. Her eyes were wet.

Adamant stepped in closer. "Thorsen? I think these two put their case very well."

Earthenhouse stared down at the balor. "Well." His shoulders sagged. "Case or no case, I'm afraid the genie is out of the bottle."

Perpetua took a deep breath. "We'll see about that!"

Fergus looked at her, hopeful. "You got an idea?"

"Kind of." Abruptly, she kissed him.

He pulled his head back. "What was that for?"

She flashed a smile. "For whatever happens." Hefting her pickaxe, she ran up the corridor, away from the pit and toward the worksite.

Cracks fissured across the ceiling. Rocks fell. Perpetua covered her head until she reached the wide shaft leading up. She looked up and saw the silhouettes of goblins and trolls ringing the edge, looking down.

"Hey!" She let the pickaxe fall and jumped up and down, waving her hands. "Hey! Who am I? Who am I!"

Slowly, like the rumble of an oncoming train, the goblins and trolls called down. "Boss Lady." "Boss Lady." "Boss Lady!"

"Yes!" She grinned fiercely and tried not to think about the picture she made: a small person in a big space, shouting a desperate plea that could barely be heard. She shut the thought away. This was too important to mess up.

"I need your help!" she cried. "You've got to bury that creature! I can't do this myself! We've got to collapse this tunnel before the balor gets out!" She waved backward, toward the tunnel she'd come running down.

The silhouettes turned and shifted. Stray words and phrases filtered down through the uproar. "But Earthenhouse said—" "Boss." "Boss Lady!" "We work for him!" "She helps us!"

"If that thing gets out,"—she pointed behind her into the tunnel—"you won't be working for Earthenhouse anymore. There won't be people to pay for your jobs anymore. A lot of people will die, and no one will trust you ever again!"

The silhouettes froze.

"Please?" No response. She sagged, defeated.

A shadow fell over her. She looked up and saw Howard standing by her shoulder. He looked past her, up at the goblins and trolls at the top of the shaft. He growled low and then bellowed. Perpetua clamped her hands to her ears. *What was that? A call to war?*

But the goblins above didn't move. Howard snorted, then looked at her apologetically.

She smiled sadly and touched his arm. *Good old Howard*.

Her breath caught. Silhouettes shifted. Dark shapes detached themselves and began climbing and jumping down the wall of the shaft. More than a dozen trolls landed on their feet in front of her with earth-shaking thuds. They formed a ragged semicircle before her, fixed their eyes on her, and waited.

She hefted her pickaxe with a grunt of effort and smiled at the line of recruits. "Come on!" She headed down the tunnel with the trolls shambling behind.

Earthenhouse, Adamant, and Fergus stared as Perpetua and the trolls marched to the ledge overlooking the cavern. The trolls fanned out. They clawed at the walls and the ceiling. Stones and dirt rained down. Perpetua ran to the nearest wall, swung up her pickaxe, and stabbed it into the rock. Pieces of the wall cracked and broke free.

Earthenhouse grabbed Perpetua's arm. "Miss Collins, what are you doing?"

"Putting the balor back to sleep!" She swung the pickaxe with a grunt.

Fergus grabbed her other arm. "Perpetua, you'll be killed!"

"They're right," Adamant shouted. "Goblins couldn't survive a balor for long. What makes you think a human would?"

"Are you going to lecture me, or are you going to help?" She shook herself free and hacked at the wall again. The pickaxe stuck, and she struggled to pull it free. It came loose suddenly, and she fell back. She shoved herself up and aimed another strike at the tunnel wall.

There was a guttural rumble, then a rush of hot air. Perpetua looked up to see the balor leap into view, landing solidly on the ledge, knocking down several trolls. It opened its mouth and let out a breath like a blast furnace.

Fergus shoved her against the back of the nearest troll. She closed her eyes against the heat and thought her tears might boil. The cool, stony bulk of the troll heated up like a brick oven. Then, as suddenly as it started, the fire stopped.

Perpetua looked up from her shelter and saw the balor crouched low, clutching its head while chunks of rock fell from the ceiling. It staggered back, dazed, and almost fell back into the pit. It looked up, and the swollen eyelids parted. The eye within glowed with the intensity of suns.

"Keep digging!" she yelled. She grabbed her pickaxe, then dropped it with a cry. The handle was *hot*!

"Miss Collins!" Earthenhouse grabbed her arm again. "Perpetua! Please stop what you are doing and get out while you can."

She shook him off and tore strips from the hem of her dress. She wrapped the fabric around her palms. Grabbing up the pickaxe, she attacked the wall again. "I'm not leaving until it's buried!" she grunted. *Hack! Swing!* The trolls redoubled their efforts. Rocks rained down. The air became thick with dust.

The balor straightened up. It snarled and snapped its teeth. Its swollen eyelids parted further, and the tunnel filled with daylight. The temperature rose like a kiln. It gathered its breath to roar.

"Keep going!" Perpetua shouted to the digging trolls. "Everybody, keep digging!" She smelled burning hair and hoped it wasn't hers.

Behind her, Earthenhouse stared at Perpetua. Finally, he cleared his throat. "Howard, please hand me Miss Collins's axe."

"He won't listen to you!" She coughed in the deepening dust.

Earthenhouse tapped Howard on the arm and beckoned him

down. He whispered into the troll's ear. Howard straightened up and plucked the pickaxe from Perpetua's hands.

"Hey!" she shouted, betrayed.

Howard handed the axe to Earthenhouse, who stepped forward and swung it at the wall, sending up a spray of shattered rock.

Perpetua gaped. "Mr. Earthenhouse, what are you doing?"

"I'm going underground, Miss Collins. Goodbye." Earthenhouse swung his axe again. "Howard, save Perpetua and her friends."

She gasped. "But—"

Taking her by surprise, Fergus hauled her over his shoulder and ran. She shouted and flailed. Adamant followed. Howard loped after them, waving his arms to fend off falling rocks.

The trolls clawed at the walls and ceiling. The rain of stone became a torrent. Behind it, the balor opened its gigantic eye. The tunnel flared white. Then the glow dimmed and faded as dust and stone blocked the view. The balor roared furiously.

With a cracking roar, the ceiling of the tunnel collapsed. The quaking floor shook Perpetua out of Fergus's arms, and she grabbed his hand and ran. The torrent of stone became a wave that tracked after the four as they raced for the shaft. The tunnel opening grew larger, and they were suddenly out in the open.

They charged up the shaking stairs, clawing their way along. Perpetua thought her lungs would burst, but she knew they couldn't stop. They weren't safe yet. They were just a quarter of the way up, closing in on halfway.

The ground pitched, and the stairs crumbled. Howard stumbled on the shaking surface. Fergus tripped and fell hard. Perpetua grabbed his wrist to haul him up.

A blast of air made her look round. She was staring across the shaft, straight into the balor's tunnel. The rock face above the tunnel crumbled. A tsunami of stone barreled forward, fast as an oncoming train.

Fergus grabbed her. They held each other close.
The wall of stone hit, and Perpetua knew no more.

# Chapter 38
# Who Knows upon What Soil

Perpetua woke, choking and struggling to breathe. A weight pressed down on her chest, and she couldn't move. Around her, stone clattered against stone.

Clarity set in with a jolt, along with an urge to scream.

Suddenly, the weight lifted off her. Howard stood over her, a big rock in his hands. He tossed it aside with a crash.

Adamant leaned into view. "Are you all right?"

She was lying against the stairs, or rather, what was left of them. The rock pile that had buried her up to her chest still held her legs. She could hardly hear the question past the ringing in her ears. "Wha—What happened?" Then she remembered and struggled to sit up. "Where's Fergus?"

"Hey, take it easy!" Adamant pressed her down, but Perpetua yanked at her legs, though rocks still pinned her ankles and gouged at her shins.

"Where is he?" she gasped. The last rock clunked aside, and she struggled up. "Fergus!"

Then she saw him, camouflaged by dust, pressed against the wall, buried up to his chest in rubble. She shouted and scrambled for him, clawing at the stones and tossing them aside.

His arm jerked. He coughed, then choked, as he struggled to

sit up. Perpetua steadied him while Howard cleared the heavier rocks away. He coughed some more.

A lead weight tugged at Perpetua's heart. "Fergus," she said, desperately calm. "What's your name?"

His brow wrinkled. "It's Fergus. Didn't you just tell me?"

"Your whole name!"

"Aloysius Fergus," he said promptly. "That's what you said when I woke up in the alleyway. Remember?"

"Oh, thank God!" Relief flooded through her, and she threw her arms around him.

His arms went around her, too, tentatively. "Um . . . sure, I guess."

Adamant rolled his eyes. "Well, clearly, there are no bones broken."

Perpetua pulled back, her cheeks heating up.

Above them, people shouted, then started to cheer.

She looked up. "What's going on?"

"Haven't you noticed?" Adamant sounded ironic. "The worksite's still standing. The construction workers are happy to be alive."

"Oh." Perpetua looked across at the expanse of broken stone sealing the balor's tunnel. Earthenhouse and his troll recruits were nowhere to be seen. Exhaustion settled over her skin like rock dust. She was bone tired. Her world had shattered around her, and she didn't know how to put it back together, or even where to start.

"Is Christina still here?" she asked.

"I didn't see her leave."

"Then this isn't over." She struggled upright. "We have to talk to her."

Howard held out an arm, and Perpetua leaned on it. He held out the other hand, and Fergus grabbed it to haul himself up. Together, they climbed slowly up the remaining steps to the construction site.

The human workers were still cheering, hugging each other

and slapping each other's backs. Chim and Chum and the other goblins stood more quietly, huddled together close to the brink of the shaft, looking down at the debris. Fred . . . Fred wasn't there. Perpetua realized with a sinking heart that he was buried with the other trolls.

*They sacrificed themselves to save us. It wasn't even their war.*

Christina squared her shoulders as Perpetua approached, leaning on Howard. The faerie glanced down at Perpetua's ripped dress, her scraped and bloody hands and legs, her limping gait, and then looked her in the eye. There was something new in her look. Perpetua frowned at the unfamiliarity of it. *Is that . . . respect?*

"Where's Earthenhouse?" Christina asked.

Perpetua cleared her throat. "Underground."

Chim and Chum drooped.

Christina set her mouth in a thin, tight line. For a moment, she looked almost sad. Then her chin tilted up again. "And the balor?"

*So, she'd heard*. "Taken care of."

Christina nodded. "I am sorry about Earthenhouse."

"Thanks," said Perpetua, curt. "But what are we going to do now?"

"What are you talking about?" Thompson stepped away from his colleagues. He frowned at Perpetua. "You said whatever it was that was down there was taken care of."

"It's not what's down there that we have to worry about." Perpetua pointed up. "It's what's out there. The veil is still gone. Humans can still see the goblins, faeries, and trolls."

Christina's agents stood ramrod-straight, eyes glittering. Christina, herself, held Perpetua's gaze for a long moment, and then softly released her breath. "You have a point." The agents looked at her. Their eyebrows quirked—for them, it was almost a shout of consternation.

"The way I see it . . ." Adamant stepped out from behind Howard and gestured at the other goblins, "we have folks here from every group affected by what's happened today. If we want to start talking about what happens next, the people who can start talking about it are all right here."

Thompson's colleagues looked nervously around.

"Um . . . okay," said Joe.

"We'll do our best," said Stu.

"Answer me honestly." Perpetua stared hard at Christina. "Can you re-magic the world and restore the veil? How long would it take? What would happen to your people in the meantime?"

Christina worked her jaw. "Years. Assuming we start right away with making people forget about the events of today and yesterday."

"I'm not going to let you tamper with my friends' memories," said Thompson, stepping in front of his coworkers.

Christina narrowed her sparkling eyes on him. He glared back. She shook her head and focused on Perpetua. "What do you propose?"

"That we use Fergus's plan," Perpetua replied. "That goblins, trolls, and faeries live among humans. Ultimately, humans will have to deal with that reality, no matter what. We just have to convince them that they can."

"The news media heard Earthenhouse's ultimatum," said Christina. "They know he made a threat. How do we deal with that?"

"I'm sure the St. Brigid Society has experience in coming up with . . ." She bit her lip. She'd come to Toronto on a matter of honesty, but . . . this seemed like another of those rare times where it was maybe good to lie. "A good cover story?"

Christina nodded slowly.

Perpetua reached back and felt Fergus's hand slip into hers. She tugged him forward. "Fergus gathered a list of people we can call, and ideas for how to campaign after a reveal."

"Fine!" Christina snapped. "Where is this plan?"

"Back at Earthenhouse's office. I'll go get it."

Christina looked away. Her mouth twisted. "Three thousand years, we've hidden away. Three thousand years of fear and distrust. Do you honestly think we can set that aside in one night?"

Perpetua sighed. "I hope so."

Christina curled her lip. "You *hope* so?"

"Yeah, I do. Because I don't think we have any other choice."

Christina turned to Thompson. They started talking about how to handle any reporters who might be snooping about upstairs. Adamant joined them.

Before Perpetua joined the group, she limped over to Chim and Chum. Looking around to make sure no one else could overhear, she knelt down to talk to them, face to face.

"Chim, Chum?" she said, her voice low. "The balor. Is there more than one?"

Chim and Chum glanced at each other. They looked at her and bobbed their heads, simultaneously, for once.

Her throat tightened. "Do the goblins know where they're buried?"

Again, Chim and Chum glanced at each other. Again, they looked at her and bobbed their heads.

She sucked her teeth a moment, and then smiled. "Good. Let's keep this to ourselves, for now. If we have to, we'll let certain people know that we know. You know?"

The two goblins gazed at her, serious. They bobbed their heads.

Perpetua straightened up, still grimly smiling. *That's our ace in the hole.*

When Thompson and his crew emerged into the station, they faced emergency workers worried about possible building collapses, reporters wondering what the hell was going on, and city officials demanding the same thing. The subway was shut down. The city was in commuter chaos.

Thompson was put in charge of handling the media. He was good at talking people down. Engineers surveyed the worksite and saw no evidence of imminent collapse or the hole that Earthenhouse's trolls had dug. With officialdom reassured, the subway reopened in time for the afternoon rush hour.

Later, leaving Fergus in the care of Adamant and the skills of Amnesia House, Perpetua took the first southbound train to the Financial District. The homebound crowds slipped by around her as she entered the Underground City.

On the plasma screens, reporters were talking about the earthquake that had shaken the city early that morning. Thompson's pleasant, unremarkable face appeared on every screen, assuring everyone that there was no structural damage to the subway.

Perpetua headed down to the office as the crowds thinned out. She heard the soprano's voice echoing around the corridors. She heard the scraggle-scrape of approaching skateboarders, and Skater Girl zipped past. Spiky Hair followed. He grinned over his shoulder at Perpetua before vanishing around a corner.

Next came a storm of running footfalls, and the three security guards bounded past. Patrick slowed and half-turned as he ran. He gave Perpetua a quizzical look. She nodded at him. He nodded back, turned, and ran on.

*Strange how the new world feels so normal*, she thought. She pushed through the door to the stairs and headed for Subbasement Three.

Perpetua stepped carefully through the gaping window into the office. Glass crunched underfoot. Two chairs lay with their legs in the air, but the rest sat sedately in their usual places against the walls. Nothing moved. Perpetua stood in the centre of the reception area, her breath loud in her ears.

"You look like you could do with a nice cup of coffee!" lilted a chirpy voice.

Perpetua staggered back, hand to her chest. She glared at the corner where the coffee maker sat. "Well, it's nice to know that you made it out unharmed. Has anybody been here since last night?"

"Nobody has asked me for coffee!" the coffee maker replied.

"Huh. I guess that's as good an indication as any."

She picked her way through the debris to Earthenhouse's door. It opened easily, and she entered the dimly lit room. Everything was as it should be. Even the fruit basket on the desk, with the pile of fruit now overripe and attracting fruit flies.

A squeak made her whirl nervously, but it was only Scooter, trundling forward out of a shadowy corner.

"So, you're still here, too!"

Scooter squeaked happily.

With a lighter heart, she crossed to Earthenhouse's desk to look for Fergus's folder.

The desktop was clean and bare. She opened and closed the desk drawers, felt underneath the desktop, but found nothing. She sucked her teeth, frustrated. *I don't have time for this!*

Scooter squeaked. She looked up and saw a pile of papers, including the folder, rolling across the room to her on Scooter's seat—which had been empty just moments ago.

She raised an eyebrow before taking the pile and setting it on the desk. "Thanks."

"*Squeak, squeak-squeak*!"

Fergus's folder was on top. Everything was there: photos, medical reports, contact information. Bono's autograph and cell phone number. She was midway through a contents check when her eyes fell on the rest of the pile. Everything was here . . . and more. Including a handwritten letter in Earthenhouse's flowing cursive script.

She read it, and her heart beat faster with each line.

*Miss Collins:*

*If you are reading this, then it is likely that my venture has backfired, and I am no longer present to run the business.*

*Assuming you are willing, I am transferring control of my company and all of its assets to you. The proper papers have been filed with the authorities. I ask that you take over my job and operate the company as you see fit, for the benefit of all our clients—human, goblin, and troll.*

*I realize I have left a lot for you to clean up, but I know that you are more than capable of cleaning up after me.*

*I also hope you will forgive me. I have struggled to understand humanity. Perhaps, they are just too complicated to fathom. But you do understand them, it seems. And, more importantly, you understand my people better than I could ever have hoped.*

*Take care of them, please.*

*Sincerely,*
*T.P. Earthenhouse*

"Why me?" she breathed. Then she looked at the rest of the pile of papers.

The top item was a framed photo. Perpetua picked it up, and her jaw dropped. It was her mother, looking younger than she'd ever seen her, in clothes so out of date, Perpetua would have bent over double with laughter in any other situation.

*How did Earthenhouse get this picture?*

*And whose arm is that draped around her shoulder?*

She flipped the catches off the back of the frame and pulled out the photograph. When she unfolded it, her hand flew to her mouth.

Earthenhouse had been hidden on the folded-back portion of the picture, his camera grin showing his raggedy teeth. He wore a suit and tie—a loud tie, with a paisley pattern, straight out of twenty years earlier.

She set the photograph down on the pile of papers, pulled her cell phone from her clip, and turned it on. A display popped up, showing fifty missed calls. All from her mother.

"You knew!" Her breath caught. "You both knew, and you didn't tell me. You—" She bit back the word and covered her mouth with both hands. She took a deep breath, held it, and let it go. She took another. Then one more. She swallowed and cleared her nose with a sniff.

Scooter squeaked. It felt to Perpetua like it asked, "*What now?*"

She looked down at the pile of papers on the desk. She closed her eyes, then opened them. The future stretched before her, with all its terrifying uncertainties.

"I . . . I don't know."

Her chest felt tight. Her eyes stung. She didn't know what to do next. She only felt the urge to scream.

*The screaming clause. I could activate that, couldn't I? Just walk away?*

She took a deep breath, then closed her mouth on it.

Her eyes tracked up to the fruit bowl at the corner of the desk. An apple sat on the top of the pile. She picked it up and turned it over in her hands. It was in pristine condition, unlike the other fruits, and Perpetua wondered if Earthenhouse had placed it there just for her.

She let out the breath she was holding.

"'We must not look at goblin men, we must not buy their fruits,'" she muttered.

The future stretched out before her. All she could do was work to change it as best she could. For the better.

She faced Earthenhouse's chair. "All right," she said. "I'll do it."

She brought the apple to her mouth and took a big bite.

After making an appointment with a glazier to fix the windows, Perpetua left the office, leaving Scooter to keep watch. She paused on the stairs to look through the folder again.

It was detailed. It had timetables, notes, more than enough to give her an idea of how to proceed. But there were things that even Fergus hadn't been sure of.

She ran her hand along a page of media contacts. Some were underlined. Some were circled with question marks beside them. At the bottom of the page, Fergus had written one word: "HOOK?" With an extra question mark.

She climbed back to the shopping level in the Underground City, deep in thought, wondering about that word.

*What was he looking for? Something to catch and hold humanity's attention?*

*Maybe. Something to show that goblins are people, and not monsters to be feared.*

*But what could that hook be?*

As she walked through the corridors, folder tucked under her arm, she became aware of the distant soprano singing. She stopped to listen.

*Casta Diva, che inargenti*
*Queste scare antic he piante*
*A noi volgi il bel sembiante*
*Senza nubs e senza gel . . .*

She focused on the voice and followed it, away from her usual route and down a smaller corridor that bent and turned. The singing grew louder with every step.

*Tempra, o Diva*
*Tempra tu de' cori ardent*
*Tempra ancora lo zelo audace.*

She came to the pair of glass doors in front of the dark corridor. She pulled the handle and stepped through. The singing drew her on.

*Spargi in terra quell pace*
*Che regnar tu tai bel ciel . . .*

And there she was—the source. At the far end of the dark corridor, standing in the spotlight of a single halogen lamp. When the last bars faded, Perpetua cleared her throat.

The goblin whirled with a gasp. She was wearing a pink satin ball gown that shone against her green-tinged skin. She gaped at Perpetua and backed away.

Perpetua raised her hands, palms outward. “It’s okay. I just . . . I just wanted to say . . . you’ve got a wonderful voice.”

The goblin tucked her head and smiled. “Th-thank you.” Her speaking voice rasped, a surprise after that performance.

“You’re welcome.” Perpetua licked her lips. Could she make this work? “And there’s something else. If you want, that is . . . I think I know a few people you might want to talk to.”

## Chapter 39
# Fergus Journal Entries: Day One

Fergus picked up the black, hardcover book with the word "JOURNAL" embossed on the front in gold. He glanced at the Post-it Note in his handwriting that said: "My Journal! Keep Out! Fergus."

He glanced over to where Perpetua lay on the couch, murmuring in her sleep. He placed the journal in his lap and, clicking his pen, began to write.

*Tuesday, August 27*
*Dear Self,*

*So, here are some things that I've come to know. I am a taxi driver. I have $1,300 in my bank account, and no balance on my credit cards. I live at 108 Albany Avenue in Toronto, and my cell phone number is (416)555-9681. Rent is due in the next five days.*

*And, apparently, I've been keeping a journal.*

*I found it after they brought me to this place they say is my apartment. It has my name on the cover, so I guess it must be mine. It's also in my handwriting. I know this because I've compared the earlier entries with what I've written right here.*

*The girl named Perpetua (funny name) is sleeping on my couch. I have a lot of questions, but I think I'll let her sleep. She's had a rough day; more than most, even on a day like this. She cried out once as some nightmare took her, but for the most part, she's been sleeping peacefully.*

*So, here I am, a stranger in my own life. It's a weird feeling, and I hope it goes away. I pick up things, and I know how they work, but they don't feel like they belong to me. I feel like any minute, some other person could walk in the door and take these things away from me.*

*But he isn't here yet. He might never return.*

*And he, whoever he is, sent me a message in this journal.*

*He told me that I am a stranger. That there are things he wanted kept private. He told me that there are things in this life that I'm just going to have to find out about for myself.*

*But he hinted, at least, that there's joy in finding out.*

*Perpetua's stirring in her sleep. I think she's about to wake up. I'll go make breakfast.*

*Something tells me she likes eggs and bacon, and lots of coffee.*

## Chapter 40
# Coming Out

At 8:55 a.m., on a Monday morning in late September, the people of Toronto stopped what they were doing and looked up.

*My heart at thy dear voice*
*Wakes with joy, like the flow'r*
*At the sun's bright morning.*

The people walking through the King-Bay intersection found themselves staring at the low roof where they'd passed the tenor every single day. This time, he stood to one side, hands clasped behind him, beaming proudly as his new protégé, the goblin soprano, stood in her pink satin finery and sang to the crowds.

*But O, my dearest one,*
*That grief may lose its pow'r*
*Say 'tis mine, thy heart's yearning.*

The people stared, mouths agape, as they saw the goblin and heard her voice. But as they stared, they listened. Mouths closed.

Hands clasped. The crowd stood rapt as her voice carried clear across the public square.

Perpetua stood beside Fergus on the low roof and watched. Howard stood nearby, holding Trixie's hand. Others stood in the background, watching and listening while the goblin coloratura filled the morning with song.

*O, bide here at my side!*
*Promise ne'er thou'lt depart!*

Across the street, the hot dog vendor felt someone tug at his apron. He looked down to see an impish figure pointing at his menu, specifically at the veggie dogs he'd never been able to sell. The goblin held up a five-dollar bill.

The vendor hesitated, then shrugged and grilled up the veggie dog. He slathered on the condiments as per the goblin's instructions and gave him correct change. As the goblin ambled away, the vendor turned back to his cart and found himself staring at a lineup of five goblins and one troll.

He clacked his tongs happily.

Through it all, the goblin coloratura sang.

*Once more those vows so loving*
*Let me hear from thy heart!*
*Breathe that mine still thou art!*

The music died away to one last high, clear note, and then silence. The crowd held its breath for a moment before letting it out. First in isolated pockets, people in the intersection began to clap. Some even began to cheer.

The tenor kissed his protégé's hand. And then another man stepped forward.

With arms folded across his chest, Bono beamed behind his sunglasses. The band behind him launched into the beat, and he leaned into his microphone and began to sing.

Perpetua leaned over and spoke in Fergus's ear, over the music. "Who knew the Edge was a goblin?"

"A lot of bass guitar players are, apparently," he replied. "And drummers. Remember Ringo Starr?"

Around the intersection, on the cornices that had been empty until yesterday evening, the goblins stood up and waved to the crowds. Some took bows.

People gaped. Some backed away. Others shouted. But more looked up at Bono, cheering loudly.

There were people looking up who weren't cheering. People who looked nervous, yet determined. Gradually, one by one, then more together, they reached out to their friends, tapped arms, or gripped elbows, to get attention.

"Phase two," Perpetua muttered.

She couldn't hear the conversations down below, but she could imagine how they might go. She saw two businessmen walking along the street, one pale-skinned and one brown, but otherwise almost identical in their conservative suits and ties. The brown-skinned man was shaking his head, bewildered. His friend tapped him on the shoulder.

"Mike," he said. "We've been friends for twenty years, right?"

Mike looked back at him, frowning. "Um . . . yeah. Why?"

"I've been trying to think of a way to tell you this for a long time. But now seems like the best time to just say it, so . . ." The other man pulled a set of false teeth from his mouth, revealing the raggedy ones beneath. "I'm a goblin."

Mike staggered back, nearly stepping into the road. "Jake, are you for real?"

Jake nodded. "Yeah. I am." He held his breath.

"But . . . but . . . but . . ."

"What?"

"But we play racquetball!"

Jake nodded slowly. "Yeah . . .?"

A young couple passed by, arm in arm.

"So, you're a faerie," said the young man, looking nervous.

The redheaded girl nodded. "Born and raised."

"You don't have wings."

She gave him an enchanting smile and touched his nose with the tip of one slim finger. "Wings? That's a myth, sweetie. You have a lot to learn."

"Yeah, but . . . wait a minute. Have you been putting spells on me?"

Perpetua stepped back to a bank of television screens they'd set up earlier that morning, broadcasting the news on several stations. "Phase three," she muttered.

"They're coming out of the woodwork," said the BBC News announcer. "Goblins, trolls, and faeries, egged on by the public acknowledgement of their existence in Toronto, Canada, are making themselves known to passersby in London, New York, and San Francisco."

"Goblins and faeries!" shouted a portly media commentator. "They're a culture synonymous with swindlers! It's in every fairy tale, from King Gobb to Oberon to Rumpelstiltskin! They're coming out to rob us again, as they have done in Europe for centuries!"

"Yeah, I worked with them," said Patrick, flanked by his security guard comrades, staring bedazzled at the cameras. "They want to earn an honest living, just like everybody else."

"In the Vatican, the Pope met with a group of visiting goblins and gave them his blessing," said another reporter.

"—protests in a dozen cities as placard-waving crowds chanted: 'Keep the stoners out.' Police described these gatherings as small, but vocal." Behind the CNN reporter, a dozen people stood on a street corner, hoisting crudely drawn red, white, and blue signs blaring: "GOD HATES TROLLS."

On CityTV, a young man sat in an armchair on the set of a talk show. He pulled his hair back, revealing his pointy ears. "I'm so glad I don't have to hide these anymore," he said. "Yeah, the other kids would tease me about my long hair and big, floppy hats, but it was better than the alternative. My friends had no idea, until now."

On the street, conversations continued. Some people stared at their friends in stupefaction, while others stepped forward, amazed but smiling, and offered hugs. Mike slapped Jake on the back and hugged him. But the faerie woman watched, despondent, as her boyfriend stormed away.

Two young men wearing metal-studded leather coats and hobnailed boots looked at the festivities in disgust. They shook their shaved heads and folded their heavily tattooed arms defensively.

The skinheads looked up, spotted Perpetua looking down at them, and glared at her. They turned and headed for the stairs, going underground. They passed the fountain where Gunther had sat, still empty.

Perpetua glanced up at a balcony across the street. Christina stood there, flanked by two of her agents. *She looks smaller than before*, Perpetua thought. Christina frowned as she watched the skinheads go. Then she shot a grim look across the street.

Media trucks were pulling up, adding to the traffic jam. Reporters and camera crews piled out and advanced on the crowd. *Like a wave? Or an army?* She couldn't settle on the metaphor.

"Well, that's it. There's no going back now." And she crossed her fingers.

Fergus took her hand. She looked at him, found his dark eyes looking back. Her breath caught.

"Hey . . ." He took a deep breath before launching in. "I found a diary. My diary. From before I went . . . underground."

Perpetua felt the blood leave her cheeks. She knew where this was going.

"So, you're Perpetua." His eyes narrowed. "There are not, like, two of you with that name?"

She snorted. "With a name like that, you think there'd be two?"

He laughed with her. But then he grew serious. He touched her arm. "So . . . so, we were in love."

She couldn't meet his gaze. Instead, she watched the scene below. "Yeah. We were." She moistened her suddenly dry lips. "I am."

"I wish I remembered that."

"So do I."

"The thing is . . ." He scratched the back of his head. "I left a note for myself. It said that, if I forget, I should get to know you again. Because you're totally cool."

A smile bent her lips. "I think the word used was 'gorgeous.'"

"Um . . ." He blushed and looked away. "Yeah. Either way, after these few weeks, I think I really would like to get to know you." Then he looked back at her and stuck out a hand. "Aloysius Fergus. Pleased to meet you."

She clasped it. "Perpetua Tallulah Collins. A pleasure."

He raised an eyebrow. "Tallulah?"

Her eyes narrowed. "What of it?"

"It's a nice name," he said quickly.

She laughed and shook his hand. They paused, still holding on, looking each other in the eyes. The moment stretched.

Then, at no signal either could have identified, they leaned forward. Their lips met. Howard ostentatiously looked up at the sky as Perpetua and Fergus held each other close. The kiss lengthened.

Behind them, U2 launched into the last verse.

And below them, the goblins danced on King Street.

**THE END**

# Night Girl Second Thank-You

I've never had to write a second afterward for a book before. I'll thank Edward Willett for that.

Writing may be a solitary vocation, but writers never work alone. Dozens of people are involved with the journey that takes a book from germinating idea to publication, and *The Night Girl* has taken this journey twice. So, let's start with those people I thanked the first time around: thanks to Kisa Whipkey and Ashley Ruggirello at REUTS Publications for making this story the best it could be. Thanks to J.M. Frey, Cameron Dixon, Brienne Wright, Christopher Ramsey, Tim Niveau, Sarah Bowman, Doug Thomas, and Rob Quehl for their hard work beta-reading earlier drafts and offering comments and suggestions. Thanks especially to Marsha Skrypuch and all the participants at her Private Kidcrit group for spending a lot of time with this story and improving it. Thanks to Damian Baranowski for his support and work on the book trailer, and thanks to my former agent, Emily Gref, for steering this story through a major rewrite that made *The Night Girl* what it is today. Thanks especially to my wife, Erin, and my kids for their love, support, and deep editorial suggestions.

I would also like to thank Steve Ellis and Andrew Boughner,

who took me on a tour of the back rooms and maintenance areas of the Sun Life Financial Tower, part of the underground city in downtown Toronto. Thanks to Brad Ross, Lori Mignone, and Carla Basso of the TTC for their support and encouragement of my map of the Toronto subway system, as dug by trolls. In my first acknowledgement, I thanked the politicians of the City of Toronto and the Province of Ontario for making the issue of Toronto's lack of new subway development as relevant to local readers in 2019 as it was when I started writing this book in 2003 —except that Toronto's rapid transit network is finally about to see a big expansion, including a long tunnel beneath Eglinton Avenue. The Eglinton line should be open by the time you read this. Maybe.

New thanks must go to Cory Doctorow and his friends, lawyer Ren Bucholz and the *Toronto Star's* David Nickle, who came to my rescue when the Canada Lands Company Limited (CLCL) sent a cease-and-desist letter on *The Night Girl*'s day of release due to the image of the CN Tower that appeared on the cover. Thank you, Cory, Ren, and David for reminding people that you can't copyright a building under Canadian law, and that trademark only applies when there's any possibility for brand confusion or damage (which, as CLCL is not active in the business of publishing fantasy novels, and as I clearly wasn't writing an unlicensed guidebook that suggested that the building was full of goblins and trolls, meant that I was not infringing on or damaging any of CLCL's trademarks). In any event, I guess I should thank CLCL for adding their own bit of excitement around my initial launch and for handing me the opportunity to bring my title to the attention of more readers.

All of these thank-yous apply to this new edition of *The Night Girl*, and to that I also thank the designer of the book's new cover, Alisha at Bibliofic Designs, and my editor at Shadowpaw Press, Edward Willett, whose tenacious publishing house is giving *The Night Girl* a new lease on life.

Finally, thanks to you, the reader, for picking up this book and reading this far. I hope you've enjoyed the story and that you feel that, while its resolution may be optimistic, it's not wholly unrealistic. I am an optimist and, at times, a hopeless one, but I believe that achieving an optimistic world starts with envisioning it. I hope you found my vision compelling, or at least fun to read.

***James Bow***
***June 2025***

# Lyrics Reference

The lyrics printed in this novel are all real songs, and are in the public domain. They are as follows:

- Chapter 5 (ii) - "Queen of the Night," from *The Magic Flute*, by Mozart, first performed in 1791. Note: these lyrics translate to English as follows: "Then you will be my daughter nevermore / Disowned be you forever / Abandoned be you forever."
- Chapter 40 - "*Mon cœur s'ouvre à ta voix*," from *Samson and Delilah*, by Camille Saint-Saëns, first performed in 1887.
- We tried to get permission to use real lyrics from U2, but they weren't amenable.

# About the Author

James Bow writes science fiction and fantasy for both kids and adults. He's been a fan of science fiction since his family introduced him to *Doctor Who* on TV Ontario in 1978, and his mother read him classic sci-fi and fantasy from such authors as Clifford Simak and J.R.R. Tolkien. James won the 2017 Prix Aurora Award for best YA Novel in Canada for *Icarus Down.*

By day, James is a communications officer for a charitable land trust protecting lands from development in Waterloo Region and Wellington County. He also loves trains and streetcars.

He lives in Kitchener, Ontario, with his two kids, and his spouse/fellow writer/partner-in-crime, Erin Bow. You can find him online at jamesbow.ca.

# About Shadowpaw Press

Shadowpaw Press is a traditional publishing company, located in Regina, Saskatchewan, Canada and founded in 2018 by Edward Willett, an award-winning author of science fiction, fantasy, and non-fiction for readers of all ages. A member of Literary Press Group (Canada) and the Association of Canadian Publishers, Shadowpaw Press publishes an eclectic selection of books by both new and established authors, including adult fiction, young adult fiction, children's books, non-fiction, and anthologies, plus new editions of notable, previously published books in any genre under the Shadowpaw Press Reprise imprint.

Email: publisher@shadowpawpress.com.

facebook.com/shadowpawpress

x.com/shadowpawpress

instagram.com/shadowpawpress

# More Science Fiction and Fantasy Available or Coming Soon from Shadowpaw Press

**For Young Adult Readers**

*The Sun Runners* by James Bow

*The Headmasters* by Mark Morton

*I, Brax: A Battle Divine* by Arthur Slade

*Blue Fire* by E. C. Blake

The Shards of Excalibur series by Edward Willett

*Song of the Sword, Twist of the Blade, Lake in the Clouds, Cave Beneath the Sea, Door into Faerie*

*Spirit Singer* by Edward Willett

*Soulworm* by Edward Willett

*From the Street to the Star*s by Edward Willett

**For Middle-Grade Readers**

*Fireboy* by Edward Willett

The Canadian Chills Series by Arthur Slade:

*Return of the Grudstone Ghosts, Ghost Hotel,*

*Invasion of the IQ Snatchers*

**For Adult Readers**

*Gods of a New World* by Ryan Melsom

*The Downloaded* by Robert J. Sawyer

*The Traitor's Son* by Dave Duncan

*Corridor to Nightmare* by Dave Duncan

*The Good Soldier* by Nir Yaniv

*Shapers of Worlds* Volumes I-V

*Duatero* by Brad C. Anderson

*Ashme's Song* by Brad C. Anderson

*Paths to the Stars* by Edward Willett

*The Legend of Sarah* by Leslie Gadallah

The Empire of Kaz trilogy by Leslie Gadallah

*Cat's Pawn, Cat's Gambit, Cat's Game*

The Peregrine Rising Duology by Edward Willett

*Right to Know, Falcon's Egg*